Ensnared

THE SPIDER'S MATE #1

TIFFANY ROBERTS

Ensnared

He's spent years as a hunter, but now he's the one ensnared in a creature's trap.

Ketahn did not want a mate. Fate has a different plan for him. When the queen he despises declares her intention to claim him, he retreats into the jungle.

What he finds there changes his world.

Small, delicate, and pale skinned, Ivy Foster is nothing like the females Ketahn has known. She's not of his kind at all. Yet the moment he sees her, he knows the truth in his soul—she is his heartsthread.

And now that he has her, he won't let anything take her away. Not the jungle, not the gods, not the queen and her warriors.

Whether Ivy agrees or not, their webs are entangled. No one will ever sever those threads.

Check the author's Website for content warnings.

Cover by Poppy Moreaux

Art by Kitsune Hebi & Fadhila Ines

Ornament and Divider Art by Anna Spies

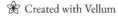 Created with Vellum

Dedicated to you, my heartsthread.
And to all our fellow monster lovers.

Chapter One

Moonfall Tunnel was all but deserted as Ketahn strode along it. The soft glow of the spiritcap mushrooms growing on the rough-hewn stone could not banish the dancing shadows cast by the blue-green spinewood sap flames, which burned in bowls carved into the tunnel walls. The only sounds were the soft crackles and pops produced by the fires.

Silk hung from the entrances of the quiet dens in both raw strands and woven fabric, most of it worn thin and tattered. All but a few of those dens were dark inside. Even the crafters' chambers, which were wider, more open spaces, were deserted.

A breeze flowed over Ketahn from ahead, carrying the merest hint of warm jungle air scented by sweet jesan flowers and damp wood. As always, he would rather have been out there, roaming the Tangle. He favored the twisting roots, gnarled branches, and cloying plants over Takarahl's carved stone and dim blue light; he would rather cross hungry mires and knots of grappler plants than these echoing passages.

But there was little choice today—it was Offering Day, when the vrix of Takarahl gathered in the Den of Spirits to make their offerings to the Eight.

Ketahn paused at the entrance to one of the dens. The swath

of silk hanging over the opening was long, tightly woven, and dyed with vibrant colors in intricate patterns, serving as a display of its crafter's skill for all who strode down Moonfall Tunnel.

Keeping his barbed spear resting over his upper left shoulder, Ketahn raised a foreleg and extended it, sweeping the silk aside.

Darkness greeted him, but it was familiar darkness. He slipped into the small den, bracing his lower left hand on the stone shelf beside him without looking at it. In all the years Ketahn's friend, Rekosh, had kept this den, he'd never left a single object out of place. Ketahn could navigate it in the dark by instinct alone.

Ketahn lowered his spear, dropping the coiled rope attached to the blunt end onto the floor and standing the weapon against the wall. Next, he swung his yatin hide bag off his back. He held it between his lower hands as he opened it and reached inside to remove a thick, leaf-wrapped bundle.

After ensuring the rawhide strips binding the bundle were secure, he placed his bag beside his spear, exited Rekosh's den, and continued deeper into the tunnel.

Though the bundle was light, it bore an implied weight that could not be measured by any scale. To most vrix, this offering would appear generous. Mender roots were rare, and there were few known places in the Tangle where they could be foraged. Medicines made from the roots cured many ailments and eased pain. A gift of mender root was a sign of selflessness, honor, and compassion.

He hoped they'd send a different message to the queen.

Ketahn slowed as he neared the entrance of another den, this one much larger than Rekosh's—it had been sized to accommodate a female and her brood. Though he did not recognize the wispy strands of silk dangling from the arched entryway, he knew the shape of the stone itself, knew the smooth spots worn into it where his mother used to lean with one of her thick forelegs crossed in front of the other as she spoke to other vrix who had dwelled in Moonfall Tunnel.

He placed a hand upon one of those spots. The stone was cold and hard under his hide, as smooth as if it had been caressed by a river for a hundred lifetimes. He recalled how his broodsister, Ahnset, had always tried to mimic their mother's stance. Ahnset had been like Ishuun in miniature, right down to the way she'd moved her legs when she walked.

But Ahnset had dwelled with the Queen's Fangs these past seven years. Ketahn had denned in the Tangle for just as long. And their mother, Ishuun...she had been dead all that time. This hatching den had been granted to a new female years ago, a female who would use it to raise her brood. Ketahn and his broodsister had no claim on it.

Removing his hand from the stone, Ketahn continued onward, striding with purpose. He had not returned to Takarahl to reminisce—though he fully intended to rouse the spirits of the past.

Ketahn found Rekosh and Urkot just beyond Moonfall, awaiting him in a large, round chamber where eight separate tunnels converged. He'd known them since all three were broodlings, but Rekosh and Urkot made an odd pair even in Ketahn's eyes.

Rekosh was nearly as tall as Ketahn, his body lean and limbs spindly. His movements displayed an effortless grace that was enhanced by his fingers—the claws at their tips were sharpened to fine points to better aid his work. The silk pouch slung across his chest and over one shoulder bulged with what was undoubtedly his offering, and Ketahn could see a few wooden spools of thread and bone needles in their leather sleeves also tucked within.

Urkot was nearly a third of a segment shorter, but his body was thick and powerful. Since he'd been a broodling, other vrix had jested that Urkot was sculpted like a female—had the sculptor been working with half the usual amount of clay. He always seemed firm and grounded even though the absence of his lower left arm should've made him appear off balance. The lower portions of all six of his legs and all three of his hands

3

were coated in a layer of stone dust that paled his black hide to white.

Mandibles spreading wide, Rekosh lowered his jaw and snapped it shut. His red eyes gleamed in the glow of the chamber's crystals like eight bloodstones. "We shall be fortunate to reach the dais and make our offerings before next Offering Day by now."

"I made haste," Ketahn replied, stopping in front of his friends. He extended his forelegs; Rekosh brushed his own against one while Urkot did the same to the other. The tiny hairs on Ketahn's hide picked up his friends' scents; silk and stone.

"Had you denned understone yesterday, we would already have finished our part in this," said Rekosh.

"I cannot sleep understone."

Rekosh's mandibles twitched, and he tilted his head. "Cannot or will not?"

"Ketahn cannot sleep without fresh leaves stuffed in his slit," Urkot said, thumping the floor with one leg. He dropped his left hand to the satchel hanging at his side and adjusted the bag, producing a clack of stone against stone from within.

Ketahn snapped his mandible fangs together. "Better leaves in my slit than rocks."

Urkot chittered. "Pebbles in places they do not belong is a small problem. Barely notice them anymore." His humor faded quickly, and his eyes—glowing the same blue as the markings on his hide—hardened. "You should not have come, Ketahn. I would have made an offering in your stead."

The weight of Urkot's words formed a lump in Ketahn's chest, but he would not waver in his purpose now. "She made her wishes clear."

"Has that ever mattered to you before?"

Ketahn tapped the side of his foreleg against Urkot's. "I would not have you risk your life on my behalf."

Urkot's mandibles rose and fell hesitantly.

"You must be warned, Ketahn," said Rekosh in a low voice.

His markings shone red, contrasting Urkot's blue. "There have been whispers along the web while you've been away."

"Are there not always whispers?" Ketahn asked. The roots in his hand felt heavier than ever, but he ignored their weight.

"She means to take a mate."

Ketahn glanced down the adjoining tunnels, each of which glowed with the gentle light of crystals and spiritcaps. Takarahl seemed ominously still and empty.

"She has taken many males," he said. "It does not concern me should she take another."

"A *mate*, Ketahn." Rekosh narrowed his eyes. "It is whispered that she desires a brood of her own. She lacks only a mate worthy of siring her eggs."

Clenching the bundled roots, Ketahn turned his head to stare down Heartsthread Tunnel, which led to the Den of Spirits. He had known this news would come eventually. It would have brought him to sever the final threads binding him to Takarahl long ago were those threads not so strong and meaningful.

Queen Zurvashi had never hidden her desire for Ketahn in the years after her war against the thornskull vrix of Kaldarak. If ever he might've felt honored or prideful due to her attentions, the chances of it were as dead as his mother, sire, and eight of his nine brothers and sisters.

Urkot bent his forelegs inward, scraping the hooked claws on their tips across the stone floor. "You still mean to go?"

Ketahn raised his hand to display the leaf-wrapped bundle. "I must make my offering to the Eight. Zurvashi would want nothing less."

Rekosh eased forward, dipping his head until his face nearly touched the bundle, and drew in a deep breath. His eyes widened, and he straightened quickly. "Mender root?"

"Ketahn, you fool," growled Urkot.

With a chitter, Rekosh spread his forelegs and sank into a shallow bow, all four arms spread wide. His long black and red hair, woven into a thick braid, fell over his shoulder. "As ever, Ketahn, time spent with you proves nothing if not thrilling."

"You should not encourage him," Urkot scolded. "The queen is unlikely to find humor in this."

"She is not meant to find humor in it," Ketahn replied.

"It is not worth her wrath."

"Zurvashi has made clear her wishes," Ketahn snapped, gnashing his mandibles, "and I am obeying!"

"That is the reason for your late arrival," said Rekosh. "You were searching the Tangle for that root just to spite her."

Urkot stared up at Ketahn, mandibles moving from side to side as though he were struggling to keep them from clamping together. The question in his eyes was as clear as though he'd spoken it aloud.

Is this worth your life?

"I have lost most everything because of her," Ketahn said, keeping his voice low despite the flare of angry heat in his chest. "If she takes anything more, it will be on my terms."

Urkot released a huff and scratched his chin with the tip of a claw. "If this is what you wish, Ketahn, I shall stride with you."

"As will I," said Rekosh. "But the High Claiming will be upon us soon. She is unlikely to forgive a rejection this year."

"Even queens must learn to accept disappointment." Ketahn relaxed his mandibles and opened his mouth to let out a huff of his own. The air he drew into his lungs was cold and stale, so unlike the hot, damp, fresh air of the surface. "I do not seek to throw my life away when so many others have been destroyed already. I want only to return to the Tangle and fulfill my duty."

Ketahn tapped his friends' forelegs with the ends of his own and tucked the mender roots against his side. "For all you have complained of me being late, where is Telok? He should have arrived before either of you."

Rekosh and Urkot exchanged a glance; brief as it was, Ketahn knew exactly what it meant.

6

"Do not withhold what you know," Ketahn said, letting his mandibles droop.

"The Moonfall matrons bade Telok and the other hunters enter the Tangle to find fresh quarry last sunfall," Urkot said, his voice a low rumble. "They are not expected to return until next suncrest."

Ketahn straightened, curling his hands into fists. He longed to have his barbed spear in hand, though he knew it could do him no good now, that it would bring him no comfort. "The night before Offering Day?"

"Because we have had nothing to fill our bellies but roots and mushrooms these past three eightdays, at least."

"There is no meat in Moonfall Tunnel," said Rekosh, "save that rotting on the bones of our neighbors. The rest is spitted over the queen's cooking fires."

Anger swelled in Ketahn's chest. The tiny hairs on his limbs stood on end, and his hide thrummed with restless energy. Though he rarely worked alongside the other hunters, he knew they were fulfilling their duties—they were bringing fresh meat into the city daily, enough to ensure that every vrix had some to eat.

"You speak true?" he asked.

Rekosh bent his arms at their elbows and crossed his forearms in the air in front of his chest, creating the sign of the Eight.

No vrix invoked the gods lightly—and Rekosh rarely did so at all.

"The same whispers come from all over Takarahl. Only those close to the queen have ample meat."

Even when he'd been a broodling, Rekosh had possessed a talent for gathering information—and gossip. Ketahn was never sure just how his friend managed to know everything that was going on in Takarahl and all the rumors spreading amongst its inhabitants, but Rekosh's information was rarely incorrect.

The Tangle was nearing the end of the current calm season. With the flood season looming, many of the jungle creatures were in a state of migration, seeking out new dens that would keep them out of the flood waters that would ravage the land. This was one of the most bountiful times of year to hunt—more creatures on the move meant more opportunity for kills.

There was no reason for the vrix of Takarahl to be suffering a meat shortage now.

Ketahn tightened his hold on the bundled roots, making the thick leaves around them creak. "We cannot allow this to continue."

"You are not the only one who feels that way," said Rekosh.

"Silence yourselves," Urkot hissed. His words echoed along several of the nearby tunnels, bouncing back to the chamber in eerie fragments. "We risk enough talking as freely as we have been, so go no further. Her web runs ever wider and is woven far more intricately than yours, Rekosh."

Rekosh and Ketahn snapped their mouths shut. Urkot's rebuke did not lessen Ketahn's anger, but it granted him focus—enough focus to understand the ultimate impotence of his rage.

Ketahn drummed his fingers on the upper segments of his legs. His mandibles were low, but they were unrelaxed. Though he was agitated, he wanted to be sure it was clear he wasn't angry at Urkot. He brought his forearms flat together, side-by-side, in a brief gesture of apology.

"Come," he said, turning toward Heartsthread Tunnel. "I must make my offering to the Eight that our queen might better understand my loyalty."

Chapter Two

THE ONLY SIGN that Ketahn and his companions were making forward progress along Heartsthread Tunnel was in the stone carvings on the walls—depictions of dozens of long-dead warriors and the many queens descended from the city's founder, Queen Takari, all of which had been worn over the long years. But the weblike writing on some of the carvings was still readable.

They had long since passed Prime Fang Jalar tes Unei'ani Ul'okari, who had slain two score warriors from another city in defense of Queen Vexii and died of her wounds. The carvings of Queen Ashai and Prime Fang Zeera had likewise been left behind, along with those of so many other queens and champions whose names were remembered now only in ancient writings kept in the queen's records.

Between the depictions of the females were smaller carvings, all of which were so faded that Ketahn had always wondered if the damage had been deliberate. None of those carvings bore writing that could be read, but Ketahn had always noted something interesting—most of the indistinct figures within them seemed to have six legs rather than four. That marked them as males.

But Ketahn could not recall having ever learned of a male

who'd been honored like this, who'd been worthy of remembrance in the same space as champions and queens.

The tunnel was wide and tall, with stone supports standing at regular intervals along its length. Large crystals glowed from their places in hewn alcoves, bathing the crowded vrix in soft blue light, and the swaths of dyed silk hanging between the supports swayed in the gentle flow of air from the Den of Spirits ahead.

Hundreds of vrix were packed in the tunnel as tightly as the threads of the most intricately woven cloth. The males' eyes and markings glowed in the light of the crystals, creating splashes of blue, green, red, and the far rarer purple everywhere.

The females, though outnumbered two to one, stood head and shoulders above the males, each of them nearly a segment taller than their counterparts. Though their hides lacked any colorful markings, most wore eye catching adornments—gold bands and rings, polished gems, decorated belts, beads, and pieces of brightly dyed silk.

The buzz of conversation was strong enough for Ketahn to feel it through the stone floor. All those voices came together to form an indecipherable sound, as primal as the ceaseless calls of tiny, unseen creatures in the Tangle. The only lulls in the conversations immediately around Ketahn came whenever he neared one of the many Queen's Fangs who were positioned along the walls.

Each of the Fangs stood tall and imposing, her right hands clamped on the shaft of a war spear with a broad blackrock head. Those spears were longer than Ketahn was tall. Each of the females wore a fanged club on her hip, as well, weapons that had the pointed teeth of various beasts and shards of blackrock embedded in their hardened wood.

None of the Fangs needed either weapon to kill, especially in so crowded a space.

Most of the other vrix, males particularly, seemed to avoid looking upon the Fangs directly. The elite warriors were only one part of the queen's vast web Urkot had mentioned—they just happened to be the most visible part.

Ketahn looked each Fang in her eyes. These warriors did not frighten him, though he knew any one of them could've brought about his end. Most of them knew him. Some he'd even fought beside in the war against Kaldarak. But he did not find the one Fang he sought—not yet.

A thousand years passed between each step forward, but the pace did not diminish Ketahn's resolve. His determination only grew with each segment closer he came to the Den of Spirits. The same clarity that suffused him during hunts settled upon him, sharpening his focus.

His place was in the Tangle, stalking dangerous beasts, exploring the dark, dank places never touched by sunlight, fighting through the jumbled plants and the hot, sticky air. Today, he would make that clear. He would make the queen understand without room for doubt.

Neither Rekosh nor Urkot spoke; they understood as well as anyone could and knew Ketahn would not be deterred.

Ketahn's eyes turned ahead more and more once they passed the carving of Queen Lyris, who had been only three generations removed from Queen Takari. He couldn't see far due to the females in the crowd, but there was a hint of more intense light ahead.

He was drawing close.

The end of Heartsthread Tunnel finally came into view. Gaps cut out of the wall allowed the light from the Den of Spirits to stream through and cast the huge carving of Queen Takari above the entryway in bold relief.

Urkot tapped a knee joint against one of Ketahn's rear legs, the gesture quick and firm and its message plain—he was with Ketahn. A moment later, Rekosh tapped Ketahn's hindquarters in a similar manner.

Three Queen's Fangs stood at the entryway, stopping the vrix seeking entrance. Their hulking forms were shadowed by the light from the cavern behind them, though their gold and gems gleamed as they moved.

One of the Fangs shoved a male back against the wall with one hand and dropped another to his waist, ignoring the pained chirrup he released. She plucked something off his belt. The object was too small for Ketahn to identify immediately—not until its sharpened edge caught the light.

It was a blackrock knife, the sort weavers like Rekosh often used in their work. The blade wasn't even long enough to span across the female's hand; the fangs of her mandibles were likely just as large as that blackrock shard, if not larger.

Ketahn moved forward instinctively, unsure of what he intended to do but certain that he could not merely watch. He had to act. Fang or not, no vrix in Takarahl had cause to treat the others as enemies.

He was halted by a strong hand on his arm and a spindly leg stretching in front of him. Ketahn didn't know whether to be grateful for or frustrated by Urkot and Rekosh's intervention.

"Weapons are not permitted in the Den of Spirits," the Fang declared in a voice at once hissing and booming.

The male forced his mandibles down, bowed his head, and brought his forearms together slowly in a sign of supplication—at least as much as the crushing hand pressed against his chest allowed him to.

For a few moments, the crowd around the entrance was silent, and the buzzing voices from ahead and behind Ketahn seemed muted and distant. The air was thicker, heavier, and crackled with the same sort of energy one could sense in the Tangle just before a lightning storm.

An unspoken question hung in the air between all those silent vrix—why were the Queen's Fangs permitted to carry weapons in that sacred cavern if no one else was?

A second Fang joined the first, extending her foreleg to brush it along the side of her companion's. "It is a tool, Irekah," the second Fang said in a familiar voice—she was Ahnset. "He is a weaver."

Irekah released a clicking growl and shoved away from the male, who sagged and seemed about to fall until Ahnset caught him by the arm.

"Weaver or not, he is a fool," Irekah snarled, "and our queen has no time for fools." She slapped the flat of the blackrock knife onto Ahnset's open palm and stalked away to take the central position in the entryway.

Ahnset helped the male regain his balance. "What are you called, and where do you dwell?"

The male's response was too low for Ketahn to make out.

"I cannot allow you to enter the Den of Spirits with this knife, Gahren," she said, tucking the tool behind her broad belt, "but by the Eight, I shall see it returned to you when this day is through."

Gahren offered another bow with forearms together.

"Would that the queen had more such as your broodsister in her ranks," Rekosh whispered.

"A hundred such as Ahnset is far more than any of us deserve," Ketahn replied, "and would still not be enough to change anything."

Ketahn watched as Ahnset said something more to the male and sent him on into the Den of Spirits. She was attired the same as her sister Fangs—gold bands around her upper arms, leather strips adorned with red beads on her wrists, a yatin hide gorget with large, thin bands of gold running from the base of her neck up to her jaw. Strips of red silk hung from her belt, which was decorated with pressed gold and more beads in weblike patterns. Her braided black hair was pulled back to hang in a bundle at her back, adorned with more beads and golden rings.

And, of course, she carried a spear and a fanged club. However gentle Ahnset could be, she was a warrior to her core, exceptionally skilled amongst the queen's elite. She'd proven herself more than most in the battles against Kaldarak.

Ketahn angled his path toward Ahnset and, soon enough, was standing before her.

Her eyes flashed purple with reflected light from the nearby crystals, and her gold adornments glinted. "My broodbrother."

She slid her forelegs toward Ketahn and sank into a bow that nearly put her face level with his.

Ketahn hooked his forelegs around hers and leaned forward. They both opened their mandibles wide as he tipped his head-crest against Ahnset's.

"Broodsister."

Her mandibles, half again as large as Ketahn's, closed lightly over his. He had seen females—Ahnset included—use their mandibles in battle. There was no question of the strength she could exert if she chose to do so. But she was one of a few vrix he trusted wholeheartedly.

Those thoughts faded as her scent washed over him, drawn in both through the air and the brush of the hairs on his legs against hers. For a short while, he forgot Zurvashi and Offering Day, forgot the cold, unyielding stone around him, forgot what he intended to do and the expected consequences of it.

Ahnset straightened, angling her head to look down at Ketahn. "You should have sent word when you arrived in Takarahl, broodbrother. It has been long since last I laid eyes upon you."

Withdrawing his forelegs, Ketahn bent them and knelt on their lower joints to bow, drawing his forearms together. "I am sorry, Ahnset. The Tangle binds me tighter each time I venture into it."

She tapped the butt of her spear on the floor. "May the Eight keep their many eyes upon you, Ketahn, and ensure the day does not come when the Tangle refuses to release you."

As he rose, Ahnset shifted her gaze to look past him. "Rekosh, Urkot. I am glad to see you, also."

"Ahnset," the two males said in unison.

Her mandibles and eyes relaxed. Ketahn could almost pretend

that all was as it had been while they were broodlings, before their lives had been complicated by the demands of Takarahl and its queen.

"Though I am sorry to deny you the pleasure of throwing me against the wall, Ahnset, I must tell you I left my knife in my den," Rekosh said, leaning forward—which made the red markings on his back glow a little stronger.

Ahnset chittered softly. "As always, Rekosh, I am sure I will find reason to do so as long as you keep talking."

Rekosh's mandibles twitched, and his forelegs drummed the floor. "Ah, to be so known by another is a thrill."

Another chitter escaped Ahnset. Then she adjusted the grip of her right hands along the shaft of her spear, raised her chin, and squared her shoulders. Her lower left hand fell, its thumb hooking on her belt just above the club.

No matter how many times Ketahn had seen it happen, Ahnset's transition from caring broodsister and friend to Queen's Fang always amazed him.

"You are welcomed on behalf of Queen Zurvashi tes Kalaa'ani Ul'okari, Queen of Takarahl and Guardian of the Ancestral Crystals," she intoned. "Our queen bids you to make offering to the Eight that our city may remain prosperous."

Urkot eased closer and sank into a reverent pose, arms intersected in the gesture of the Eight which, for him, would always be incomplete. Rekosh and Ketahn did the same.

Ahnset flicked her gaze toward Irekah. Dipping her head closer to Ketahn's, she whispered, "After you have made your offering, hasten out the Deepdelve Tunnel. Do not delay. The queen is in foul temper today."

As Ketahn and his companions proceeded past Ahnset, his thought was given voice by a low whisper from Rekosh.

"Has she any other temper?"

The fullness of the Den of Spirits' light struck Ketahn before he could reply. He slitted his eyes against the glare, and the cavern gradually came into focus. As much as he'd come to dislike being understone, Ketahn always felt a flare of wonder when he entered this cavern.

The ceiling was so high that it was lost in hazy, bluish darkness, a darkness both broken and enhanced by the sunlight streaming in through the hole at the ceiling's peak. From the floor, that hole looked too small for even a hatchling to pass through, but Ketahn had peered into it from the surface. It was at least five segments across, big enough to swallow the largest female with room to spare. Looking through that hole in the dark of night to see the blue crystals glowing far below had been an awe-inspiring experience.

Now those many-faceted crystals were catching the sunlight and shattering it, spraying rainbows across the cavern walls and stonework. Crystal formations stood throughout the cavern, some of them larger than Ketahn; they grew from the floor, hung from the ceiling, and jutted from the walls. Shaped stone flowed around those crystals in many places, taking advantage of their light to make clear the writing etched everywhere.

Here were recorded the stories of Takarahl, its queens, and the Eight, available for all vrix to read—though some sections had been blocked off for as long as Ketahn could remember so stoneshapers could repair the wear they'd accrued over the years.

Ketahn had never seen any stoneshapers working in those areas, and Urkot had never met another shaper who claimed to have done so. There was only one ongoing piece of stonework in the Den of Spirits—a new statue that had been taking shape over the last few years.

There were not merely carvings here—there were statues and sculptures, the most prominent of which depicted Queen Takari in ten-segment-tall stone. She was surrounded by eight pillars that towered over her, each of which bore eight gemstone eyes.

The eyes of the Eight, looking down upon Takari to fulfill her oath.

Zurvashi's statue would be twice as tall when it was finished.

The old stories said Queen Takari had discovered the Den of

Spirits as she'd been leading her exiled people in search of a sanctuary. She'd fallen through the brambles that had grown over the hole overhead, and by the grace of the Eight, had landed unharmed. It had been their will that guided her to this place, their will that had safeguarded her.

Once Zurvashi's statue was complete, anything that fell through the hole was likely to be caught not by the gods, but her gigantic stone hands.

Those stories claimed Queen Takari had sensed the spirits of her ancestors here. She had sworn to protect the Den of Spirits from that day onward, had sworn her entire bloodline to uphold that sacred duty. She'd become the first Guardian of the Ancestral Crystals.

But Ketahn had never sensed any spirits in this cavern. Perhaps it was because the last of Queen Takari's bloodline, descended over countless generations, had been slain by Zurvashi in this very cavern sixteen years ago.

Queen Zurvashi stood upon the uppermost portion of a broad stone dais at the center of the cavern, backed by towering columns, carved archways, dangling banners, two of her Fangs, and a single Queen's Claw—one of the males who served as her personal hunters and scouts.

Ringlets adorned the small braids into which Zurvashi's hair had been arranged, and her belt made Ahnset's look plain. She wore enough gold that she seemed to emit her own light. All that metal—along with her many beads and gems—was polished to shining. Where she was not clad in metal, her body was swathed in sheer, purple silk, some of which was so long that it hung over her hindquarters and brushed the floor.

She did not move save the occasional twitch of her mandibles or forelegs, observing the vrix making their offerings to the nearby spiritspeakers with unsettling indifference. When it came to the queen, boredom was dangerous.

Ketahn sank into a lower stance, putting himself on level with most of the nearby males, and continued following the procession. Vrix were streaming toward the central platform from four different tunnels, guided by Fangs positioned at regular intervals.

Silk-shrouded spiritspeakers moved along the dais, their flowing white coverings lending a sense of softness and grace to their large bodies. They collected offerings from the approaching vrix and gave blessings in return. Only Archspeaker Valkai, who alone wore intricate gold bands around her arms and neck, was not taking offerings. She stood just below and to the side of the queen with her arms bent and forearms crossed in the sign of the Eight.

To Ketahn, she seemed to be avoiding looking at anything directly, especially the males with yellow sashes and flattened strips of bark who were alongside her spiritspeakers—the queen's scribes, who were noting the name and offering of every vrix in attendance.

Ketahn glanced at the unfinished statue nearby, which already loomed larger than anything in the cavern even though it lacked two arms and a head. He found himself suddenly torn between his anger and his urge to leave, to return to the jungle, to delve deeper into the Tangle than ever without leaving so much as a frayed thread for the Queen's Claw to follow.

Another meaningful tap came from Urkot, followed by one from Rekosh. Only eight vrix remained between Ketahn and the dais; perhaps he might have taken that number as a sign rather than an inevitability were his attention not otherwise occupied.

The queen stirred.

Zurvashi's amber eyes glinted as boldly as her metal adornments as she swung her gaze to Ketahn. He had faced down bloodthirsty beasts that hadn't looked half as predatory as the queen. Her mandibles opened wide and rose, and her mouth parted enough for her tongue to slip out and trace one of the pointed tips on her upper jaw.

She turned her head and spoke to the nearest of her Fangs—Prime Fang Korahla, the head of her elite warriors.

Prime Claw Durax watched the exchange from behind the

females with his pale blue eyes narrowed. When the queen had finished, Durax turned his head to glare at Ketahn. One of his hands dropped to clasp the haft of the blackrock axe slung on his belt.

Korahla strode forward, halted at the edge of the dais, and banged the butt of her spear on the stone, making a hollow clacking that echoed through the cavern. "Ketahn tes Ishuun'ani Ir'okari, approach the dais so our queen may honor you by accepting your offering."

Ketahn was aware of the hush that had fallen over the Den of Spirits; the cavern was so quiet he could hear the air flowing in through the hole overhead as clearly as he could feel it across his fine hairs and hide. Some might have called it bravery, others foolishness, but he felt no fear—and he did not hesitate to move forward.

The queen's heavy, hungry gaze did not intimidate him. It only filled him with fresh determination.

"Finally learning your place, Ketahn?" Zurvashi asked, her voice low and buzzing.

"My queen demanded my presence." Ketahn stopped at the base of the dais, tilting his head back even more than usual to hold her gaze.

"Ketahn, sweet one, I have yet to make a demand of you." Her mandibles snapped toward each other, their tips touching before she spread them again. "When I finally do, you will not look quite so smug."

"As you say, my queen," he grated, barely stopping himself from bristling at the truth of her words.

"I shall never understand why you choose the hardships of the Tangle over the luxuries of Takarahl." Zurvashi lifted her upper arms, turning her hands so her palms faced away from Ketahn. The gold and gems on her wrists and the backs of her hands flashed with blinding reflected light. "My request remains, Ketahn. Become my chief hunter. Lead the Queen's Claw. Such would be a much more sensible use of your skills."

Durax stepped forward with a growl, mandibles wide and hand rising as though he were about to tear his axe free. "My queen, you cannot choose this jungle worm to—"

Zurvashi flicked a hand toward Durax, not even glancing in his direction. The Prime Claw's mouth snapped shut, and he released his weapon. He dropped his gaze as he retreated a step.

Ketahn released a slow breath. The air he drew in afterward was laden with jungle smells from above, but they were overpowered by Zurvashi's heady scent, a particular feminine fragrance that struck him on an instinctual level well beneath his waking mind.

Her scent had never overcome him before; it would not do so today.

"With respect, my queen"—he took the leaf-wrapped bundle in his lower hands, lifting it toward her—"I seek only to give thanks to the Eight. For allowing me to live during the reign of the greatest queen Takarahl has ever known."

Her mandibles clacked together, their fangs striking with enough force to have crushed Ketahn's skull. She rose higher, and her shadow, cast by the beam of sunlight slanting in from overhead, stretched long over the dais' stone.

"You are not half so clever as to veil your insults in mock praise and have it elude my notice, Ketahn," she rumbled.

Faint tremors crept through the stone floor as she strode toward him.

She descended to the level just above Ketahn, looming over him like a storm cloud over an already flooded jungle. "Present your offering, that I may best decide your fate."

Her scent was even stronger now, and the pieces of silk hanging from her belt had fallen aside to reveal the long seam of her slit, now just above his eye level.

Clamping his jaw shut, he forced his mandibles down, shifted his rear pairs of legs back, and bowed. He unraveled the bundle with his upper hands.

"I offer the same gift I made seven years ago, my queen."

22

The leaves fell away to reveal the mender roots, which were still oozing their purple juices.

"Fresh enough for my queen's dye masters," Ketahn said, keeping his gaze locked with Zurvashi's.

She narrowed her eyes, and her hide stretched as her muscles tensed. One of her legs slid forward, but Ketahn did not back away even a finger's span. A low hiss sounded from the queen's throat. The Fangs flanking her moved forward, leveling their spears. At a gesture from Zurvashi, they halted two segments before reaching the edge of the dais.

"Forgive me, my queen," Ketahn said, "but I had forgotten. Your favorite shade requires something more."

Ketahn brought his upper arms together and stabbed a claw into his left palm. It sank deep. The pain was far off and yet oddly thrilling; it was not lost upon him that it might have been one of the last sensations of his life.

Blood welled around his claw. He turned his hand and let the blood drip onto the mender roots. The dark red droplets mixed with the purple juices, creating blotches of darker color.

The queen's mandibles pressed together. The scrape of their fangs against one another was the only sound in the whole cavern.

"Such things cannot go unpunished, Ketahn," she said, her voice a low growl that vibrated across his fine hairs. She bent forward and reached out with a hand, snatching the roots away from him.

His hearts quickened, and tension rippled through his body. Fear sizzled up from his gut, hot and unsettling, but it had never stopped him before.

Zurvashi squeezed the roots in her fist. Purple juice ran over her hide and spattered the floor between Ketahn's forelegs, joined by a few fresh drops of his blood.

She leaned closer still, bracing her thick, powerful legs to either side of Ketahn. Her heat pulsed into him, and her scent wrapped around him like a cocoon, laced even more heavily with her desire.

Ketahn's stem stirred behind his slit. He clenched his jaw against the sensation, refusing to give her such a reaction.

"You provoke my ire, Ketahn." Her lower arms encircled him, and her large claws grazed his back lightly enough that he nearly shuddered.

He kept his mandibles low. If she meant to end him now, there would be no stopping her—but he was quick enough, at least, to inflict some damage before he was through.

"Clever as you think yourself, do you not realize what you are accomplishing?" she asked.

Ketahn's claspers drew tighter against his pelvis, pinching his slit closed more firmly as the seam bulged with the insistent press of his stem. He held her gaze without wavering.

"You do not," she continued with a chitter. One of her hands rose suddenly, and she grasped his bound hair in her fist, yanking on it to force his head back. "Your every act of defiance, Ketahn, serves as proof that you are to be my mate. You alone are worthy of that honor."

Ketahn was aware of eyes upon him—dozens, hundreds, the eyes of every vrix in Takarahl, perhaps even the eyes of the Eight. But he could see only Zurvashi's.

"But you are not worthy, Zurvashi," he said.

Her hold on his hair strengthened, producing sharp pain on his head, and her claws pressed hard enough against his back to threaten piercing his hide.

Had he come here to seek his death? Did he possess an eagerness, tucked somewhere in the hidden recesses of his mind, where his darkest secrets were shrouded in webs even he could not penetrate, to meet his end?

"Shall I make my demand, then?" she whispered, stroking the sides of her mandibles up and down his neck. "Shall I test you once and for all, sweet little Ketahn, and prove the choice has always been—and will forever remain—mine?"

"Even you, my queen, cannot have everything you want," he replied.

"For all your prowess and skill, Ketahn, you lack understanding." Her mandible fangs scraped his neck, producing a dry rasp. "I am the *only* one who gets what I desire—always."

Ketahn's forelegs curled, their claws raking the floor. He strained to expand his awareness, to place part of his focus on his surroundings and the many onlookers, or on the crystals, the stonework, on anything, but Zurvashi commanded his full attention.

"May the Eight bless you, my queen," he said thickly, "and ensure you receive all you deserve."

His hearts pumped wildly as Zurvashi stared into his eyes. Her fangs paused just beneath his jaw, their deadly tips resting against the soft, vulnerable hide there. Finally, she shoved him away. Ketahn remained upright only by spreading all six of his legs to assume a wider stance.

"Enjoy the Tangle, Ketahn," she said, turning away and displaying the backs of her hands dismissively. "Your time there will soon be at its end. And remember the threads that bind you to this city. I will not hesitate to sever them one by one should you give me cause."

A strong, rough hand clamped around Ketahn's upper arm. "Move, you damned fool," rumbled Urkot.

Ketahn tugged his arm free, and stared at the queen until she had taken her place at the peak of the dais. When her attention flicked toward him, he crossed his forearms over each other and dipped his head.

She responded by lifting her gaze to look past him.

"You have done enough," Rekosh whispered, tapping Ketahn's rear leg. "Much as I admire the way you made your statement, it is best not to linger."

Ketahn felt little as he and his friends strode toward Deepdelve Tunnel. His hearts did not ease, even as the soft sound of conversation resumed, and his muscles were stiff and restless. But nothing else remained—not pride or satisfaction, not fear or relief, not foreboding or hope.

"Zurvashi tes Kalaa'ani Ul'okari," a female called, her voice booming through the chamber, "I challenge you under the eight-fold eyes of the gods. Your reign shall end this day, and Sathai tes Sorak'ani Tok'okari will become the new queen of Takarahl."

Uncertain clicks and trills swept through the crowd like wind through the jungle boughs.

Halting, Ketahn spun to face the dais; Rekosh and Urkot did the same.

The two Fangs who'd been flanking Zurvashi had moved forward to level their spears at the challenger, a female with a scarred hide and only a few scraps of adornment. Durax stood between the Fangs and the queen, axe in hand, as though he were not entirely outclassed by the females surrounding him.

Sathai's mandibles were raised, and she had her arms to the sides, making her appear even larger. She was looking directly at Zurvashi, past the blackrock spearheads that were within a handspan of her face.

"An eventful Offering Day," Rekosh said. "Perhaps your display was inspiring, Ketahn."

Ketahn's mandibles twitched. He folded his arms across his chest as his fine hairs rose again; he could still smell Zurvashi, making him long more than ever for the thick jungle air. "I hope you are wrong, Rekosh. No more vrix need die meaninglessly."

"But it would have been fine had you done so?" asked Urkot, folding his upper arms to mimic Ketahn's stance. His lower arm reached across his torso so he could settle his hand over the scarred hide on his side.

"We need not watch this," Ketahn replied, trying to ignore the sting of Urkot's words. "As Rekosh said, it is best we do not linger."

"This may be the challenge that changes everything," Rekosh said with too much excitement. "We must bear witness."

The queen lifted a hand. Even from a distance, Ketahn could see the purple juice staining her hide—and a bit of his dark blood mixed with it.

The Archspeaker moved from her place, her long silk wrappings trailing over the floor. The shifting fabric seemed to change color in the rainbow light of the crystals. "Your challenge is recognized by the eightfold eyes, Sathai tes Sarak'ani Tok'okari," she called in a high, clear voice that nonetheless reverberated through the cavern. "The Eight bear witness. Our ancestors bear witness. Takarahl bears witness."

Queen Zurvashi made a harsh, hissing growl and snapped her mandibles together. The Fangs at the edge of the dais withdrew, moving several segments away from the queen. Durax did the same, but only after a long hesitation that earned him a glare from the queen.

Zurvashi stomped on the stone and spread her arms. "Come then, Sathai. Add your name to the ranks of my slain challengers."

The other female leapt onto the dais smoothly. Her hind legs flexed, and her hide pulled taut. Ketahn recognized the scars she bore—they had been left by spears, knives, and fanged clubs, by claw and fang.

"Let us be off," Ketahn urged.

"What if the Eight finally take action, Ketahn?" Urkot asked. "What if you compelled them to do so? This...this may be justice."

The note of hope in Urkot's low voice nearly broke Ketahn. He could not bring himself to say what he knew to be true—this challenge would be no different than any other.

Sathai reared back, balancing herself on her hind legs to lift her front pair off the ground in a display of size and strength. Her mandibles parted wide, and she answered the queen's prior growl with one of her own.

The challenger charged. Only as Sathai crashed into her did the queen move, shifting her huge body aside with deceptive speed as she grabbed hold of the challenger.

Zurvashi twisted, redirecting Sathai's momentum just enough to disrupt her balance. As she tumbled to the floor heavily, Sathai latched onto the queen, dragging Zurvashi down with her.

Two of Sathai's fists slammed into Zurvashi's face in quick succession, the dull thumps of impact echoing through the otherwise silent cavern. All eyes were upon that dais, and it seemed the same sense of longing and hopefulness Ketahn had heard in Urkot's words thrummed in the very air. Takarahl's fate dangled by a single frayed thread.

But they all knew. They *had* to know. Since claiming rulership of Takarahl, Zurvashi had faced at least ten such challenges... and before ever she'd seized the title of queen, she'd been Prime Fang to the prior ruler.

Zurvashi herself had led her Fangs into battle against Kaldarak.

The queen pressed the tips of two legs onto the floor and rolled atop her challenger, golden adornments clinking. Wrapping her other legs around Sathai's middle, Zurvashi hammered her fists into her challenger's face and torso, using her lower arms to divert Sathai's attempts at shielding herself. Sathai's defenses crumbled, and there was a wet crunch as the queen's next blow landed.

Now Zurvashi had more than one hand bloodied.

Without ceremony, Zurvashi grasped Sathai's head, wrenched it aside, and brought her mandibles down around the defeated female's throat.

Ketahn balled his hands into useless fists.

The sound of the queen's mandibles closing made the wet crunch from a moment before seem mild and unimportant; it was a sound Ketahn had heard far too many times in his life, but he'd never been able to shake how much it unsettled him. Sathai's body stiffened. Her legs curled in toward her hindquarters, her claws raked across the floor, and then she was still.

Zurvashi grasped the long hair on Sathai's head with one hand and the challenger's chin with another. She pulled the head up and twisted it to the side. The muscle, hide, and bone holding

28

Sathai's head onto her body gave up their fight after two heart-beats. Dark blood pooled atop the dais and spattered across the stone as the queen rose.

The Archspeaker Valkai kept her gaze averted from the scene. Her silk coverings rippled as though she'd shuddered, and she lifted the cloth with her lower hands so it did not touch the spreading blood. "The Eight have made known their will. The sacred rite is concluded. Long reign Zurvashi, Queen of Takarahl and Guardian of the Ancestral Crystals."

Zurvashi turned her face toward Ketahn, meeting his gaze and holding it for a moment. Then she tossed the severed head aside and returned to her place on the uppermost part of the dais. "Proceed."

The spiritspeakers hurriedly resumed their collection of offerings as a pair of Fangs marched forward to collect Sathai's remains.

Durax stared at Ketahn from his place at Zurvashi's side, mandibles twitching. He still held his axe in hand.

"Shaper, shelter us," Urkot said, voice laden with sorrow and despair.

"Weaver, shroud us," Rekosh said, his voice filled with disappointment and frustration.

"The Eight hold no power here," Ketahn growled, turning toward Deepdelve Tunnel. "Not so long as she rules."

Chapter Three

THE TANGLE BREATHED AROUND KETAHN. Leaves rustled, branches creaked, and vines swayed lazily, moving as though the air were as thick as mire muck. Twigs fell here and there, snapping and cracking and shaking more leaves. Unseen creatures made their calls of warning, of mating, of hunger.

Shafts of orange-tinged light pierced the canopy in places, but few managed to reach all the way to the jungle floor. The shadows between the mighty tree trunks and their jumbled roots and branches were already deep. The sun would light the sky for a while longer, but inside the Tangle, it was all but sunfall.

Ketahn crept along thick branches high over the ground, knowing full well that neither height nor distance could cleanse the unease that had festered in him since the events in the Den of Spirits earlier.

He was no longer in Takarahl. He could breathe easier now, could fall back into the life he'd chosen, the life he found most fulfilling...

But he couldn't help envisioning long threads, each thin and delicate, glistening silver in the failing light, running from his arms and legs back to the city. He could almost feel their pull.

Long ago, there had been many more of those threads, and they'd been strong together—just as sticks were stronger in a bundle.

Zurvashi's threat was nothing new. Ketahn had always known his connection to Takarahl—through the vrix he cared for—was at the queen's mercy. Yet the reminder had been a smoldering coal in his chest as he'd navigated the intersecting corridors on his return to Moonfall Tunnel. It had persisted as he'd gathered his belongings from Rekosh's den, and it had only strengthened when he'd departed from his friends and strode toward the nearest exit from the city.

Even now, after traveling hundreds of segments away from Takarahl, he'd not shaken the feeling.

Tucking his barbed spear's shaft along his forearm, he leapt off the branch, throwing his arms forward to grab a nearby bough. His lower half swung beneath him, dangling briefly in empty air.

His stomach sank, but he hauled himself up, hooking his rearmost legs around the underside of the thick bough to find additional purchase. His claws sank into the bark, and he paused to allow his mind to clear. Any distraction out in the Tangle, even if it existed only in his mind, increased the danger eightfold.

Ketahn forced himself onward, selecting his path along the wide branch with care. His den was not far; he'd traversed half the distance between it and the city already. The wisest choice would have been to go there and rest, allowing the solitude and isolation to soothe him until he could shed his worries.

Today did not seem a day for wise decisions.

He continued deeper into the Tangle, beyond his isolated den, to seek solace in the hunt. The shadows thickened rapidly as the sun, hidden from Ketahn by the dense jungle growth, continued its fall into the realm of spirits and darkness.

New sources of light appeared in the sun's absence, first in the deepest hollows and recesses and then spreading with the onset of night. Ketahn's vision sharpened. Vrix eyes were best in the half gloom of the nighttime jungle, drinking in the soft light.

Jesan flowers emitted their pale purple light as they bloomed to the darkness, staining the leaves of their vines with new color. Clusters of mushrooms glowed in greens and yellows on the ground and along tree trunks. The broad leaves of spiritsong trees gave off their deep blue light, bright enough only to distinguish themselves from the deeper darkness. Like the crystals in the Den of Spirits, those trees were said to hold spirits within them, and vrix avoided damaging them—an angered spirit was a dangerous thing that could not be overcome with any weapon.

With the sky gone black, the trees and their branches were like the walls and ceiling of a vast cavern choked with plants—but they lacked the oppressive air of Takarahl's tunnels.

Ketahn stalked along the branches, eyes sweeping his surroundings ceaselessly, and listened to the Tangle's night sounds. The darkness had been ushered in by droning calls of reclusive creatures, and beasts that did not normally stir during the day now added their voices to the night.

The air hung heavy and still, and the whisper of leaves over-head was muted. Ketahn had spent so many nights like this in the jungle, so many nights in warm air under peaceful skies, so many nights of quietly appreciating the world around him. The towering trees and their mighty roots served as a reminder that there were always bigger things—the vrix, male and female alike, were small compared to the Tangle. The overgrown brush and vines, the leaves and branches, the mushrooms and flowers, were all in their own ways signs of something more.

Perhaps they were signs of the Eight, who, according to the tales, had wrought this world. Perhaps they were signs of life's perseverance. Perhaps it was both. The answer made little differ-ence to Ketahn.

Only out here could he set aside the past. Only out here could he imagine any sort of future.

One beast call rose over the rest, high and undulating, pulsing smoothly between a howl and a whistle.

Halting, Ketahn turned his head to listen, the fine hairs on his legs standing up to better sample the air. With little wind, he could scent only the plants immediately around him. But that call had come from nearby—a few hundred segments at most. And it had been made by a soota; their hides were particularly supple, their meat especially flavorful and tender.

What better way to return to his den than with a fresh soota skinned and carved?

He passed his spear into one of his upper hands, ensured his bag was fastened snugly to his back, and altered his course to follow the soota's call, angling toward suncrest, the direction from which the sun would rise at dawn to resume its battle against the darkness.

That call had come from near a place the other hunters avoided, somewhere said to be haunted by malevolent spirits that were no friends to the vrix. Ketahn had always found the area around it to be a bountiful hunting ground. At its core was a place the sun would never touch, a place where darkness welled in defiance of light—a huge pit that devoured anything that fell in.

The call sounded twice more before Ketahn glimpsed the soota. It was high in the trees, even higher than him. Its sleek hide, which was covered in soft, blue-gray fur, shimmered in the faint glow cast by the red glands set behind its large, yellow eyes on either side of its face.

Ketahn stopped in the shadow of a tree, peering up at his prey. The soota lifted its front legs off the branch, rearing back on its two pairs of hind legs, and called again, its throat briefly swelling and displaying that red glow as it did so.

The soota eased down again and trundled forward, its hooked claws easily grasping the branches around it.

It was heading directly for the pit.

Carefully, Ketahn climbed higher. As he gained height, diffused starlight broke through the canopy to fall upon him, making his markings glow purple.

He moved in the direction the soota had gone with even greater care, testing each branch and vine before trusting them with even a little of his weight; the plants were more delicate here, not merely because they were thinner but because they were more exposed to the wind.

Soon, Ketahn could make out the edge of the pit below, where the ground jutted up slightly and jagged, moss-covered stones stood like the teeth of a lurking predator.

The Tangle had done its best to swallow up the circular pit. Hardy plants grew from the steep walls amidst the exposed rock and dirt, and thick roots extended out and down into the darkness. A web of plant life had grown across the entire pit farther down, the creeping vines engulfing any debris—or unfortunate beasts—that happened to fall in.

Even when the sun passed directly over the pit, there was only darkness to be seen beneath the tangled growth spanning it. When the rocks Ketahn had tossed into the pit hadn't been stopped by the plant web, they'd fallen for another few heartbeats before landing—either with a dull thud or a splash.

The boughs of the surrounding trees had strained to span the hole, but it was too wide. The branches only extended about ten segments in the air over the pit, less than a sixth of the way.

As Ketahn passed directly over the pit, he felt a change in the air. Some unseen energy, faint but impossible to ignore, thrummed around him. It had always reminded him of that lightning storm energy, though this was always present, always constant.

Legends told that long ago the vrix had been assailed by a huge, fiery beast that had required all the Eight to overcome. The Shaper and the Delver had dug this pit, and the Hunter had lured the beast here, far away from the vrix, whose injuries were tended by the Broodmother. The Protector and the Flamebearer had used all their might to banish the monster to the darkness below. Then, the Weaver had assisted the Rootsinger in creating the web of plants to keep the creature trapped forever.

Takarahl's other hunters feared rousing the beast from its slumber.

Ketahn was not sure he believed all that, and he'd been tempted to find a way down to discover the truth of it—but he could not deny the unnatural energy this place emitted, and he swore he had seen a light below on a few occasions, the merest hint of fiery orange.

He flattened himself along a thick bough and searched the trees for his prey. A flash of red caught his attention ahead, only slightly above him now. Leaves rustled as the soota leapt from branch to branch. Ketahn followed.

Glancing down, he glimpsed the soft blues and greens shed by leaves in the darkness, making the pit seem almost welcoming. But there was something beneath it for an instant—that orange glow, like a fire smoldering in the deep, there and gone in an instant.

Though it should have reinforced his misgivings, though it should have lent weight to the stories, that glimpse only intrigued Ketahn. If nothing else, the bottom of a cursed pit would've made a good place to hide from Zurvashi and the Queen's Claw.

Not far away, the soota worked its way along a thin, trembling branch that extended past the rest into the open air over the pit. Throat swelling, the creature released another undulating howl into the night air, as though it were calling directly to those glimmering stars.

Ketahn crept closer, shifting the coil of silk rope attached to his barbed spear into his lower hand. The boughs shook beneath his weight, which was much greater than the soota's, but he needed only a clear path to make his throw.

The soota howled again as a gust of wind swept over the Tangle, shaking the trees. The dark clouds blocking out a portion of the night sky shifted, revealing the two full moons just over the canopy. The soota's fur took on a silver sheen in the moonlight.

Ketahn hefted his spear, closing his fingers around the familiar groove worn into the shaft. He waited only for the swaying branches to ease...

A tremor pulsed through the bough upon which Ketahn was

perched, faint but distinct from the vibrations caused by his weight and the wind. Pressing the tips of his mandibles together, he turned his head to glance back toward the trunk.

Several dark shapes were moving in the shadows of the leaves. A set of four eyes briefly caught the moonlight, flashing yellow. Those eyes were not directed toward Ketahn—they were focused on the soota.

Ketahn stilled himself, watching as more of the xiskals crossed the broken patches of moonlight. Their tough, mottled hides were covered with long, backswept quills along their spines, and their front legs—four in total—were longer than their rear pair, all tipped with hooked claws ideal for climbing.

This was a small pack—he only counted five—but xiskals were dangerous in any number, despite being only half the size of a full grown male vrix.

The xiskals prowled toward the soota, focused intently on their prey. The surrounding branches creaked and groaned under the new weight, dipping more with every finger length the xiskals advanced. Something tightened in Ketahn's chest, squeezing with as much force as the queen could've mustered.

The soota turned abruptly, fur bristling and long ears snapping up.

That energy in the air intensified, pulsing along Ketahn's hide. He did not know which of the Eight he had angered—the Protector or the Broodmother, perhaps—in his confrontation with Zurvashi, but it seemed the gods were keen to test him tonight. And he knew with a certainty as solid as Takarahl's stone what was about to happen.

The xiskals darted toward the spooked soota as Ketahn turned back toward the tree trunk, wrapping the end of his spear's silk rope around his hand. Branches cracked and snapped, leaves shook violently, and the tenuous support beneath Ketahn fell away.

He threw the barbed spear at the trunk, but he was already plummeting amidst the broken boughs and panicked chitters from the xiskals. Ketahn found himself looking up through a mass of tangled branches, falling leaves, and thrashing beasts at a purple and blue sky sprinkled with stars that looked like glowing larvae dangling from a cavern ceiling far, far above.

Something darted through the intact boughs overhead—a blur of blue-gray, a flash of red—and vanished.

Ketahn might have offered a prayer to the Eight in that moment, as he tumbled backward and the world inverted so he was staring straight down into the gaping pit, but he'd only ever been able to rely upon himself.

The silk rope went taut, constricting his hand painfully. The strain on his arm was immense as it took his full weight. Branches and twigs slapped and raked his hide as they fell around him.

Ketahn swung toward the edge of the pit. His body spun around in time for him to see the pit's wall rushing toward him.

The rope jolted. The strain on his arm ceased, and his insides lurched as he fell again.

Ketahn hit the wall hard, releasing a pained growl he barely heard over the noise of chittering xiskals and crashing branches below him. He clawed for purchase with his arms and legs, but the dirt and plants were too loose, the slope too steep.

The sounds from the xiskals ended suddenly, along with all the crashing.

Ketahn slipped, knocking loose a torrent of clumped dirt and small stones that clattered down the slope.

From somewhere overhead, the soota made its high call into the night as though nothing had happened.

"Damn your eyes," Ketahn snarled, uncertain of whether he was directing the words at the soota, the Eight, or the queen.

In a jumble of dirt and stone, leaf and root, Ketahn fell again.

Chapter Four

THE SOUND of branches breaking and leaves thrashing were deafening as Ketahn hit the plant web. Wood scratched and pricked Ketahn's hide, so much of it at once that he couldn't identify any single point of pain.

The stronger branches and vines jolted him, not enough so to halt his fall but enough to slow it. His body was twisted and whipped around wildly, destroying his understanding of up and down; was he falling into the pit or into the sky?

Bramble claws raked at Ketahn from all directions, a thousand hands all trying—and failing—to catch hold of him. The tangle of plant growth seemed endless, but all too soon, he'd smashed through to a layer of dead, brittle, particularly biting branches. He lashed out with arms and legs made numb by pain in search of something, anything, to grasp, but all the branches broke off in his hands or shattered against the hard hide of his legs.

He glimpsed only darkness below—darkness bearing that strange orange light.

Ketahn plunged into that darkness. His body rotated again, and he found himself looking up at a large gap broken through the plant web, its edges lined with jagged branches.

He could not help noticing the glimmering stars through the opening, or the tuft of dark cloud lined with pale moonlight. The Eight must have decided his fate truly was to die in some dark hole, after all.

At least it wasn't Takarahl.

The silk rope cinched around his hand, bringing Ketahn to an abrupt halt with all his weight on that arm. He growled; this pain was unique to all the rest, and he doubted his shoulder could take much more of such punishment. Would the rope give out first, or his body?

Dangling in the air, Ketahn reflected briefly upon his choices today, found no reason to regret any of them, and pulled himself up high enough to grasp the rope with his other hands. His movements set him to swinging, and soon he was also slowly rotating.

The branches creaked and groaned overhead, and the leaves shook when he tugged himself higher and clamped the claws of his forelegs down on the rope, pinching it between them. With a drawn-out crack like rolling thunder, a series of branches snapped overhead. The rope dropped by a full segment, dropping Ketahn an equal distance and making his insides lurch again.

He refused to suffer another fall.

Keeping himself as otherwise still as possible, Ketahn glanced down. His eyes took a moment to adjust to the gloom—which was now somehow absent of that orange light—before he could make out the bottom of the pit. Much of what he saw was deep black, but there were shimmering points of faint light closer to the pit wall—reflections upon the surface of standing water. Fortunately, there seemed to be solid ground directly below him, strewn with countless branches and other debris.

Climbing any higher now would only result in a longer fall to the bottom of the pit, which was at least ten segments down already.

As delicately as he could, Ketahn curled his hindquarters and shifted his rear legs to gather the silk from his spinnerets. His body pulsed as he drew out the thick thread, and he began to swing again, gently—but not gently enough to prevent more groans and cracks from above.

He passed the silk thread into one of his lower hands and tied it off to the spear's rope. Slowly, he lowered himself, unraveling the rope from his hand as he moved and drawing more silk from his spinnerets. As soon as he was close enough to the ground, he stretched his rear legs, setting their tips down to reduce the strain on the rope.

Cutting off the thread, Ketahn settled his other legs on the ground and studied his new surroundings as the punishments his body had endured echoed and throbbed. The ground was damp, blanketed not only with the twigs, leaves, and vines that had fallen with him but a thick layer of rotting leaves and debris. Only a few segments away, the ground gave way to black water. The air smelled of wet dirt, decay, and stagnant water, but there was something more, a tang almost like that left in the aftermath of a lightning strike...

And the pit's energy was stronger than ever, coursing up through Ketahn's legs and across his body in steady, buzzing waves.

Thick shadows dwelled outside the shaft of moonlight streaming through the break overhead. Ketahn could make out more scattered rubble, stones, overgrown vines, and dangling moss, but it was all indistinct, as though he were peering through a veil into the land of spirits.

Orange light flared behind him, bathing his surroundings in an eerie glow that cast long, deep shadows. He glimpsed everything more clearly—untold years of rotting plants and leaves, piles of broken branches, boulders and roots coated in muck and moss, standing puddles outside the surrounding water, and even bones amidst it all.

Ketahn spun toward the source of the light and stilled.

His mouth opened, and a sound might have come out—a

gasp, perhaps, or some oath to the gods—but he couldn't be sure; just as he couldn't be sure of what was before him.

Something huge jutted up from the ground, big enough that part of its base was in the water, something far too big for the orange light to fully illuminate. Ketahn couldn't even get a complete sense of its shape. It was simply too large.

The light was positioned at least eight segments above the ground. It came from a small circle, as steady as the sun without any of the heat or intensity. In seven years of wandering the Tangle, Ketahn had never seen anything like it. Reminiscent of sunlight or the glow of a wood fire, it was entirely unlike either, and though it wasn't particularly bright, it was almost blinding relative to the surrounding darkness.

Ketahn lifted a hand to shield his eyes from the light. At a glance, the thing it was attached to seemed to be made of stone, overgrown with clinging moss and draped with pale vines. But the texture was unusual, and there were bits of it gleaming in the light—almost like the gold so popular with the females of Takarahl.

Releasing the strand of silk hanging from overhead, Ketahn crept toward the strange stone. The reflected light on its surface moved as he did.

The orange light went out.

Ketahn stopped, barely keeping himself from trembling as the unknown energy coursed over him in the darkness. The huge stone thing took shape again when his eyes readjusted, outlined now in the dim light of moons and stars that penetrated the tangled web overhead.

Though much of it was covered by dirt and plants, this thing dominated the base of the pit, spanning almost from wall to wall. Ketahn had come down on a relatively narrow stretch of ground between it and the water. At its top, the stone seemed to touch the web of vines, roots, and branches. It must've served as a support for those plants to grow across the pit.

Even if it could somehow be moved there, he doubted the massive stone would fit in the Den of Spirits.

Far away and unimportant, the soota called again; it might as well have been in another world.

Ketahn continued forward. The air hummed around him, vibrating over every one of his hairs, across every threadspan of his hide, and down into his bones.

He extended an arm and brushed his palm across the face of the rock. Flecks of dirt and a hard, brittle, abrasive substance broke away.

"By their eightfold eyes," he rattled.

It wasn't stone beneath that grime. Gold remained his closest comparison, but he knew that was wrong; at best, this was some distant cousin of gold, some other metal. It was cold, solid, unyielding, and impossibly smooth beneath the crust that had formed upon its surface. And it was abuzz with that energy and something much deeper—a rumbling that could only be felt, not heard.

The orange light flashed on.

Ketahn snapped his hand back and retreated. This close, he could see the object's surface gleaming between the dirt and those rough patches, between the clumps of moss and dangling vines.

As he tipped his head back, his eyes caught on something above his eye level. He shifted to the side and stretched up on his rear legs, tearing away some of the vines and wiping away more dirt, working quickly—he didn't know how long that unnatural light would last.

Once a wide enough piece of the surface was cleared, Ketahn eased back.

There were markings. Deliberate markings—lines forming unfamiliar shapes that had no meaning to him but undoubtedly had *some* meaning. When he looked at them directly, they were black, but when he shifted his head to either side, they took on a sheen like sunlight reflected on the surface of a pool.

What was this? His mind raced, sifting through every detail

he could recall regarding the monster that had been cast into this pit by the gods. Was the orange light cast by one of its fiery eyes as it opened and closed, searching for whatever had disturbed its slumber? Had the beast's skin been described as gold but not gold? If he were walking in a place where the gods had done battle...

He was uncertain of what that meant or how he should have felt about it. Perhaps he'd simply disrespected the Eight a few times too many, and they'd tossed him into this pit to rot like the flame beast of legend?

The orange light died again. A reddish afterlight lingered in Ketahn's vision like an angry gash on the beast's unnatural hide, but that afterlight didn't fade as his eyes readjusted.

Ketahn's mandibles twitched, and he found himself longing suddenly for his spear, which was still lodged in the web of plants above.

There really was a gash in the side of this...thing.

Ketahn approached the opening. It was nearly twice as tall as him, wide enough to allow a female vrix through at the base but barely stretching a handspan across at the top. The outer material was mangled and bent all around the edges. Thick vines and moss hung over it in places, but there were other things dangling and protruding within—some of them vinelike, some bonelike, most of them hinting at that odd metal luster through the grime.

Dirt and debris had flooded in at the base, which was angled slightly downward from the ground. This was like the mouth of a cave—not that he'd ever seen a cave like it.

As large as that opening was, the damage and debris made it difficult to see far inside. Ketahn had the impression of a cavern beyond—or, perhaps, a chamber.

He must have recognized the foolishness of what he did next. He must have realized he was beckoning death, but something deep and mysterious drove him, something beyond explanation or understanding.

Ketahn brushed aside the hanging plants and entered the cave.

Though the dangling, vinelike things inside gave way easily as he passed, he occasionally felt the scrape of sharp edges against his hide. The red light strengthened as he navigated the debris around him, and so did the thrumming in the air. It was relentless now, and it was everywhere, even in the dirt beneath him.

He emerged in a large chamber that was flooded with red light, making everything seem dark. The floor, ceiling, and far wall were broken, split along the same line as the gash through which he'd entered. To one side, a sharp decline led below ground level. To the other, it was on a far more gradual incline. More of those bone and vine-like things jutted from the breaks, but the tearing here was less jagged; much of it seemed to have come apart in rectangular sections along the wall and floor.

The dirt from outside continued well into the chamber, where it created the washed-out look of a dried stream bed. It was piled highest at the base of the sloped side of the chamber—which also happened to be partially filled with murky, unmoving water. There were weathered branches and rotted leaves scattered across the floor.

The air was thick, but the stench of fetid water, the slime on its surface, and mushrooms wasn't as strong as it should have been.

Ketahn crept farther into the chamber. The walls, ceiling, and floor were not of the same material as the exterior, though it was impossible to tell what they'd been crafted of in the red lighting and through all the dirt.

Still, he'd never seen such clean angles in a structure, had never seen pieces that fit together so smoothly and sleekly—as though they'd been woven from the finest silk rather than shaped of stone or some other solid substance.

But most curious of all were the large objects along the walls. Some of them had been tipped over or displaced, but many more were lined up in neat intervals, covered in dust and dried mud.

47

Ketahn might have guessed they were cocoons of some sort, left behind by unknown creatures, as some of them appeared to have opened, but that didn't seem right. There was nothing natural about this place.

Ketahn approached one of the open objects. A significant portion of the inside was hollowed out, like some sort of basket, but it seemed large enough to fit a broodling within—even a broodling on the cusp of maturity. It was at least a segment and a half long and half as wide.

The inside was caked with muck and slime, some of which glistened in the red light. The pit likely filled with water in the flood season—and it did not seem this chamber was spared.

Moving to the next of the cocoon things, Ketahn placed his hand atop it to wipe away the dirt. The buildup flaked away to reveal something smooth and slightly curved beneath.

Ketahn's mandibles clacked together as he cleared away more of the dirt. The smooth material was clouded, but light passed through. Had it somehow been shaped of colorless crystal? He leaned down to look closer, but the interior was too dark for him to make anything out.

Perhaps these were...eggs of some sort? He could not imagine the size of creatures that hatched from such huge eggs.

Ketahn lifted his gaze and searched the walls for some sign, some symbol, some writing, some clue as to what all this was, but there was nothing. Nothing save a narrow opening in a recess along the wall, through which more of that red light was visible.

He walked to the opening, feeling cool air flow from it as he neared. That must've meant there was another entrance somewhere that was allowing the air to move.

After a brief examination, he determined the recess was actually a doorway—one that was mostly blocked by a slab cut to match the opening almost perfectly. Bracing his shoulder against the entryway frame, he clamped two hands on the slab and pushed.

The slab groaned, creaked, and clanged, the sounds all

bearing an unusual reverberation that Ketahn felt in his bones. Once the slab had slid into the opposite side of the doorframe, disappearing completely, he eased his hold, ducked his head, and slipped through.

He found himself in a tunnel that had a curved ceiling and walls but a flat floor. To one side was the break, carrying through from the prior chamber, beyond which the tunnel sloped sharply down until it hit dark water. Though there was plenty of dirt and grime, it was less abundant here.

Ketahn's fine hairs flattened and stood up as he realized there were more entryways along the tunnel, each crested with a red light. From where he stood, he could see that only one of those doors was open—the one directly across the tunnel.

"Delver, guide me," he said; his voice echoed along the tunnel, stretching into something unfamiliar.

If ever the Eight heard the pleas of their children, Ketahn doubted they would answer in places such as this. Places such as this shouldn't have existed.

He crossed the tunnel, braced his hands to either side of the doorway, and leaned forward to peer inside.

The large chamber was like the first in all ways but two—the grime here was not quite so thick, and the implied flood line didn't quite reach as high, leaving several of the cocoon things uncovered.

One of those cocoons near the break in the floor had split open. Dirt coated the bits jutting from its shattered shell, but they did not command half as much of his attention as what he saw through the top, where that clear, crystal-like material had broken away.

Bones. Old and darkened and unlike anything he had ever seen—though *nothing* in this place was like anything he'd seen. He could not imagine what that rounded skull with its two gaping eye holes and straight, flat teeth must've looked like with muscle and hide still attached. He'd encountered no such creature, whether living or dead. The skeleton was partially out of its cocoon, the head and one arm sticking through the shattered top.

The skull was cracked, a wedge of it having fallen away, and there were shallow gouges in the arm bones as though left by deep cuts.

Ketahn checked the other cocoons. Though most were too hard to see through because of their clouded covers and the poor lighting, he glimpsed a few more of those strange skeletons in a few.

It seemed impossible that his confrontation with Zurvashi had occurred earlier this very day, impossible that Takarahl lay less than half a day's travel behind him. Again, there were no markings on the walls, no carvings or sculptures to offer insight regarding the nature of this place or these creatures. Perhaps...it was a burial chamber?

The vrix had such chambers in the deepest parts of Takarahl, where countless holes had been bored into the stone for dozens of segments down. Dead vrix, wrapped in raw silk shrouds traditionally spun by their kin, were laid to slumber in those chambers forever under the care of the Eight. Did this place serve a similar purpose for these odd creatures?

A thoughtful trill sounded in his chest. He'd explored many dark, hidden places, and he'd discovered a few old burial chambers and abandoned dens in the process, but he'd seen nothing like this place—and each of his questions about it seemed only to spawn three more without ever being answered.

What did this place have to do with the ancient story, with the fiery beast overcome by the Eight?

Exiting the chamber, Ketahn glanced along the tunnel, first toward the portion that was lost beneath the water, then toward the other, where sealed entryways lined the corridor on either side. He tilted his head and turned to face that side of the tunnel. All the doors had red lights over them but one at the limits of what he could see—that door had a green light that was barely visible in the red glow.

His legs were moving before he made the decision to check that door, and he didn't fight them. Why was one light green? What did it signify?

Within a few segments, he'd passed the thick band of dried mud and residue that marked the flood line. The floor beyond was surprisingly clean, as though yet to be touched by the ravages of the Tangle. The air flow was a little more pronounced, a little cooler, the scents upon it more muted.

He stopped in front of the green light door. It was closed completely, and though the frame was separated from the sealing slab, there was no apparent gap—not even anything significant enough to work the tip of his smallest claw under.

Ketahn tried anyway, poking and prodding around the inside of the doorframe, pressing his claws against it in search of purchase. He needed only a strong enough grip to force it open. But the door slab was smooth and hard, and it refused to yield to his efforts. Even when he curled his fingers and raked his claws against it, he failed to leave the smallest mark.

Spreading his arms, Ketahn slapped all four hands on the door frame and bowed his head.

There was a strange noise from somewhere around him, a soft but startling tone that made him recoil from the doorway and dart his gaze around.

It wasn't until his attention returned to the doorframe that he noticed the faint green glow emanating from beneath one of his hands. Slowly, he lifted that hand.

The section of the doorframe he revealed was set apart from the rest by a thin black line, and it was now glowing the same green as the light over the door, though it was pulsing slowly. A glance along the corridor confirmed that each doorway had one of those little rectangles, but none of the others were lit up.

There was a long, soft hiss overhead. Ketahn's eyes darted up in search of the source but he could see nothing on the solid, curved wall.

The door in front of Ketahn slid open with a sound not

unlike that of the wind blowing through tall rock formations and disappeared within the wall. But the real wonder wasn't a door moving by itself and vanishing—it was the chamber beyond.

The space was completely devoid of dirt and debris—not even a speck marred the gleaming floors and walls. Neither was there any plant or mushroom growth to be seen. The light was pure white, cast by large, glowing circles on the ceiling; it seemed even brighter, briefly, than the sun. The air that flowed from the chamber was clean, cool, and almost entirely scentless. He wasn't sure how that was possible, but that lack of understanding applied to everything here.

For the first time since he'd entered this place, Ketahn knew its true colors. The floor was polished black with large square patterns etched into it. The walls were white as a peaceful cloud, with faint depressions in them at regular intervals, but their lower thirds were dark gray.

Several large, rectangular patches on the walls looked almost like paintings, but the images and symbols within them were crisper and more vibrant than anything painted by vrix hands, and these gave off their own light.

Some of them also happened to be moving.

The blend of uncertainty and curiosity within Ketahn resulted in a jagged, hot feeling in his torso as he approached the nearest painting. There were twenty images within it, lined up in two even rows. Each was a simple depiction of a being with two arms and two legs, like malformed vrix. Half of these were slightly different from the others—a little smaller, a little curvier in their shape.

Twelve were dark red, the color of spilled blood. Eight were bright green. The latter were the source of the movement in the images—meaningless symbols similar to the ones he'd seen outside were below all twenty images, but the symbols beneath the green images were changing every few moments.

"This magic must be of the Eight," Ketahn said as he lifted a hand to touch a set of changing symbols.

The tip of his claw passed through the image as though it were formed of mist. Before he could react to that, the painting changed. A square containing countless symbols appeared, blocking out everything else.

Ketahn snapped his hand back and retreated from the painting, fine hairs bristling and hearts thumping. There was another image now—not a simple drawing, but something so real that he was sure, for a moment, that he'd summoned a bizarre creature from nothingness.

It was only the creature's face. It had a pale, soft looking hide, dark hair atop its head—with more short hair along its jaw, around its mouth, and in a strip above each of its eyes. Those eyes, its nose holes, and mouth were arranged similarly to a vrix's, but it only had two eyes, and there were no fangs or mandibles to be seen. Just two plump, pinkish bits of flesh comprising its mouthparts.

Was this what those dead creatures had looked like? They were ugly things.

Ketahn turned and swept his gaze around the chamber. The cocoons here were unsoiled, allowing him full view of their dull gray exteriors, precise planes, and smooth contours. The sections of see-through material were larger than he'd realized, stretching almost two-thirds of the way across the tops of the cocoons. Though the overhead light reflected heavily on those surfaces, Ketahn could make out the figures laid in each cocoon.

There were twenty in total—ten along one wall, ten on the opposite.

He looked back at the moving painting, which still displayed the creature's face and all those symbols. Tentatively, he extended an arm, bringing it nearer and nearer to the painting. With a flick of his wrist, he raked his claws through the image and immediately withdrew his hand, which had touched nothing but empty air.

The symbol-filled square vanished, revealing the original

image. Were the creatures in the painting somehow related to the cocoons?

Turning away from the painting, Ketahn strode to the far end of the chamber, glancing at the cocoons as he passed. Eight of them had small squares of light filled with more symbols on their fronts. The rest were blank—and each of the blank cocoons contained remains. Three held only bones. The other nine creatures seemed somewhat fresher and more intact, though their hides had a leathery look that reminded Ketahn of dried strips of meat.

Ketahn studied each of them as he walked toward the doorway, trying to hold back the many questions forming in his mind; he doubted any of them would be answered now, if ever.

The cocoons with lights on their fronts all seemed to contain creatures that were so recently dead they almost looked alive—but could anything living be so utterly motionless?

Though not all of them had pale hides and dark hair like the one that had appeared on the painting, they all looked small, soft, and delicate, like they wouldn't survive a day out in the Tangle.

Ketahn halted as his gaze fell upon one of the creatures. He noticed first its long hair, which was gathered around its head in shimmery strands that were like gold spun into thread. Vrix had smooth, silken hair on their heads, but this creature's hair seemed softer and fuller, and it wasn't straight—waves ran through the strands like ripples on the surface of a pond.

He crept closer, leaning forward to study the creature. It was one of the smaller, slighter ones, pale of hide and lithe of limb. Like the others, it was clad in some sort of cloth that covered its torso, upper arms, and the upper portions of its legs—two separate pieces of fabric, as far as he could tell. He knew just by the look of the material that it wasn't silk.

The pink flesh around the creature's mouth was full and plump, like a pair of juicy larvae laid together, and rounded mounds pressed up from its chest, pulling that white fabric taut. The creature's eyes were closed, and lush, dark hairs—from its eyelids—rested upon its cheeks, in bold contrast to the pale hide. There were also two thin strips of dark hair above its eyes.

These creatures were bizarre, even repulsive in some ways, but there was something about them that intrigued Ketahn.

That wasn't right. There was something about *this one* that fascinated him. Some sort of beauty that could not be placed, unlike anything any vrix had encountered, something that...that didn't belong in this world.

Were these creatures from the shadowy world of spirits? Was it possible for spirits to take flesh forms and walk as living beings?

Ketahn shifted his gaze to the creature's limbs. They, like everything else about the creature, were small. Its fingers were slender, the claws at their ends were short and blunt, and it had an extra finger on each hand—but somehow, those five-fingered hands didn't seem odd and unbalanced. There were vinelike things sprouting from its wrists, legs, and neck, some of which were thin enough for Ketahn to see the fluids flowing through them—some dark as blood, one dull amber, the rest colorless.

His time out in the Tangle had taught him better, but he longed to touch this creature. He longed to know if it felt how it looked, if its hide was smooth and yielding, if its hair was softer than fluffed silk. Succumbing to such urges out in the jungle only invited danger. Anything that appeared so harmless, so inexplicably alluring, could only bring pain and doom. Nothing good could come of it.

Still, he braced his arms on the exterior of the cocoon to lean even closer—not immediately realizing that his lower left hand had settled directly atop the patch of light on the cocoon's front.

A light flared to life in the cocoon, illuminating the creature inside fully and making its hide seem so thin and pale that Ketahn glimpsed disturbingly blue veins running just under its surface.

From everywhere and nowhere came a soft, smooth voice unlike that of any vrix, speaking garbled, meaningless words.

"Kahlohnist Ayvee Foztor, numburr too wun oh. Normul vytalz. Kunfurm eemur jensee uh waykening see kwens."

Kethan pushed himself away from the cocoon, inadvertently pressing the square of light on its front again. An unfamiliar tone sounded, as gentle as the one he'd heard at the door but twice as startling. Raising his forelegs, he searched for the source of that voice, for the new, sudden threat.

"Eemur jensee uh waykening ee nih shiated," the voice continued. Something thrummed under the floor, sending gentle pulses up along Ketahn's legs. The vines connected to the creature emptied abruptly and withdrew from the creature just before the inside of the cocoon filled with mist, obscuring his view.

"Suhb jekt beeng uh waykened wih thout rehk omended uh just-mant peer eeyod. Maye suhferr tempor eree lethargee, nawzhuh, dih zeeness, disoree entashun, fuh teeg, end difi kultee konsen trayt-ing. Pleeze kon sult uh mehdikal tek nishun too ree port eh nee ish yoos."

By the Eight, what was this spirit saying? Had Ketahn

provoked its wrath? He was reminded again of his empty hands, of his barbed spear caught in the plant web, and he growled.

Even if a spirit could not be harmed by such a weapon, Ketahn would not succumb without resisting.

The cocoon hissed, long and loud. Ketahn retreated by another segment before the cocoon broke open. The clear top—just a lid, he suddenly realized—lifted until it was standing straight up. The mist swirled and dissipated as the inner portion of the cocoon, rumbling faintly, rose and tipped forward so the creature inside lay at a slant.

But the creature itself hadn't moved a muscle.

"*Kahlonist too wun oh, welkum too*"—the disembodied voice changed suddenly, becoming stiffer, deeper, less...alive—"*nah vee gayshun daytuh kor uptid. Kurrint lo kayshun un noen. Eemur jensee signull inoprativ.*"

The spirit fell silent, leaving Ketahn to stare at the creature.

A new scent teased him, something clean, exotic, alluring. Something sweet and, somehow...feminine.

Ketahn shifted nearer to the cocoon, lifted a foreleg, and carefully brushed it against the creature's arm. An appreciative trill sounded in his chest. That intriguing scent absolutely belonged to this pale little thing, and it was only stronger and sweeter now that he was closer.

He extended an arm next, watching both it and the creature's face as he brushed his fingers over that long, golden hair. It was even softer than he'd imagined. His hand followed the strands of hair down until his palm settled on the creature's shoulder.

The creature made the faintest of movements—its chest swelled, and the white fabric stretched over those chest mounds, which now hung a little lower, as though they possessed more weight and flexibility than he could've guessed.

Ketahn stilled but did not pull away. The creature's chest relaxed, and he felt a faint flow of warm air against his hide. Breathing. The strange being was alive. And its hide was smooth.

57

Yielding. Warm. Better than silk beneath his palm, and somehow thrilling.

Sliding his hand down its arm, Ketahn nearly shuddered at the rasp of his rough hide against the creature's—against *hers*.

Because this thing was a female, he knew it instinctually—the scent was merely further confirmation. There were many creatures in the Tangle that were not like the vrix in that respect, many creatures for which the females were smaller and weaker.

And this unique creature was *his* female. She belonged to him. Many vrix had tamed wild creatures as pets; why should he not have one of his own?

Another of his hands rose, and he cupped the underside of one of those mounds. It certainly had some weight, and it was even more yielding than her flesh elsewhere. He squeezed, testing its give; it had some measure of firmness. He'd never felt anything like it. Vrix were thick of hide and didn't carry excess flesh; they were as hard as stone compared to his little creature.

Curious, he lowered his hand, meaning to take hold of that white fabric and peel it away so he could see what those mounds looked like uncovered.

"*Og zillaree powurr nyntee fyv pursent dee pleeted. Tohtul siztum faylyur in uh proximet lee too yeerz, nyntee sehvin dayz, end twellv owrs,*" the spirit announced, back to its prior calm tone. "*Pleez ehvak yuate eemeedi etly.*"

Though Ketahn still had no idea what the spirit was saying, he stilled his hand and forced his mandibles down. Perhaps this place wasn't as dangerous or evil as many of his kind believed, but he could no longer argue against the truth—it *was* haunted, infested by powerful spirits. It was even possible this creature and her kin had somehow been trapped here by the spirits, and Ketahn was granting her freedom she might otherwise not have had.

Regardless, this wasn't the place to study his new pet.

He needed to find a safe route out of the pit, which promised to be a challenge even for a seasoned vrix climber—especially while carrying another living creature.

Carefully, he reached around the creature's body with all four hands and lifted her off the cocoon upon which she'd been laid. She was limp; she tipped against him, her slight weight barely noticeable against his hide. But he could not ignore the feel of her —warm, soft, tiny.

Ketahn hooked an arm under her legs, which bent over it. Her unsegmented limbs were unsettling to him; every part of this female was connected beneath her hide, the joints all but hidden.

He stopped himself from studying her further. This was still not the place to do so, especially with the spirit roused.

Gathering her securely to his chest, he turned for the exit. "Whether with the aid of the Eight or not, I will unravel the tangled threads of this mystery."

The last thing he noticed before leaving the chamber was the painting. One of the green creatures drawn upon it had turned gray—the eighth. Another sign? Had he been meant to fall into this pit and find her, just as Queen Takari had been meant to fall into the Den of Spirits and discover the crystals ages ago?

He looked back down at the female and brushed the strands of hair from her face.

"Perhaps you shall be called Eight," he offered thoughtfully.

Eight made no reply.

Chapter Five

KETAHN GRASPED a thick root with one hand, clamped another on the exposed rock overhead, and dug the tips of his legs into the dirt. With a final heave, he drew himself over the rim of the pit. The damp layer of fallen leaves beneath him was a welcome change; it was flat, for one thing.

He allowed himself a few moments to recover from the climb, though he only slightly relaxed his hold on Eight, who was cradled in his lower arms. He'd lashed some silk thread around their torsos to ensure she'd remain in place for at least a little while if he had sudden need to utilize his lower arms for something else.

His muscles burned, and it seemed there was no part of his body that did not ache now that the excitement of his discovery had cooled. The Tangle had battered him tonight, but it had surrendered a wondrous bounty—or at the very least an intriguing one.

Again, he reminded himself this was not the time to examine her. The pit had offered shelter from the Tangle's many dangers, but now Ketahn and his little female were exposed. No matter how curious he was, no matter how weary and worn, he needed to return to his den with all possible haste.

He turned toward the pit, tipping his head back to look skyward.

The greater and lesser moons were nearing the far side of the break in the canopy now, well on their way toward moonfall. Each was a swollen orb, one silver, one pink, against the dark backdrop of the sky, their light hitting the pit in a wide beam that enhanced the shadows of the surrounding jungle.

With the direction of moonfall determined, he untied his spear from his bag, taking it firmly in hand, and delved into the Tangle with Eight.

Ketahn slowly worked his way higher. Remaining close to the ground would've been easier on his abused body, but the danger was always greater on the jungle floor—not merely due to predators, but harmful plants, deadfalls, hidden pits waiting to swallow up unsuspecting creatures, and patches of murky water and mud deep and hungry enough to trap even the strongest vrix.

His eyes dipped toward Eight briefly. How could anything like her ever have survived here? She couldn't be more than a segment and a half tall; he doubted the top of her head would even reach his chest if she were standing on her two legs—*if* she could stand on them to begin with.

How could any creature balance itself on two legs? How could anything move with any speed or agility with a body like hers?

He'd not gone far before Eight stirred. Ketahn stilled, glancing down at her as she tensed and released a heavy breath. She made a soft, pained sound that produced the faintest of vibrations in her chest, but it didn't have any of the buzzing or clicking that usually accompanied such sounds from vrix.

The thin strips of hair over her eyes drew closer together, forming a crease in her hide between them, and the corners of her mouth shifted back, pulling those bits of plump pink flesh taut. Her eyes squeezed tighter shut. Her nose holes—which were on the underside of an odd, fleshy protrusion that sloped down from between her eyes and ended at a point just above her mouth—flared wider.

Ketahn's mandibles twitched, and he tilted his head.

Vrix could open and close their eyes and mouths, could raise and lower their mandibles, but otherwise the hide on their faces was firm and unmoving. It seemed every part of this creature's face could move and change in some way. The result was as intriguing as it was unnerving.

Ketahn moved his free hand to her face and gently pressed the pad of his thumb to the fuller, bottom flesh around her mouth. The soft hide yielded to his touch, contouring itself to the shape of his finger until it flattened against the hard teeth hidden behind it.

Eight turned her face away, making her golden hair brush his forearm. His hide thrummed as though charged with thrilling energy from that delicate touch. Tiny beads of water had gathered on her skin on her upper chest and above her eyes. They reflected the moonlight in tiny points that made even the small, flickering stars overhead seem large and bright.

One of her elbows—surprisingly hard—braced against his chest and pushed. Her whole body twisted slightly so she was directed skyward. The fabric on her torso caught between their bodies, pulling tighter still over her chest mounds, enough so for Ketahn to see the outlines of their smaller, defined peaks.

"*Mmph*," she said.

He attempted to reproduce the sound. It rumbled in his chest, but he knew immediately it was not the same. *Mmm* wasn't a sound he'd heard from a vrix before, and he wasn't sure how she'd produced it. And she'd ended it with a breathy noise—one that the spirit in the pit had used in some of its words.

Somewhere nearby, leaves shook, and a branch snapped. Ketahn turned his face away from Eight, seeking the source of the disturbance.

A large creature was prowling along one of the massive roots just a few segments below Ketahn, pushing through the vines and

63

branches that grew nearby. Though the beast was mostly hidden in the shadows, Ketahn knew it simply by its size and the way it moved.

A grel. Its upper body was broad and powerful, with thick arms and long claws, its muscular neck leading to a blunt head that had jaws strong enough to rival a female vrix's mandibles. Its four small eyes shone with tiny points of reflected moonlight.

The grel huffed and snorted, turning its head from side to side—and most of its upper body along with it—as it scanned its surroundings.

Ketahn held Eight closer to his chest and eased along the bough he was standing upon, moving into the deeper shadows near the trunk. Grels had poor senses of smell, so as long as he kept out of sight and quiet, he could avoid an unwanted encounter.

Eight shifted, making another *mmm* sound, this one more pained and troubled than the first.

The grel raised its head and snapped it toward Ketahn, its long, fleshy ears standing up.

Shaper, unmake me.

Bark crunched under the grel's claws. The beast opened its jaws, baring its sharp, inward angled teeth—the sort of teeth that hooked in with a bite and didn't let go. The grel's growl was deep enough to make the air vibrate.

Though the grel did not likely stand any taller than Ketahn, it was far broader, and undoubtedly outweighed him by no small amount. He'd killed such creatures before, but their strength, speed, and toughness made them deadly predators, even to vrix.

Something slapped his chest. Ketahn angled his gaze toward the female to find her hand pressed against him, its heat sinking into his hide. It sent a thrill through him. She was growing more restless, and those strips of hair above her eyes had fallen lower.

The grel would tear her apart in an instant if given the chance.

Ketahn raised his upper arms, forelegs, and mandibles,

spreading them wide to make himself look as big as possible, and hissed.

The grel's ears twitched and flattened, and the beast retreated half a step, making an uncertain, chuffing sound.

Eight stiffened in Ketahn's arms. Her eyes fluttered open, calling his attention away from the immediate danger. Those eyes were, like the rest of her, strange. They rolled in their sockets for a moment, which was made disquieting by the white around their edges, before turning toward Ketahn.

He could only stare back. The whites of her eyes surrounded inner rings of blue, but the night was too dark for him to tell the exact shade. And within that blue were large, black circles, directed at Ketahn. Her eyelids opened wider, and the strips of hair over her eyes shot up.

Eight opened her mouth and screamed. The sound was high, piercing, and loud enough to echo between the trees and make Ketahn recoil and nearly lose his balance.

Ketahn hurriedly lowered one of his arms, clamping a hand over her mouth. Hot air blew against his palm as she continued to scream, but the sound was greatly diminished now—though its echoes lingered in his head.

She grabbed his wrist with one of her little hands and struggled in his grasp, kicking those odd legs and trying to pull her face away from him. He tightened his hold on her. For a creature so small and seemingly delicate, there was surprising strength in her resistance.

He glanced at the grel, turning his raised barbed spear toward the beast. The weapon was unlikely to fell the creature in one blow, but it could inflict a wound dire enough to make the grel flee.

But the grel had backed farther away, its ears now fully flattened along its thick neck and hulking shoulders. It had its head lowered, and its teeth were still bared.

Ketahn's mandibles twitched, and he tilted his head. He looked briefly at Eight, who was still wide-eyed and thrashing, before returning his gaze to the grel. With a thoughtful chitter, Ketahn removed his hand from his female's mouth.

She screamed even louder than before.

The grel scrambled back with a broken growl. Its rear legs lost their purchase, and the beast slipped, its front claws tearing gouges in the wood as it fell. Before it could recover, the grel shoved away from the root, crashed amidst the undergrowth below, and darted away. Snapping branches and huffing breaths marked its flight into the shelter of the Tangle's nighttime shadows.

Ketahn had seen grels flee a few times, but he'd never seen one in such terror.

He lowered his hand toward Eight's mouth again. She slapped and clawed at it, turning her head from side to side to evade his touch.

"*Noh! Dohnt tuch mee!*" Eight's words were similar to those the spirit had used, but her voice was different. It was higher than the spirit's, rougher, and it was filled with feeling. With...emotion.

He realized only then that her scent had changed subtly; it contained a sour hint of fear. If her screams hadn't been enough to attract the attention of other predators in the Tangle—which they certainly had been—then the hint of fear in her smell would surely do so.

Using a bit more force, he pressed his palm over her mouth. She grasped his forearm with both hands, digging her blunt claws into his hide, but her grip caused him a flare of excitement rather than pain.

"Silence," he said.

Eight stilled immediately but for her trembling and panting breaths, which made her shoulders and chest heave and blew the strands of her tousled hair up and down. Her eyes glistened as though filling with water, more of which had gathered on her pale skin, and the fabric of her upper garment was damp.

"Be silent, Eight." Ketahn lowered his mandibles to look as unthreatening as possible. "Be calm. It is not safe for you to make so much noise."

She stared at him, eyes wide and uncomprehending, and made more of her unfamiliar word-sounds against his palm. They made no more sense to him muffled than they had when she'd spoken unhindered.

Ketahn ground the tip of a foreleg against the tree bark. The journey ahead wasn't a long one, but it was dangerous—even more so if she could not follow his instructions. Any creature that had spent more than a few days in the Tangle should have known to keep quiet, to stay high above the ground, to be alert.

Eight fell silent again. The passing time was marked only by the beating of Ketahn's hearts as he waited for her to speak again, each moment intensifying both his curiosity about this little female and his urgency to reach the security of his den.

Slowly, he lifted his hand away from her mouth.

"Pleez, ay dohnt noe wut—"

With a huff, he covered her mouth again. "Be silent."

She whimpered but didn't fight him this time. He wasn't sure if it was because she'd understood him or she'd exhausted herself, but he didn't like it—just like he didn't like the fear in her scent. She was trembling in his arms, faintly but noticeably.

Drawing in another breath, Ketahn removed his hand from her mouth again, halting it barely a finger's length away.

Eight's mouth opened, those plump pieces of flesh parting, and her pink tongue slipped out to trail across them. Ketahn's arm tensed, ready to silence her again, but she simply drew that little tongue back into her mouth and pressed those plump bits together. She dipped and lifted her chin twice in quick succession.

That seemed like some sort of gesture...but what could it mean? Had she run her tongue around her mouthparts like that to signal her hunger?

He couldn't ignore the possibility that her kind were cunning, deceptive predators of some sort...

Ketahn cast his questions to the back of his mind, where they could weave their own webs for a while. His fixation with this creature was dangerously distracting.

Holding her more snugly against his chest, he continued his journey. She squeezed her eyes shut, wrapped her arms around herself, and curled up. When she spoke again, he didn't bother admonishing her; her voice was barely a whisper.

"Pleez bee uh dreem. Pleez bee uh dreem. Pleez..."

The significance of her speaking, even if her words had no meaning to Ketahn, struck him as he traveled. He'd never met a creature capable of speech apart from his kind. The Tangle's beasts had their calls that communicated so much, but none of it was as intricate as the language spoken by the vrix...and Eight's language seemed just as complex.

Not vrix, not animal, not spirit...what was she?

His.

If nothing else, she was his. He would unravel her mysteries one thread at a time if necessary. But he would *not* take her to Takarahl, would not bring her before the queen. He would not share her with anyone.

She remained in that position for the rest of their journey, trembling and tensing further as he climbed steadily higher. Her occasional whispers were too soft for him to make out, not that he would've understood them anyway, and the jungle was mostly quiet, leaving Ketahn far too much time to battle his thoughts and the endless questions dominating them.

When he finally neared his den, Ketahn was ready to collapse. It felt as though a hundred years had passed in the span of this single day, as though the events of the morning had happened in a different lifetime. He looked upon his den gratefully. It had taken him many eightdays to determine the best way to weave together all the silk, vines, and branches to make the den strong enough to remain in place and serve as a shelter. He'd destroyed his initial construction by failing to properly secure it to the supports.

But this den had hung for years near the Tangle's leafy canopy, suspended by a wide silk web that fastened it to the surrounding boughs and spread its weight between them. Any creature unaccustomed to climbing vrix webbing was unlikely to reach it.

Ketahn did not hesitate to tie his barbed spear to his pack and climb the trunk leading up to the web; allowing his aching body even a moment's rest would have rendered him unable to move until morning, at the very least. Eight made an abrupt, alarmed sound as her weight was forced against his chest, wrapped her arms around his middle, and held tight.

He chittered softly and took hold of the web with his upper hands. Eight's alarm only increased as he released the tree and, hanging with his back toward the ground, crawled along the web toward the den at its center.

"*Naht gunna luhk*," she whispered, raking his hide with her blunt claws. "*Naht reel. Eetz naht reel. Oh gahd, aym gunna bee sik. Pleez bee uh dreem.*"

"We are safe, Eight," he said.

He'd meant to comfort her, but his words seemed to do the opposite; she clung to him, her body shaking. "*Dohnt wanuh fahl. Dohnt wanuh bee eetun. Pleez dohnt eet mee.*"

He held her more firmly as his den came within reach, but it wasn't enough to prevent her screech as he latched onto the den's exterior and turned upside down to move toward the entrance on its lower portion. The den bounced and swayed with his movement, but the supports were strong; it would not fall.

Her hair fell into his face, striking him with her fragrance all over again. A rumble sounded deep in his chest. Eight's scent was as alluring as it was strange. It would be a welcome presence in his den.

Thankfully, she didn't thrash or struggle, though she did keep speaking her meaningless language in a fast, panicked voice. She was still speaking as he pulled himself through the low opening on the side of the rounded den and entered the comforting, familiar darkness.

As soon as he had his legs braced on the floor, he reached up and removed the hide covering from the crystal he'd mounted amidst the woven branches, filling the space with a soft blue glow. The relief of being home was overwhelming—almost as strong as the relief he was about to experience when he finally let his body relax.

He removed the silk strand binding him and Eight together and gently placed her on the floor.

She scrambled back from him until she was pressed against the curve of the far wall, her legs drawn close to her body. Her eyes were wide, she looked far paler than when he'd first seen her, and the hair around her face was damp and sticking to her skin. "*Oh mai gahd, pleez dohnt eet mee.*"

That fear scent wafted from her; apparently, shelter and security was not enough to ease her terror.

Chapter Six

THEY'D TOLD Ivy there would be dreams aboard the *Somnium* —vivid dreams. And she knew there'd been many, even if they were all hazy and far away now, but this...

This was a nightmare.

Ivy squeezed her eyes shut and hugged herself tighter. Her body trembled, wracked by fear and chills. The last thing she remembered was lying in the cryochamber, staring at the technicians as they prepped her for cryogenic sleep. She'd been apprehensive but excited to be taking part in the *Somnium's* voyage, to be amongst the first colonists to leave Earth and form a new colony on Xolea—to make a new home, a new life, a new start.

She wasn't supposed to wake up to *this*.

I'm not awake. I'm still sleeping, still dreaming. This can't be real.

Ivy pressed her lips together, grasped her forearm, and pinched hard. A cry tore from her. She let her forehead fall against the woven branches of the wall and drew in one heavy, ragged breath after another. The air was thick and humid, smelling of earth and wood and something more, something spicy, like mahogany.

The thing that had carried her in here made a low, uncertain

73

rumble, one she might've thought expressed concern were it not so close to a growl.

"This can't be happening. It's a nightmare." Ivy brought her hands up to her hair and clenched the strands close to her scalp, producing another flare of pain. Tears stung her eyes, and she released a soft whine, but she only grasped harder. "Not real, not real, not real."

The nest swayed. Ivy felt the monster moving closer, but she didn't want to look anymore, didn't want to see it. She curled up even further and nestled against the wall; she would've squeezed herself right through it if she'd been able to.

A large, rough, strong hand caught her wrist and drew it away from her head. She flinched, opened her eyes as she turned her face toward the creature, and yanked her arm out of its grasp.

The creature retreated, making the nest sway more harshly, and stopped with its body bathed in the soft blue light cast by the crystal on the wall. Ivy's eyes widened. Eight glowing violet eyes stared back at her.

Monster.

Spider.

Nightmare.

Those words and a thousand others tumbled through her foggy brain as Ivy raked her gaze over the creature. It was huge, even hunkered down as it was now. Six and a half, maybe seven feet tall, its body was a blend of hard angles and lean muscles. The torso was humanoid, with a broad chest leading down to a narrow waist, but its backside... It was like the rear end of a spider.

The monster had two sets of arms, one over the other, and *six* legs—long, multijointed spider legs, plenty long enough to reach her from anywhere within this nest. Its hands each had three fingers and a thumb, all of which were tipped with black claws. There were more limbs, smaller ones, tucked against its lower abdomen between its two front legs.

A thick neck led to the creature's head, and its face... The

74

parts were arranged like a human's might have been, except it was anything but human. Its face had a hard, almost masklike look, with two pointed crests sweeping up and back from its forehead and two more layered beneath, positioned behind its temples. Its mouth was a slash cutting across its face broken only by a pair of fanglike protrusions on either side, but those were nothing compared to the powerful mandibles jutting from between where the cheekbones and temples would have been on a human. Strands of long black hair with white streaks flowed from behind the headcrest and hung over the creature's shoulders.

Despite all that, there was an immediate beauty to this monster. Its skin was black, but there were markings on it—on its headcrest, at the joints and tips of its front legs, even around the upper portions of the wicked fangs on its mandibles. And those markings were glowing cool white and intense purple in the same way some things glowed under ultraviolet light.

Ivy cradled her hands against her chest and shook her head, unable to take her eyes off the creature. "Y-you're not real. You're just a...a dream. A nightmare."

"*Kir ven'dak unir kess'ani ikarahl,*" the creature said. Its voice was low, layered, raspy, and run through with subtle clicks and gentle buzzes. Though its jaw opened as it made the sounds, its lips didn't move.

It didn't *have* lips.

But it did have sharp teeth inside its mouth, and a long tongue that was the same color as its purple markings.

Ivy shuddered. Then she remembered. This wasn't the first time it had spoken to her. She vaguely recalled it speaking when she'd first woken to find herself in its clutches. It...it had covered her mouth as though it wanted her to be quiet. What was the word it had repeated?

Sheevix?

She released a shaky breath. Maybe...maybe it didn't plan to eat her? It hadn't hurt her yet.

Keyword there is yet, *Ivy.*

This creature appeared more...curious than anything.

"What are you?" she asked quietly.

Its head dipped slightly, and though Ivy couldn't tell for sure, she swore its eyes were on her mouth. The mandibles on the sides of its face twitched, rising just a bit before relaxing again. The spikes at the ends of those appendages were at least as long as her palm, and each ended in a deadly point.

"Are you going to hurt me?"

Why was she even bothering to speak to it? It wasn't as though this creature could understand her.

Because talking is calming me down.

Talking was also helping clear the fog away from her mind. Yet more than either of those reasons, it seemed to be keeping this monster at bay, at least for now. The creature clearly didn't understand her, and she couldn't understand it, but it seemed fascinated by her words.

The creature's spidery legs bent, lowering its body closer to the floor. That was good, wasn't it? It didn't seem tensed to pounce or anything. As long as it remained calm, Ivy would have time to think.

She was supposed to have been awakened by a medical tech after landing on Xolea, which had been described as a deep-space paradise. Ivy and the other colonists had been told... *What* had they been told? They'd be asleep for the entire journey, dreaming in stasis. If there was an emergency, there were protocols in place to ensure everyone's safety.

But where were the others, where were the techs and crew? Where was the ship? What had happened?

A sharp pain lanced through her gut. She winced, closed her eyes, and dropped a hand to her stomach, pressing down as though it would relieve her discomfort.

"*Arvok elad kess'ani zikarn,*" the creature said. Something in its tone sounded questioning.

She opened her eyes to see the creature leaning toward her

with its lower arms braced on its legs and its shoulders hunched, those violet eyes still gleaming in the eerie blue light.

Thankfully, some of the tightness had eased in Ivy's chest. Breathing slow and deep, she raised a hand, palm out. "Stay."

The creature tilted its head to the side, mandibles shaking briefly. "*Sss-tay?*"

Her eyes widened. "Did you...did you just understand me?"

"*Arvok elad et unixt sss-tay, Vel?*" the creature asked. "*Kir ven'dak unir kess'ani ikarahl.*"

It adjusted its front legs, shifting its body toward her.

Ivy's heart quickened. She thrust her palm at it again. "No. Stay back."

The creature stilled, eyes dipping to look at her hand. Tentatively, it extended one of its arms. Ivy watched as the creature straightened its fingers, flattened its palm, and pressed it against hers.

That hand was twice as long as hers, with thick, powerful, claw-tipped fingers. The skin was rough and hard, but it was warm, and the creature's touch was surprisingly gentle. For a few seconds, Ivy stared at the comparison. Her pale, tiny hand against the creature's, so different and yet somehow...somehow similar.

Then she realized that the giant spider-thing was touching her.

She gasped and yanked her hand back.

The creature's fingers bent slightly. It turned its palm toward its face, staring as though in awe before curling its hand into a loose fist and lowering it.

"*Kess elad ahn'vi, ahn'jesh. Noth ven kess elgath, Vel?*" The creature's voice was softer now, still wholly alien but tinged with wonder and curiosity.

Ivy shook her head with a frown. "I don't understand you."

There was intelligence in its eyes. She couldn't deny that no matter how frightening the creature's appearance was. It was speaking a language—one she couldn't understand, but a language all the same. Surely if it meant to hurt her, it would have done so already?

She struggled to recall the months of training she'd received before boarding the *Somnium*, but it was still lost in that cryosleep haze...not that there was likely to have been anything about establishing first contact with an alien species in those seminars and workshops. Xolea was supposed to be uninhabited. That was part of why it had been chosen, wasn't it?

A baseline understanding—that was what she needed with this creature. Some starting point from which they could develop communication. If they could both speak, they could both find ways to better imply their meanings.

She touched both her hands to her chest. "My name is Ivy."

The creature reached toward her again, moving very slowly. A tremor swept through Ivy. She tensed and pressed back against the wall as firmly as she could.

Keeping its fingers bent so its claws were directed away from her, the creature tapped her shoulder with its knuckle. "*Vel.*"

Vel? It had said that before. Relaxing only slightly, she kept her eyes locked with the creature's and shook her head. "No." Swallowing thickly, she touched her fingers to her chest again. "Ivy."

Another of those rumbles sounded from the creature's chest as it dipped its face closer to her. Its eyes narrowed—at least the larger, central ones. Those big mandibles squeezed as though about to close. The creature tapped her with its knuckle again, this time on the center of her chest. "*Ay-vee.*"

She nodded. "Yes. Ivy."

"*Ay-vee. Ay-vee...Fawz-tor?*"

Ivy gasped. "You know my name? Ivy Foster?"

"*Ay-vee Fawz-tor,*" the creature repeated, turning her name into something exotic with its deep, inhuman voice. It tilted its head so its eyes were more directly angled toward her face. "*Et althai'ur ikar Ay-vee Fawz-tor. To wun oh.*"

Had she gone insane in the cryochamber, or had this alien

spider really just told Ivy her name and colonist number? That... that wasn't possible, was it? How could it know?

Her brows creased. "Do you know where the *Somnium* is?"

The creature's mandibles sagged as it lowered its hand. "*Kess'ani ikarahl, Ay-vee, othan elad tharashi. Kir ven'dak unir othan.*"

Okay, we're losing that moment of understanding. Let's step back.

She lifted her hands and touched her chest, repeating her name. Then she gestured toward the creature, palms up, and lifted her eyebrows.

The creature glanced at her hands. It raised two of its own, mimicking her palms-up gesture before touching its own chest—which looked more like armored plating from this close. "*Ketahn tes Ishuun'ani Ir'okari.*"

Ivy blinked. That...was a lot. "Ketahn tes Ishuun a...uh..."

The creature extended an arm again and, with the same gentleness as before, took hold of Ivy's wrist. Whether due to fear or curiosity, she didn't resist as the creature shifted closer to her and guided her trembling hand to its chest.

"Ketahn," it said, bowing its head.

"Ketahn," Ivy repeated. Her gaze was fixed on her hand and the alien flesh around it. Ketahn's skin had a thick, leathery feel, but it was surprisingly supple. There was definitely hard muscle and bone beneath, but on the surface, it was warm and even had a little bit of give. Her thumb twitched, brushing across that skin.

She wasn't sure how she knew, and had no reason to believe it so firmly, but she was certain Ketahn was male.

Another noise vibrated in Ketahn's chest, one Ivy felt more than heard—part content purr, part tiger's growl, but so much lower and quieter than either.

Tipping her head back, Ivy slowly lifted her gaze until her eyes once more met his. He cocked his head, spilling more of his hair over his shoulder to brush across her forearm. That touch tickled, sending a tingling thrill up her arm, and she flinched, withdrawing her hand from his grasp.

Ketahn displayed all four of his palms to her and eased back, keeping himself low to the floor. "*Kir kala'dak zakash kess, Ay-vee.*"

When he'd reached the far wall, he twisted his torso to draw a piece of cloth across the nest's round entry hole. Ivy wasn't sure if she was grateful to have that barrier, however thin, between herself and the alien forest outside, or if it was a terrifying confirmation that she really was trapped in here with this thing.

No...with him.

He kept his eyes on her as he removed the bag that had been slung over his shoulders—and the weapon along with it. The spear was nearly as long as she was tall, with a coil of white rope attached to it and a large, barbed shard of what looked like sharpened obsidian for its head. Ketahn stood the spear against the wall and placed his bag on the floor.

Ivy leaned against the wall and wrapped her arms around her legs, hugging them to her chest. She glanced around for the first time since Ketahn had carried her in here. The place was like a hanging bird nest on a huge scale, shaped like an oval, but she doubted an animal could've built anything so intricate.

The branches and vines comprising the walls were woven in repeating patterns like a huge wicker basket, with more of that white rope stuff threaded through it. Tentatively, she ran her fingers over one of the ropes on the wall beside her. It was surprisingly soft to the touch, nothing like what she'd imagined, but it had little give.

There were pieces of cloth with a silken sheen hanging here and there, and the floor was padded with soft furs. Higher up were numerous baskets woven directly into the wall that held clay pots and jars, pieces of fur and hide, and more tools and weapons, some of which were made of the same materials as Ketahn's spear.

Between the craftsmanship—craftsspidership?—of this place and the items within, Ketahn's spoken language, and his mannerisms, it was clear that he was part of an intelligent species. Obviously, they were a bit far from being a spacefaring people...but they weren't exactly living in caves and worshipping fire.

She hunched forward and rested her forehead on her knees. There was a dull throbbing in her head, concentrated behind her eyes, and even though she'd done little more than try to wrestle free of Ketahn's hold earlier, she was exhausted. Had the cryosleep not been enough?

How long *had* she been in stasis?

Her chest constricted as she recalled another piece of information—she and the other colonists had been told many times that the journey to Xolea would take sixty years. By the time they arrived, many of the people they'd known on Earth were likely to have died.

Ivy pushed those thoughts away. She'd known the consequences when she'd decided to sign on for this journey. But she couldn't help but wonder...

Had her parents missed her?

Her eyelids drooped, and her head lolled, but she forced her eyes open, fighting the weight dragging her down. This wasn't time for sleep—there was a spider monster ten feet away from her, and she wouldn't be able to defend herself if she was unconscious.

She tried to ignore the sounds coming from Ketahn, the soft trills and rough, low mutterings, but she couldn't. She was torn between wanting to pretend he wasn't there, that he wasn't real, and wanting to remain vigilant.

But eventually, her body relaxed, and her eyelids grew too heavy. The last thing she was aware of was a long, sighing breath escaping her before she succumbed to sleep.

Chapter Seven

IVY WOKE WITH A PAINED GROAN. Before she could so much as gather her wits, her stomach cramped. Agony bloomed through her abdomen, and she curled up on her side, muscles tensing and sweat beading on her skin. She felt hollow and nauseous, in danger of emptying her stomach—not that there was anything in her stomach to begin with.

She pressed a hand to her belly, willing the sensations away with deep, even breaths. She was hungry and thirsty, and her body was suffering the aftermath of cryosleep. She'd heard the medical techs refer to it as stasis sickness.

But someone was supposed help her. That was the protocol. The med techs would assist everyone after they'd been woken from cryosleep, would help manage the pain and discomfort of anyone suffering stasis sickness, would ensure everything returned to normal.

And then it would be sunny days on a beautiful new world where Ivy could be whatever she wanted to be.

All she had to do was endure this a little longer...and wasn't this pain a small price to pay for a fresh start?

Something brushed over her ankle—something warm and rough. Ivy's brows knitted as a large hand cupped her heel, lifting her foot into the air delicately. Why would a tech start a med exam with her feet?

That something—a finger?— lightly swept across the bottom of her foot, tickling her. Ivy jerked her leg and raised her head to look over her shoulder. Her breath caught in her lungs as her eyes fell upon the creature behind her.

Everything came flooding back in that instant.

She wasn't on the *Somnium*. She wasn't being tended by technicians and doctors. She wasn't on Xolea.

She'd been taken by a spider monster to its nest, where it was going to...to...

To what?

Ivy forced herself to really see what was happening. The creature—Ketahn, he'd said—held her foot in one of his four hands with a long finger from another hand extended, having trailed that finger across her sole. He was staring at her with eight violet eyes, his head tilted slightly as though to ask, *what the heck, woman?*

She'd been taken by a spider monster to its nest, where it was tickling her feet.

Keeping his gaze locked with hers, Ketahn reached forward with a third hand, delicately took her big toe between his forefinger and thumb, and wiggled it.

Ivy arched a brow. "Are you playing piggies now too?"

The whole situation struck her as bizarre, though she could understand his curiosity considering he didn't have toes—or even feet.

"*Noth ven kess lenaal kuix ithin?*" he asked, dropping his gaze to her foot again. He wiggled her remaining toes then stroked her sole once more with the pad of his finger.

His touch was so light that it made her shudder and sent a tremor up her leg—an oddly delightful tremor.

Her breath hitched, and she scrambled back, wrenching her foot out of his grasp. She sat with her back to the wall, legs drawn up to her chest, and feet flat on the fur covered floor. She wagged a finger at him. "No. No tickling."

Ketahn released a huff, mandibles drooping. "*Tih-kling*?"

She had no idea how she was going to explain tickling. Instead, she pointed to her foot. If he was curious, she could give him an anatomy lesson. "Foot."

A clicking rumble vibrated his chest. He extended his arm and pointed to her foot. "*Voot*," he said, making a chuffing sound closer to a *v* in place of the *f*.

"Foot," she said again, emphasizing the *f*.

Ketahn shifted his attention to her mouth. "*Ikar et ikarahl vana, Ay-vee. Vhoot.*"

"Okay, so maybe you can't make that sound because you don't have lips." She pointed to her mouth. "Mouth." She tapped her bottom lip. "Ivy has lips."

"*Nowth.*" He gestured to his own mouth. "*Shev.*"

"Shev," she repeated.

There was a chance that Ivy and Ketahn really would be able to communicate with each other. She should've been scared out of her wits, but that chance...she had to cling to it, and to the hope it signified. Because if he'd found her, he had to know where the ship was, didn't he? She just had to figure out how to ask him to show her. To bring her back.

Monstrous spider-person or not, Ketahn was all she had right now. And as long as he didn't plan to eat her...

Ivy didn't back away when he leaned toward her, expecting him merely to point at her mouth, but his hand did not stop until the pad of his thumb had stroked her lower lip. She tensed, eyes locked on him, as her lips parted. She might not have backed away, but him being this close put into perspective just how big he was compared to her—and how scary he looked.

"*Lit*," he said with a click of that purple tongue.

"Close." She placed a hand hesitantly over his and pushed it away. Ketahn dipped his chin toward their hands, lifting hers a

87

little. "*Hani.*" He displayed his other hands with fingers splayed. "*Hani.*"

Ivy repeated the word, out loud and in her mind, storing it away as she'd done with the other, and raised both her hands. They trembled slightly. "Hands." She closed the fingers of one hand until she was holding up two fingers. "Two. Ivy has two hands. One"—she lowered one finger and lifted it again—"Two. Two hands."

His mandibles twitched, and he tilted his head aside, watching her curiously.

"Ketahn has four hands." Slowly, she reached out and lightly touched each of his hands as she spoke. "One, two, three, four." She held up four fingers. "Four hands."

She had no idea if he would remember any of this. Was she going too fast?

"*Hvor* hands." Ketahn turned his palms toward his face for a moment before looking at Ivy's hands. "Two hands."

Okay, so maybe he will remember.

He curled two of his upper hands into loose fists and raised his fingers one by one, reciting a word with each. "*Ul. Tok. Ir. Set. Gon. Het. Urd.*" With the eighth finger, he dipped his head toward her. "*Vel.*"

Ivy recognized that word. He'd said it many times, mostly in question, when speaking to her. Eight? Had he been referring to her as eight? Why?

"No *vel.*" She tapped her chest. "Ivy."

He placed his hand on her chest, his splayed fingers easily spanning from one of her shoulders to the other. "Ivy."

Her eyes flared, and her heart hammered against her ribs in response to his closeness and his touch.

"*Kess elad* Ivy. *Kir unir ithin.*"

Ivy shook her head. "I have no idea what you're saying."

Ketahn grunted, seemingly put out by this, but they resumed the anatomy lesson, each pointing to parts of their bodies, saying the words in their own languages and repeating them in each other's language. Some of his words were difficult for her to say, and she knew she wasn't pronouncing them right—knew that she couldn't when some of them contained subtle buzzes and clicks. Ketahn continued to struggle with sounds Ivy made with her lips, but they both seemed pleased to be making progress.

Finally, Ivy gathered a portion of her hair and lifted it. "Hair."

He hooked some loose strands of his hair with his finger. "Hair. *Sutra.*" He leaned close to her, holding his hair toward her as though wanting her to touch it.

Brows low, she glanced from his eyes to his hair, then slowly reached up and grasped the strands. Her lips parted in surprise at its feel; it was like silk. She rubbed it between her finger and thumb, then ran her fingers through it, marveling at its color.

"It's so soft," she said.

That low purring sounded in his chest. He lifted a hand to her hair, took a lock of it between his fingers, and rubbed it. "*Kess'ani sutra alvos iln huthaal, varsi ree shendar iln syth.*"

Ivy lowered her arm and watched him. There was almost a... reverence to the way he was touching her hair.

"I don't know what you're saying, but at least it sounds nice."

After a few moments, he released her hair. "*Kess elad ahn'jesh,* Ivy. *Kess elad'dak iln kir.*" He rapped a fist on his chest, producing a dull thump. "Ketahn *elad larak.* Ivy *elad jesh.*" One of his hands moved to her chest, cupped her breast, and squeezed.

Ivy's breath hitched, and her nipple puckered beneath his touch. It took her brain a moment to register what he'd done, and a moment longer for her to react.

She slapped his hand away, the sound of her flesh striking his shattering the quiet in the nest. "No."

Ketahn snatched his hand back, spreading his mandibles wide and letting out a low, startled hiss.

Ivy yelped and shrank away, curling into herself against the wall and covering her head with her arms.

Way to go, Ivy. You're getting eaten now. You just had to go and slap the spider.

89

But he groped me!

Is that worse than being eaten alive? He was just curious! It's not like he has breasts.

"Please, *please*, don't eat me. I'm sorry, Ketahn."

"*Ven kir'ur zikash kess*, Ivy? *Elad kess'ani ukata zikahl?*" There was a light touch on her shoulder. "Ivy?"

She raised her head slightly to peek at him. He didn't look threatening—or at least he looked as unthreatening as a hulking spider person could. He'd leaned his torso forward and lowered himself so that his belly was almost flat on the floor, putting his eyes beneath the level of hers for a change, and was holding himself up with his lower hands.

Ivy slowly lowered her arms. "Ketahn no eat"—she brought her fingers to her mouth and acted as though she took a bite of something and chewed before pointing to herself—"Ivy?"

"No eat?" His mandibles fell low as he mimicked her gesture, pantomiming the act of eating—which granted her another glimpse of that purple tongue and the fangs inside his mouth. "*Kess elad vukod?*"

She stared at his mouth, at those sharp fangs, and shuddered. "Ketahn eat Ivy?"

His eyes flicked a little wider, and he recoiled. "Ketahn no eat Ivy."

Relief rapidly flooded her. "Thank you."

And just as swiftly, that pang of hunger tore through her gut with as much intensity as it had possessed when it woke her. She winced, settling her hand over her belly as it growled and a wave of dizziness crashed over her, making her lightheaded and weak.

"Ivy *elad vukod?*" Ketahn asked. He made that eating gesture again. "*Kess telenas saal ukaan?*" He repeated both the gesture and that last word, *ukaan*.

"Yes," Ivy nodded. "Ivy hungry. Ivy needs to eat."

Ketahn backed away from her and rose to a far more imposing height. "*Kir'al tavit dera kess*, Ivy. *Kir'al irel ukaanahl, vux ikesh'al ukaan.*"

Ukaan meant eat, but what was that similar word? *Ukaanahl*? Did that mean...food? She wished this whole process was faster—and wished even more that she'd never woken up to find herself in this situation—but this was a step in the right direction. Wasn't it?

Ketahn turned away from her, snatching his bag off the floor and slinging it over his shoulders before taking his spear in hand.

Ivy sat up straight, eyes wide, and despite his frightening lower half—the spider half—being on display, she crawled toward him. "You're leaving me? Alone?"

What if something else crawled into the nest while he was gone? Something that *did* want to hurt or eat her?

"*Kir ven'dak ithaa ukaanahl dun, vux kir telenas tavit.*" He turned toward her again, and his mandibles twitched and fell. He gestured at her with a flattened palm. "Ivy, sss-tay."

She stilled. He'd understood and remembered. He was learning. She curled her fingers against the wood beneath her and nodded. "Okay. Ivy stay."

Not like I have anywhere else to go anyway.

"*Kir'al saavix dun ursh ul vi selyek.*" Ketahn pulled aside the cloth hanging in front of the opening.

For a moment, Ivy had to squint against the light that streamed in; the jungle had been dark when she'd awoken in his arms, but that was no longer the case. How tightly woven was this nest to prevent any of that light from leaking through?

But the instant her eyes adjusted, she wasn't concerned with the sunlight any longer—her attention was fully upon Ketahn. This was her first glimpse of him in bright light, and it was like seeing him anew...just without that initial terror.

His skin was black and had a slight leathery texture to it, and the purple and white of his markings was even more pure and vibrant than they'd seemed when they were glowing. His long black hair shimmered, and its white streaks lit up like strands of silver—and now she could see that there were violet streaks within it, also, too subtle to have spotted by the eerie blue light of the crystal. The hard planes on his torso and arms were inhuman, but there was an undeniable grace to his shape.

And she could not deny the humanity in his alien face.

Not humanity, I guess, but...intelligence and compassion.

His mandibles closed, the fangs at their ends lightly clicking together. "Sss-tay," he hissed softly before slipping out through the hole.

The nest rocked and bounced with his movements. Ivy's stomach lurched, and her heart quickened. She clutched at the woven wood beneath her, seeking stability that she knew she would not find. Outside, branches creaked, and leaves rustled. Unfamiliar animal calls drifted on the air. She heard light scrapes on the exterior of the nest as he climbed along it.

As Ketahn's rearmost legs slipped out through the hole, and the cloth covering fell back into place, plunging the interior of the nest into relative darkness until her eyes readjusted to the light of the crystal.

The nest violently swayed once more before it slowed to a halt. On trembling limbs, Ivy crawled toward the exit, her palms and knees brushing over the furs on the floor. She grasped the cloth and lifted it, peering out. She was immediately struck by a wave of vertigo as she looked down at the jungle below. The branches, leaves, and vines were so thick and jumbled that she couldn't even see the ground, and everything was so *big*. She'd never seen trees so tall or immense in her life. Even this high up, many of the branches looked wide enough to be used as walkways, and some of the leaves were big enough that they would've covered her from chest to ankles if she held one in front of her.

Steeling herself, she lifted her gaze. Straight ahead, the tangled boughs and leaves formed a canopy that the sunlight pierced in brilliant shafts. But it was what she saw directly overhead that truly stole her breath.

A spiderweb. That was the only way to really describe it. A massive web spanned the trees and branches overhead, its many threads converging on the hanging nest. Just like the walls of the nest itself, the web was interwoven with the thick branches, but it was that silky material that was predominant in this case. And what appeared to be chaotic at first took shape as she angled her head to see more of the web; it was arranged in a neat pattern, with the primary threads and intersecting support threads spaced evenly throughout. Here and there, dewdrops sparkled in the sunlight along the web. There must've been many more before he'd climbed out.

Ivy let out a slow, shaky breath as she sat back and let the cloth fall into place.

I'm caught in a spider's web.

Chapter Eight

WITH IVY OCCUPYING his every thought since he'd found her, Ketahn had all but forgotten that his nighttime hunt had yielded no meat—at least not the sort for eating. His choice to relocate to the Tangle, to live apart from his people, had been made with full understanding of the expectations it would place upon him.

A hunter must provide.

He was to provide meat to the vrix of Takarahl, each of whom did their part to aid the survival of their city. Failure to deliver would be noted. The queen had imposed no mandate upon the hunters, but her scribes monitored everything—including the food brought in by the city's roving hunters.

There was no doubt that Zurvashi would use any excuse at her disposal to draw Ketahn back to Takarahl at her whim. He had no intention of giving her another reason to do so.

And yet he could not turn his focus away from Ivy. She was hungry, and he needed to provide for her. He did not have the luxury of days to prowl the branches and stalk the undergrowth. As small and delicate as she was, he feared Ivy would not last that long without fresh food. And this morning's hunt couldn't even be considered a hunt at all—he'd found only a few animal signs, all days old, at least, and the calls he'd heard from creatures large enough to provide adequate meat had each come from hundreds of segments away. It was as though Ivy's scream last night had scared away everything in the Tangle.

Fortunately, the Tangle had other bounties obtained easily enough for those who knew the way, and he'd filled a small pouch to bulging with food. Perhaps it was little better than the roots and mushrooms of which Urkot and Rekosh had complained, but a full belly was better than one turning in on itself in hunger any time.

What he'd managed to forage thus far could scarce be considered a meal for a vrix, but he hoped it would be enough for his Ivy, if only for a little while. He'd be far less distracted if her gut wasn't making odd, gurgling, growling noises that she'd implied indicated hunger.

Ketahn climbed the broad trunk of a leaning grubwood tree, using the claws on the tips of his fingers and legs to latch onto the rough bark. His every muscle still ached, and climbing required more effort than usual, but his rest had dulled the discomfort and refreshed him enough for it to be bearable.

The Tangle was a different place by day. The sunlight breaking through the roof of leaves overhead set off the greens, browns, blues, and purples in a way at once far subtler but more vibrant than their nighttime glows, and different animals were active and calling.

He paused high off the ground to listen to those calls, turning his head aside. The hot, thick air hung around him without the slightest breeze to disturb it; he welcomed it after the stale, cool air in the tunnels of Takarahl.

After the impossibly clean, crisp, scentless air in the chamber where he'd found Ivy.

His mandibles twitched as he recalled what she'd communicated to him earlier this morning—she'd asked if he meant to eat her.

The thought might've made him chitter in amusement had it not been so sickening. He'd sampled meat from many jungle creatures, but he would never eat the flesh of a creature like Ivy. Even though she looked nothing like a vrix, she was more like his kind than any other animal he'd encountered. She was intelligent—intelligent enough that they'd already begun to learn one another's languages in the short time they'd spent together.

Ketahn brushed the pad of a finger across the line of his mouth.

Lips. Pronouncing the word was difficult, but he longed to say it himself—to say it in a way she'd understand. Those plump little strips of flesh intrigued him for many reasons, only one of which was the way she used them to shape her words.

He twisted his torso away from the trunk, hanging from it precariously as he swung his gaze in the direction of the cursed pit. He understood that it had not been a cave in which he'd discovered her, but what could it be called, then? A temple, like those that had been erected in some of the other vrix cities? An elaborate burial chamber?

Ketahn couldn't begin to imagine how the place had been built. His people had metal—gold—but there wasn't enough of it in all the world to build something so large, with so many intricate and complex pieces.

Cocoon was the only word he knew for the things Ivy and the other creatures had been sealed in, but he knew that wasn't right. Were they really eggs? Nests? Something more sinister? Someone or something had built that place with materials and methods far beyond anything Ketahn or his kind possessed, possibly even beyond the capabilities of the gods themselves.

Until he could communicate clearly with Ivy, he would have no answers. She—a strange, frail, unknown creature—was his only hope for information. She had to know somethi—

Ketahn stilled as a sound echoed between the trees—the clack of stone against stone in a short, quick rhythm. A familiar rhythm. Hunters from Takarahl had used such means of communication in the Tangle for generations. Though nearby animals were alerted by the sounds, they were far less often as frightened as they would've been by vrix shouts.

The simple method of communication had proven valuable in the war against the thornskulls, during which many of the males who'd been drawn into service with the Queen's Claw had spent long times in the thickest parts of the jungle with poor visibility.

He slid his hand up the shaft of his spear to grasp it just beneath its head and reached back to retrieve his knife from his bag. With both weapons in hand, he brought the flats of the blackrock blades together, producing a clacking beat.

The answer came within a few moments, another staggered rhythm just off from the first two. Two hundred segments away, perhaps three hundred.

Ketahn climbed around to the opposite side of the trunk and dropped onto a wide branch. He moved in the direction from which the signals had come. He did not often encounter other hunters in the Tangle, and he wasn't necessarily in the mood to speak with anyone, but he could not ignore such signals.

After a short while, he repeated the signal. When he received the answer, it came from far closer, and he altered his course to follow the sound.

Movement ahead soon caught his attention—a figure stalking along a branch that was higher than Ketahn's, gliding through patches of shadow and shafts of sunlight as it approached. Ketahn knew those bright green markings anywhere.

Telok.

Ketahn halted on a wide portion of the branch, where it was braced by another bough crossing beneath it.

Telok used the nearby vines and branches to swing himself down onto Ketahn's level, keeping the shaft of his spear tucked along his straightened arm. The angle of the sunlight striking his hide gave his pale scars long, deep shadows.

Old wounds that Ketahn had nearly forgotten throbbed

dully. Many of those wounds, many of his scars, had been suffered during the same battles in which Telok had collected his own.

"I did not think you would still be so far out," Ketahn said, extending his forelegs as Telok drew near. "Urkot told me you were due back in Takarahl at suncrest."

Telok stretched his forelegs, tapping their lower segments against Ketahn's. "The others began their return just before suncrest."

"And you were content to wander?"

Telok chittered, withdrew his legs, and rested his lower forearms atop his uppermost leg joints. "I do not wander, Ketahn. That is you. I travel ever with purpose."

With a soft chitter of his own, Ketahn asked, "And what purpose is that?"

"I sought you."

Ketahn spread his arms to the sides. "And you have found me."

"I did not expect to."

Tapping the side of Telok's leg, Ketahn said, "If any hunter from Takarahl could, it is you."

Telok huffed and clicked his mandibles together. "I know all your tricks, Ketahn. I could track you through a mire without a handspan of ground above water if I had to. That was not my concern."

"What, then?"

"I knew you would return to Takarahl for Offering Day, and I feared you would do something to provoke Zurvashi's ire."

"Your fears were founded."

"Yet here you stand." Telok raked his gaze over Ketahn, leaning back slightly. "Though you look as though you did not have a pleasant night."

"It was..." Ketahn's mind raced. He trusted Telok without question, had known him for most of their lives, and he longed to speak to someone about what he'd found last night—especially someone who'd also roamed the Tangle and had undoubtedly seen unnatural things out here.

But at the same time, Ivy was Ketahn's, and he had no desire to share her with anyone. At least not until he knew more.

"It was long," Ketahn said, "and I am still sore."

Telok's mandibles twitched and rose. "Did she..."

"No. I stalked a soota high in the branches, and just before I could make the kill, a pack of xiskals tried to attack my quarry. The branches could not hold their weight. They happened to be the same branches upon which I was perched."

"And the soota?" Telok asked.

"I heard it howling in the trees, completely unbothered, as I picked myself up off the ground."

Telok chittered, and Ketahn couldn't help but join in. He could find humor in such things in hindsight—and that was easier than thinking about what had happened after that fall.

"Xiskal meat is tough, but they carry much more of it on their bones than soota," said Telok. "Perhaps it was a blessing, in the end?"

"The xiskals were lost to the Tangle," Ketahn replied. "All I gained for my efforts and pain is the story." And the strangest, most intriguing creature in the world. "What of your hunt?"

"Enough to grant each of Moonfall's broodlings a portion of meat, at least," Telok replied. "So long as the others manage to bring it home without catching the notice of the queen's eyes."

Something tightened deep in Ketahn's chest and slowly twisted. "Her eyes?"

Telok thumped the tips of his forelegs on the branch, and his fine hairs bristled. "The queen's scribes have been awaiting us each time we've returned from the hunt these past few moon cycles. They collect the meat, take measure of it down to the smallest bit of sinew, and record it. When they are through, they haul it away.

"The first few times, we thought it odd but did not suspect anything more. Then the others in Moonfall began asking us about it, saying they had received little despite us bringing in a steady supply. This season has been bountiful. There should be meat in every den."

Telok tipped his head back to look skyward, folding his arms across his chest and tucking his barbed spear along the top of one forearm. "We asked the scribes. We were told only that the food was going to where it was needed the most, and were thanked for our hard work in trying times. The next time we delivered meat, the keepers were accompanied by Claws who tolerated neither questions nor delay."

Fire blazed inside Ketahn, building heat without any means of venting it, filling his limbs with restless energy for which he had no immediate use. He did not doubt Telok's story at all, though he could not understand Zurvashi's motives. What did she stand to gain by angering and weakening the vrix of Takarahl?

The answer might well have been as simple as a belly full of meat whenever she pleased.

Blind anger would do Ketahn no good now—it wouldn't do anyone any good. Thus far, Ketahn's rage had not brought about disaster only because of the queen's desire for him, and he knew her patience was not unending. For a moment, he allowed himself to wonder...what would happen were he to submit to Zurvashi?

A foolishly hopeful part of Ketahn imagined her respect for his willpower being enough to grant him some influence over her, allowing him to slowly convince her to improve the lives of the many vrix who'd suffered under her rule. Though he would have hated every moment of it, would it not be a worthy sacrifice? What did his joy matter compared to that of hundreds, thousands of his kind?

But he wouldn't do that. He wouldn't forsake his freedom for anyone—so, perhaps, it was those who'd seen him as some sort of hero after the war who were the true fools. Ketahn had fought for what little he had now. Everyone else could wage their own battles.

And it would never have worked, regardless. The queen was

not the sort to be swayed much by anyone, not even a male she claimed was nearly her equal.

He again found himself longing for those simpler days when he, his friends, and his brothers and sisters had been free of such worries. When they'd spent their days in each other's company, chittering and teasing good-naturedly, wrestling and playing at being warriors, learning the trades of their broodmothers and sires, and exploring the many tunnels, both used and forgotten, that comprised Takarahl.

Ketahn straightened his leg joints to stand higher. "Do you recall the undertunnel we discovered as broodlings? The abandoned path under Moonfall we explored, when the den beside Rekosh's collapsed?"

Telok's eyes widened. "I have not thought about it for many years."

"Nor have I. But it led to the surface, and if it has not caved in... The queen would not have eyes or scribes there. Perhaps a stoneshaper could burrow down from the den of a friendly vrix?"

"Urkot could dig clean through in a day," Telok said with a thoughtful chitter. "You should come, Ketahn. Your efforts would be of great help."

Extending a foreleg, Ketahn flattened it along the side of Telok's. "My place is out here, my friend. My presence in Takarahl would only draw Zurvashi's attention to Moonfall Tunnel, and your efforts would be for nothing."

"So, the whispers Rekosh has been hearing are true, then?"

Ketahn released a huff. "The queen declared her intentions before everyone within the Den of Spirits. She has left no question of it."

Telok tilted his head, angling his gaze toward the jungle floor, which was somewhere far below and out of sight. A tremor rippled through his body, making his hairs rise and fall in quick succession. "I do not envy you, Ketahn."

"You need not fear for me. I will cut my own path through whatever is to come, regardless of the queen's desires."

He could almost envision that path in his mind now, running straight through the dense plant life, leading him back to his hanging den. Back to...Ivy.

She needed him more than anyone else did. She was depending upon him. And that was his purpose this morning— to provide for her. As delicate as she seemed, there was no telling how quickly her body would fail without food. Telok at least had his fellow hunters for support, the vrix dwelling in Moonfall Tunnel had one another, but Ivy had no one except Ketahn.

Telok thumped Ketahn's leg with his own. "You must tell me how it went. I can only imagine what you said to her, Ketahn."

"Another time, my friend," Ketahn replied, offering an apologetic bow. "I am certain Rekosh would thrill in recounting the tale, but should you wish to hear it from me, it will have to be another time. If I do not resume my hunt, I will have hungry days ahead."

Sliding back, Telok sank into a bow of his own. "Allow me to accompany you. I will gladly teach you to hunt properly."

Ketahn chittered. "Have you forgotten already, Telok, that you are the one who taught me all those years ago? All my failed methods were learned from you."

Curling his hands into loose fists, Telok tapped them against his chest. "Your words pierce more surely than a spear, Ketahn. I must demand the chance to prove myself the more skilled hunter."

Ketahn bowed deeper still. "You will have your chance soon enough, but I will not allow an unfair contest between us. It must wait until you have recovered from the hunt you have just ended."

"You are the one who fell through half the Tangle," Telok replied with a chitter. "I shall allow you time to recover. And then I shall make you wish you had remained a weaver."

"Or you shall wish you had become a weaver instead." Ketahn rose from his bow. "Be safe, Telok. May their eightfold eyes look upon you favorably."

Telok straightened also, drumming his forelegs on the branch. "And you, Ketahn. I am glad she did not eat you alive."

"Had she done so, I would have used my final breath to ensure she choked."

"You must at least hold out until I am there to witness it. I would not want to miss such a display."

Telok departed, heading in the direction of Takarahl, while Ketahn turned toward his den.

Keeping alert, Ketahn searched for more food as he traversed the jungle, all the while battling his conflicting, chaotic thoughts about Ivy, the queen, and the situation in Moonfall Tunnel. The joy of encountering Telok faded as time passed, and Ketahn's mind turned increasingly toward Ivy as he neared his den.

Before long, he'd forgotten about Zurvashi and her cruelty. There were countless mysteries to contemplate regarding Ivy, more than enough to drive away his worries and drown out his concerns with bubbling curiosity and excitement.

He recalled the words Ivy had taught him in her language. Some, like her word for food and the one that meant the pink flesh around her mouth, had those odd sounds in them that he had trouble recreating, but he enjoyed the challenge. She'd not pronounced many vrix words properly, either, but the two of them were building understanding.

When he reached the area below his den, he climbed high, barely noticing the many gouges he'd left in the wood over the years. The climb had become instinctual, though it certainly felt different this morning because he wasn't hauling fresh meat up with him.

The den was swaying gently in the breeze, and the surrounding branches were creaking their familiar songs. Drops of dew still glistened on the webbing overhead. The sunlight cocooned the den in pure light, making it seem otherworldly— though it could never appear as otherworldly as the place he'd found Ivy.

Ketahn fastened his spear to the side of his bag and ascended, crossing the web eagerly. The den was already bouncing and swinging when he reached it.

He repeated Ivy's unusual words in his mind as he climbed toward the opening, determined not to forget them.

Determined to show Ivy that he was hungry to learn from her, hungry to teach her.

Ketahn swept aside the hanging cloth, grasped the edges of the opening, and pulled himself into the den. He stilled with only half his body through the opening, muscles tensing. Ivy, who'd kept herself huddled against the far wall since he'd brought her here, was nowhere in sight.

His hide prickled with blooming panic an instant before movement flickered at the edge of his vision.

Something hard and sharp pressed against his neck.

Chapter Nine

INSTINCT SEIZED CONTROL OF KETAHN. Faster than he could've made the decision to act, his hand darted up, grasping the weapon by the flat of its blade and forcing it away from his neck. In the same instant, he pulled himself fully through the hole and lunged at his attacker, tearing down the cloth at the opening as he moved.

He wrenched the weapon from his attacker's grasp and caught a pair of slender arms in his hands, driving the creature back. His mind only recognized Ivy's face—her eyes wide and filled with terror—as he slammed her back into the wall, pinning her wrists over her head.

Ivy gasped and struggled against his hold, shaking her head from side to side. Her golden hair spilled over her face and shoulders. "*Aym sahree! Aym sahree! Ay dih dunt noe eet wuhz yew!*"

Ketahn tossed the weapon aside and moved closer to Ivy. Her alluring scent filled his den, and between her nearness and her struggles, it was growing stronger by the moment, clouding his thoughts. One of his forelegs brushed against her leg, drawing in more of that scent and her taste. He leaned toward her and breathed her in. The combined smells of the jungle and sweet, fragrant, warm female flooded his senses.

She stilled, her chest rising and falling with her rapid breaths. *"Pleez, Ay dih dunt noe. Aym sahree."*

He dipped his head, burying his face between her shoulder and neck and brushing it over that pale, soft flesh. Her hair delicately swept over his hide, sparking tingles across its surface. A rumble sounded in his chest, vibrating through him to the tips of his limbs.

Behind his slit, his stem stirred, pulsing with the beat of his hearts.

His claspers unfolded and reached forward, sliding over the rounded spots where Ivy's legs met her torso—ready to draw her against him and lock her in place.

Ready to mate.

"Ketahn," Ivy whispered next to his ear. *"Pleez dohnt hert mee. Pleez,* no."

Ketahn halted, not allowing himself to even draw breath for several moments. The sound of his name from her lips had pierced that haze, but it was that final word, that *no*, that shattered whatever trance he'd fallen into.

He raised his head and looked down at Ivy.

She was trembling in his hold, her eyes were closed, and her face was turned aside. Her cheek glistened with moisture. A clear droplet flowed from the inside corner of her eye and rolled down her face, following that wet trail to her lips and, finally, her chin.

"What is this?" he asked, staring at the droplet hanging on her chin.

Ivy opened her eyes and slowly turned her face toward him. The white parts of her eyes were pinker now, the tiny veins within more visible than ever. More water shimmered within them, and the dark hairs on her eyelids were spiked and coated with moisture like blades of grass laden with dew.

Ketahn lifted one of his lower hands, carefully wiped that drop from her chin with the pad of his finger, and brought it to his face. He could barely make out its scent when he inhaled—water, but something a little more.

Opening his mouth, he extended his tongue and touched it to the tip of his finger.

Water, yes, but there was a saltiness to it—and a hint of sweetness. He needed more.

He dipped his head closer to her and ran his tongue from the bottom of her jaw up to her cheek, licking away that salty-sweet moisture and sampling her flesh.

She made a mewling sound and turned her face away, squeezing her eyes shut as her trembling intensified. "*Wut arr yew doo eeng?*"

His stem pressed hard against the inside of his slit, threatening to force its way out, and his claspers tightened their hold on her. Ivy's scent and taste were driving everything else out of his mind, were plunging him back into a lustful haze that would become a mating frenzy soon enough.

He licked her cheek again, and another rumble rolled in his chest. She shifted her body against his slit. A tremor of pleasure raced through him as he drew his tongue back into his mouth. His slit parted, and the tip of his stem emerged.

"*Yew sed yew wud naht* eat *mee*," she said quietly.

Eat? She thought he was about to eat her?

Ketahn jerked his head away from her, bringing his mandibles together and keeping them closed. Immense heat flowed through his body, and the pressure building behind his slit...

By the Eight, he wasn't about to eat her, he was about to mate her!

He was about to mate this...this *creature*.

It made no difference that she was intelligent, that she could speak and learn—she was not a vrix, and the desire she'd awoken in him was wrong. It...it would be like mating an animal.

With a hiss, he released her and retreated, snapping his claspers firmly against his pelvis and forcing his stem back into his slit.

She fell to the floor and huddled there against the wall. Her trembling had not subsided. The skin of her forearms was red and irritated where his hands had been clasped a moment before.

"What are you, Ivy? A spirit of temptation?"

She turned her face toward him, her eyes wide and fearful, her cheeks glistening with salty sweet water. Ketahn flattened his tongue against the roof of his mouth as the urge to lick her struck him again.

It was her fear that held him back. The sight of it unsettled Ketahn just enough for him to reclaim control, for his disgust with himself to twist into something closer to shame.

Ivy inhaled shakily and raised her hand to her chest. "Ivy." She shook her head. "*Naht* food. Ivy Ketahn's...*frend*."

"Ivy *naht* food," he said gently in her language. "Ketahn no eat Ivy."

Her head fell back against the wall, and she closed her eyes. Her lips pressed together, but something like relief shone upon her face as the strips of hair over her eyes relaxed.

Backing a little farther away from her, he grasped his bag and swung it off his shoulders, setting it on the floor. He had to force himself to move slowly; his muscles thrummed with tension, and his body had yet to fully settle. He wasn't sure if it could settle at all, not while her scent enveloped him.

Tugging the bag open, he reached in and took out the bulging water skin he'd refilled from the dew collectors this morning. "Drink."

Once she'd opened her eyes, he pretended to open the water skin and pour some into his mouth before holding it out to her. "Drink."

Ivy leaned forward with an outstretched hand and took the water skin. She glanced at it, repeated the word, and spoke another in her own language, "*Dreenk.*"

She opened the top, brought it up to her nose, and sniffed. Seeming satisfied, she pressed it to her mouth and tipped her head back. Her throat worked as she drank long and deep. She paused only to take a breath before tipping the skin up again.

Ketahn watched, fascinated. The way her lips curled around the end of the water skin allowed no water to escape. He never would have guessed two plump little pieces of flesh could be so useful.

Her eyes flicked toward him, meeting his gaze. With a start, she lowered the water skin, causing some water to trickle out and run down her chin. Her pink tongue darted out, licking the moisture from her lips.

"*Sahree.*" Her cheeks darkened as she raised a hand and wiped the excess water off her chin. Closing the water skin, she offered it to him. "*Wahnt sum? Thair iz morr.*"

His eyes lingered on her lips. He would have liked to lick away that water himself, to have another taste of her skin, to—

Barely suppressing a growl, he extended an arm to accept the water skin, taking it on his upturned palm so as to keep as much distance between his hand and hers. He opened the top and raised the skin to his face. A hint of her scent wafted from it.

Ketahn poured water into his open mouth. Some of it ran

down the sides of his face, but he ignored it. He sealed the container and set it aside. Dropping his attention to his bag again, he removed a pouch from within, untied the leather strip that held it closed, and dipped a hand inside to scoop out a handful of wriggling grubs.

He held his hand out to her. "Food."

Ivy recoiled, her face scrunching as she stared at the squirming grubs. "*Oh, grohs.*"

Mandibles twitching, Ketahn tilted his head and moved his hand closer to her. "Eat, Ivy. Food."

One of the grubs wiggled free and fell onto the upper segment of her leg. Ivy shrieked. The piercing sound was like a spike being driven through Ketahn's ears. She slapped the grub away, and it landed on the fur rug in front of him.

Ketahn plucked the grub off the floor with his lower right hand. Its pale, plump yellow body pulsated as it weakly attempted to escape his hold.

Why was she not accepting his food? Did she not understand?

"This is food," he said. "Eat." To demonstrate, he opened his mouth and tossed the grub inside, biting down on it. The plump body popped between his teeth, filling his mouth with juices.

Ivy's lips parted, and she gagged. She quickly covered her mouth as her cheeks puffed out and a shudder coursed through her. "*Oh, thahtz nastee. Ay em naht eating thaht.*" She gagged again, this time against her hand. Her skin looked paler than normal.

Ketahn swallowed, glanced at the grubs still in his closed hand, and looked back at Ivy. When he moved that hand toward her again, she shook her head vigorously and recoiled.

He hadn't seen enough of her kind to know for certain, but she looked unwell. She appeared sickly compared to how she'd looked even in her terror a short while before. He dumped the handful of grubs back into the sack and tied it closed, sliding it aside but keeping his gaze on Ivy.

There were many creatures in the Tangle that did not eat the flesh of other animals. Was her kind the same way?

Bracing his forelegs to either side of Ivy, Ketahn dragged himself closer to her. She stared at him with those wide eyes, which, thanks to the sunlight streaming in through the den's opening, were a brighter blue than the clear sky. He cupped her jaw with one hand.

"Ketahn," she said, clutching his wrist with both of her hands as she tried to pull away from him.

"Calm, Ivy," he replied gently, maintaining his hold on her. "I need but a moment."

Ivy's nose holes flared with her heavy breaths as he touched her lips with the fingers of another hand, peeling them back to reveal her teeth. Her body tensed, and her grip strengthened, but she did not resist him.

Four of her front teeth were pointed, but they weren't nearly long or sharp enough to be considered fangs. The others were flat and straight. He squeezed her jaw lightly; when she did not react, he opened his mouth wide and squeezed again.

The strips of hair over her eyes slanted down toward her nose, and a fiery gleam sparked in her eyes. "*Ihf yew puht* one *uhv thohz nastee theengz en mai* mouth, *Ay wil byt yew.*"

She opened her mouth wide, flattening her little pink tongue.

Ketahn leaned closer and angled her face to better peer inside her mouth. The teeth running along the sides were wide and also fairly flat, closer to those of creatures that survived by eating plants than those that ate only meat.

Apart from those white teeth, her mouth looked soft, its flesh an even deeper pink than that of her lips. His urge to slip a finger between her lips was alarming in its suddenness and strength, and it wasn't even half as strong as his desire to slide his tongue along hers, to discover what this part of her tasted like.

He released her and withdrew before those thoughts could fully take root and command his actions. His only purpose in studying her that way had been to determine what sort of food she could eat. Fascination was not the same as attraction.

And he had no interest in taking a mate, regardless—not a vrix, and certainly not a...a whatever Ivy was. However intelligent this female was, she was a pet. Nothing more. A curiosity to occupy his time.

"Stay," he said in her language, turning away from her to collect an empty sack from one of the baskets on the wall. "I will find new food. Plants."

Ivy nodded. "*Ay wil* stay."

Ketahn mimicked her gesture, accepting that nod as a *yes*. "I will return quickly this time. Drink more if you want. Water." He pointed to the water skin on the floor as he moved to the den's opening.

She looked at the water skin. "*Wahtur.*" Curling her fingers around it, she drew it closer. "*Thaynk yew.*"

Tilting his head, he regarded her for another moment. Her softly spoken words and demeanor conveyed appreciation. Was she thanking him?

A gentle trill sounded in Ketahn's throat as he exited the den. They had far to go in their journey toward understanding one another, but every bit of progress was encouraging—their growing knowledge was like the strands of an immense web being woven into place one at a time, slowly creating something far greater and stronger than any individual piece.

I'M GOING TO DIE.

Ivy was on an alien planet with a big alien spider creature staring at her and an array of alien food spread out in front of her. She flicked her gaze over the plants laid on the floor.

There were white roots similar to carrots, palm sized, purple maybe-fruit balls with bumpy skin, thick leafy plants that looked like succulents, long stringy ones that reminded Ivy of an air plant she once owned that had died—because apparently you still needed to water air plants—a couple heart-shaped pink fruits with gnarly purple spikes growing off their skins, a cluster of pale growths that looked like bean sprouts, and several thin, golden ovals that might have been some kind of mushroom but were reminiscent of honey combs.

Eating any of this would be like playing Russian roulette.

Every colonist had been given a series of injections to help their bodies adapt to Xolea's environment, to protect them against diseases and bacteria both known and unknown, and to even make them resistant to toxins that might've been present in food on their new planet, but nothing was guaranteed. That was why the *Somnium* had been stocked with ample food stores, equipment, and supplies to grow crops of their own. That was also why every colonist, regardless of their intended duty on-planet, had been trained in the use of electronic chemical analyzers that had been included with the tools—so they all knew how to determine what was safe for consumption.

Ivy didn't have any of that here. All she had was chance.

"Eat, Ivy," Ketahn said, drawing her attention up to him. He raised his hand to his mouth and pantomimed taking a bite. His teeth made a clicking noise as they snapped together. "Food."

The *f* sound was still off in his pronunciation, produced with an airy rumbling from the back of his throat, but it was a big improvement over his earlier attempts.

Ivy nodded. "Yes. Food." She returned her gaze to the plants. It was in that moment that her stomach cramped again, making her wince and reminding her that she needed to eat. The water had helped a little, but it wasn't enough. She was literally starving.

She released a long, slow breath. "Okay. At least none of it is moving."

Ivy picked up the spiky pink fruit, which reminded her of dragon fruit, and held it up. "What is this?"

He reached forward and took the fruit from her, using a

thumb claw to slice the fruit's thick skin near the top. Then he grasped one of those spikes and peeled it down. As the skin broke away, it revealed the interior of the fruit, which was a lot like a pomegranate—though the seeds clustered within were vibrant blue instead of red.

Ketahn handed the fruit back to her. "*Seiki'larak.*"

Ivy repeated the name as she took the fruit from him. Holding it on her palm, she scooped out a few of the seeds and brought them to her mouth. She tensed and mentally prepared herself, half excepting them to be insect eggs or something considering what Ketahn had tried to get her to eat before, but she was pleasantly surprised by the taste. The seeds were coated in a jelly-like substance that was flavorful on its own, but once the soft arils had broken, sweet juice flooded onto her tongue.

She lifted the fruit to her mouth and scooped out more seeds, eating swiftly. Before she knew it, she was scraping the empty skin to get the last of the jelly.

"*Kess'ur nahani seiki'larak?*" Ketahn asked.

Lowering the fruit, she looked up at Ketahn to find him watching her. Her lips stretched into a smile. "*Seiki'larak* was good."

He tilted his head, his attention fixated on her mouth. His mandibles rose slowly, spreading wide, and his eyes narrowed just a little.

Was he...smiling? She could only assume so; he'd have to do it with his mandibles, as his mouth was hard and seemed mostly inflexible.

Setting the empty skin aside, Ivy picked up the lumpy purple ball next, holding it out to Ketahn. "And this?"

"*Ekkai'uta.*" Ketahn brought two of his hands together as though holding an invisible ball and then broke it apart.

"Simple enough." Placing her thumbs near the stem, she dug them in and tore the two sides outward.

What she'd expected to find inside was nothing like the reality. Instead of some pulpy meat like an orange or a peach, the fruit contained a thick, creamy, yogurt-like substance. She dipped her finger in and brought it to her mouth, sucking the dab off. Her brows rose—it tasted like a vanilla pudding.

"Oh my God," Ivy groaned. "This is delicious."

Ketahn tilted his head, bent his front legs more sharply, and rested his forearms atop his knees. Well, his upper knee joints, anyway. "*Ven kess'ani ikarahl unixt thuun kess nahani ekkai'uta kota?*"

That word, *kess*, had come up often when he spoke to her. She couldn't be sure, but she had a suspicion that it meant *you*. That didn't help her figure out what he was asking, but one obstacle at a time, right?

Still holding the shells of the *ekkai'uta*, she moved her hands closer until only an inch or two separated them. "Small. Use small words, Ketahn."

With his upper hands, he imitated her gesture. "*Vi*? Smoll?"

Ivy nodded. "*Vi*. Small." She widened her hands. "Big."

He did the same. "Vig. *Valai.*"

"Big," she repeated, emphasizing the *b* sound.

Ketahn tried again, producing something a bit closer with a strange clicking in his throat.

"Ivy is small. Ketahn is big."

"Ivy is hong-ree. Eat."

She chuckled. "Yeah. Ivy is hungry."

He leaned back, regarding her anew, and once again raised his mandibles and narrowed his eyes. This time, he produced a chittering sound. It should have been like any other sound from an unknown creature—alien and indecipherable, perhaps even unsettling—but somehow she knew that it was laughter.

Ivy raised the *ekkai'uta* to her mouth and slurped out its creamy inside, clearing both halves in a matter of seconds before grabbing the other one he'd brought, tearing it open, and devouring it. Then, though it went against all the survival training she'd been through before boarding the *Somnium*— they'd been advised to wait at least a little while after eating alien food even with a favorable analysis—she sampled several of the other foods.

She was simply too damn hungry to wait. As she ate, she and Ketahn continued to learn from one another.

The sprout-things were called *jugan'telth*. They were crisp, with a satisfying crunch, and a hint of spiciness that was reminiscent of horseradish though it wasn't as strong. The roots were called *ashok'tika*, and they were surprisingly tender. There was an earthiness to their taste, but it was overwhelmed by starchiness. Biting into those roots was like chomping on a raw potato.

She'd have to figure out a way to cook those and try them again.

Her favorites were the honeycomb-things, *huthaal'rok*, which indeed were some sort of mushroom upon closer inspection. They melted on her tongue and tasted just how they looked—as sweet as honey.

She and Ketahn shared another *seiki'larak* after the *huthaal'rok* were gone. By then, she was full, and Ketahn gathered the remaining food to put away, sealing some of it in crude clay jars and dropping others in baskets on the wall.

As she watched him clean up, Ivy realized she was relaxed. Almost...content. Secure in the knowledge that this spider-man-creature wasn't going to hurt or eat her, that Ketahn was friendly enough to provide her water, food, and shelter despite his reaction when he'd returned earlier.

Ivy couldn't blame him—she'd held a spear to his throat. She'd picked up the weapon shortly after he'd left, having spent who knew how long jumping at every sound and freaking out every time the nest swayed a little more than normal. Holding the spear had helped ease her until the nest had really started shaking and she'd heard claws scraping the exterior.

She'd reacted in fear and instinct, her subconscious deciding she'd at least attempt to put up a fight against whatever terrifying monster had been about to eat her.

Ketahn had moved so fast—faster than she could even register that it was him and not some nameless horror.

Sucking in her lower lip and biting it, she ran her eyes over him. He wasn't a spider or an insect, but the resemblance was undeniable—and she'd never been a fan of bugs. If she looked at him too hard, her mind hitched on all those inhuman characteristics. It told her to be afraid.

And she had been when he'd pinned her against the wall, when he'd wrapped those smaller appendages around her hips and run his tongue across her cheek—she'd been so sure he was going to eat her right then and there. But there were many times when he looked at her and there was almost a...tenderness in his eyes.

Just thinking that was almost enough to make her believe she really had lost her mind in cryosleep.

She needed to keep her focus on what was important—surviving and finding the *Somnium*. Finding other people. If she was alive, there had to be others, right? Other people who were in need of help? And if they found the *Somnium*, there had to be a chance of rescue, right?

If only Ketahn could tell her where he'd found her.

In time. They were making progress. She just...needed to be patient and hope that the others were okay.

That she wasn't the only human left.

Chapter Ten

IVY CLUTCHED the steering wheel as her stomach twisted into knots. Those knots coalesced in a cold, dense ball of dread, so heavy it threatened to drag her down, down, down, and she knew she'd fall forever and ever into darkness and no one would hear her screams, no one would come save her.

Because right now she had no one.

And she really, really needed someone.

How could she have been so naïve? So stupid?

She closed her eyes. Young and dumb—that's what she'd been at seventeen. Too young and too trusting, with her head in the clouds and her heart on her sleeve.

She hadn't listened to reason, hadn't listened to the people she should've trusted, the people she'd run away from a year ago. Instead, she'd trusted someone else, someone who she thought loved her, someone she'd given up everything for...

When she opened her eyes, she was standing on the sidewalk in front of her parents' house. But it was so much bigger, darker, and more imposing than she remembered—not at all the place in which she'd grown up. The windows stared at her with judgment gleaming in their panes, and the eaves looked like harshly angled eyebrows.

Her feet moved on their own, and she glided along the walkway with a slowness that gave her anxiety plenty of time to amplify.

Why had she come here? After everything, why here?

Because this is home, isn't it? Somewhere has to be home...

And they are my parents.

Suddenly she was at the door. It towered over her, making her feel like a little kid again, telling her she was as small and naïve and stupid as she felt. Her hand weighed a thousand pounds as she lifted it to knock.

Thud. Thud. Thud.

The sound echoed in the house and outside, but it built instead of diminishing, folding over itself again and again until it was as violent and powerful as thunder and she couldn't even block it out by clamping her hands over her ears because it was inside her and it was going to tear her apart.

The latch clicked, and the thunder ceased as though it had never existed.

The door opened, and there stood her mother, her bright blue eyes so much like Ivy's. Except Angela's eyes were cold and empty as she stared at Ivy.

"What do you want?" *Angela demanded.*

Ivy had never heard her mother's voice sound so unfeeling, so aloof. She'd known before coming that she shouldn't have expected a warm welcome, especially not after the way Ivy had left, but this...

"I wanted to see you and Dad," *Ivy said, her throat tight.* "I...I wanted to say that I'm sorry, that you were right. About everything."

Angela's eyes narrowed. "A little too late now, don't you think? You made your choice."

"I know, and I'm sorry. Sorrier than you know. But right now, I'm just so lost, so alone. I...I need you."

I need someone.

Her father, Jason Foster, appeared beside his wife. His beard had more gray in it than the last time Ivy had seen him.

His thick brows furrowed as he stared down at her. Ivy had never thought of her father as intimidating, but there was something unnerving in his presence now. "You don't belong here."

Tears spilled from Ivy's eyes.

Where do I belong?

"I made a mistake," she whispered, her voice broken. "I was young and stupid. I should have listened to you both."

Though her parents were standing right there in the doorway, right in front of her, they seemed to be getting farther and farther away, as though an impossible distance were opening between them and Ivy.

"And proof of your mistake *is all over the internet now," Jason said.*

"All of our neighbors know," Angela said. "All our friends. All our family. They all know that you're a whore."

Shame and despair crashed down upon Ivy, making her knees tremble. "I didn't know! I trusted him. I loved—"

"What do you know of love?" Her mother sneered, grasping the cross hanging around her neck. "You left us so you could live in sin and spread your legs for a man who never wanted anything more than to take advantage of you. Bad enough you destroyed your reputation, but now you've damaged ours."

A sob tore from Ivy's throat. "I know. I know. Please. I have nowhere else to go."

"You should have thought about that a long time ago," her father said.

Jason and Angela were so far away now that they seemed tiny with the distance, but Ivy could still see their cold eyes, their disapproving frowns, and the hard sets of their brows with crystal clarity.

"Please don't turn me away. I'm your daughter."

"We don't have a daughter," Angela snapped.

The door slammed shut with another peal of thunder. Ivy tumbled backward into shadows, into impenetrable darkness, into nothingness.

Alone.

Ivy jolted awake, and for a moment, she still felt herself falling into that nothingness, still felt that emptiness inside her like an unbridgeable chasm. She rolled over onto her back and opened her eyes to stare up into the darkness. Her cheeks were wet with tears she must've shed in her sleep, her breaths were short, and she was trembling.

Why did she have to dream of them? Why now, after all these years, did she have to be reminded of that rejection, that abandonment? Of how truly alone she'd been for so, so long. Ivy rubbed her chest.

But those old memories and the tightness in her chest didn't matter compared to the unbearable ache in her bladder. It felt like it was going to explode if she moved again. The pressure was so immense, so unrelenting, that she clenched her jaw and held her breath to contain a pained cry.

She'd awoken from a nightmare just to face a new one.

Without food and water in stasis, her body simply hadn't had anything to expel—but she'd stuffed herself with fruits, vegetables, and water yesterday, and now everything had been kick-started into motion.

And she had nowhere to go to relieve herself. At least, not without help.

With a groan, she rolled over and pushed herself up on her hands and knees, clenching her thighs as she sat back on her heels. She wasn't sure which way she was facing with how dark it was, but she knew Ketahn was somewhere near the entrance of the nest.

"Ketahn?"

Ketahn's voice rumbled from the nearby shadows. "*Sheevix, Ivy. Etorri'ven.*"

Ivy pressed her hands down upon her thighs and dug her fingertips into them as the pressure in her bladder increased. "Ketahn, I need you to wake up."

"*Arvok elthan* you?"

A moment later, a blue glow filled the nest; Ketahn had uncovered the crystal that emitted its own light. It still startled her to see him appear out of the shadows. He was lying on his back with his hindquarters pointed toward her, his legs folded and drawn in against his body, his arms crossed over his chest, and his shoulders leaning against the curved wall. A pile of furs beneath him served as his bed. Because of the lighting, most of his body was dark, like a shade caught in pale moonlight, but his eyes and those purple markings were vibrant and glowing.

She pointed toward the cloth covered hole behind him. "Out."

"*Dak.* No."

Ivy stared at him. "Spider man, did you just tell me no? I need to go out. Now." She pointed to the exit again.

"*Ree elad selyek dera etorrahl.*" Ketahn released something from his hand—the leather cover that had been hiding the crystal. It fell with a soft rasp, plunging the nest into darkness again.

"Are you serious right now?" she asked, brow furrowed and mouth agape.

Squeezing her thighs together, she stood up and waddled through the dark with one hand out in front of her. As soon as her fingers bumped the crystal, she yanked the cover off.

Ketahn, still lying against the wall with his spindly legs folded up, lifted his head. His violet eyes gleamed at her, reflecting the weak light. He snapped his mandibles. "*Arvok elad* you *ven? Etorri'ven*, Ivy. No...out. *Ursh.*" He pointed to the floor where she'd been laying.

Etorri'ven could be nothing else but *go to sleep*, especially given his commanding tone.

"Yes, out." She jabbed her finger at him. "Ketahn take Ivy"—she turned her finger toward the entrance—"out now."

A decidedly irritated growl sounded in his chest. "Ivy stay. No out."

"Oh, you big jerk." Ivy crossed her legs and pressed her fists against her pelvis. She bounced slightly, a whimper escaping her as the pain and pressure increased tenfold. Tears flooded her eyes. "I need to go out! I need to go out now!"

Ketahn narrowed his eyes and lifted his torso upright, tilting his head. His tone was much gentler—and much more concerned —when he spoke again. "*Arvok elthan* you, Ivy? *Elad* you *zikahl?*"

"Out. Oh, God, please. I have to pee, Ketahn! Just take me *out!*"

But it was too late; she couldn't hold it any longer.

Shame blazed through her as hot urine soaked her shorts and ran down the insides of her legs to pool on the fur rug at her feet.

Mortified and defeated, Ivy stood there with tears spilling down her cheeks as she sobbed. "I hate you. I *hate* this."

How could one bad choice I made as a dumb teenager lead me to this?

Ketahn rolled over, unfurled his legs, and rose with alarming smoothness and grace. He stepped closer to her. Ivy tried to back away from him, but he simply swept one of his front legs behind her, blocking her only escape route.

He dipped his head toward her and inhaled. His mandibles twitched, and he narrowed his eyes, sniffed at her again, and dipped lower still to look down at the wet spot on the floor. Even in the dim light, she could make out the fine hairs on his legs standing on end.

"*Arvok ven* you *ur ven?*" he asked, straightening to look into her eyes. Now he was the one who jabbed a finger—down at the soaked fur. His voice was quite a bit more exasperated when he said, "*Ursh kir'ani tovuun? Ven* your *lavil krax ursh* your *tovuun?*"

He was scolding her like she was a naughty puppy!

"Don't you dare take that tone with me." She leaned toward him, the anger simmering in her just as strong as the shame that had her eyes brimming with fresh tears. "You have no right being angry. I told you I needed to go out"—she pointed to the entrance—"but *you* didn't listen!"

"I *ven'dak unir* your *ikarahl*—"

"Ivy needed to go out! Out, out, out, *out*!"

"*Ova* I *unir thuun* out *ven'dak unixt krax ursh* my *tovuun*," he growled. Ketahn eased back from her just enough to spread his legs and lower himself closer to the fur rug.

She heard him inhale again, heard him mutter something. Her skin burned.

Ketahn rose with a frustrated huff. Before she could say a word, he hooked his left arms around her—one at her back, the other just beneath her ass—and yanked her off her feet and against his side. She gasped, throwing her arms around his shoulder and neck in reflex.

He shifted his lower hand to palm her ass, pushing her pelvis firmly against him and forcing her legs around his waist—so her wet crotch, thighs, and shorts were in full contact with his warm, leathery skin.

Ivy wanted to cry more.

"*Ahgan ikesh telenas nek* out," he grumbled. He spread his legs to either side, bracing them against the curved walls to lift himself completely off the floor, and reached down to snatch up the rug. He rolled it up hastily with his right hands.

"You're not allowed to be grumbly with me, spider man. This is your fault," Ivy muttered.

"Ketahn. No *stider* man."

"Caught on to that one quick, huh? And it's spider, not stider. *Puh.* But I guess we've pretty well established you have a problem with pee, huh?"

Low blow, Ivy. Low blow.

"You *ikar kalakaxx*," he snapped. Tucking the fur rug under one arm, he turned and strode to the opening, yanking away the cloth over it. There was no sunlight to be seen—only darkness deep enough to make the crystal's cool blue glow seem dazzling in comparison.

Ketahn didn't slow; he pulled himself through the opening, latching onto the outside of the nest.

Ivy's eyes flared as he turned to climb toward the web, and she found herself suddenly looking down. She let out a squeak and tightened her hold on him, pressing her face closer to his shoulder. It wasn't completely dark out here—she could see hints of huge branches and dangling vines barely etched in the faint light, and there were ghostly glows scattered around in various colors, but straight down there was only impenetrable black.

The same void she'd found herself in during that nightmare.

She squeezed her eyes shut and clung to Ketahn, pushing aside everything that had just happened—at least for now. She wasn't alone. That was all that mattered at the moment. She wasn't alone in that darkness.

Though Ivy felt their bodies swaying and bouncing along

with the nest, the web, and the branches as Ketahn climbed, he was solid and dependable, grounding her despite everything. His hold on her strengthened when he turned belly up to traverse the underside of the web, and he twisted his torso to allow her body to rest against his more fully.

Her damp thighs felt like they were sticking to his skin, and her soaked shorts were miles beyond uncomfortable, but Ketahn made no further complaint. She didn't know whether to laugh or cry about this situation.

After that sense of helplessness, of feeling and being treated like a child in that nightmare-memory, waking up and pissing herself was a perfect new low.

Ivy kept her eyes closed for a while even after she and Ketahn were upright again. Like that, she could almost pretend everything was okay. She could almost pretend that she had begun her exciting new life on the other side of the galaxy, that she'd finally arrived in the place where she could unlock all the potential she'd thrown away as a teenager.

But her curiosity eventually won out; she'd only glimpsed bits of this world so far, and it didn't matter how hard she closed her eyes and hoped—it all wasn't going to go away.

Ketahn was traveling steadily downward, crossing immense branches and scaling thick tree trunks, hauling her through an alien landscape that was made all the more bizarre because so much of it *almost* looked familiar. Silver moonlight broke through the canopy, which was now far overhead, in several places, and the eerie sources of light amidst the tangled vegetation were more prevalent now that they'd gone lower.

So much of this jungle seemed to glow by night—leaves, mushrooms, beautiful flowers, and small, fluttering bugs. It was like a magical fairy land. She'd been too disorientated and scared that first night to see it. And Ketahn fit right in with his glowing violet markings and eyes.

A new sound joined the night music of the alien jungle—the trickling of running water, somewhere ahead and below. A swath of jungle opened before Ivy suddenly, lit by the largest concentration of bioluminescent plants she'd ever seen, all of which were clustered along the banks of a wide stream. The water's surface wavered with reflected light.

Here more than anywhere else, she got a sense of otherworldly magic.

Ketahn climbed down to the ground. Instead of stopping and setting her down, he strode toward the water.

"Ketahn? What are you doing?" Ivy drew back and pushed at his shoulder, but he held firm. Her gaze flicked between him and the fast-approaching stream. She wriggled in his arms. "Ketahn, stop!"

Without slowing his stride, he tossed the rolled-up fur onto the streambank and carried Ivy straight into the water.

The warm water rose around her quickly, past her legs, hips, and chest until it was nearly touching her chin. Her wide eyes met Ketahn's. Finally, he adjusted his hold on her, settling a pair of hands on her hips.

He dunked her under.

The water enveloped her, muffling her hearing and blinding her. Ivy fought him, but even his seemingly casual grip was too strong to overcome.

As soon as he released her, she kicked up, sputtering and gasping for air when her head broke the surface. She swept her hair from her face and glared at him as she treaded water.

"You...you...asshole! Are you trying to drown me? Is this punishment because I peed on your precious rug? I told you I—"

"*Sheevix*, Ivy," he said with a snap of his mandibles.

"Don't you hush me! And don't go snapping those"—she pressed a thumb to each of her cheeks and curled her fingers, wagging them to mimic his mandibles—"at me."

Ketahn cocked his head, eyes narrowing. He lifted a hand to his mouth and opened and closed his fingers and thumb repeatedly as he made a series of nonsensical sounds.

"Did you just... Are you mocking me, spider man?"

He growled low. "Ketahn."

Maybe it wasn't smart to tease a spider alien who could easily tear her apart with his bare hands, but she couldn't help herself. She was just so damn angry—and underneath that, she was stressed, upset, afraid, and still exhausted. And this was just one harmless little way of getting back at him for her humiliation.

Notching her chin up, she smirked at him. "Spider man."

His mandibles drooped and came together slowly, and though he neither narrowed nor widened his eyes, his gaze seemed suddenly quite dry. Without a word, he placed a hand atop her head. Water streamed off it, running down her face, and she blinked it away.

"Ketahn, don't you d—"

He pushed her under again.

Her words were cut off as water filled her mouth. She came back up splashing and coughing. Once she'd expelled the water she'd nearly drowned in, she shot Ketahn a death glare.

He chittered, spread his mandibles wide, and raised them, narrowing his eyes. He was laughing at her. That dang spider man was laughing and grinning at her.

"Sure. Laugh it up, spider man. I'll pee on another one of your rugs. See how you like that," she muttered as she swam toward the bank, giving him a wide berth. As soon as her feet touched the bottom, she stormed to the shore, sloshing water around her legs. "Big ole jerk."

Even if she hadn't been able to hear the water moving behind her, she would've known he was following her closely just by feel —Ketahn's presence was impossible to ignore. If she hadn't been so angry, she might've wondered if that was merely her instincts recognizing the nearness of a dangerous predator, but she didn't care about any of that now.

If he intended to hurt her, he would have done so a long time ago.

Once her feet were on the grassy bank, Ivy spun to face him. Her wet hair slapped her in the face, and she yanked it aside, ignoring the water streaming down her legs. "The next time I say out, Ketahn takes Ivy out. Understood?"

But Ketahn made no indication that he understood—he didn't even make any indication that he'd heard her to begin with. His eyes were fixed upon her body with a curious gleam.

Looking down, Ivy realized that not only were her white shirt and shorts clinging to her like a second skin, but they were practically transparent. She could see her pink areolas clearly through the material.

She brought her gaze back up to Ketahn. He was still staring at her body.

Her brow creased as she crossed her arms over her chest, feeling vulnerable and naked. "Umm...Ketahn?"

"*Arvok elad* you, Ivy?" His voice was even lower than normal, even more inhuman, as he moved toward her. "You *elad iln zet* I *ur losak.*"

He took hold of her wrist with a big, clawed hand and tugged one of her arms down before reaching for her chest. His fingers grazed her nipple, making it harden, and Ivy gasped, smacking his hand away.

"No," she said.

With a sound that was somehow a grunt and a hiss at once, Ketahn closed the remaining distance between them and caught her other wrist. He forced her arms wide apart. "*Enevet'ven.*"

Ivy's eyes rounded. She yanked her arms, trying to free them from his grip, but she couldn't budge them. "Ketahn, let me go."

Ketahn leaned down as his lower hands caught the hem of her shirt and lifted it. His knuckles brushed across her belly.

Ivy inhaled sharply, flinching against the tickle of his touch as he peeled her shirt up. She leaned away from him, trying again to pull her wrists free, but she was trapped as he bared her breasts. "What are you *doing*?"

He kept one hand on her shirt, holding it up, as he moved another to her breast. His hand covered it completely. Ivy stilled, her breath quickening.

"*Arvok elad ithin*?" He watched his hand as he squeezed her breast.

The rasp of his palm over her hardened nipple elicited a jolt of pleasure that speared Ivy straight to her core. She clenched her thighs in shock.

Oh my God. No. What the hell was that?

Ketahn dipped his head lower still as he shifted his hold on her breast to cup it from beneath. He lifted it slightly and stared at her nipple. He said something, but the words were lost on her when he stroked the pad of his thumb across the taut bud. The ache in her core expanded.

No. No, no, no, no. This can't be happening.

She was not getting turned on while this spider creature touched her. It...it was simply her body's natural reaction, something she had no control over. It had nothing to do with attraction because...because...he was a spider! Their bodies were completely different, and he was just satisfying his curiosity. That was all.

He switched his hold to her other breast and stroked his rough thumb over its nipple, causing it to harden as well. A tremor wracked her, and her sex clenched.

"Oh, please stop," she whimpered.

"*Dak akar tes* you *elad* soft," he said, his rumbling voice thoughtful. "*Dak akar et selyek.*"

Ivy struggled to focus on his words instead of his touch; she was so close to understanding a few more of them, but he was making her feel things that she shouldn't have felt, things that made it impossible to think straight.

"Y-Yes. Ivy soft. You can let go now," she said.

"No. No soft." He pinched her nipple between finger and thumb as though to prove otherwise.

It didn't hurt, but it sent a bolt of pure pleasure straight to her clit that made her knees weak. She drew her lips into her mouth and bit down on them to lock in a moan.

What's happening to me? This can't be happening. This can't *be happening.*

Ketahn tilted his head, mandibles twitching. He drew in a deep breath and stilled. "Your *jurrahl...*"

His long legs spread to the sides, and he sank low, sniffing at her as his face dipped below her head, as his cheek brushed her right breast, as his breath fanned across her stomach. He stopped with his gaze directly upon her shorts.

Ivy opened her mouth, meaning to tell him to stop, but his lower hands had already hooked the waistband of her shorts. He peeled them down without hesitation, baring her sex. When he released the shorts, they fell to pool around her ankles.

"Hair *dun, kota*?" Ketahn shifted his face forward, so close that the hard crest of his forehead bumped her belly, and inhaled.

"Oh God." Ivy pushed back on her toes to put distance between them. "Yes, I have hair there. Now let go. Examination over."

Ketahn did not seem to agree. With a growl, he tugged on her arms, drawing her closer still, and settled his lower hands on her hips. He brushed a thumb downward over the small patch of hair above her pussy several times, like he was petting it—until he touched the apex of her sex.

Ivy's breath hitched. She squeezed her thighs together to deny him further access, but as she'd learned so many times already, Ketahn was not so easily deterred.

His front legs slid forward, their tips slipping between her calves, and hooked around her legs. Effortlessly, he swept his legs to either side—forcing hers apart as though she'd made no attempt at resisting. Her skin flushed with embarrassment. He eased her back, directing her thighs to rest on his legs.

The night air was warm against her exposed sex, but Ketahn's breath upon it was like sweet fire. Unbidden, her imagination pictured him extending that long, purple tongue and licking her.

Panting softly, Ivy swiftly pushed that perverse image away and struggled to free her arms or close her legs, but she was thoroughly trapped, her body quivering not in fear, but in need.

I'm going to hell.

Chapter Eleven

THAT SCENT... By the Eight, it was driving Ketahn mad. It was Ivy's fragrance, the same one he'd first smelled after opening her cocoon in the pit, but it was so much stronger, so much sweeter, and undeniably feminine. Before, it had been alluring but subtle. Something had changed over the last few moments.

Not even the queen's scent, which was nearly as powerful as Zurvashi herself in its own way, had been able to cloud Ketahn's mind like this. His stem was thrumming behind his slit, and tremors pulsed through his claspers and threatened to force them outward.

What had changed? Why was Ivy emitting this heady scent, and why was it centered on her slit?

His chest vibrated with another growl as he shifted his hand, placing a finger along either side of Ivy's slit. Her flesh there was hot, soft, silken, and he had the sense that it was damp not merely because she'd just left the water.

Unable to look away, he spread his fingers. Her slit opened like the petals of a blooming flower, revealing slick flesh that was even pinker than her lips.

Had he any doubt she was female before, it was destroyed

now; there was a small, tight opening at the bottom of her slit, beckoning him, tempting him.

What would it feel like to push his stem inside her, to feel her clench around him? What would it feel like to have her soft hide sliding against his? His stem pulsed, pushing unrelentingly against his slit, and his claspers stretched forward reflexively, brushing along the upper segments of her legs.

Higher up, near the apex of her slit, was a small bud, hooded by a delicate fold of flesh.

He could feel the throbbing of her heartbeat under his fingertips, and heat poured off her, welcoming and enticing. How hot was she within? Ketahn trailed a finger along her slit, gathering the glistening dew from those pink petals. Ivy gasped, and her legs tensed, her toes curling down. More nectar gathered at her center, and her scent strengthened.

Vrix females did not produce their own secretions—it was the males whose slick eased entry. This, like everything else about Ivy, was something new. Something unexpected. Something...intriguing.

What did her dew taste like? Would it be as sweet and heady as it smelled?

His finger reached for that bud, which was firmer than the surrounding flesh but gave way to his touch more than the peaks of her chest mounds had. He circled it, pushing that hood of flesh away.

Ivy cried out, bucking her hips against his hand. "Ketahn! No! *Oh gahd, stahp!*" She wildly fought his hold and twisted her hips. "*Thisiz rawng. Thisiz soh, soh rawng.* No *morr!*"

Something in her voice pierced the lustful haze that had seized Ketahn. He tore his eyes away from her slit to look up, past her heaving chest and its soft, rounded, fleshy mounds, to her face. Her cheeks were pinkened, her eyes were wide and pleading, and her lips were parted. There was a crease in the skin between her eyebrows.

Though he did not fully understand how to read the signs on

her face, he knew the panic in her eyes—and he recognized a glimmer of hurt.

He'd again been on the verge of mating with her. He'd been moments away from his stem emerging to plunge into her hot, soft flesh.

And not once during his exploration of Ivy had Ketahn thought of her as anything but a tantalizing female.

Keeping his upper hands around her wrists, he hooked his lower pair under her knees and lifted her off his legs, carefully guiding her feet to the ground. As soon as she was standing on her own, he released her and backed away, bowing his head and pressing his forearms together. "I am sorry, Ivy. I did not mean to frighten you."

She stumbled back, nearly tripping over her own feet, and yanked down the upper cloth to cover her mounds. Her pale golden hair was a tangled mess around her head and heaving shoulders. She thrust a hand between her legs, cupping her slit as she hunched over, body trembling.

"This *kant bee hapin ing*," she said, speaking quickly, breathlessly. "I *kant bee ternd awn bai* a *spider man.*" She whimpered. *"Oh gahd, hee wuz naht uhbowt too mayk* me *kum.*"

"Ivy?"

Ivy snapped her face toward Ketahn and thrust a finger at him. "I am *naht hapee wihth* you *ryt n'ow.*"

Ketahn tilted his head and narrowed his eyes, clicking his mandible fangs together. Though he didn't understand most of her words, her tone wasn't hard to translate—she was angry.

And that didn't feel any better to him than her upset and hurt had only moments before, intensifying the constricting feeling in his chest. He wasn't even sure what manner of creature Ivy was, but he knew that he wanted her to be content. Not angry, afraid, or hurt.

She withdrew her hand from between her legs, turned away, and walked toward the stream. His gaze dropped to her hindquarters. The flesh there was round and plump. Her soft, pale hide should have revolted him, but something about it invited his touch, begged him to run his tongue over it and sample its taste.

Ivy crouched and plunged her hands into the flowing water, scrubbing them together before splashing her face and holding her palms to her cheeks.

Was she angry with him because he'd removed her covering, or because he'd touched her? Because of the *way* he'd touched her?

He scraped the tip of a leg across the ground. She was intelligent, capable of deep emotion and complex thoughts and language, and he had treated her like nothing more than an animal.

No, that wasn't right. He'd been driven by curiosity, but even more so by instinct. Her scent had called to him, had crashed over him and swept his mind away just as the waters of a flooding river might have swept away his body.

She was so different from the vrix, fascinatingly so, and those differences grew more appealing with each passing moment.

Ivy was no animal—and she wasn't a pet. She was...something else. Something more. Something for which neither Ketahn nor his kind had a name. And if he could not tell her directly, he needed to show her that he wanted her to feel at ease. To feel...equal.

"Ivy?"

She ignored him and splashed her cheeks again.

Ketahn huffed and stalked over to her. She turned away from him, but he caught one of her wrists and hauled her up to her feet.

"*Stahp! Lhet goh!*"

She tugged on her arm and tried to lean out of his reach. He grasped her other wrist and turned her to face him, guiding her hands toward his chest. Ivy bared her flat, white teeth in a *not* happy expression, growled, and tore her arms out of his hold.

"Ivy," he said, lunging forward to grab her wrists again before she could retreat. "*Pleez*. I will not hurt you."

"*Wut?*" She stared up at him with her eyebrows tilted down and her lips pressed together firmly.

He tugged her closer, placing her hands on his chest. "You can touch me." He slid her hands slowly toward his shoulders. "You can explore."

Ketahn released her wrists, lowered his arms, and bowed his head toward her.

This time, she didn't pull away. Her palms remained upon his hide. Her expression eased, taking on a hint of confusion.

"*Arr* you *wahnt ing* me *too tuch* you?" she asked. She slid her right hand back down his chest. "*Tuch?*"

"Yes, touch," he said first in her language, then in his own.

Her eyebrows dipped again, and she hesitated, as though she were about to pull away. She drew in a deep, shaky breath and seemed to find some resolve.

"*Fiyn.*" Ivy rolled her eyes in their sockets, displaying an alarming amount of their whites. "You *prahblee wohnt stahp til* I *doo.*"

She flattened her palms on his chest and spread her fingers. Her eyes were focused on her hands as she moved them up, over the smooth, hard planes of his chest and the raised scars upon it, then over the ridges of his collar bones, which ran down from his shoulders. Those hands dipped to the more tender flesh of his neck, where her fingertips sparked thrills across his hide that were like tiny bolts of lightning.

Ivy paused there and flicked her gaze up to his.

"Touch, Ivy," he rumbled.

She trailed her hands up the thick cords of muscle on the sides of his neck, following them to his mandibles. Her fingers were hesitant as they brushed along the soft hide where his mandibles connected to his face and swept down to the tips of their fangs.

"*Theez arr sharrp.*"

Ketahn curled his hands into loose fists and forced his mandibles to relax. Her scent filled the air around him, and it still

145

bore that extra sweetness that had driven him mad before. He did not allow himself to look down, but he knew her slit was close—so close he almost swore he could feel its heat. When his claspers twitched, he drew them in as snug as he could, pressing them over his slit to keep it closed.

This touching was not for him, it was for Ivy. But that didn't stop it from feeling good. He enjoyed the soft rasp of her skin on his.

Ivy reached higher and cupped his jaw. She used her thumbs to trace his mouth.

"*Oh'pen,*" she said, then opened her mouth.

He glanced at her pink tongue and her straight, white teeth, and he might easily have lost himself staring at her lips for a long while, but he'd apparently maintained enough discipline to comply. He said the word for *open* in his language before opening his mouth wide.

Her eyebrows rose. "You *hav reelee sharrp* teeth." She applied a little pressure to the underside of his jaw, making him close his mouth. "*Klohz.*"

"Close." He snapped his mouth shut with a click of his teeth.

One corner of her lips rose. "*Guhd theeng* you *dohnt plann too* eat me."

His mandibles twitched, and he lifted a hand to pluck up a strand of her damp hair, which he stroked between finger and thumb. In her language, he said, "Ketahn no eat Ivy."

Her lips curled up fully as she met his eyes. "Ivy no eat Ketahn."

Ketahn spread and raised his mandibles and narrowed his eyes slightly, letting out a soft chitter. The thought of this little creature eating him was amusing, but in his spirit, he knew it was not impossible—there was an admirable fierceness at Ivy's core, a hint of predatory instinct that was weak but not entirely dormant.

Ivy cocked her head. "You *arr smy'ling, arrent* you?" She drew a hand back and traced her finger across her mouth, tilting its corners higher. "*Smy'l.*"

"Yes." He ran a fingertip straight along the line of his mouth and said in her language, "Ketahn no lips."

Ivy nodded, her eyes dipping to his mouth. She touched her fingertips there again, tracing them lightly, testing their flexibility. "*Eetz ohkay.* You *kan* smile *yor w'ay.*"

Her hand moved higher, following the edges of his headcrest before threading into his hair. She combed her fingers through it until the strands fluttered down to rest over his shoulders. He wanted her to do it again.

Instead, she flattened her palms on his chest. Her eyebrows fell. Leaning forward, she turned her head and pressed the side of her face against his chest, sliding her hands toward his sides.

Ketahn stilled, uncertain of what she was doing or how to react. Face-to-face touching was something intimate to his kind, performed only between vrix who trusted and cared for one another fully, and though this wasn't quite that, it felt incredibly close. He could not ignore the warmth of her hide or of her breath, which teased at his chest. He could not ignore the feel of her little hands on his sides or her damp hair brushing against him.

And it was becoming increasingly difficult to ignore her scent.

"You *hav morr thann* one *harrt,*" she said, her voice vibrating into him. Pulling back, she settled her hand on his chest again and tapped her fingers. It took him a moment to realize she was matching the rhythm of his hearts.

Taking hold of his left lower wrist, she brought his hand up and pressed it into the valley between her chest mounds. Ketahn tilted his head, regarding her questioningly, but just as he was about to ask her what she was doing, he felt it. The steady *thump-thump, thump-thump* beneath his palm. Ivy's heart.

"*Harrt,*" she said again. "Ivy *haz* one *harrt.*"

Ivy has one heart.

That understanding didn't come with any surprise. She was small, and even if she stood as tall as a female vrix, her body shape

147

still would've meant there'd be less of her. It was reasonable that she could survive only with one heart.

But what did it mean for her strength of spirit? Every vrix possessed a heartsthread that linked their hearts and spirit; did having but one heart make hers weaker?

As he stared down at her and that strange pulse continued under his palm, he had the sudden urge to weave her into his own heartsthread—to keep her safe, to keep her supported, to keep...*her*.

Tilting her head, Ivy continued to study his body, running her fingers along his upper shoulders, following the muscles of his arms before exploring where his lower shoulders connected to his sides. Every moment spent with her hands upon his hide made it harder to suppress his urges; his instincts were rising again, threatening to take control.

"You *arr naht soh skairee eh nee morr*," she said softly.

She trailed her hand down his abdomen, lower and lower, and his muscles tensed beneath her touch. His claspers shifted in anticipation, defying his will. His stem swelled within his slit, creating swift, torturous pressure.

When her hand was a finger's span from his slit, he caught her wrist and snatched it away, breaking that contact. She looked up at him with wide eyes.

"No. Not there, Ivy."

She glared at him, then rolled her eyes, letting out a *pfft* sound. "*Hippuh krit*. You touched me." She pointed down, and his eyes dipped to her slit.

A growl clawed up from his chest, and his claspers twitched, stretching toward her. Ketahn slammed his forelegs on the ground and thrust himself away from Ivy. "It is too much. I cannot control myself if you touch me that way."

He spun away from her, a tremor coursing through his limbs as the pressure behind his slit flared. He sucked in a breath and pulled his claspers in tight enough that their tips painfully dug into the hide of his pelvis.

Queen Zurvashi had frequently tried to tempt him, to lure him in with her scent, her body language. This pale little creature had come closer to getting him to submit to his instincts in two nights than the queen had in seven years.

He forced his gaze to anything, to anywhere, but Ivy—and thankfully, it landed on a cluster of cleanleaf growing along the streambank. They were exactly the reminder he needed of his purpose for bringing Ivy here.

Ketahn strode to the plant and plucked off several of the thick leaves with two of his hands. Once he had enough, he made his way back toward Ivy, keeping his eyes averted from her. She had her lower cloth covering in hand and was bending down as though about to put them on. He snatched them from her grasp; even without bringing the cloth to his nose, he could smell a hint of her piss on it.

Of course, there was a hint of something else on it, too, but he wasn't going to acknowledge that sweet scent now.

"*Hay!*" She held out her hand. "*Giv* me my *shortz*, Ketahn."

"This needs to be cleaned," he said, twisting away from her to keep the cloth out of her reach as he stepped to the water's edge —beside the spot where he'd dropped the rolled-up fur. "Before your piss-scent lures every animal in the jungle to us."

She stood beside him with her arms folded across her chest as he crushed some of the leaves in his fist, bent down, and plunged her cloth into the stream to scrub it. Her form lingered at the edge of his vision. He tried—and failed—to pretend his face was not again level with her slit.

"*Stuh bern spider man*," Ivy muttered.

He lifted one of his rear legs, hooking it behind her to brush across her rounded hindquarters. She yelped and hopped away.

"Ketahn," he said, smiling.

Chapter Twelve

Ivy's breath hitched as she rocketed out of sleep, sitting up before her eyes were fully open. Cold sweat was beaded on her skin, and her heart was racing. The nest rocked wildly, making her stomach lurch, and the sounds of the howling wind and pouring rain outside were overpowered only by one other—a crash of thunder she felt right down to her bones.

The cloth covering the nest's entrance blew inward as lightning briefly illuminated the jungle, casting everything in harsh, bluish light and impenetrable black shadows. Cold air flowed inside and swept around Ivy. She shivered.

Shifting, she drew her knees to her chest and wrapped her arms around her legs, staring at the flapping cloth. Being in this confined space in the middle of a raging storm reminded her of something that had happened when she was nineteen and living in her car. She'd always hated storms—the downpours, the raging winds, the rolling thunder—and being in Kansas, there'd been plenty of them. But that time...

She'd seen the tornado. She'd watched it destroy the buildings around her like they were made of paper, had watched it tear massive trees out of the ground with roots still intact, had seen it fling cars aside like they were grains of rice. And it had been coming right toward her.

There'd been nowhere to go, no shelter to take. Ivy had done all she could—make sure her seatbelt was secure, pull her coat over her head, duck down, and pray. She'd prayed for the first time in three years as the wind blasted her car, as debris pelted the car's exterior, as the vehicle rocked fiercely on its shocks.

She'd been desperately alone since her boyfriend had betrayed her and her parents had turned their backs on her, but never more so than in those moments as that tornado tore across the ground on its way to devour her.

Would anyone have cared if she'd died? Would anyone have even noticed?

Within a few seconds, not even prayer had been possible—the roar of the tornado had been too strong for her to hear her thoughts, the motions of the car too turbulent for her to feel anything in her heart but terror.

She'd screamed. She knew that much, even though she hadn't been able to hear it in the cacophony.

And then she was suddenly aware of a great calm, of silence so complete that she'd wondered if she had gone deaf. Her throat had been raw, her eyes had burned, her muscles had been sore from tension, and her cheeks had been wet with spilled tears. She'd thought she had died. That was all that could explain that silence, that stillness.

When she'd finally found the courage to sit up and tug down her coat, she found herself in her car. The windows were peppered with cracks and chips, and the road just outside her door was covered in debris. Not fifty feet away lay a pile of shattered rubble that had been a four-unit apartment complex before she'd ducked down.

She'd survived. And the relief that flooded her at that realization had brought more tears to her eyes, a deluge of them. She'd cried even harder when she'd realized that sixteen-year-old Ivy would've thanked

God for his mercy...but nineteen-year-old Ivy could only attribute it to blind, stupid luck. She'd known at that young age that the universe wasn't about compassion and justice, but choices and chance.

And that most of it fell on the latter.

That had been six years ago already.

There was a sharp pang in her chest.

No, not six years. She only perceived it as that. There was no way of knowing how long she'd been in cryosleep—decades might've passed, for all she could tell. Everyone she'd once cared for...was probably gone.

Another boom of thunder rattled the nest. A high-pitched cry tore from her throat, and she hugged her legs tighter. Her skin prickled with goosebumps as a gust of wind rushed inside. No matter how many years had passed, her fear of storms was undiminished.

"Ivy?" Ketahn asked, his inhuman voice somehow cutting through the noise.

The sky lit up again, and her eyes fell upon Ketahn for an instant, focusing on the dull flashes of purple that were his markings and eyes. She ducked her head, burying her face against her knees as thunder shook the nest again.

"Come, Ivy," Ketahn said. "I vill...*kumeak*. Ketahn am *kumeakahl* for Ivy."

Ivy didn't hesitate; she unraveled herself and crawled toward him. The nest swayed violently, and she stopped, clenching the furs between her fingers, squeezing her eyes shut, and pressing her lips together. Her heart leapt into her throat.

We're going to fall. The webs and branches are going to break and we're going to plummet to our deaths.

Strong hands slipped under her arms, and the long, hard sections of Ketahn's lower legs hooked behind her thighs. He lifted her toward him smoothly, so strong and yet so gentle. She opened her eyes as he eased back and drew her atop him with her legs on either side of his hindquarters, which were facing up. His torso was upright, with his abdomen now against her chest, and he circled the small of her back with his lower arms.

Ivy watched him—little more than a shadow amidst shadows —reach aside and tuck down the flapping cloth so the opening was covered again. Darkness swallowed the nest.

She shivered, wrapping her arms around Ketahn and pressing herself closer to him.

But the dark had not persisted for more than a few heartbeats before Ketahn uncovered the crystal. The dim blue glow that filled the nest was a pale imitation of the flashes of lightning, but...it was comforting.

"Ivy oh-kay," Ketahn purred; she felt his voice even more than she heard it. He reached up, feeling around for one of the baskets woven into the wall, until he pulled out a wadded cloth. It looked purplish in the light, but Ivy had the sense that wasn't its true color.

Ketahn unfurled the cloth, spread it wide, and draped it over Ivy from behind like a blanket—which it was certainly large enough to be. The soft, silky material was cool at first, but it warmed quickly as Ketahn's heat radiated into her.

He wrapped his upper arms around her, cocooning her in his hold, and leaned back against the wall, guiding Ivy to rest her upper body against his chest. A pair of his legs curled in to cover hers, their weight a comforting counter to the nest's merciless shaking. Shifting a hand up, he slowly combed his fingers through her hair. His claws lightly grazed her scalp.

Another crash of thunder shook the nest, and Ivy tensed, her fingers digging into the thick hide of Ketahn's back.

"Ivy oh-kay," he purred again, one of his hands sliding down to curl around her hip. "Ketahn am *kumeakahl* for Ivy. Ivy no hurt."

Kumeakahl. Did that mean...guardian, or protector?

Ivy forced herself to relax against him, to allow his heat to ease into her. She closed her eyes and focused on the gentle petting of

Ketahn's hand, on his arms and legs securely around her, on the steady rhythm of his hearts.

It was strange to lie against him like this, to feel so...safe, so comforted by a creature that had been a nightmare when she'd first seen him. But he held her like she mattered.

For the first time since waking up—for the first time in years —she didn't feel so alone.

Ketahn had touched her over the last six days—he had to if she wanted to get in and out of the nest, and she sure as heck couldn't climb trees and branches like him—but he'd not done so with the intimacy and boldness he'd displayed at the stream that other night. He'd seemed almost reserved since he'd pulled away from her just before her fingers would've touched his slit.

She knew now without a doubt that he'd told her *not there*.

Ivy didn't know why; he'd touched her between the legs as though it had been of little consequence. He'd simply been curious about her body.

But his touch wasn't something Ivy could forget. No matter how hard she tried to push the memory away, she recalled perfectly the feel of his thumbs stroking her nipples, of his rough yet gentle fingers caressing her sex, circling her clit.

She recalled perfectly how *good* it had felt.

It'd been years since anyone had touched her intimately. And to have been caressed by a spider creature, to have been brought to the verge of coming...

And here in the dark, with his arms and legs around her, his breath warm on the top of her head, and his hand stroking her hair, his alienness didn't matter. All that mattered was the two of them, the comfort he gave her, the care and attention—all the things she had gone without for so, so long.

Ivy released a sigh and shifted, raising a knee to tuck her leg more comfortably around him and rubbing her cheek against his chest.

His hand slid down from her hip, and his fingers curled just beneath her backside, hitching her closer. Ivy's breath caught. His fingertips were so close to her sex. Involuntarily, her core clenched, and arousal bloomed within her.

She squeezed her eyes shut, trying to push away the sensation, but it was too late. All she could think about was those fingers creeping higher and stroking her through her shorts, was Ketahn touching her as he'd done before, caressing her without any barriers, sliding through her wetness and bringing her to climax.

Ivy pulled her bottom lip into her mouth and bit it, hoping the pain would divert her thoughts.

It did not.

It's because I've been so lonely. Because I've yearned for someone to hold me, to care for me. Because it's been so long since...since anyone has touched me like that.

It's because no one has ever *touched me like that. With such...reverence.*

But...but it was *just* a touch.

A touch in the darkness, where no one could see, where she could imagine him as anything, as anyone...

No. It was still wrong. He wasn't human!

She shifted in an attempt to put distance between her ass and his hand, but only succeeded in grinding her pelvis against the ridges of his abdomen. A shudder coursed through her.

"Ivy..." Her name rumbled from Ketahn's chest, deeper and stronger than the thunder, and his hold on her tightened. One of his legs slid along her backside, teasing the skin of her thighs with those fine hairs and coaxing another shudder from her. Not a moment later, she felt the claspers that were normally tucked against his pelvis slide forward to hook around her hips.

She turned her face into his chest, pressing her forehead against his hard hide. "I'm sorry. This is wrong. My thoughts are wicked and unnatural. Oh God, I am so depraved."

"You be *ahn'seiki*, Ivy," he said, his voice rough and thick. "It am *zoruk saal gurashar. Ahn'zoruk.*"

His claspers squeezed her closer still, until her skin was flush with his and she felt the slit between those limbs against her sex—

and the hard thing pressing against it from underneath. The hard thing that seemed to long for freedom.

It had piqued her curiosity since that night at the stream. She should've been terrified when he'd restrained her, when he'd touched her. But part of her...*liked* it. Part of her wanted more. Part of her wanted to see what would emerge from that slit so she could wrap her hands around it, so she could find out what it felt like.

So she could imagine what it would feel like inside her.

Oh God, I'm sick, sick, sick.

Ivy clenched her jaw and curled her nails into his hide. "I'm sorry. I'm sorry, Ketahn, I don't mean to—"

"Shh," he hissed softly—a sound he'd learned from her a couple days ago. Though his body was always hard, it was even more tense than usual now, and his breathing was deep but ragged. "No sorry. Sleep."

His arms held her more securely, and he produced a strange

sound in his chest—one part purr, one part hum, all parts alien. But it was gentle, soothing, and oddly melodic.

Ivy turned her head to the side, listening to the music he was making, to his beating hearts, to the storm; soon her fear, desire, and shame were far off things. She was warm and safe, wrapped in a protective embrace. A soft sigh crept past her lips as she was lulled to sleep.

Ivy wasn't home...but this was the closest she'd felt to it in years.

Chapter Thirteen

Ivy blew a rogue strand of hair out of her face and glared at Ketahn. "This isn't working."

Water flowed around her knees, cool only compared to the warm, humid morning air. The stream's surface glittered in the sunlight, offering her fleeting, wavering glimpses of the creatures swimming lazily along the bottom. Of course, the fishes' movements weren't so unhurried any time she tried to spear one of them.

She knew these creatures weren't technically fish—just like the animals that flitted around the trees and sang songs into the jungle air weren't *really* birds—but they were close enough. The creatures in the stream looked like crosses between catfish and stingrays.

"Eyes and hands as one," Ketahn said in accented, stilted English. He pointed to his eyes. "See." Then he pantomimed jabbing downward with a spear.

"Yeah, I know. You said that the last twenty times. And I'm seeing just fine, but the fish are too fast."

"You be more fast. See as they will to be, not as they am."

Broken English aside, she understood what he meant, but that didn't make her task any less challenging. He was basically

161

telling her to develop precognition and figure out exactly where the fish were going to move as she struck. That sounded super easy.

Not.

She released a huff and returned her attention to the water, readying the spear in her hands. It didn't help that Ketahn's spear was almost as tall as she was with an uncomfortably thick shaft and a heavy head made from obsidian-like stone.

"Be a fish," Ivy whispered as she locked her gaze onto one of the creatures.

The fish glided closer, slowing right in front of her.

She adjusted her grip on the spear. "Be a fish."

The fish stopped, its fins flapping leisurely as it hovered in place.

Pressing her lips together, she thrust the spear into the water. The spearhead sank into the streambed, kicking up a cloud of mud that obscured everything around Ivy's feet.

That cloud didn't hide the totally unharmed fish as it darted away.

Ivy growled, kicked the water, and tried to yank the spear out of the streambed. The effort only managed to make her already tired arms burn; the spear remained stuck. "I am not a stupid fish!"

Ketahn chittered. The sound wasn't malicious or dismissive, but it certainly didn't ease her frustration.

He'd spent the week since that terrifying thunderstorm teaching her various survival skills—identifying plants, ways to collect rainwater, starting a fire, mending nets, and weaving baskets. Today's first lesson happened to focus on fishing.

And she was horrible at it.

Not that she was very good at much of anything he'd tried to teach her so far.

Ketahn's demonstration when they'd first arrived at the stream this morning had been so smooth and effortless. He'd strode to the bank, jabbed his spear into the water, and pulled it out with a fish wriggling on its end.

Ketahn moved toward her now, his legs barely disturbing the water as he entered the stream and grasped the spear with one hand. He plucked it up as easily as Ivy might've picked a dandelion.

Ivy swept back her damp hair and scowled at him. Sweat dripped between her breasts, down her back, and glistened on her skin. "Why can't we just use your net?"

"This water is much small," he replied. "No net. And you must take lesson for spear, Ivy. Must know to use. We no have net *akar'selyek*."

She groaned. Ivy knew what he was doing and why. He was trying to teach her to live out in this jungle, to survive. This was also breakfast—in the jungle, you had to work for what you ate. So, if she wanted to eat, she had better catch something.

And she was determined to succeed because of the temptation of more meat.

She wasn't even going to think about how hard it had been to convey to Ketahn that she needed her meat cooked before eating; it had been the most difficult game of charades in her life.

Ketahn raised his spear, keeping its head less than a foot over the water's surface. He pointed to his eyes with a free hand and then down to the water. "See."

Ivy followed his gesture with her gaze. Another of those fish was drifting along the streambed, perhaps the one she'd just missed. The fluid movements of its fins were so unhurried that she swore the darned thing was taunting her.

He positioned the spear directly over the fish and then altered the angle slightly, as though aiming in front of his target. "*Zok.*"

She was fairly certain that word meant strike, or attack.

His arms barely seemed to move, but the spear thrust down like a bolt of lightning, striking so fast that the splash from it breaking the water's surface seemed delayed. When he lifted the weapon, it came up with another splash.

"Eyes and hands as—" Ketahn halted the spear and his words at the same instant. The only thing on the spearhead was water, sparkling in the sunlight. No fish.

A loud snort escaped her. It was followed by uncontrollable laughter that had her doubling over as she pointed at his spear. "Not as good as you think, huh?"

Ketahn glared at her and gnashed his mandibles, the fine hairs on his legs briefly bristling. "Cannot catch *akar'selyek*," he grumbled. Considering the way he used it, *akar'selyek* probably meant always or every time, something along those lines.

She snickered. Her cheeks hurt from grinning so wide, and her stomach ached from her laughter. "See! It's not as easy as you make it sound."

He turned his eyes back to the water. His mandibles twitched as he scanned for a new target; Ivy had barely spotted the fish he was looking at before his spear darted into the water again. With a triumphant growl, he turned his head to meet her gaze and lifted the weapon from the water.

Two catfish-stingrays were flopping and flapping their fins on the end of the spear, impaled side by side—one still on the spearhead, the other pushed back to the shaft.

Ivy stared at the fish, dumbstruck. Brows furrowing, she flicked her gaze to Ketahn. "Now you're just showing off."

Ketahn grasped the fish with his left hands, pulled them off the spear, and twisted to toss them into the basket waiting atop a nearby rock, where they joined the first fish he'd caught. When he turned back to Ivy, he held the spear toward her. "Yes, I show. Show you to do it."

Ivy glared at the spear and pushed it back toward him. "You know what? I don't need the spear."

He tilted his head and made a questioning chirrup.

Turning away from him, Ivy widened her stance and bent her legs, lowering her hands until they hovered just above the water. Her shadow blocked the sun's rays, giving her a clear view inside the stream. Patiently, she waited.

Movement from the corner of her eye caught her attention. She looked toward it just as another catfish-stingray darted up to eat something that had been floating on the water's surface, making a *bloop* sound and sending out a small ripple. Lazily, it coasted along the stream's bed toward her. Ivy's fingers flexed.

Focus, Ivy. You can do this.

With her eyes locked on the fish, she pressed her lips together and waited until it was just beneath her.

Ivy's hands moved faster than her thoughts could match. They closed around the fish, and she yanked it out of the water. It wiggled in her grasp, rubbing its slick, rough scales against her palms.

She stared at it with wide eyes. It didn't immediately register that she'd caught it.

"I got it. Oh my God, I got it!" She grinned wide and held up her prize, letting out a little squeal as she looked at Ketahn. "I caught the fish with my *hands*!"

Ketahn was wearing his vrix smile, and though the expression was so simple, the light it sparked in his eyes filled her with an immense sense of accomplishment. He was proud of her.

The fish—presumably unhappy about its current situation—swelled slightly, as though it were drawing in a deep breath, and then it released a spray of what Ivy could only hope was water directly into her face.

Ivy flinched and stumbled backward—and unfortunately caught her heel on a rock. She gasped, eyes flaring, and released the fish to desperately wave her arms in a vain attempt to regain her balance.

She landed on her ass with a big splash that sent up a torrent of water around her. It streamed from her hair and down her face. She blew the water away from her lips and raised her hands to wipe the soaked strands out of her face.

Ketahn was chittering, the light in his eyes now mirthful.

Ivy arched a brow at him. "You're laughing at me now?"

"Yes."

165

"Oh, I see. Well...laugh at this." She swept her arm across the surface of the stream, sending a wave directly into Ketahn's face.

He raised a hand—much too late to shield himself—and shook his head sharply, twisting away from her. As he used his palm to brush away the water from his face, he chittered again. Leaning closer, he slipped a hand under each of Ivy's armpits and lifted her out of the water, setting her on her feet.

Keeping his hands upon her, he met her gaze. "Ivy do good. You make catch."

She smirked. "Don't expect me to catch another. I'm all fished out. You're sharing yours."

"Oh-kay," he replied. That amused light still danced in his gaze. "You must make fire."

"Are you serious?" Ivy let her head drop back. "Uuuuugh! Fiiiiiine." Stepping away from him, she trudged toward shore. "Guess we're playing *how long before the human starves* today."

His only response was to chitter at her again.

Chapter Fourteen

IT WAS no surprise to Ketahn that his mood fouled when he entered Takarahl; he was never in good temper while understone, at least not during the last seven years. The only surprising thing was that he'd kept his spirits so high all the way up until his arrival.

Ivy was to blame for that. She'd kept his mind occupied these past four eightdays, leaving little space in his thoughts for anything else. With each new thing he learned about her, four new questions sprouted. The immensely improved grasp he and Ivy had on each other's languages had still proven inadequate for his insatiable curiosity.

Through practice and experimentation, he'd learned to make most of the strange sounds in her words. It took creative use of his throat, chest, and tongue to shape noises that were easy for her due to her lips. But her language was complex and confusing. Sometimes it seemed as if each of her words had a hundred variations, each of which had very specific uses. Worse, there were many words in her tongue that defied either her ability to explain or his to understand—sometimes both.

Ivy had been learning the meaning of Ketahn's words very quickly, but her body simply could not create many of the subtle clicks, chitters, and buzzes used in vrix speech. He understood her, but other vrix would do so only with great difficulty and patience.

He drew in a deep breath as he reached the junction chamber that would lead him to his friends. The air was cool, smelling far too much of damp stone and burning spinewood sap for his liking. He longed already to fill his lungs with jungle air—though the only scent he truly craved was Ivy's. Ketahn didn't care if it were likely to drive him mad; he would never tire of her fragrance.

This Offering Day could not reach its end soon enough.

But by the Eight, had it really been an entire moon cycle since he'd fallen into the cursed pit and found Ivy? Had it really been a moon cycle since his last confrontation with the queen?

Perhaps he should simply have taken to denning with Ivy in the pit, nearby what little remained of her people, who were called humans. Better a dark place full of bones and restless spirits than anywhere within a thousand segments of Zurvashi.

As he turned toward the entrance to Moonfall Tunnel, Ketahn paused. Since entering Takarahl a short while ago, he'd seen no one apart from the two Fangs who'd been guarding the cave mouth through which he'd entered, but there was someone ahead now—a male vrix approaching through the gloom.

As the other vrix neared, Ketahn clenched his jaw, though he prevented himself from making any other outward signs of agitation. He knew that male—Durax, the queen's Prime Claw—and it took a great amount of willpower to keep from raising his spear.

Durax rolled his upper shoulder, making the black fur draped over it seem to bristle for an instant, and dropped a hand to the grip of the blackrock axe slung on his belt. His pale blue markings glowed in the tunnel light. "Strange for you to be wandering these tunnels alone, jungle worm."

Ketahn released a slow, silent breath. Though he'd hoped to complete today's trip without incident, he'd known it would be impossible to do so. But he couldn't have guessed the inevitable incident would come so soon.

"I would say the same of you, Durax, but it would be stranger still to see you out in the Tangle actually hunting."

The Prime Claw halted a few segments away from Ketahn, squeezing the rawhide grip of his axe hard enough to make it creak. He lifted his chin and directed his blue eyes at the bulging bundle tied to the top of Ketahn's pack. "What are you carrying, jungle worm?"

"My offering to the Eight."

"Would it not have been more efficient to enter Takarahl closer to the Den of Spirits?"

"I enjoy passing through the place of my birth on my way to the Den of Spirits." Careful to keep his barbed spear down, Ketahn lifted one of his empty hands and gestured down the tunnel. "Do you mean to deny me passage?"

"What are you carrying?" Durax repeated.

Ketahn narrowed his eyes. "I have told you."

"I will tear it off your back myself if you do not te—"

"Furs," Ketahn said with a snap of his mandibles. "Cured furs to give in offering."

"And the meat?"

"The meat was divided and delivered days ago." Ketahn spread his hands to either side—all but the one holding his weapon—and turned their palms up. "Check with our queen's scribes. They have tallied all I have delivered to them."

Durax huffed, mandibles opening wide in agitation, and strode forward, closing the distance between himself and Ketahn until barely a segment remained. "We Claws have been wondering whether you would come today. Most believed you would stay in the Tangle, that we would never see you again. But I knew. I knew you were too foolish to stay away, too foolish to understand that you will not win this war you are trying to wage."

"I do not know of what you speak, little Durax. I have come to fulfill my duty to the gods, nothing more."

"I am the Prime Claw," Durax growled. "I am the chief hunter, I am the queen's eyes and ears, I am her blade, guided by expert hands. I am the heartsthread of her web, and *I* am the only one worthy of her."

Ketahn chittered and tilted his head. "So why did she ask me to lead the Claw again last Offering Day?"

Durax tore the axe from his belt, raising it as though to strike even as he lifted his forelegs off the floor in challenge. "I am your better in every way!"

"Yet you hesitate," said Ketahn, stepping forward to eliminate the last bit of distance between them. He felt nothing—not fear or sorrow, not anger, joy, or confusion. Nothing but a blossoming warmth in his gut, a sensation both calming and anticipatory. He knew it now, after experiencing it so many times over the years, as the stillness before a battle, and he embraced it.

Durax's fingers tightened on the grip of his weapon, producing another creak. "I serve the queen. It is her will alone that shields you. But you will not enjoy her favor much longer. She will tire of you soon, and then she will finally do as she should have long ago—she will rid herself of you."

"She would have been rid of me seven years ago, had she respected my wishes," Ketahn said.

"And what are your desires compared to those of our queen? Of what significance are you?"

"No more than anyone else." Ketahn leaned forward, opening his mandibles wide. Their fangs glinted in the dull crystal light. "But I know this, Durax—your hesitation is not due to your loyalty to the queen. Battle has taken its measure of us both, and you know as well as I in whose favor the scales are tipped."

"Much has changed since we last saw battle, grub belly," Durax rattled. "Your arrogance is not warranted."

"And yet my days are spent prowling the wilds to bring food to our people, while yours are spent in Takarahl with Zurvashi dangling you from a string by your stem like a toy with which she's grown bored. You are no hunter. You are merely a collector of rumors."

Durax hissed as he spread all four of his arms, assuming an extremely aggressive pose, but he didn't move any nearer to Ketahn. "I am in Takarahl to serve the queen. I do her bidding. She keeps me where my skills are most valuable."

"Perhaps she is merely aware of your many limitations. If nothing else, she's always been a keen judge of a vrix's capabilities —or lack thereof."

The fine hairs on Durax's hide bristled, and he brandished his axe again as though on the verge of striking. "I will cut you down where you stand, jungle worm, and leave you in too many tiny pieces to be wrapped in a death shroud."

"Then do so," Ketahn growled, leaning so close that barely a finger's breadth remained between him and Durax. "Attack me or stand aside, Durax, for I have not the time to remain here as you spin webs of meaningless words."

The silence surrounding the two vrix was as thick and tense as a rope braided with ten thousand strands of silk. Ketahn's muscles were coiled, ready to strike, but his body did not betray his preparedness—and he did not give in to the part of his mind that longed for this confrontation to turn violent.

He did not for a moment believe Zurvashi had any true attachment to Durax. Were she to finally obtain Ketahn, she would toss Durax aside without a second thought. But that did not mean killing the Prime Claw would go unpunished. In fact, it would be one of the surest ways for Ketahn to find himself trapped in the city, completely at the queen's mercy, before this day was through.

That was unacceptable. The last moon cycle had taught him much about Ivy, enough to know she might eventually develop the skills to survive the Tangle on her own, but she had a long journey ahead before achieving that.

And even if she were to accomplish that, he was not prepared to let her go.

Finally, Durax's mandibles twitched and drooped, and he lowered his arms and legs. Axe dangling from his hand, the Prime Claw stepped aside. As Ketahn moved past him, Durax said, "You believe yourself clever, jungle worm, but you will be crushed. Just like all the rest. Her misguided desire for you will not last. It will not protect you forever."

"Nor will your undeserved title protect you," Ketahn replied without looking at Durax. He strode along the tunnel, keeping his movements smooth despite the anger dancing in his chest like licks of overfed flame.

Behind him, Durax growled.

Ketahn followed the corridor as the wall mounted crystals gave way to small spinewood sap fires, which shed the familiar blue-green light that had been predominant in Moonfall Tunnel for as long as he could remember. Each step away from Durax only irritated Ketahn further—because it was another step closer to Zurvashi.

Offering Day was no surprise—it came every four eightdays, just as it had throughout Ketahn's life, and the lives of his ancestors before him. Once a moon cycle, the vrix of Takarahl gathered to make their offerings. He'd known it was coming. That was why he'd set aside a few of his finer furs two eightdays ago. That was why he'd kept track of the passing days with little line-marks on a flat stone in his den.

Yes, it meant time away from Ivy, but he'd already spent time away from her. An entire moon cycle without delivering meat to Takarahl would have drawn unwanted suspicion onto Ketahn, so he'd hunted and foraged regularly; he'd fulfilled his duty. And he'd provided for Ivy in doing so.

Learning that she ate meat—but only if it had been cooked or thoroughly dried—had been as confusing as it was exciting, but he'd noticed the change in her within days of first providing her with some. Her color had taken on a subtle but healthy pink undertone, her eyes had seemed a little brighter, and she'd been more energetic than ever.

His days with her had been amongst the most fulfilling of his life. Apart from his minor preparations regarding Offering Day, he'd scarcely thought about anything outside the little world he and Ivy had been sharing. It had just been the two of them and the enormity, danger, and beauty of the Tangle. They'd fallen into a comfortable routine together, one that he could not see himself tiring of any time soon.

Upon waking with the morning sun, Ketahn would carry Ivy out of the nest to relieve herself—sometimes up in the trees, sometimes on the ground. They'd fill water skins from the dew and rain collectors he had positioned in the trees around the den afterward. On particularly hot mornings, they would journey to the stream and enjoy its water while it was still cool. Then came a meal. Ivy seemed to prefer lighter food in the mornings, favoring nuts and fruits, only sometimes adding meat.

Following their meal, their day would begin in earnest. She called that time her *lessons*, which was a human word that meant he was teaching her—and in addition to sharing important skills and knowledge with her, those lessons had helped distract Ketahn in both body and mind. It had grown more and more difficult every day to ignore her scent filling his den, to resist his constant urges to touch her. At least while he was teaching her, there were other things upon which to focus.

He'd shown Ivy various jungle plants and taught her which were useful in various ways, which were edible, and which were dangerous to vrix or other animals, though Ketahn had nearly ended those lessons forever after she'd eaten some sweetfang root one afternoon. She'd complained of stomach pain not long afterward. By sunfall, she'd been huddled on the floor of the den, her skin paler than ever but with wild blotches of color on her cheeks and a sheen of sweat covering her.

She'd explained sweat to him before then—he'd noticed her skin leaking water while they were out in the jungle on many occasions, and she'd assured him it was normal for humans. But her sweat that night hadn't been the same. It had been cold, and excessive, even when night had fallen and the air had cooled, and its salty-sweet scent had been fraught with a bitter tang of sickness.

For two days and two nights, Ketahn had tended to her as best he could. He'd wrapped her in cloth when she shivered, had helped her remove the cloth when she'd cried out that she was burning inside. He'd helped her drink, and though he'd offered her food, she'd refused to eat. When she'd retched, he had supported her, holding her body securely as she leaned through the opening to empty the meager contents of her belly out into the Tangle.

And when she'd moaned in pain, when she'd writhed and muttered words he either hadn't understood or couldn't make out, he'd just held her. She'd clung to him with desperation, her grip sometimes deceptively strong though her body was weak.

For those two days and nights, Ivy had suffered, and Ketahn had felt...helpless. He'd felt fear. Fear that he would lose his Ivy. None of his efforts had chased away her pain. Nothing he'd done had cured her—and nothing he could've thought to do would've helped any more. Only mender root might've eased her, but he'd had none in the den and the nearest patch was half a day's travel away. He refused to leave her for an entire day while she was in such a state.

On the third morning, he'd jolted awake, having fallen asleep leaning against the wall without intending to, and his hearts had raced in immediate panic because Ivy was no longer in his arms and there was sunlight streaming in through the uncovered opening.

And she had been there, on her knees, looking out into the jungle.

When he'd said her name, she'd turned her head to look back at him. Her skin had still been too pale, but for the first time since falling ill, she'd smiled.

Ivy had been the one to insist he continue the plant lessons. She'd said something about an *injek shun*, about it changing the way her body worked. The thought of going through that helplessness again, of watching her suffer without any means of aiding her, had been more frightening than anything Ketahn had faced in his life, but he could not deny her.

She was hungry to learn, and he was eager for any reason to spend his time with her.

He'd taught her the basics of trapping small animals, how to find safe trees and branches to climb—though he wasn't sure how to teach her to climb them, considering her limited limbs—and how to craft and maintain simple tools. He'd taught her to read tracks and follow beasts through the Tangle, even in the trees, and they'd spent a lot of time—especially at night—identifying animal calls and what they meant.

She'd mastered none of the skills he'd taught her. Ketahn hadn't expected her to; it had taken him years to perfect some of his methods, and he always felt as though there were more to learn. In the Tangle, anyone who did not constantly find new lessons was likely to find death instead.

But she had demonstrated something else—determination. He'd watched her time and time again when she failed a task; her face would scrunch up and she'd mutter her unintelligible human words in frustration. He'd seen her throw rocks and sticks, had seen her grasp her hair and tug on it, and a few times, had seen water—tears, she'd called it—build up in her eyes. Sometimes her frustration was amusing, and even Ivy admitted it afterward. Other times...it produced a pain in Ketahn's chest. She was overwhelmed, struggling to adapt to what she had called a new world, and sometimes she seemed to be hanging on only by frayed threads.

Yet every time that had happened, she'd taken a few moments to ease her breathing, to lift her chin, to clench her fists and say she was going to figure it out. Setting and lighting a fire on her own had taken her an entire morning. Her hands had been red and irritated, her blunt little claws had been chipped and filthy, and dirt had streaked her face by the end, but her smile after finally succeeding had been so bright and endearing that it had flashed in Ketahn's mind's eye over and over again ever since.

Ivy was not a vrix. She did not have the size, strength, or commanding presence so many female vrix possessed. She did not have long, powerful legs, an elegant headcrest, or clever mandibles as capable of caressing as they were crushing. She was not a warrior. She was not a protector. At best, she was a clumsy weaver, and she could not even produce her own silk. He doubted she knew how to work gold or shape stone, doubted she knew how to sculpt clay into pots and containers, doubted she knew how to do anything concerning a great many crafts that were vital to vrix survival.

According to everything his kind held important, Ivy was... useless. She would have struggled to contribute her due in Takarahl. He knew that, given time, she'd become competent in many of those tasks, but even that wouldn't change the simple fact that she was not vrix—she was *other*.

And somehow, that made her irresistibly alluring to him.

Her golden hair was unlike that of any vrix he'd ever seen, so soft and full with gentle waves. He combed his fingers through it as often as she allowed, and it seemed to soothe them both. Her eyes, which had disturbed him at first, held new beauty in their depths each time he gazed into them. They were as blue as the sky at a glance, but there were different shades of blue within—some darker, some lighter. The black parts of her eyes shrank and expanded depending on the light, getting so big at night that he sometimes worried they would swallow up that entrancing blue.

Her pale skin was so soft and smooth, so receptive to his touch. And her lips...he did not understand why they fascinated him so much, and yet he often found himself staring at them.

Ivy was slight and fragile, but there was a toughness to her that he could not define. Though she could not match him in physical strength or speed, her mind was sharper than the most finely-honed shard of blackrock. And as odd and unbalanced as her two-armed, two-legged body appeared, he'd seen hints of grace in it, especially as she'd grown stronger and more accustomed to life in the Tangle. Her hands were especially clever. Those thin little fingers of hers possessed surprising dexterity.

Dexterity he could not ignore while those fingers were touching him.

Growling, Ketahn quickened his pace. The spot where Moonfall Tunnel widened into a dwelling space finally came into sight ahead.

Thinking about Ivy would only further befoul his temper—because he was not with her. In the back of his mind, he recognized that their time apart, even this time, was a good thing. He'd had to take great care when they touched one another lest he grow excited beyond control, and that struggle had only become more difficult with each day. But he'd come no closer to understanding why.

Why did he have such an attraction to this human? To something so different from him, something so small and delicate, something so strange looking?

Why did he even now yearn to hear the sound she made when she was amused, that high, musical sound she called *laughter*?

He didn't know what Ivy was to him, didn't know what she could be. Ketahn didn't know what he wanted. And that experience was as new to him as Ivy had been the night he'd found her.

All Ketahn did know was that he no longer wanted a life without Ivy in it.

Chapter Fifteen

"You should have sent another in your stead," Urkot said.

"We need not repeat all that," Ketahn replied as he set down his spear and tugged his fur-laden bag off his back.

"Each time you return, you challenge her to keep you."

"And if I do not return, I challenge her to hunt me."

Telok folded his arms across his chest and leaned his shoulder against the wall. "And who in her service could accomplish that? Durax?"

Rekosh chittered. "He would have to first determine how to unravel himself from the queen's hindquarters to even begin hunting anyone."

"If anything can pry him from her side, it is his hatred for me," Ketahn said.

"And even then, what would you have to fear, Ketahn?" asked Telok. "Unless she were to convince me to track you, you'd never be found."

"I would scent your arrogance from a thousand segments away, Telok. You would never catch me." Ketahn lowered his bag to the floor and set at the knots to detach the bundle of furs from it. "Either way, it is unpleasant, but at least my returning to Takarahl shows Zurvashi I do not fear her."

"Which only makes her desire you more," said Rekosh with another chitter.

His small den was cramped with all four friends inside; even were they still broodlings, it would've been a snug fit. Ketahn and Telok were on either side of the entrance, Urkot stood before the flat slab of stone Rekosh used as a workspace, and Rekosh was lounging atop the pile of furs and silk cloth that served as his bed.

"If anyone could hide forever in the Tangle, it is Telok," said Urkot, "but you would be the next most likely, Ketahn."

"As always, I am bolstered by your confidence. But let the queen—or at least her interest in me—be my concern." Ketahn hefted the furs off the bag and checked the rawhide ties keeping them bundled together. "But as to the Prime Claw...why did I encounter him on his way out of Moonfall?"

"Because the Queen's Claw believes there is meat being brought in without going through her scribes," Rekosh said. He had a long piece of thread looped and woven around the extended fingers of his lower hands, the taut strand creating intricate patterns in the air between those hands. "Such is the nature of webs spun of rumors."

Ketahn glanced at Telok and tilted his head in question.

Telok freed an arm, pulled aside the cloth hanging over the entryway, and peered out into the tunnel. Once he'd leaned back and let the cloth fall into place again, he said, "Not here. But the passage was clear."

Ketahn nodded, only realizing after he'd done so that the gesture held no real meaning to his companions. To humans, it meant *yes*, or *I agree*, or *you are correct*—though sometimes it also seemed to mean *I am impressed*, or *I approve*. "Durax was dangling threads to see what he could snare."

"The Claw have been frequent visitors to Moonfall this past eightday," said Rekosh without looking up from his silk thread. "Their questions betray their suspicions, but they know nothing as yet."

Urkot absently scratched the scar on his side, creating a soft rasp. "I have scouted a few locations to open additional entrances. Changing between them regularly would keep the Claw's attention divided."

"That will allow us more time, yes, but it will be discovered before long regardless," said Telok. "Durok and his Claws are not especially skilled hunters, but they are stubborn beyond reason."

"As am I," Ketahn said with a chitter.

"And all of you think I am the one with a head full of rocks," said Urkot.

"But at least Ketahn is entertaining from time to time." Rekosh hooked a claw under the thread where it spanned between two of his fingers to pull it back into the weave, layering another bit of complexity into the pattern.

The humor in the den wilted like a dying flower.

"Vrix who seek only to feed their families will be the ones hurt if we fail in this," Urkot rumbled. He braced a dust-covered hand on the stone slab behind him and leaned upon it, his hindquarters tucked in the open space beneath the slab.

Ketahn clenched his jaw, pressing his tongue against the backs of his fangs. He could not ignore the plight of his kind, could not ignore the danger his friends were placing themselves in for their parts in this, and he could not ignore the guilty pang in his gut for keeping himself far from the entire situation.

This went beyond discontent with the queen's rule. It went beyond the grumblings of hungry vrix, beyond complaints whispered in dark corners, beyond angry, fearful glares cast at members of the Queen's Fang and Claw. The air was thick with it —tension, restlessness, bitterness, all building toward some terrible, explosive peak.

And still, Ketahn wanted only to put Takarahl at his back and return to the Tangle. To Ivy.

"Telok spoke true." Ketahn ran a hand over his headcrest and combed his claws through his hair. "The Claw will discover this in time, no matter how carefully it is done. Especially if Durax is involved."

"His presence in this could only be due to the queen's orders," said Rekosh. The thread looping and crisscrossing around his hands was nearing the point of chaos—a tangle that seemed somehow far larger than it really was.

Ketahn grasped his hair that was gathered in a tie and tugged on it, producing a faint flare of pain on the back of his head. "Durax will go to great lengths to prove himself to the queen. No amount of cruelty will be too great. He will soon enough find a vrix he can break, and he will learn all he needs."

"So what, then?" Telok drummed his claws on the hide of his arms. "We stop?"

Ketahn met Telok's steady gaze. "No. You spread it."

Rekosh drew his torso suddenly upright, mandibles twitching excitedly. "Spread the idea to every tunnel being deprived of meat. Convince them all they can do as we have."

Stepping forward, Ketahn leaned down to brush the back of a finger along the silk stretched between Rekosh's hands. "Weave a web so tangled the Claw won't know where to begin unraveling it."

Urkot's fangs clacked together. "And when they decide to simply hack through the threads, how many will die?"

"She cannot have all of Takarahl executed," Rekosh said. "Our greatest safety is found in our numbers."

"It will not do us well to underestimate her savagery." Urkot pounded a leg on the floor, producing a small cloud of dust, and lowered his mandibles. "But I will find out if there are more hidden pathways below other parts of the city."

"I will whisper into the web," Rekosh said with too much excitement.

"You will feast yourself to death on gossip one of these days, Rekosh," said Telok.

"I have not yet had my fill, Telok. My appetite will never be sated."

Telok chittered. "I will speak with the other hunters to determine where we may find allies beyond Moonfall."

184

Ketahn grasped one of the sturdy ties fastening the furs and heaved the bundle onto his shoulder. "And I will remind the three of you that we have offerings to make. I will not allow Zurvashi to keep me understone, and neither will I be held by your chatter."

With a chitter of his own, Rekosh swept his hands together and dipped them to free them from the thread in one smooth motion. "Without us, Ketahn, who would you ever talk to? Our chatter sustains your spirit, my friend."

Though he chittered in response, Ketahn again felt another twinge of guilt—he had someone else to talk to, and he craved conversation with her even here, in the company of his closest and oldest friends.

"He probably speaks to the trees," Urkot offered, pushing away from the stone slab. "All hunters do."

Telok straightened and grasped the entryway cloth. "And how would you know that?"

"What else would you talk to if you are not surrounded by rocks all day?"

"Perhaps we should have asked Ketahn to send some of the females he's rejected over the years to us," Rekosh said. "Then Telok would not also have to speak to trees, and Urkot..."

"He would continue to speak to rocks," said Telok.

Urkot chittered. "I cannot deny that."

"I would rather speak to rocks and trees than endure the queen's company," said Ketahn. "Come, let us be off before I am convinced we should delve into the deepest tunnel to befriend the stone."

The four exited Rekosh's den and walked together to join the crowds awaiting entry to the Den of Spirits. The mood was almost the same as it had been on the last Offering Day, but there was something more in the air this time—a hint of the restlessness and anger Ketahn had sensed from his friends. The crowd was less talkative than normal, and the silence that settled over them whenever they were near a Fang seemed as motivated by frustration now as by fear.

It was impossible to miss the Claws who were posted with the Fangs; few male vrix wore anything for the sake of adornment, so the black furs on the Claws' shoulders stood out.

Ketahn and his friends talked and jested as they slowly advanced, avoiding any mention of the queen or the discontent in Takarahl. It was pleasant to speak as though there weren't a huge, dark shadow looming over them, as though their lives had gone exactly as they'd hoped it would when they were broodlings.

Of course, Zurvashi remained in the back of Ketahn's mind throughout, lingering like the ache of an old wound that refused to fully heal. But this time he had something to overpower those thoughts—Ivy.

His desire to return to her intensified with each moment, wearing his patience unusually thin. More than once he was tempted to hand the furs to one of his friends and take his leave. It was only the thought of the queen's potential fury being directed at Urkot, Rekosh, or Telok that kept Ketahn from doing so.

He would learn before long that Urkot had been correct— Ketahn should have sent someone in his stead.

They did not find Ahnset in Heartsthread Tunnel. That disappointed Ketahn despite his eagerness to leave as quickly as possible, but that disappointment was nothing compared to his confusion when he and his friends entered the Den of Spirits and looked upon the central dais.

The queen was not atop it.

Spiritspeakers and scribes were in their usual places along the edge of the dais and within the crowd, and there were a few Fangs and Claws standing nearby, but the queen herself was not in her customary position. She wasn't anywhere.

Ketahn's confusion gave way to dread. Zurvashi's absence didn't bode well for anyone; she'd treated Offering Day as a day of her subjects showering her in gifts and praise for many years, and would only have missed it for dire reasons.

The journey back to Moonfall Tunnel after Ketahn and his

friends made their offerings was quiet. He was certain their thoughts all concerned the queen, but none dared speak those thoughts aloud in the open. With Durax and his Claws creeping around Moonfall, Ketahn couldn't suppress a gnawing fear in his gut that the plot to sneak meat into the tunnel had already been discovered.

When they entered Moonfall Tunnel and crossed into its wider portion, Ketahn's muscles tensed, and his hearts stuttered.

There were Fangs positioned about halfway down the tunnel. Occasionally, pairs of Fangs would patrol these outlying passageways, but this wasn't a pair—there were six of them there. Not a patrol but a retinue.

"I knew something wasn't right," Telok whispered.

"This is no surprise." Ketahn didn't allow his stride to falter. His dread and foreboding twisted, becoming frustration that would flare into rage with enough of a spark. Takarahl was Zurvashi's domain, but Moonfall Tunnel...this was where Ketahn, his friends, and his siblings had spent their youth. Even if it had never felt the same—could never feel the same—as it had all those years ago, this place had seemed untainted to him in many ways.

From this direction, Ketahn and his friends would reach Rekosh's den without crossing paths with the Fangs. That was fine. He could collect his belongings and leave by a longer route to avoid the females. This did not need to end in confrontation, it did not need to become another delay keeping him from his human.

He'd not made it halfway to Rekosh's den before a few of the Fangs looked toward him. Ketahn and his friends stopped. One of the Fangs turned to face Ketahn fully and stepped into the center of the tunnel, but she was halted by an order from another.

Even from that distance, he knew the Fang who'd stepped forward was Ahnset—just as he knew the Fang who'd stopped her was Prime Fang Korahla.

Ahnset stiffened, keeping her gaze on Ketahn for a moment,

before retreating to her place against the wall and assuming the rigid stance of a vigilant Fang. Korahla and another female approached Ketahn instead, their long legs devouring the distance.

"You can outpace them," Rekosh said. "We will leave your belongings elsewhere for you to—"

"No," Ketahn said.

"Then we will stand with you," grumbled Urkot.

"You will return to your dens. You need not risk yourselves in this. You have a greater purpose to fulfill. We will speak again soon enough, my friends." Ketahn strode forward, fighting the urge to look back at his friends. He could almost sense their struggles, their longing to follow, but they knew he'd spoken true. They had to know.

A familiar calm settled over him, reducing his dread, frustration, and blossoming rage to a dull, distant noise in the back of his mind.

"Ketahn tes Ishuun'ani Ir'okari," Korahla said as she and the other Fang drew within a few segments of Ketahn, "our queen requests your presence."

Ketahn halted, tilting his head to meet Korahla's gaze. "And if I refuse?"

"You are more a warrior than any male in Takarahl, Ketahn, but you cannot stand against the Queen's Fang."

"So, it is not a request?"

"My duty is to enforce her will," Korahla said, clacking her mandibles. "Yours is to obey. If any respect remains between us, let this ill will be between yourself and our queen."

Snapping his mouth shut, Ketahn released a heavy breath through his nose holes, pressed his forearms together in a brief gesture of apology, and continued forward. Korahla and the other Fang flanked him, their steps heavy on the stone floor, their metal adornments clanking with their movements.

Though Ketahn and his friends had fought primarily alongside other males during the war, they'd sometimes joined with female warriors when open battle had been unavoidable. Korahla had proven herself a dependable, skilled warrior and an effective leader. Ketahn was glad to have had her on his side.

But she'd also proven herself obedient and dutiful, following the queen's commands without question or fail. Ketahn trusted Korahla and her word—but he did not trust the female who commanded her.

As they proceeded down the tunnel, Ketahn narrowed his eyes and raised his mandibles, and the fine hairs on his legs stood up. The Fangs had been positioned around the entrance to a particular den. A den with familiar smooth patches worn into the stone around the entryway.

He looked at Ahnset, who was standing across the tunnel from the entryway, her posture rigid. Though she maintained her hard stance, her eyes softened when they met his.

"Inside," Korahla said, striding past Ketahn to sweep aside the silk hanging in the entrance. She did not look at him as he moved past her to enter the den.

Something constricted in Ketahn's chest as he crossed the threshold. This den was so familiar to him that he could almost sense every piece of it, every carved alcove, every crack, every bulge in the stone, as though it were all touching his hide at once. But it was also strange—as strange as the place where he'd found Ivy, if not more so.

All the belongings and decorations were different. The air itself was different, carrying the scents of vrix he did not know.

The cloth fell back into place behind Ketahn, and he turned to look deeper into the den. His chest constricted as his eyes fell upon the female standing in front of the far wall. It would have been unsettling to see any female in the place his mother used to stand all those years ago, but seeing Zurvashi there...

It was crushing, and infuriating, and it only rekindled his long-burning hatred of her.

"Your broodsister says this is the den in which you were raised," Zurvashi said, turning her amber eyes to Ketahn. Reflections of the glowing crystals on the walls danced along her gold and gemstone adornments as she stepped toward him. "It reminds me of the den in which I was hatched. Just the same as all the rest."

Ketahn curled his hands into fists. "I thought you were spawned from the loins of some fiery monster."

Zurvashi waved a hand. "Such insults are unbecoming of you, little Ketahn. They demonstrate your courage, yes, but also your foolishness."

"Perhaps I am a fool. I returned to Takarahl today, after all."

"Durax would have thrilled in a chance to hunt you." Zurvashi turned toward a loom on the wall, where countless silk threads were stretched. The tails of her long silk wrap whispered over the floor. "I would say he is a greater fool than you, but you both seem equally eager to rush to your deaths."

The space between Ketahn and Zurvashi felt far too small; she could cross those five or six segments as quickly as he could blink, and though he knew he was faster than her, he had nowhere to retreat but into a tunnel full of Fangs.

"Why me, then?" he asked. "Why a common fool to sire your brood?"

The queen brushed the backs of her fingers down the strands, making them vibrate and produce soft, tiny sounds. "Because there is potential in you, Ketahn. There is strength, courage, and brilliance, though the latter must be coaxed out of you by circumstance. Were you hatched a female, you might well have been the only one to prove a true rival to me."

She stilled her hand, keeping her gaze on the threads. "Your broodmother was a weaver, was she not?"

Ketahn forced his straining mandibles down. "She was."

"I would have liked to have met her. I understand that the rest of your brood is dead, along with your broodmother's first two broods, but the legacy she has left behind..." Zurvashi turned her head to settle her gaze upon Ketahn again, shifting her body a moment later to face him in full. "Between your broodsister and you, Ishuun has left the most fascinating offspring. Two of Takarahl's greatest warriors—hatched by a weaver."

Zurvashi's scent struck him then, overly sweet and strong, dominating his breaths. Unbidden, his body stirred.

Ketahn stilled, muscles stiffening as he fought that response. "I was to be a weaver, also."

"And what a waste that would have been." She extended a foreleg, setting its tip down beside Ketahn, and swept it aside, forcing him away from the exit.

He turned, putting his back toward the corner, and Zurvashi turned with him. Her mandibles twitched. Ketahn raised his arms and forelegs as instinct smashed into his fury.

"Little Ketahn," she purred, "are you challenging me?"

Her scent only strengthened, threatening to cloud his mind, to rouse even deeper instincts that he would not be able to resist.

He growled, "Until one of us is slain."

Zurvashi's eyes flashed an instant before she lunged at Ketahn. He wanted to fight despite his many disadvantages, wanted to finally end this, one way or another, wanted to put this behind him forever—whether forever meant the rest of his life or eternity in the realm of spirits. Only one thing stopped him from acting, and it also happened to be the one thing capable of battling back the power of Zurvashi's scent.

Ivy.

One of the queen's large hands clamped around Ketahn's throat, and she caught three of his wrists in crushing grips. She lifted him off the floor and slammed his back against the wall, jolting the breath from his lungs.

"Your defiance is no longer necessary," Zurvashi snarled, leaning her face close to his and spreading her mandibles wide. "You are the only suitable mate for me in Takarahl. The only one worthy of siring my brood. Your disrespect and disobedience has held my attention for a long while, but now it is time for you to submit to my will, Ketahn."

Ketahn grasped her forearm with his only free hand, but he

191

knew without trying that he could not break her hold. "My defiance...dies only with me."

The queen tightened her grip on his neck, shifting closer still, filling his vision as thoroughly as her scent filled his nose. "Together we can craft a legacy to surpass that of the gods themselves." She released one of his lower arms and cupped her hand over his slit.

Ketahn's mandibles opened wide, and he forced his claspers firmly against his pelvis, refusing to relent to the allure of the pressure at his core.

Zurvashi only pressed harder before dragging the pad of a finger up along his slit. "Our offspring would be the pinnacle of our kind, the greatest vrix to stride this world. And my name will be the first in a new dynasty to span a thousand generations. I will eclipse Takari and her worthless descendants."

By the Eight, the smell she was emitting was as close to a mating scent as he'd ever detected from her, from *any* female. He could no more ignore it than he could ignore her forceful touch or her crushing grip—or how the unwanted pleasure she was causing him threatened to part his slit.

But he wanted Ivy. Her scent was the sweetest, and only her touch sparked true excitement within him. Ivy's fragrance was a delicate lure, coaxing him closer as it sank slowly deeper and deeper into him, as it caressed his instincts and roused real desire. Zurvashi's was a stone hammer, bludgeoning him into submission, inflicting damage until he could do nothing but relent.

And he had not forgiven Zurvashi for all she had done. He could not.

Drawing in a choked breath, Ketahn chittered. It was all he could do to maintain his tenuous self-control, to keep his body's responses from growing strong enough for her to notice. He chittered in the queen's face, and her eyes darkened.

With a roar, Zurvashi swung Ketahn aside and threw him. His legs dragged across the floor for an instant before he landed on his left shoulders, tumbled, and crashed into the far wall. Pain burst across his torso and throbbed in his arms and neck.

"These games are through, Ketahn. The flood season draws near, and with it the High Claiming." She stalked across the chamber and lifted a leg, jabbing its thick end against his chest and pinning him against the wall. Her claws pricked his hide. "You will return to Takarahl and perform your duty. You will show the vrix of this city that you desire me, and you will outperform every other would-be mate who attempts me. You will bring me the finest gifts, you will spin the finest web, you will dance the finest dance."

The queen leaned on Ketahn more heavily, forcing the air from his chest. He clamped all four hands on her leg, but she was too heavy to move. He flared his mandibles as he stared into her burning eyes, his body thrumming with unreleased anger, with bristling defiance.

"You will obey your queen, little Ketahn, or you will pay a high price."

"I...do not...fear...death," he rasped.

"Not your own," she replied.

Those words hung in the air, heavier than the queen herself, more solid and imposing than all the stone in Takarahl. Ahnset, Rekosh, Urkot, Telok—she knew of all of them, knew of his connections to them.

But there was one thread of which neither the queen nor any other vrix was aware. There was one thread she could not knowingly sever—but her demands would cut it all the same.

Ivy. She needed him the most, and she would not survive this world without him. He could not abandon her. He would not abandon her.

But he could not risk the lives of his friends and broodsister, either.

Zurvashi shoved away, briefly crushing Ketahn even harder against the wall. She turned and strode toward the entryway. "It is time to set aside your foolish notions, Ketahn, and become what you were meant to be."

She tore the hanging cloth aside and exited the den.

Ketahn's head fell back against the cold stone wall as he sucked in another breath. The air was still laden with Zurvashi's overpowering scent, but it couldn't command his focus anymore. Pain pulsed through his body, and his new aches would likely plague him well into the night.

She'd been right; he was a fool. He had been for a long while. Zurvashi was not a problem he could ignore. He could not play this game in which he split his life between the Tangle and Takarahl, could not pretend that everything was fine the moment he emerged from understone.

Though he'd not yet fully caught his breath, he spread his legs, flattened his hands on the wall, and struggled his way upright. Zurvashi was forcing him to choose, just like he'd always known she would.

He staggered through his first few steps toward the entryway, catching himself on the stone frame and halting before he passed through. There were voices in the tunnel, accompanied by the sounds of heavy legs striking stone and metal jingling.

Ketahn had to return to the Tangle. Had to return to Ivy. He knew neither would bring him solace today, but he would not be able to think here...

And the longer he lingered in this place with a barbed spear in hand, the more dangerous his thoughts would become.

194

Chapter Sixteen

KETAHN HAD BEEN GONE FOR, well...who knew how long? Ivy couldn't really keep track of time like she had on Earth, not that it really mattered anymore. There was simply night and day. Because of the dense jungle canopy and the orientation of the nest's opening, it was hard to tell the sun's position most of the time. And she had no idea how long the days and nights on this planet lasted regardless—though they did feel a little longer than those on Earth. All she knew was that her body seemed to have adjusted well enough to this alien day-night cycle.

She sighed, lowered the half-finished grass basket she'd been working on, and looked out through the nest's entrance.

Where is he?

Sunlight pierced the canopy in rays of gold, setting the multi-hued leaves aglow. Vegetation rustled in the soft breeze, beasts made their calls, insects buzzed, and birds sang sweet songs. If not for the alien wildlife, Ivy could easily have imagined herself somewhere in the Amazon rainforest.

She gathered her hair and swept it off her neck, moaning as the breeze flowing in through the opening caressed her sweat-dampened skin. With all the humidity, it sure felt like the

Amazon. Her cheeks puffed out as she released a slow breath through her mouth.

"Though I'm definitely not some Amazonian warrior princess."

She'd been on her own for six years before applying for the Homeworld Initiative. During that time, she'd endured cold, hunger, hopelessness, loneliness, and fear. Her training before boarding the *Somnium* had been hard in different ways—learning about things she'd never heard of before, undergoing incessant physical and mental evaluations, striving to be good enough in a pool of tens of thousands of applicants.

Yet nothing she'd faced in her life had been as difficult or trying as her time stranded in this alien jungle. Everything had to be caught, harvested, and crafted, and all of that required skills she never would've dreamed of needing. The basic survival training she'd received had barely prepared her for any of this—especially considering that the manmade tools she'd been taught to use were unavailable to her now.

But her time in this jungle had been infinitely better than any other point in her life—because Ketahn was with her. He'd been there to teach her, to guide her, to admonish and praise her. He was there through it all.

Ivy drew her hair over a shoulder and got back to work on her basket, determined to finish it before Ketahn returned, to show him her progress.

That desire triggered a heavy, sorrowful pang in her heart. Though the memories were fuzzy, she could recall a few times while she was very small—seven years old, at most—when she'd waited, brimming with excitement, to show her parents an arts and crafts project she'd made at school. Wanting so desperately for them to be proud of her, to praise her. To tell her she was doing good.

They'd nodded and said things like *good job*, but even at that age she'd sensed their disinterest. She'd realized that they hadn't really looked. That they hadn't seen her art...hadn't seen *her*. So, after only a few attempts, she'd decided to stop sharing such things with them. That felt better than their hollow, meaningless praise.

Even when she'd lived with them on good terms, Ivy's parents had always been kind of...distant. They'd been loving in their own ways, she supposed, but it had never come through as affection, and it had never resulted in any sort of bond between parents and daughter. They'd put all their energy into their first child, Evan. Having already been fourteen by the time Ivy was born, he'd moved out long before she was old enough to get to know him; he'd made his own life before she'd even finished elementary school.

By that point, her parents had been ready to focus on themselves. Ivy had been unplanned for, an accident baby, and her parents hadn't expected to raise another child. They'd given more of their time to their work, social circles, church gatherings, and hobbies than they'd ever given to her, but Ivy had been happy for a long time despite that. She'd dedicated herself to school and had been an excellent student, and she'd found a myriad of ways to entertain herself during those long hours spent alone.

Ivy had never resented her parents for their distance, but it had been especially hard as a teenager, when she'd been faced with so many changes. She'd never spoken to her mother about any sensitive issues, had never asked her father for advice. Her parents had provided food, clothing, and shelter, and she'd had to figure out all the rest.

So, when Ivy had attended one of the late-night parties thrown by her classmates and met Tanner, she'd been drawn in by his attentions. After a single night, Ivy had known he was the one she wanted to spend her life with. He'd been a few years older than her, but who cared about age? What was a five-year difference when she was going to be eighteen in a year?

Tanner had been so handsome with his wavy brown hair, his dashing smile, and his dark, dark eyes. He'd treated Ivy as though she were the most important girl in the universe. He'd made her laugh, had taken her out to eat, had gifted her pretty flowers, and had touched her in ways that made her feel so, so good—intimate ways that Ivy's parents had told her were wrong. She'd reveled in it all and had been eager to reciprocate. Tanner had become her world.

After being with Tanner for a couple months—and thinking herself in love—she'd told her parents about him. They'd been livid and had forbidden her from seeing him. That had been the first time Ivy raised her voice to them in anger. She'd refused to listen, refused to live without Tanner. She could not and would not wait until she was eighteen; that was too long to go without seeing him.

So she'd run away, dropped out of school, and moved in with him. He was all she'd needed. He was going to take care of her.

Tanner had insisted on waiting until she was eighteen before they had sex. Of course, they'd done other things while they waited, but he'd always been very careful with her, had always held back. In her naivety, she'd thought it was because he was sweet and caring.

How naïve and stupid she'd been.

The truth was that he'd needed her to be of legal age to keep himself protected before he took what he really wanted.

Her first birthday surprise from him on her eighteenth birthday had been a paper to sign. He'd told her it was to add her name to the apartment lease since she was old enough, and she'd stupidly signed without reading a word—it had been hard to worry about the document and its legal jargon while he'd been kissing her neck and rubbing her shoulders.

Her second surprise had been far more exciting. Tanner had set everything up, and it had been so romantic—the soft flickering hololights, the rose petals scattered across the floor and bed, the chocolates. He'd wanted to make the night of her eighteenth birthday something she'd never forget, the night when they'd finally make love.

He'd simply failed to inform her that it had all been a ruse.

That there had been cameras in every corner, recording from every angle as Tanner had Ivy perform sexual acts upon him, as he performed them upon her, and finally, as he took her virginity.

Tanner had changed in that moment. He'd been rough, and it had hurt. He'd ignored her cries of pain, had even laughed as he used her body. Ivy had known the first time would be uncomfortable, but she'd thought Tanner would have been gentler, would have stopped or slowed down. He hadn't. It was like...like he'd *wanted* her to cry.

It wasn't until it was all over, after he'd come inside her and then on her, that he'd stopped. There had been no sweet words, no apologies, no kisses. She hadn't felt sated or loved. She'd felt... used. Dirty.

After Tanner had withdrawn from her, his demeanor had become that of a complete stranger. As she'd lain there with tears running down her cheeks, he had told her it was over between them and he wanted her out. Confused, hurt, *crushed*, she'd sat up, pulled the bedding to her chest, and asked about her name being on the lease. He'd laughed in her face and informed her that she'd actually signed a waiver by which she'd agreed to forgo legal action.

Even more confused by that, she'd gathered her things—mostly just clothing—and left the apartment feeling utterly numb. She'd just reached the bottom of the stairs when the first text message came through from a once-close friend.

Wow. I can't believe you actually did that.

Did what? Ivy had replied.

Ivy had discovered exactly what after her friend sent the link —*Rough Cock Makes Virgin Teen Cry.* Tanner had livestreamed their time together, and it was out there for the world to see. Over and over and over again.

She learned not long after that several former classmates who she'd thought were friends had discovered the livestream in progress and helped spread it around. By the next day it felt like the entire town knew.

Shamed, hurt, and alone, Ivy had gone back to her parents. But they'd already known, and what meager affection they'd shown her during her childhood had long since dried up.

Grass bent between Ivy's clenched fingers. She blinked and hurriedly loosened her grip.

"Way to take a stroll down memory lane, Ivy," she muttered, smoothing out some of the bent strands.

Regardless of how painful those memories were, Ivy's prior thoughts were true. Ketahn had no obligation to care for her, provide for her, or teach her. He could have abandoned her at any moment. Heck, he could have eaten her that first night he'd found her. She knew it wasn't always easy on him, especially with the language barrier between them, but he'd remained by her side. He'd encouraged her when she felt like giving up, he'd comforted her when she was scared, he'd taken care of her when she'd felt like she was on the verge of dying.

This strange spider creature, this wholly inhuman male, genuinely cared about her. More than any human ever had.

Ivy sighed and lifted the basket to eye level. Her brow creased, and she frowned. The basket was lopsided, with one side higher than the other, the weave was loose enough in some spots that she could have stuck her pinky finger through the gaps, and it was *definitely* not a circle.

"Not an Amazonian warrior princess or a basket weaver." She sighed, lowered the basket to her lap, and wiped the sweat from her forehead.

And now she had to pee. She shifted on the fur to take some pressure off her bladder.

Ivy turned her face back toward the entrance. Ketahn had said he hoped to be back by nightfall, but would return sooner if he could. That could be five minutes, thirty minutes, or hours from now.

Like the other occasions when he'd left her alone here, he'd assured her she was safe. Nothing could get in but him. So far, that had proven true, but that didn't mean her time without him was relaxing. She always found herself restless, anxious, and bored, and the beast calls that often echoed through the jungle still unsettled her even though she knew what creatures made many of them.

But she also spent that time alone worrying for Ketahn.

She spent that time...missing him.

As crazy as it was, she enjoyed Ketahn's company. Ivy never lost sight of his alienness, but he was still a person. He was intelligent, cunning, kind, and even had a sense of humor.

She smirked as she recalled all the times he'd laughed at her mishaps. Well, he didn't really laugh, not like a human would. He made this chittering kind of sound, but it was deep and rolling. It was...warm. He'd tried to mimic her laughter a few times, but the result had been stiff, unnatural, and decidedly hilarious. And even when he laughed, she never detected any malice from him—he'd just give her advice on how to avoid failure on her next attempt and praise her for the effort she'd put in.

"Where is he?" she asked again without meaning to speak aloud. "Ugh. Come on, Ivy. He'll get back when he gets back."

But what if he doesn't come back?

Ivy swiftly shoved that thought to the farthest recesses of her mind. Ketahn *would* come back.

There was little with which to occupy herself here. After finishing her basket, she tidied up the nest, peeked into the pouches and baskets sewn into the walls, and nibbled on some goldcrests, the honeycomb-like mushrooms that were called *huthaal'rok* in Ketahn's language. She debated starting another basket but one glance at her malformed previous attempt dashed that thought. Mostly, she sat by the entrance and gazed upon the outside world.

And tried to ignore the discomfort in her bladder.

She was this close—*this* close—to just sticking her ass out of the nest to do her business. Who was around to see her, anyway? She snorted at the mental image that thought presented. Not a flattering one, that was for sure. And she could just imagine her mortification if Ketahn decided to return at *that* moment.

Ivy leaned against the wall and let out a slow breath. With nothing else to do, she felt sleep tugging at her consciousness. She fought it—if only to entertain herself. Just as she was losing that fight and her eyelids were beginning to flutter, the gentle swaying of the nest became more of a jostling bounce.

She started, instantly alert, and withdrew from the opening. Her hand itched to reach for the spear near the wall, but she'd learned that lesson—she just needed to trust Ketahn. Only he could get inside.

The soft scraping of his hands and legs against the outside of the nest was familiar now, and it went a long way toward putting her at ease, but he was certainly making the nest shake more than he usually did.

He appeared at the opening, blocking out the fading daylight. For the moment he was silhouetted there, his form took on a menacing air, and he was a shadowy monster out of nightmare—but that nightmare no longer held any horrors for her.

Ketahn pulled himself into the nest with a huff and tore his bag off his back, tossing it aside with uncharacteristic carelessness.

Ivy frowned as she looked from the bag to Ketahn, who grumbled something she couldn't make out and dropped his spear beside the bag. "Ketahn?"

He snarled, spinning to face her with his mandibles flared wide and his eyes glowing viciously. His front legs rose off the floor and his arms spread to the sides, claws splayed.

Ivy's breath lodged in her throat, and she flinched back, bumping into the wall as her eyes rounded. Her heart stuttered, and every little hair on her body stood on end. Ketahn had never acted like this with her before.

Something flashed in his violet eyes. His mandibles drew together, their fangs clicking softly, and then drooped to hang at the sides of his face. Ketahn's whole body sagged immediately afterward, all that threat and menace vanishing in the space of a heartbeat.

He strode across the nest to stand before her, took her wrists, and pressed her palms against his chest as his upper hands smoothed over her hair. All eight of his eyes closed. Ketahn bowed his head, and a soothing rumble vibrated in his chest.

Ivy's brow furrowed. His hearts thumped against her palms. She curled her fingers slightly and rubbed at the hide of his plated chest. He shuddered and continued petting her hair, maintaining his loose grip on her wrists. Whatever tension he'd been carrying slowly eased. It was as though touching her...calmed him.

She spread her fingers wide as her own fear bled away. "Ketahn, is something wrong?"

"Everything," he said. "Everything but this."

Warmth blossomed inside her at those words. She stepped a little closer, tilting her head back to gaze up into his face. "Do you want to talk about it?"

He stiffened, tightening his hold on her.

Ivy caught her bottom lip between her teeth. Now that her initial startlement had passed, she knew he wouldn't hurt her. She continued stroking his chest. "You don't have to, but sometimes talking about things that bother you can make you feel better."

Ketahn opened his eyes and moved a hand to her cheek, hooking his thumb under her jaw to tilt her face more toward his. "You make me feel better, Ivy. And I will not trouble you with my *utodok*."

"Where do you go when you leave me here?"

"To hunt. And to *Takarahl*, to give food."

"*Takarahl*? Is that...is that your home? There are others like you there?"

"It is where my people live. There are many vrix there, and many more around the jungle." He caressed the underside of her jaw with the pad of his thumb. "But *this* is my home, Ivy."

Ivy's breath hitched, and a shiver swept through her. "What... what can I do to help?"

Ketahn leaned down, tipped his hard forehead against hers, and breathed in deep. Another rumble rolled through his chest. "Be you."

Chapter Seventeen

Ivy closed her eyes and hummed as she tipped her head back and scrubbed her fingers through her wet hair. While the *nath'-jagol*—which literally meant cleanleaf in Ketahn's language—didn't lather like shampoo or soap, it made a fizzy sound and sensation when in contact with water, similar to an activated bath bomb. She enjoyed its strong fragrance, which was a like blend of gardenia and lemon.

Water gently flowed around her hips, and the sun shone hot upon her skin. This day, like many others in the jungle, was warm and humid, but the stream was cool and refreshing. She enjoyed it every time Ketahn brought her here to drink, bathe, and lounge.

Tossing aside the remnants of the cleanleaf, Ivy drew in a deep breath and dipped under the water. She rinsed her hair before resurfacing. Smoothing her hands over her face and sweeping her hair back, she opened her eyes.

Her clothes—which were becoming quite worn—were already cleaned and laid out to dry on a large, flat rock that jutted out into the stream. It had taken a couple weeks, but she'd overcome her self-consciousness about her nudity around Ketahn. She was just as alien to him as he was to her, and whatever cultural standards of beauty they'd both been raised with couldn't rightly apply to one another. Though he stared at her plenty when she was undressed, often quite intensely, he'd never given Ivy the sense that he was judging her.

But there was always something in his violet gaze, something deep, something smoldering, something...hungry. And whenever she saw it, her body intuitively reacted.

The fact that he didn't wear any clothing had helped somewhat to ease her self-consciousness. She wasn't about to go traipsing around the jungle naked, but times like this...it was okay. Of course, with as fast as her clothes were breaking down, it wouldn't be long before she had no choice but to run around bare-assed. A couple more weeks, and her shirt and shorts would be little more than tattered rags so discolored that no one would ever be able to guess they'd once been pristine white.

Maybe she could convince Ketahn to let her cut some of his spare cloths to fashion a makeshift dress or something.

Next to her clothing was a small pile of cleanleaves from which she plucked another leaf. When Ketahn had first given her the plant, its long, thick, pointed leaves had reminded her of aloe vera, but these were spongier and more bulbous.

Breaking the thick leaf open down the center, she spread its sides and turned it over onto her arm. It immediately began to fizzle. She used it to wash her upper body.

Ivy turned her head and peeked at Ketahn over her shoulder. He was sitting atop a large rock—the vrix version of sitting, anyway, with his legs folded inward and his underside flat on the stone—as he rubbed some sort of oil into his hide with three of his four hands. In his fourth hand he held the clay jar containing the oil. His spirits had improved since he'd returned from Takarahl two days ago.

Her gaze followed his hands as they glided over his chest and abdomen, and she only turned her face away when those hands dipped toward his slit.

Her cheeks flushed, and something in her core warmed. Ivy's curiosity hadn't waned since she'd first felt something stir behind that slit. If anything, her curiosity had grown, especially when Ketahn held her against him during the nights. Nothing had occurred between them since that stormy night all those weeks ago, and he'd been extremely careful when handling her since. But that didn't stop her body from yearning for touch.

Ivy squeezed her eyes shut.

His touch—she'd yearned for *his* touch. The touch of a spider creature.

Had her parents known about this, they undoubtedly would've tried to drown her in holy water.

She didn't even know how to process her desire. His touch should've been wrong on so many levels, it should've been perverse, it should've disgusted her, it...

It felt right.

She opened her eyes and vigorously scrubbed the rest of her body. Ketahn's touch shouldn't have felt right. Every logical, reasonable part of her mind screamed *wrong, wrong, wrong* but that couldn't silence the powerful, pervasive whisper.

That couldn't silence the truth.

Ivy dipped into the water and rinsed off her skin, twisting to look back at Ketahn. Even after over a month with him, she was still figuring out his body language, was still piecing together the way his kind expressed themselves, but she knew something had been troubling him for the last couple days. She'd seen it in his stance, seen it in the way his mandibles twitched and fell.

Ivy sighed and walked toward the streambank.

Ketahn reached behind himself to rub oil on his back. As his hands worked their way toward the center of his back, he apparently reached the limits of his flexibility. He strained for a moment, jaw clenched, mandibles drawn together, and muscles bulging beneath his hide.

He let out a soft hiss as he shifted his arms to his front and settled his right hand over his left shoulder, rolling the joint and rubbing his hide as though in pain.

Frowning, Ivy stepped out of the water and onto the warm,

dry rock of the bank. She picked up the large silk cloth waiting for her. Hurriedly, she dried herself off and wrapped the cloth around her body, tucking the corner between her breasts. "Are you okay?"

Ketahn turned his head and settled his gaze on her. Though his lack of irises and pupils made it hard to tell exactly where he was looking, she felt his eyes roving over her, she saw that intensity rekindle within them. But there was a hint of something else in his gaze now. Something...vulnerable.

"I cannot move as I used to," he said, gesturing toward his back with one of his lower hands.

"What do you mean?" she asked as she approached him.

He bent his arm back, reaching in vain for the spot he'd missed. "I cannot touch."

Ivy climbed onto the rock next to Ketahn and moved behind him. There was at least a foot long expanse of skin between his four shoulders that was untouched by the oil.

Ketahn looked at her over his shoulder.

She held her hand out. "I could do it for you."

His eyes dropped to her hand, and his mandibles twitched. He twisted his torso to pass the jar to her. She took it and brought it to her nose, taking a sniff. The oil smelled earthy and woodsy, with a spicy mahogany undertone. She dabbed her finger into it and rubbed it between her finger and thumb. It wasn't greasy, but smooth and satiny.

When she returned her attention to Ketahn, he was watching her, waiting.

"Did you hurt your shoulder?" she asked.

He tensed, legs drawing closer in toward his body, and she could see the fine hairs on them bristling, each like a ghostly silver thread in the sunlight.

Ivy frowned. "Is it part of the stuff you don't want to talk about?"

Ketahn huffed and turned his head away from her, body

relaxing. He was silent for a time before he finally spoke. "I was hurt by another vrix. Our *jikarai*."

"*Jikarai*?" Ivy eased closer. With the way he was sitting and the position of his legs, she'd have to lean against him to reach the spot on his back, though it would still be with some difficulty. Unless...

Bracing a hand on one of Ketahn's knee joints, Ivy threw her leg over his hindquarters and climbed onto him.

Ketahn stiffened, legs unfurling slightly. "What are you doing, Ivy?"

She caught herself with a hand on his back as his movement pitched her forward. She'd never ridden a horse before, but she imagined this was a similar experience. The corner of her mouth curled up. She was bareback riding an arachnotaur.

Ivy shifted, scooting her ass backward a little. The backs of her thighs rasped over his thick hide. Water dripped from her wet hair, running down her back to be absorbed by the silk towel wrapped around her. "It's so I can reach better. Are you...okay with this?"

He dipped his chin in a curt nod and settled down.

"You can trust me, Ketahn," Ivy said.

"I know, Ivy." He rolled his injured shoulder again before crossing his arms over his chest, making the hide on his back taut.

Her eyes settled on his back. The large marking there was solid purple outlined in a strip of white, its pattern swelling and shrinking in smooth curves as it led down his back and across his hindquarters. There were scars here, just like there were on his chest, arms, and legs, though these were fewer. Some looked as though they'd been inflicted by claws, some by blades, but all were old and faded.

"So what is a *Jikarai*?" she asked, pouring some oil onto her palm.

"*Jikarai* is...one who leads. The one who leads Takarahl. A strong female who controls everything."

"Oh! Like a queen." Ivy placed her hand between his shoulders and began massaging the oil into his hide. "Is it only the queen who leads?"

"Yes. She has killed all those who have tried to take her place."

Ivy frowned as she moved her hand higher. "Did...you try to take her place?"

Ketahn hunched forward, pressing his back more firmly against her hand. "No. No male has ever led the vrix, and I do not want her place. But she...she wants me."

Her hand stilled. "Wants you?"

"She wants me as her *luveen*. So she may mother a *okari*. So she may have eggs."

Ivy hadn't yet learned those two words, but she could infer the meaning of one of them. *Luveen*... Mate. The queen of the vrix wanted Ketahn to be her mate.

She caught her bottom lip between her teeth as she resumed massaging the oil into his back, unable to help the sudden flash of jealousy that struck her. She had no right to feel jealous. Ivy was a human, and Ketahn... Ketahn was other. He was a vrix, as was his queen.

"I told her no," Ketahn continued, "as I have many times for years. She was...not happy."

Ivy drew back and lowered her hand, eyebrows rising. "You don't want the queen?"

"She has made much death." He glanced at Ivy over his shoulder with four of his eyes. "I have lost much because of her. Takarahl has lost much. But her strength is great, and she does not fear its use."

"So she hurt you," Ivy said softly.

"It is a small hurt." One of his legs brushed against her calf. "I am still a strong male."

His fine hairs were soft, and his touch sent a thrill up her leg to her core, making it clench. Trying to ignore the sensation, she poured more of the oil onto her palm and tucked the jar between her thighs. This time, she brought both hands to his back, pressing her fingers and the heels of her palms into his hide to massage his muscles and rub the oil in as she worked her way up.

"Is that why she wants you? Are you...the strongest?" she asked.

Ketahn made an appreciative sound that was between a groan and a growl. His remaining tension melted away beneath Ivy's touch. "Yes."

That was it—no hesitation, no doubt, and, somehow, no arrogance. Just a simple statement of fact.

"I see," Ivy said, tilting her head. Her hands reached the spot between his upper shoulders. "Is...there another female you're wanting as your mate?"

He made another of those pleased sounds, which rumbled into her through every place their bodies were touching. "There is no vrix I long to take as my *nyleea*."

Hooking her ankles over his legs, she tightened her legs and dragged herself closer to his torso. The action caused her bare sex to slide over his hide. Her breath hitched.

"Oh," she said a little breathlessly. Ivy brought her hands up to his injured shoulder and kneaded the joint and the muscles around it. "And *nyleea* also means mate?"

"Yes," he purred. "*Luveen* is male, *nyleea* is female."

"*Nyleea* sounds pretty."

Ketahn was silent and mostly still, but his stillness only made Ivy more aware of his every tiny movement. The twitch of his mandibles, the faint tremors occasionally coursing through his arms, the slight shifts of his legs, which made those tiny hairs brush against her skin. And she could not ignore his heat—it seemed to intensify with each moment, like her touch was feeding fuel into the fire at his core.

Ivy leaned forward, pressing her chest to his back as she looked at him from the side. "How does your shoulder feel now?"

"Much gooder."

"Much better," she corrected with a chuckle. "You were close."

He grunted, his body vibrating against hers. "Your language is difficult for no reason."

She plucked up the jar and held it out to him. "I know. It can be confusing. But you've grasped it really well."

Ketahn accepted the jar and placed the lid atop it, which he tied in place with a silken string. "And you speak my language well, also, for someone who cannot make the right sounds."

"Like *zirkita*?" she said, trying to force that higher-pitched buzzing sound out of her throat for the word *dirt*, and failing.

He chittered. "*Zirkeeta*. That is what you mean to say."

"Well, it sounds pretty similar to me. *Zirkita*."

Ketahn chittered again and repeated the word, putting the emphasis on that buzzing sound in the second syllable. "You are saying something very different, and the two things do not go together."

Ivy snorted. "And you say my language is hard. And stop

laughing at me." She caught the end of his hair and gave it a gentle tug.

"It is as you say—I am laughing with you."

"Ha! See, you still have trouble with the *f* sound, so don't get onto me about pronunciation." She smiled. Lowering her legs from Ketahn's, she carefully climbed off him, taking his offered hand when he held it out for her. Once she was standing, she made to pull her hand away, but he held it a little longer, as though hesitant to let go. Her gaze met his.

There was fire in his eyes. Deep, meaningful, and powerful, it spoke of a passion that transcended appearance, language, and culture, of a connection that people only dreamt of finding on this world or any other.

Finally, he released her, and Ivy drew her hand to her chest, making sure her makeshift towel was secure before she sat down on the rock beside him with her legs crossed.

"So what does *zirkita* mean then?" she asked.

His eyes narrowed, and that fire was replaced with humor. Those deadly mandibles lifted to the sides in a smile. "It is a male's..." He gestured toward his pelvis. "Spear."

Ivy dropped her gaze to his slit and stared. Spear. His...spear. Her eyes widened and snapped back up to his. "Oh my God, all this time I've been saying cock?" She made a circle with her index finger and thumb and inserted her other index finger through it. "Your...your cock?"

Ketahn chittered again, the sound even deeper this time. "Not mine. Just *cock. Zirkita.*"

Her skin flushed, and she lightly slapped one of his legs. "Jerk. No wonder you laughed at me every time I said it. You could have told me."

"I told you many times how to say it right, Ivy. And I knew what you meant." He extended a hand, hooked a lock of her damp hair with his claw, and tucked it behind her ear. His gentle touch lingered as he brushed the pad of a finger over the shell of her ear. "There is no hurt."

Ivy smiled up at him. "Only my pride."

"I do not know that word. What have I hurt?" He twisted toward her, sweeping his eyes over her body as though searching for a wound.

She laughed as he picked up one of her arms and then the other, looking them over. "Not that kind of hurt."

Ketahn tilted his head and narrowed his eyes. "Then what?"

"It's...kind of like...kind of like how good you feel about yourself and the things you've done. And it can be hurt when something makes you question that feeling. Like...if I am proud of the baskets I wove and then you show me one of yours and how much better it is, that hurts my pride a little."

His mandibles sagged, and he lowered her arms, though he did not release his hold on them. "I do not mean to hurt your pride, Ivy."

Ivy turned her arms and drew them back enough to take his hands in hers. "It's okay. Sometimes wounded pride is a good thing. It helps me learn to be better. And sometimes it can be done in fun"—she grinned wide—"like laughing at me while I say *zirkita* instead of *zirkita*."

"You said cock both times again. Maybe we will not talk about dirt from now on?"

His chitters joined in with her laughter.

Their humor eased, and Ivy withdrew her hands with a soft smile, though Ketahn seemed reluctant to relinquish them. As she combed her fingers through her drying hair, gazing out over the stream with the sun shining down upon her, she found herself...happy. How bizarre was it to be stranded on an alien world with a spider creature for a companion and feel like this was the most content she'd been in her life? She had shelter, food, and a friend—she'd never had all three at any one time over the last seven years. This laughter between them...it was genuine and good natured.

And yet, she couldn't help but wonder about the other colonists. She'd been friendly with several of the people she'd been training with thanks to spending twenty-four hours a day together going through classes, exams, safety seminars, and physical training. In time, those acquaintances could've become real friendships, but the rigorous schedule'had made it difficult to really get to know one another.

Those people were out there somewhere—along with five thousand other colonists.

Were they still aboard the *Somnium*? Were they even still alive?

Was anyone going to ever come looking for them?

I might be the only one left.

"Ketahn?"

"Yes?"

Ivy turned her face toward him to find him already staring at her. "Where did you find me?"

Chapter Eighteen

KETAHN'S MANDIBLES TWITCHED. He opened his mouth as though to speak, then closed it and turned his face away from her.

"Ketahn?" Ivy leaned closer to him, trying to peer up at his face, willing his eyes back toward her. "Where did you find me?"

He released a heavy breath and hunched forward, bracing his hands on the joints of his legs. "In a dark place. A place where many *althai* dwell, and other vrix refuse to go."

She furrowed her brow. "*Althai*?"

"Yes. They are..." He lifted a hand and waved it in the air vaguely. "They are not often seen, but sometimes heard. They cannot be touched, but they can be felt. Do you understand, Ivy?"

"Are you talking about...ghosts? Spirits? Things that are dead?"

"Some of them are dead. Or they are what is left of the dead. Like a... What is your word? Memory? Like a memory that is stuck in the real world. But others...they are..." He huffed and shook his head. "I do not know how to say it. They are like the trees, or the dirt, or the sky, but...the heart of those things."

"And you found me in this place?"

"Yes. You slept there, closed in a *gorahl*."

"What is that?"

"A *gorahl* is what some small animals wrap themselves in to change. But yours was not the same. It is the wrong word." He brought two hands together, cupping one over the other, and swung the top one up like it was a lid. As he did so, he made a drawn-out hiss. "It opened, and you came out."

Ivy gasped. "A cryochamber? You found me in a cryochamber?"

"Is that your word for it?"

"It's a machine, a pod that put us in stasis, which is a deep sleep that kept us alive as we traveled through space."

Ketahn's mandibles twitched again, and he tilted his head. "You are saying words I do not understand, Ivy."

She pointed at the sky. "Space, beyond the sky, in the stars. I came from there."

He tilted his head back and looked up. "Even creatures with wings cannot go so high as to reach the stars, Ivy."

"We were on a flying ship. A...a big metal..." She shook her head. "I don't know how to explain it so you'd understand. The pod that you found me in, where was it?"

Ketahn returned his attention to her. "At the bottom of the dark hole, in a place with many chambers."

Many chambers? Her heart quickened. "And were there others like me? Other humans?"

His mandibles fell. "Yes. But most were only bones."

Most. Ivy held onto that word as sadness filled her. So many lives...

She shifted onto her knees and moved closer to him, ignoring the stone digging into her skin. "Most, but not all. There are still others, right? Humans that are sleeping?"

"I do not know, Ivy. I cannot be certain."

"Can you take me there?"

His features darkened, mandibles rising and eyes taking on a dangerous gleam. "No."

Ivy's brow creased, and she frowned. "No? Why not?"

222

"It is not safe to go there, Ivy, and the spirits are the most small danger."

"But you went there before, when you found me!"

"I fell." He stretched an arm high over his head and then lowered his hand rapidly. "The xiskals that fell with me all died, and I lived only because the Eight protected me. I will not take you back to that place of death."

She placed her hand on his forearm. "Ketahn, there could be other survivors. We can't just leave them there."

"No, Ivy," he growled, snapping his mandibles. His forearm muscles flexed under her hand. "Put the others out of your mind. We will never return to that place."

"Are you serious?" She yanked her hand back and pushed herself to her feet. "I can't just put them out of my mind. You expect me to just...forget that my people could be down there? That there could be others like me still alive?"

Ketahn rose, too, in one smooth motion that unfurled his long legs and had him towering over her. "You are alive. That is enough. We cannot help any others."

Ivy glared up at him. "Why? Just because you say so?"

"Because I care only for you!" He leaned toward her, the fine hairs on his hide bristling. "I will not allow you to hunger because I must give to others."

"Then I will hunt for them!"

He snorted. "You could not find the ground if not for me."

She gaped at him. "Did you... Are you insulting me?"

"I am speaking true. You could not live one day alone out here. What use would you be to others?"

Ivy thrust a finger at him, jabbing it against his hard chest. "You are such a...a...an *asshole*!" She spun and stalked away from him, toward the trees.

"You say I am what poop comes out of?" he growled from behind her.

"Yes! Stinky, yucky poop!"

Ketahn snarled, sounding a little closer. "Where are you going?"

She turned with her hands on her hips and glared at him. "I'm going to pee, and I'm mad at you so I am taking a moment to get away from you, spider man."

"Not spider, not man. *Vrix*." He halted a few feet away from her, hands curled into fists and muscles tense. "And always you must pee."

"Well *excuse me* for being human and having natural bodily functions!" Ivy threw her hands in the air. "Maybe something will eat me and then you won't have to worry about me anymore!"

"I will not let anything eat you, human," he growled, drawing himself closer to loom over her again. "Do not speak of such things. I will be here to anger you for a very large time."

"Fine!" She stepped closer to him, tilting her head farther back. "You better be!"

Ketahn chittered softly, the menace he'd exhibited a moment before vanishing as he offered her his version of a smile. "We are bound by a strong thread, Ivy."

Ivy growled and scrubbed her hands down her face. "I can't even with you. You make it so I don't want to be mad, but I do want to be mad, and I should be mad, so I am mad."

He tilted his head to the side. "You are a confusing female."

"And you are a stubborn male."

"I do not know this word."

"Yeah, well...figure it out, spider man." Ivy turned and strode into the foliage.

"Stay close," Ketahn grumbled.

"I know!" She swept her gaze around her surroundings as she picked her way through the big leafy bushes and muttered, "I'm not stupid."

She didn't really have to pee, either, but she figured this was the only way to get Ketahn to allow her a respite. She just needed a moment of solitude. A moment to think, to ponder why Ketahn refused to take her to what she could only assume was a crash site given his mention that it had been at the bottom of a dark hole. What else could it be? And if she had survived, surely there had to be others still alive in stasis. Ketahn said it was dangerous, and she didn't doubt that—but she swore there was something more behind his refusal.

After all, he'd found a way out with her in tow. That meant he could get back down there if he really wanted to.

A splash of yellow at the corner of her eye caught Ivy's attention. She turned her head. There were several goldcrests growing on a few deeply shaded tree trunks only thirty feet away—that was deeper into the jungle, yes, but still close enough that she could call out for Ketahn if needed.

Well, if she was going to be out here pouting, she could at least be useful and gather some food while she was doing it. She moved toward the mushrooms, walking on the larger patches of soft, mossy ground. The moss was cool against her bare feet. When she reached the trees, she grasped the goldcrests at their bases, as close as possible to the tree trunks, and snapped them off one at a time.

As Ivy gathered the goldcrests on the crook of her arm, her thoughts returned to Ketahn like they often did. She understood his reluctance to rescue any other humans. It would be harder work for him to feed who knew how many extra mouths, especially when he was already bringing food to his people regularly. And he was right—she wasn't skilled enough to be much use, not yet. Maybe not for a long, long time.

Still, it was just...*wrong* to leave the others there. Even if there was next to no chance of there being other survivors, shouldn't they still look just in case? Shouldn't they figure out something —*anything*? If Ivy was willing to learn and work, she was sure the other survivors would do the same. Plus, there were colonists aboard the *Somnium* who specialized in survival, agriculture, medicine, and all sorts of useful fields—and there were loads of supplies stowed all over the ship. It didn't all have to fall upon Ketahn. And she would be able to translate.

She'd make him understand, no matter how long it took. She'd make him understand that going back was the right thing to do.

She plucked the last goldcrest off the trunk, brushing away the bits of bark and dirt clinging to its underside.

Heat flared along her spine, the hairs on the back of her neck stood up, and her heart skipped a beat. She froze before ever adding the final goldcrest to the pile cradled on her arm.

There was something behind her. She knew it instinctively, with bone-deep certainty—and she knew it was not something friendly. Icy terror flooded her veins and knotted her stomach.

It's...just Ketahn. Following too close to make sure I'm okay.

Ivy knew that wasn't true long before she drew in a deep, shaky breath and forced her legs into motion, turning at a glacial speed to face the unknown horror.

The creature before her was no vrix—it wasn't anything she'd yet seen. It was as big as a tiger, stood on four legs, and its lean, powerful muscles were evident beneath its brown and green scales. Its head, which reminded her of a velociraptor's, was supported by a thick neck. Its black claws were each longer than her fingers, and its four cold, amber eyes were fixated upon her. A bright yellow and green frill ran along its spine from its skull, with leathery skin stretched between the thin, bony spikes.

As big as the beast was, it had come within fifteen feet of her without making a sound, and the tension in its muscles and focus in its gaze suggested it had been ready to pounce by the time she'd sensed its presence.

Oh, God. It is *ready to pounce.*

The beast remained silent apart from the sound of its huge claws digging into the ground just before it leapt. Ivy couldn't say the same for herself.

She screamed. She screamed in terror and half-jumped, half-fell aside, her heart racing at a thousand miles an hour. The goldcrests spilled from her arms. She turned her head as she hit the ground, her fall cushioned by the moss and dead leaves on the jungle floor, just in time to see the huge creature pass over her. Time seemed to move so slowly that she swore she could've counted every individual scale on the beast's underbelly in that fraction of a second.

The beast twisted in midair like a cat, swinging its hind legs around as its hurtling body crashed through the brush, snapping branches and violently rustling leaves. It had spun almost in a full circle by the time it slammed into the tree, its claws snagging the bark and ripping it to shreds.

Ivy sucked in another breath and scrambled to her feet to flee. "Keta—Ah!"

She was silenced by searing pain on her calf, so hot and piercing that it made her mind blank. Thrown off balance, she stumbled forward and dropped onto her hands and knees hard enough to make her teeth clack together.

She looked over her shoulder. The beast clawed at the ground like a bull preparing to charge. Its mouth opened wide to reveal dozens of pointed teeth and a bluish, tapered tongue, all of which dripped with what she hoped was saliva and not some sort of venom.

And at the bottom of her vision, she saw bright red blood welling from the cuts on the back of her calf, in sharp contrast to her pale skin. The burning sting of the wounds renewed itself with each throbbing beat of her heart.

Oh God! I only made that comment about being eaten because I was angry! It isn't supposed to actually happen.

The undergrowth in front of Ivy went wild. Before she could even swing her head in that direction, a big, dark shape burst out of the thick foliage, darting straight over her head. The beast's attention snapped to the newcomer an instant before the two collided.

As the creatures tumbled through the vegetation in a cacophony of abused branches and leaves, Ivy glimpsed long, spindly legs and white and purple markings on the new creature's hide.

Ketahn.

He and the beast broke apart, but there was no lull in their battle.

Ivy shoved herself up again, bracing an arm on a nearby tree to steady herself as her wobbly legs threatened to give out. Her breaths were ragged, and her heart was rolling thunder in her chest as she beheld the struggle tearing across the jungle floor.

The beast was thrashing and snarling, chomping its jaws and slashing its claws and tail at Ketahn, moving with immense speed. But he was just as fast. Between the crashing vegetation and blazing speed, Ivy could barely follow what was happening. All she could tell for sure was that Ketahn seemed to be trying to subdue the beast, getting far too close to it to put her at ease.

Something thin and silvery glimmered in a shaft of sunlight as Ketahn lunged at the beast, which bent its neck around to bite at him. Those sharp teeth closed only inches from Ketahn's throat. He hissed, the sound so deep and powerful that Ivy felt it in her bones, and swung a hand up. His claws sank into the underside of the creature's jaw.

The beast made a pained growl and renewed its thrashing, but Ketahn's other hands were moving, too fast for Ivy to comprehend—winding a silken thread around the creature's muzzle. The beast spun away from him, tearing Ketahn's claws free and shedding dark blood from the underside of its jaw. There was a thick bundle of silk binding its mouth shut now.

The beast shook its head wildly from side to side. Ketahn shifted his hold on the silk thread, using his weight to yank the beast's head down. He was upon it even as its chin struck the ground, using his arms and legs to divert and restrain its thrashing limbs. Ivy only realized then that there was blood on Ketahn's hide—and she had no idea if it belonged to him or the beast.

Snarling and snorting, the creature flailed. Ketahn's body was jostled like a rider trying to hang on to a bucking horse. It seemed even his strength could not match the beast's desperation to be free.

Ivy's nails scraped bark as her knees buckled. She slid to the ground, coming down on her backside. Why was she just watching? Why wasn't she helping him?

What can I possibly do?

Ketahn roared. She had no better word to describe it, though the layered sound wasn't like any roar she'd ever heard apart from in its ferocity and dominance. His hands worked furiously, wrapping that deceptively strong silk thread around the beast's legs and pulling it taut. The tension forced the creature's head back, exposing its neck.

Ketahn's head darted down. His mandibles clamped shut on the beast's throat. The beast growled and huffed, kicking and thrashing all the harder.

Ketahn whipped his head back.

The wet sound of tearing flesh was so brief compared to all

the other sounds in the jungle at that moment, but it would stick with Ivy for a long, long time. Ketahn's mandibles ripped free, spraying blood into the air. A big, tattered chunk of the beast's throat was clutched between them. Ketahn snapped his head aside and released the chunk, tossing it into the vegetation nearby.

With a final jerk, the beast stilled.

Ivy stared at Ketahn. Despite the jungle's heat and humidity, she was cold and shivering. She brought her arms up and wrapped them around her chest. It was only then that she realized her towel had fallen and was lying on the ground beneath her, stained with blood.

Ketahn released his hold on the beast, letting its limp body fall. A troubled rumble sounded in his chest. He was in front of Ivy in a few quick strides, stretching his front legs to either side of her to sink down low.

All four of his arms banded around her, clutching her to his hard chest as he rose. Even his claspers—usually tucked securely against his pelvis—sought her out, lightly brushing her skin as though every part of him was seeking confirmation that she was here, that she was alive. His breath was harsh and heavy as he buried his face in her hair.

"Ivy," he rasped.

Ivy slipped her arms around his neck and held onto him as his warmth surrounded her, pushing away the chill. "I'm okay. I'm okay."

His embrace strengthened, and the pounding of his hearts did not ease. She focused on their rapid, steady rhythm, finding only comfort in it when she'd once thought it so strange. Between that and his heat, she could almost forget what had just happened, could almost ignore that throbbing burning in her leg.

Ketahn lifted his head and slid a hand up to smooth it over her tousled hair. He rumbled her name again and inhaled deeply. His hand stilled abruptly, and his body stiffened.

"That scent..." He shifted his front legs, crossed them beneath her, and sat her upon them.

Ivy winced. Just that bit of movement—just her own weight on her backside—was enough to make her aware of the dull aches permeating her body. Of course, none of those aches compared to the pain on her calf.

With a low, unhappy trill, Ketahn released his embrace, steadying Ivy with a pair of hands on her shoulders as he raked his gaze over her body. She didn't even care that she was naked; she just wanted his arms around her again.

"No," Ketahn whispered, dropping his body down again to take careful hold of her left ankle.

Ivy glanced down to see blood and dirt smeared all over her lower leg and foot. Ketahn lifted her leg gently and bent to inspect her wounds.

"You are not okay," he said, voice raw. "This is not okay."

Before Ivy could respond, he swept her into his arms, this time cradling her against his chest. He had two arms under her back, one curled across her ass and thighs for support, and a hand around her ankle, keeping her wounded leg elevated so nothing touched the still-bleeding cuts. His long, smooth stride didn't jostle her in the slightest as he carried her back to the stream.

He sat her gently on a patch of soft moss growing atop a boulder at the water's edge. As he drew back, his narrowed eyes met hers. "No more going alone. You only pee with me."

"What?"

"Ivy stay with Ketahn," he said, hissing on the *s* just like he used to.

Oh, he's mad.

"Ketahn, I am not peeing with you watching," Ivy said, settling her hands in her lap.

"Then you will not pee," he growled.

"You are being completely unreasonable!"

"I do not know what that means"—he leaned over Ivy, bracing his arms to either side of her and placing his face within an inch of hers, mandibles wide—"but it is better than you being dead!"

"This is the first time this has happened! I wasn't even peeing anyway. I was just...just trying to do something useful. I'm sorry. I should have been paying more attention."

"So I will watch for you. I will remain with you." Ketahn tipped his forehead against hers, voice falling low. "I do not want you to hurt. It is not useful. It is not good."

Ivy frowned. His voice was rough, almost pained, and it flowed straight into her heart, piercing it with a pang of sorrow and filling it with warmth. It didn't matter how different they were, she was sure of one thing—Ketahn cared about her.

Tears stung her eyes. She closed them, reached up to cup his jaw, and stroked it with her thumb. "I know. I'm sorry. I...hate that I'm such a burden to you. That I'm so weak."

"No," he said firmly. He withdrew from her and took her face between his upper palms. His many violet eyes met hers. "Not weak. Not a burden. It is my...pride to give for you. I said words that were untrue."

"You didn't, though. All this...I'm not good at it, Ketahn, and I would have died a long time ago on my own. I would have died *today* if you hadn't been there to save me."

Something rattled in his chest, the sound slipping into his voice when he spoke. "When I was small, my mother said many times that I must learn to...*rasyth* before I could weave."

That word, *syth*, was what he called the silk threads he made, and *sythi* was what he called the web holding up his nest. But she wasn't sure what this version meant.

Apparently, her confusion was plain upon her face, because he said, "*Rasyth* is to make a web. To stretch the threads and bind them. It is simple, but...doing it well is not easy. Making it strong is not easy. Making it...beautiful is not easy."

"You mean like the baskets I make."

He chittered gently. "They are not good, but each is better. *You* will get better."

Ivy's lips curled into a small smile.

His eyes softened, and he stroked his claws through her hair, but stilled when his gaze shifted to his hands. He released another unhappy trill. Lifting his hands away, he withdrew from her. Ivy only then noticed the dark blood glistening on his hands, mandibles, face, and chest, and she knew some of it was undoubtedly on her now, too. But her only concern was for him.

Ketahn turned away and strode into the stream, submerging himself to his shoulders. He leaned forward, splashing water on his face and scrubbing his mandibles and hide.

There was no trace of blood left upon him when he faced Ivy again, just water running down his sculpted hide in rivulets. She swept her eyes over him, seeking signs of injury, but found none.

Had he really fought that thing—that...that velocitiger—without suffering even a single scratch?

He moved to the streambank, retrieved his bag from the place he'd set it earlier, and returned to Ivy. Climbing onto the rock, he set the bag beside her, opened it, and removed a scrap of silk cloth from within. He dunked it into the water, rinsing it thoroughly before again taking hold of Ivy's ankle. At his gentle guidance, she shifted to rest her weight on her hip, turning her leg so her wounded calf was facing outward.

Ketahn's big hands worked quickly and decisively, using the cloth to clean away the dirt and blood from around the cuts. The stinging, burning sensation returned tenfold, strong enough to make Ivy hiss and reflexively try to tug her leg from his grasp. He held it firm, allowing her no escape.

Fresh crimson welled from the wounds, mixing with the water to trickle down her skin.

"Not deep," he said, setting the cloth aside. Turning his hand, he lightly stroked the back of his finger along her shin, sending a thrill through her and briefly overpowering the burn of her wound. "Such soft skin."

As he spoke, his rear legs were in motion, bending sharply toward the spinnerets at the end of his hindquarters. When he swept one of those legs forward, there was a loose bundle of sticky silk thread gathered at its tip, which he passed to one of his hands.

"I was not a warrior or a hunter," he said as he rolled the webbing into a small, puffy wad. "I was a weaver, as was my mother. She taught me for many years. I was not good when I began. I was very good when I stopped."

"A weaver?" Ivy had assumed spinning webs was instinctive for him, just as it was for spiders back on Earth. But then, the cloth he had on hand all seemed to be woven of silk, so being a vrix weaver clearly went beyond simply crafting webs.

Was that why his touch was so gentle and precise?

"Why did you stop?" she asked.

"The queen made battle with Kaldarak. With other vrix." Carefully, he separated the wad into pieces, laying the first over the uppermost cut on her leg and pressing it into the open wound.

Ivy winced at the surge of pain. He placed one of his hands on her thigh, putting just enough pressure on it to keep her leg still. It was only then that she realized what he was doing with the webbing.

"Wait! Are you...are you putting webs *inside* me?"

"It will bind the cuts. The hurt will go away fast." Ketahn tilted his head, and his mandibles twitched uncertainly. "Do humans just...leave wounds to bleed until they stop?"

"No, of course not. We treat wounds and use medicine. We just..." She pulled her lips in as she flicked her gaze down to the webbing in her leg. It already felt as though it was dulling the sting. Still, just the thought of webs being put inside her flesh made Ivy shudder. "On Earth, we have creatures that are called spiders. They...well, they look kind of like you, just without... well, without the more human-like parts, and they are much, *much* smaller, and they also make silk and webs. Most of the time, humans are...scared of them."

"Why do you fear them?"

"Because they...look scary?" After spending time with Ketahn, after getting to know him, that answer sounded ridiculous.

Ketahn stared at her thoughtfully. "Do you fear me, Ivy?"

She shook her head. "No. I did at first, but not anymore."

He raised the hand in which he held the wadded silk. "Do you trust me?"

"I do."

The rumble in his chest wasn't quite a purr, but something about it seemed...content. He gave her thigh a gentle squeeze and moved on to the next cut, repeating the process with the silk.

Though she expected it this time, the pain was just as intense. Her nose scrunched, and she hissed through her teeth. Leaning back, she braced her hands behind her and curled her fingers, scraping her nails over the mossy stone. She didn't miss how Ketahn's gaze flicked over her naked body.

"What happened?" she asked, watching his hands work. "After the queen made battle?"

"I was sent to fight. To hunt. And I was like you, Ivy. I did not know. I was grown, and I had to take lessons to hunt, to live in the jungle, to fight. I almost died every day." Ketahn moved on to the next cut to repeat the process. "But I wanted to live. So I learned. Because of the danger, I learned fast. And soon, I was good at it. Better than good.

"You have been in the jungle only one moon cycle, Ivy. You are learning fast, too, because you must. It took me longer than this to be good." His eyes met hers. "It will take you a little longer, too."

With her brows creased and lips pressed together, Ivy stared into his eyes. She knew what he was doing, knew what he was saying, and the tears that sprang into her eyes had nothing to do with the ache permeating her leg. She nodded curtly.

Once he'd treated her cuts, he dragged his bag closer and rummaged through it until he found another piece of cloth, this one dry and clean. He tore it into a few long strips, which he used to snugly wrap her wounds, tying the ends off at her shin.

Ivy eased off her hip, taking care not to allow her newly wrapped calf to settle on the ground. "Thank you."

Ketahn plucked the wet cloth off the rock, rinsed it out in the stream, and turned back toward Ivy, shifting closer. She remained silent as he touched the cool cloth to her face and wiped away the dirt, sweat, and blood from her skin. His strokes were gentle and attentive, smoothing over her every facial feature with something akin to adoration.

As the cloth reached her chin, he lifted two of his lower hands to brush her hair back, tucking it behind her ears. One of those hands cupped the back of her head. He guided her to tilt her chin up and her head aside as he ran the cloth along her neck down to the hollow of her throat.

Ivy's eyes fluttered shut. Despite her lingering pain, Ketahn's ministrations were soothing. No one had ever touched her this way, had ever tended her this way; no one had ever taken her care into their hands without want for anything in return. It was a luxury she'd never known, not even in a world full of luxuries like Earth.

Ketahn trailed the cloth back up and then reached around to clean the back of her neck. He withdrew it from her briefly, and she heard a small splash and some swishing in the water. Then the cloth was on the left side of her neck, running down to her shoulder. One of his hands circled her left wrist and lifted her arm so the cloth could continue all the way down to her fingers.

He cleaned her other arm the same way, though his movements seemed a little slower—almost exploratory.

The cloth lifted away and splashed in the water again. When it returned, it was at her collarbone. Ketahn swept it slowly across her chest, leaving droplets of water to trickle over her skin, and then down one of her breasts, grazing her nipple. The sensation sent an electric current through her that coalesced in her core.

Ivy's breath hitched, and she flinched back, her eyes snapping open. Her nipples hardened, aching for more.

Ketahn withdrew the cloth. His gaze was focused upon her breasts, which only seemed to strengthen the needy thrum between her thighs. "Did I hurt you?"

A different kind of heat swept over her, making her skin warm and her cheeks flush. Self-consciously, she banded an arm over her breasts and glanced away. "No. You didn't hurt me, Ketahn."

He curled a finger under her chin and turned her face back toward him. Their eyes locked; the intensity in his poured more fuel onto the fire inside her.

"Speak true, Ivy," Ketahn said. "You move away from my touch like it hurts."

Ivy wrapped her fingers around his wrist and guided his hand away. "It doesn't hurt. It...It..." She groaned and covered her face with her palm.

"Ivy?"

"It feels good," she said, the words coming out in a rush. "It feels *too* good."

Ketahn caught her wrist and gently tugged her hand down. His head was tilted as he regarded her, his mandibles twitching faintly. "Help me understand."

"Oh, my..." Her skin heated further. "Do...do female vrix have breasts?"

"Is that the word for them?"

Looks like it's time for human anatomy lesson two.

Ivy lowered her arm slightly and turned her palm up beneath her breasts. "Yes. These are breasts. And these are nipples."

"Vrix females do not have these parts. Why do they sometimes harden?"

"They change when we're cold or when we're...aroused."

He dipped his head to study her breast more closely—closely enough for her to feel his warm breath upon her skin. "What does that word mean?"

It took everything within Ivy to remain still, to not lean forward, press her breast against his face, and see what he would do. Just that teasing breath of his flooded her core with delicious heat.

"I...I don't know how else to say it," she said softly. "Arousal,

desire, pleasure, lust are all words you don't know. It's when...
when you feel *really* good. It would be like...oh God, I can't
believe I'm going to say this. It would be what you feel when
someone touches your... *zirkita*. Your cock."

Ketahn reeled back, mandibles pulsing as though they were
trying to open and close at the same time. His eyes dipped to her
breasts, met her gaze, and then dropped toward his slit before
settling once again on her breasts. "That is what they are for? To
feel good and ready you for mating?"

I can't believe I am having this conversation with him.

At least it's distracting me from the pain in my leg.

"Well, yes and no. Female humans make food in our breasts
when we have babies. Hatchlings? But they can also be touched
to bring females pleasure. To make us ready for sex. Mating. Our
skin is very...sensitive, but more so on our breasts and our"—she
motioned to between her legs—"our pussies."

The claspers at the sides of his slit fidgeted, straining forward,
straining toward her—though they kept drawing back in against
his pelvis, where there was a very distinct bulge. He averted his
gaze. There was a light in his eyes that spoke of deep, heavy
thoughts. Ivy longed to know what was happening inside his
mind, but something told her that he wouldn't be able to express
it in a way she'd understand—if he chose to express it at all.

When he eventually turned his face back toward her, he
seemed on the verge of speaking, but his attention abruptly
shifted skyward, and his mandibles sagged. They fell even farther
when he glanced at her bandaged leg again.

"We have stayed too long. Much longer, and your skin will
become red again, and you will have more hurt," Ketahn said, and
Ivy knew he was referring to the sun burn she'd suffered a couple
weeks ago.

He pulled his bag closer with one hand as he wrung out the
cloth with two others, folding it quickly and dropping it inside.
After tying the bag closed, he swung it onto his back and gathered
Ivy, lifting her off the rock with great care and cradling her in his

arms. When her breasts pressed against his plated chest, he looked down and stared at them. They were soft against hard, light against dark. It was...erotic.

"I will take you to the den," he said thickly as he strode to the rock where she'd laid out her clothes, snatching them up with the claws of a leg and passing them to her. "Then I must return for the unac. We will not let the meat go to waste."

Ivy clutched her clothes with one arm and settled her palm against his chest. "I'm sorry. Sorry I yelled at you and called you spider man."

His eyes narrowed, and his mandibles rose. "I know."

Ivy smirked and shook her head.

Arrogant jerk.

Chapter Nineteen

THE LATE MORNING sun streamed into the den through the opening and cast a bright patch on the floor in which Ivy was currently seated, staring outside as she slowly ate sweetseeds. There was a gentle breeze flowing in, freshening the air, but it carried a hint of cold that spoke of a coming storm.

Ketahn breathed that air deeply. He'd always appreciated the faint scent that preceded the rain; it added a new layer to the already complex blend of jungle smells, making them all seem even more alive and vibrant. But those, unsurprisingly, were not the smells upon which he focused. That breeze swept Ivy's fragrance straight toward him, and he couldn't help but take it in greedily.

He pulled the silk thread tight, wrapping it around the shaft of the spear once more before tying it off. After cutting away the excess thread, he grasped the flat of the spearhead in one hand and the shaft just beneath it in the other. The head remained in place when he gave it a tug.

Carefully, Ketahn set the weapon, which was almost half a segment shorter than the spears he was accustomed to, aside. Ivy had selected the wood for the shaft, shaped it, and hardened it herself. She had found the blackrock shard for the head and worked it into shape with her own hands. Soon enough, he'd have her wrap part of the shaft with silk to create a grip as she preferred. And, whenever she made her first kill with it, she would add a small trophy to the spear—a feather, a scale, a fang, or a tiny bone—to enhance its strength.

But he had insisted on setting and securing the spearhead. He would teach her how soon enough, would have her practice until she had perfected it, but her first weapon had to be durable. It had to be reliable. Ketahn had to know it would not fail upon its first thrust.

With his work done, he shifted all his attention to Ivy. Her hair shone like strands of pale gold in the sunlight, surrounding her head in an otherworldly glow. He watched the barest hints of muscle moving under her skin as she plucked another seed from the fruit, brought it to her mouth, and slipped it between her full, pink lips.

Just as surely as he was bound to his broodsister and his friends, Ketahn was bound to Ivy. The connection they shared was deeper than Takarahl's tunnels, more powerful than a raging storm, and more mysterious than the spirits dwelling in the jungle's darkest places. It was friendship, yes...but it was unlike any friendship he'd ever had.

He enjoyed his time with her. Enjoyed providing for her. And he enjoyed learning about her, even if so much of her life before waking from what she called a *cryochamber* had involved things of which he had no understanding. The life he'd shared with Ivy thus far had been fulfilling, enriching, and...happy.

And he could not deny that so much of what he did for her was what any vrix male would do for his mate.

At that thought, his eyes wandered, drifting over her body. In the seven days since she'd been attacked by the unac near the stream, he'd thought about that day often. Ivy had asked a few more times about the *ship*, had asked him to take her to it, had tried to explain again and again, but he'd refused her each time. The only difference was that they'd both remained calm during those exchanges, though he could tell she was far from deterred.

But the focus of his recollections was always upon the aftermath of that attack, not the cause of the argument that had preceded it. He'd thought about when he'd cleaned and tended her, thought about what she'd told him, about the way she'd reacted. Somehow, he'd kept himself from touching her breasts again, though he'd noticed more than ever when her nipples hardened and poked against the ragged fabric of her shirt. He'd been intrigued by them before, but after hearing that they brought her pleasure when touched...

He wanted nothing more than to run his hands over them, to tease those nipples with his fingers and watch them grow taut. He wanted to explore her entire body with his fingertips and discover all the spots that gave her pleasure, all the spots that coaxed a reaction from her. He wanted to learn what touch would open her slit to him and produce the heady fragrance of her lust.

Yet Ivy was not vrix. She could not be his mate.

That thought had held him back for so long, but it was a fraying thread—with each passing day, it was thinner, weaker, and Ivy being human mattered a little less. The differences between them seemed an ever-shrinking obstacle. He had seen her slit, which she called her *pussy*, had seen it open, had seen it glisten with her dew. They would fit together. He knew it.

Every day, his certainty that she could not be his mate wavered.

With a huff, Ketahn rose from his place against the wall and crossed the den to Ivy.

She looked up at him and smiled. "All done?"

"Yes," he said as he settled down beside her. "You will have more work to do on it, but only a little."

Ivy plucked out a few sweetseeds from their shell and held them out to him. "Thank you."

He cupped the seeds in his palm and tossed them all into his mouth at once. The burst of juice over his tongue was all the sweeter knowing she had picked the fruit and shared it with him. Once he'd swallowed, he extended his tongue to lick away a bit of juice that had trickled from the corner of his mouth and gestured to her leg. "It is time to tend your cuts again."

She turned her body toward him and stretched her bandaged leg out to his waiting hand.

Ketahn untied the silk strips and peeled them away. They were clean, just as they had been over the last few days—a good sign, as her wounds had not reopened. Laying the strips aside, he lifted her leg gently and bent down to inspect the cuts.

Ivy wiggled her toes, and when he peered up at her face, she grinned at him. "I can still feel my toes."

He growled at her in mock irritation and shook his head. "Not amusing, Ivy."

After he'd tended to the unac that day—they'd only just eaten the last of its meat this morning—Ivy had told him about human ailments. About what she called *infections*. She'd told him about wounds making people rot from within, about even a tiny cut being enough to kill a human under the right—or wrong —circumstances.

He knew the same was true for vrix, but humans seemed so much smaller and more fragile. So much more prone to dying.

She'd talked about humans losing feeling in their limbs because of such wounds, something Ketahn had not wanted to think of happening to Ivy. And only two days ago she had told him she could not move her foot and toes. In his alarm, he'd begun rummaging through his belongings, desperately seeking something, anything that could help—until he'd heard her laughter. He had not understood her humor at first, as it hadn't been implied in her tone, and his annoyance upon discovering she had spoken in jest had given her reason to laugh long and hard.

He had eased somewhat when she'd explained that she'd been given some sort of medicine that made her body far more capable of resisting illness. She'd claimed that she likely would have died after eating the sweetfang root were it not for that medicine. Ketahn had accepted that information gratefully, though part of him insisted such a thing wasn't possible in the realm of the living.

Ivy giggled. "Oh, come on. You know it's funny. You know you want to laugh."

"I have hold of your leg"—he slid the pad of a finger along the bottom of her foot—"and I know how to make you laugh against your will."

She squeaked and nearly pulled her foot out of his grasp in her attempt to escape him. "Ketahn, no!"

Her skin was so sensitive, and she was so responsive to his touch, that it was a struggle for him to relent, especially as his urge to touch her elsewhere intensified. He wouldn't be able to resist forever; his self-control would eventually crumble, and he'd be helpless but to submit to his desires, to give in to the mating frenzy.

For now, he'd hold strong. It was all he could do.

Withdrawing his finger from her foot, he returned his attention to her cuts. They seemed to be healing well. The discoloration that Ivy had called bruising was all but gone, and the flesh around the wounds no longer looked swollen and irritated. Each cut was scabbed over now, covered in a layer of crust that Ivy said protected the healing flesh beneath.

Though he knew he shouldn't tempt himself, he delicately brushed a thumb along the pale, unbroken skin to the side of the cuts, marveling at her softness, her smoothness, her sun-instilled warmth. "How does it feel?"

Ivy set the sweetseed shell down. "It's a little tender and still feels tight when I move it, but it doesn't hurt."

Ketahn nodded, staring at his clawed thumb against her skin. He stilled it, giving the side of her leg a gentle squeeze. "No need to bind it while we are in here."

"Very good, Doctor Ketahn."

Ketahn chittered. Since she'd explained what a doctor was,

he'd found it amusing to think of himself as one—though that amusement would fade were he to pause and consider just how much more harm than healing he'd done in his life. He forced himself to draw back and lift his gaze to hers, trying to ignore the tantalizing body it swept over on its journey.

"So what do you plan for us to do today?" Ivy asked, reclining on her elbows and tilting her head. "Or are we going to spend a lazy day in the nest?"

"It is not lazy to rest, "Ketahn said.

Ivy lifted her other foot and poked him in the chest with her big toe. "I like the way you think."

He caught that foot in one hand and smiled at her. With a grip on both of her legs, he could so easily drag her closer, could pull her right against him, and then he could hold her like he did through the nights, could continue exploring her body, or he could slide his hands up those legs, spread them wider, and tear off the fabric covering her pelvis to gaze upon the petals of her slit.

His hands tensed, eager to fulfill those desires, but the sharp sound of wood cracking from somewhere outside stilled him.

Ivy started, her eyes rounding. "That sounded close," she whispered.

Ketahn nodded. Moving slowly and silently, he reached over to grasp the cloth that usually hung across the den's opening and drew it into place. He remained confident that nothing else could get into the den, but it was best to avoid notice entirely.

"Ketahn?" someone called in a familiar voice from below—Ahnset's voice. It was strange for him to hear it amongst the trees rather than echoing dully off stone walls, but more than that, it was alarming.

He trusted Ahnset more than anyone, which was why she was the only other vrix who knew the location of his den, but he was not prepared to trust even his broodsister with Ivy. Ahnset was dependable, honest, and caring, but she was also bound by duty to serve the will of the queen...and Ketahn had little question as to what the queen's will would be regarding his human.

"Ketahn?" Ahnset repeated. "If you are here, come out. I would sooner pull your den down than climb all the way up there."

Ketahn released Ivy's legs and, still moving carefully, leaned toward her to cup her cheek in his hand. Keeping his voice low, he said, "I must go. You will be still, silent, and out of sight. You are safe."

Ivy flattened a palm against his chest as her eyes searched his. She nodded.

He shifted his hand, smoothing it back over her hair and combing his claws through those golden strands. How could he be so reluctant to leave her? It was only Ahnset out there, and the den would be well within view.

But he knew at least part of the reason for his hesitance. Ahnset had come here only a few times over the last seven years, and each time had been due to some dire circumstance. She did not have the time or freedom to visit for the pleasure of Ketahn's company.

"I saw the cloth move, Ketahn," called Ahnset. "I *will* come up."

Despite the ominous implication of Ahnset's presence, Ketahn chittered. His hand lingered on Ivy a heartbeat longer before he rose and guided her away from the opening. She crawled backward, shifting onto her knees once she was clear.

Though a hint of unease creased her brow, she seemed steady, seemed calm. Her trust bolstered him; she'd be fine. They'd both be fine.

Ketahn whipped aside the cloth and poked his head out. Ahnset stood upon a thick branch twenty segments below, staring up at the nest with her golden adornments glittering in the fractured shafts of sunlight.

"Your threats do not frighten me, broodsister," he said. "We both know you cannot climb up."

She snapped her mandibles. "But I did mention tearing your den down. Trying to climb to it would be a simple way to do so."

"I rarely complained when you tore my weaving while we were broodlings"—Ketahn pulled himself out of the nest, trailing one of his rear legs behind to stroke across Ivy's knee—"but I will not allow you to destroy my home."

Ivy's sweet, exotic scent clung to the fine hairs of his leg, a thrilling reminder of what he had to protect. Fortunately, the surprise of Ahnset's arrival had been enough to jar him from the desires that had nearly consumed him only moments ago.

Ahnset chittered. "You will always have a home in Takarahl."

Ketahn hissed dismissively as he crossed onto the web, traversing it as quickly and smoothly as possible. After climbing down a tree and following a couple intersecting branches, he was standing in front of Ahnset, and whatever annoyed comment he might've made about living in the city had died well before he could give it voice.

Ahnset shifted close, and the two tipped their foreheads together. Ketahn hooked his forelegs around hers and released a slow breath. Her familiar scent was soothing, but he wanted only more of Ivy's fragrance.

"You thought to avoid me?" Ahnset asked.

Only now that her mandibles were so close did he notice the gold band around the right one—it was new. "Never, broodsister."

She withdrew from him, standing straight to glare down in that stern Queen's Fang posture.

Ketahn could only chitter again. "Are we here as a Fang and a common hunter, or as brood siblings?"

"Duty says it should be the former." Her shoulders relaxed, and her mandibles fell. "Yet I have come as your broodsister only. I fear you will not believe that soon enough, but it is true."

Ketahn's insides twisted, and he found himself battling an urge to look back up at his den. The only duty to which he was bound in that moment was his duty to Ivy—to provide for her, to teach her, to protect her. To hide her. She was for him and no one else, and he refused to take even the slightest risk of revealing her.

So he tilted his head, narrowed his eyes, and ignored the hot, itchy sensation sparking across his back that begged him to just turn around. "If you say it is true, I believe it. What dire matter has brought you here, Ahnset?"

Her eyes softened, and she released a tired trill. She sank down so she was closer to his eye level again. "My concern for my broodbrother, who will not like what I intend to say."

"It is about her." As those words left his mouth, Ketahn felt suddenly cold and hollow, a stark change from how he'd felt a few heartbeats before.

Ahnset scraped the tip of her foreleg across the bark. "Yes."

Ketahn curled his hands into fists, squeezed tight, and relaxed them. He repeated those motions several times before speaking again. "Then you need say no more. We may simply be brood siblings and act as though nothing exists but the two of us and the Tangle."

Not that Ketahn could accomplish that—he could not forget Ivy. Just the thought of it made him feel ill.

Ahnset chittered softly, almost sadly, and bumped her foreleg against his. "There are times I wish that was true, Ketahn. But we know it cannot be, and the Tangle cannot hide us from our duties."

Drawing in a deep breath—more aware of the absence of Ivy's scent than the smells that were on the air—Ketahn dipped his chin and gestured for Ahnset to speak.

Her mandibles twitched, and her fine hairs bristled for the space of a heartbeat. "It is no secret that the queen wants you as her mate. By now, word has spread throughout Takarahl. I know you have long denied her, but..."

Ketahn's breath caught in his lungs, building immense pressure in his chest. He might've expected this from most anyone else, and it would have been meaningless to him, but from Ahnset...

She met his gaze and held it. "You should accept her as your mate."

He forced his weight onto his forelegs to keep them down, unwilling to express such rage and aggression to his broodsister, regardless of the chaos within him. "You have known me since we hatched, Ahnset," he said, his voice measured but strained, "and though our paths split long ago, you know me still. So why? Why would you come all the way out here to say *that* to me?"

"Because I do not wish to see you suffer." She leaned closer, flattening her forelegs against the sides of his. "Your resistance in this, Ketahn, it is..."

"Foolish?" he growled.

"In its way, yes," she said gently. "Yet you are no fool, broodbrother. What male would not delight in the chance to become mate to our queen?"

"Any male but Durax," Ketahn snapped, withdrawing from Ahnset. "Some of the males she has taken to her den carry the scars of her attention to this day."

"None of them are you." She stomped on the branch, producing a dull thump and sending a tremor through the wood. "There are no vrix in Takarahl who would make so strong a match as you and our queen. Your broodlings would be unrivaled, and your legacy would endure forever."

"Is that meant to concern me, Ahnset? When have I ever shown interest in being sire to a brood? And what use have I for a legacy?"

"It would be to the honor of our mother and sire," Ahnset replied in a small voice.

"By the Eight, Ahnset," Ketahn said, voice raw, "we have both done much to honor our mother and sire. My mating Zurvashi would not do so."

"How would it not?" She straightened, rising to her full height. "Zurvashi is the queen. There is no greater honor for a male than becoming her mate and being sire to her broods. And more than queen, she is strong, cunning, and bold. An unrivaled warrior. She has made Takarahl into a power feared in the Tangle. Few queens since Queen Takari herself have accomplished so much."

Ketahn turned away from her, his every muscle tense, fire flowing through his veins. The itching just under his hide persisted, beckoning his gaze upward, urging him to look toward Ivy, to go to her. Because only with her had he been able to forget. Only with her had he been able to pretend everything else really was gone—or at least so far away it didn't matter.

"I know your disputes with her," Ahnset continued. "I lost as much as you, broodbrother. I feel the pain of those losses as heavily as you."

"And yet you continue to serve her."

"I look toward the future, Ketahn, not the past. We cannot unravel threads the Weaver has already woven, but we can yet affect what is to come. We can ensure the things to come are better than what has been."

"You believe my mating with Zurvashi would make things better?"

"Accepting her...would be for the good of our city. For your own good."

A choked, bitter sound burst from him. He looked at her over his shoulder. "For my good?"

"Yes. You would not need to remain out here, and I would not need to worry for you so often."

Slowly, he turned to face her again. "You know I am here by choice, Ahnset."

She lowered her chin and folded her arms across her chest. "A choice you made in guilt."

"Guilt?" Ketahn strode forward, straightening his forelegs to push himself up to his brood sister's eye level. "Guilt did not drive me from Takarahl, Ahnset, though I carry it still for every vrix slain under my lead. *She* drove me away. All the death was because of her."

"The thornskulls would have grown more aggressive had she not acted."

"Every vrix slain in that war died for roots, Ahnset."

"Mender roots. For healing."

Ketahn opened his mandibles wide and hissed. "To make dye for her blood-cursed cloth! To serve her vanity. Our friends, our mother and sire, our brothers and sisters. If not here in the Tangle, then in the tunnels, digging deeper and deeper without time to build supports because she needed more blackrock for her warriors and more gold and gems to ensure she shines the brightest, or in her silkworks, because her dye masters tried to perfect her beloved shade and poisoned two dozen weavers in the process."

Ahnset stood firmly, though a sorrowful light had entered her eyes. "Zurvashi fought, too. She bled. All of us had to sacrifice, Ketahn."

"Not because it was necessary, but because she demanded it. Because it served her greed and her desire for power. Her rule has brought only suffering."

"You truly believe it all so terrible?"

Ketahn's mandibles sagged, and he slowly lowered himself to his normal stance. "Yes. You have always seen things as they should be, Ahnset, rather than as they are."

"I am not so blind as you believe. I see. I know she is not kind; I know she is not selfless. But Takarahl is secure because of her strength."

"She made that war, Ahnset, and it was all for nothing. The suffering now...it is all for nothing."

Ahnset placed a hand on Ketahn's shoulder. "If that is true, broodbrother, it is only more reason to accept. As the queen's mate, you could change things for everyone. You cannot do that as a hunter hiding in the jungle."

Those words stung, but he did not allow himself to show it.

Even if Zurvashi could be swayed, Ketahn knew the cost of doing so would be immense, and she was likely to bend good-intentioned suggestion into something to benefit only herself. "I cannot change life for anyone but myself. That is why I am here."

"She wants you, Ketahn, as she has wanted nothing else in all the years I have served her."

Ketahn took hold of Ahnset's wrist and lifted her hand off his shoulder. "But I do not want her, Ahnset."

He'd always known that, even before Zurvashi had turned her eyes toward him. Yes, the queen was strong, bold, and confident. She was clever, striking, and beautiful. She was even capable of humor. But those qualities had always been overshadowed by two others—her insatiable ambition and her cruelty.

Zurvashi was nothing like Ivy. Ivy was soft, warm of both body and demeanor. Her eyes were a more brilliant blue than the sky on the clearest of days, her hair was as fine as silk and lustrous as pale gold. Her laughter was high and musical, a delight to the ears, and her smile outshone the sun.

But the differences went far beyond the physical. Ivy's humor held none of the maliciousness to which Zurvashi was prone. Her teasing was good-natured, reminding Ketahn of the way he and his friends jested with one another. Though Ivy was no stranger to anger, she never bent it toward cruelty and spitefulness, and she had the humility to eventually apologize when she knew she'd been wrong.

How could he not admire the strength at Ivy's core, her determination and willpower? To Ketahn, Ivy was far more impressive for her perseverance because she lacked size and might.

And he wanted her. Regardless of their differences, he wanted Ivy. He wanted his little human.

He had a strange, sudden sense that he'd been trudging through life tangled in sticky webbing that had blinded him and restrained his movement—and that the webs had just been cut away.

Ahnset had been staring at him with open concern in her eyes, her mandibles moving erratically.

"You were in Moonfall when she summoned me to our mother's hatching den," he said. "You were right outside, Ahnset. Surely you overhead what happened."

She averted her gaze, posture stiffening. "She has always been known to have her moods. Do not we all? And with the High Claiming so near and a city to rule..."

"You know my reasons, Ahnset. You have always known." He slid his hand to the underside of her wrist and shifted it down, so their palms were touching. "My answer will not change."

But his desires had, entirely without his will, and he could not ignore them.

His only interest—all his interest—was in Ivy.

IVY HAD NOT REALIZED how slowly Ketahn had spoken to her in his language until now, as she sat there listening to him and the newcomer. But her grasp on the vrix language had grown exponentially as the weeks had passed, and though she'd never be able to speak it well, she understood much of it.

This other vrix, who Ketahn called Ahnset, was trying to convince him to mate with the queen.

Tucking the sweat dampened hair at her temple behind her ears, Ivy eased onto her hands and slowly crawled to the entrance. Once there, she pinched a corner of the cloth and drew it aside, just enough to peer out.

She saw Ketahn first. His back was toward her, displaying those familiar violet and white markings along his back and hindquarters. And in front of him... Ivy's eyes widened. She'd thought Ketahn was big and monstrous when she'd first seen him, but the other vrix was huge. He looked like a child compared to Ahnset. Ivy figured Ketahn was around seven feet tall in his normal standing position, and that meant Ahnset had to be at least nine and a half feet tall and a great deal heavier.

The newcomer's body was decorated with beads, dyed silk, and golden jewelry—bracelets, rings, armbands, hair clasps, even a neck piece that looked like stacked bands of gold attached to a thick leather backing, like a gorget right out of medieval times. The vrix wore a wide belt around its waist from which dangled a swath of cloth that covered its pelvis— not that seeing it would've necessarily helped Ivy determine whether the creature was male or female. Ketahn wasn't exactly a...a dangler.

But there were a few other differences between Ketahn and Ahnset apart from size that were immediately apparent. The larger vrix only had four legs, albeit thick, powerful ones, and there were no markings visible anywhere on its black hide.

Ivy didn't know anything about the vrix's culture or their home, Takarahl, but this vrix seemed important—and also meant something to Ketahn.

Ahnset had its hand over Ketahn's; a curl of its fingers could've engulfed his entire hand completely.

"You know what will come, Ketahn," said Ahnset. Its voice was huskier, but there was a hint of softness to it—like it was somehow in a higher register even though Ivy swore it was slightly deeper than Ketahn's voice. Strange as it was, that quality seemed...feminine.

Was this vrix a female?

"I will be fine, Ahnset," Ketahn replied.

Ahnset did close her hand around Ketahn's now. "I do not want her anger turned onto you. I do not want to see her hurt you, or be *kreshan* to hurt you myself."

"I will find my own way, *okari'kija*."

"It does not need to be like this. You can protect yourself if you *sultirin* to her."

"I will never *sultirin*," Ketahn said firmly.

"I cannot protect you from the queen, *okari'ojan*." Ahnset lowered her hand and leaned down, tipping her headcrest against Ketahn's. "I do not want to choose. Do not make me."

"I am not asking you to." Ketahn brushed his front leg against Ahnset's.

Ivy's brow furrowed, and her fingers squeezed the hanging cloth. Bitter heat rose from her belly, making her chest and throat tight. The interactions between the two vrix brimmed with familiarity and intimacy.

But why would a female who was sexually involved with Ketahn want him to mate with someone else? Perhaps they were lovers forced to keep their involvement secret from the queen?

There is no vrix I long to take as my nyleea.

Ivy shoved her jealousy aside. Ketahn had told her he didn't have a mate.

What if he did, though?

What...what business would it be of hers? What would it matter to her?

Deep inside, she knew it would matter. It *did* matter.

"I...must return to Takarahl," said Ahnset, straightening and pulling back from Ketahn. She pressed the sides of her forearms together and bowed her head. "I am sorry I did not come for pleasant reasons."

"Whatever the reason, *okari'kija*, it is always good to see you." Ketahn offered Ahnset a bow, making a gesture with his arms that Ivy could not see because of his position. "May the Eight see you back safely."

Ahnset turned and started to move away from him, but stopped after a single stride. "Think upon it, Ketahn. If not for yourself, then for those who care about you."

As Ketahn rose from his bow, he turned his head as though glancing over his shoulder. Ivy caught only a glimpse of his violet eyes before he faced forward again. He said nothing more, and Ahnset continued on her way, her heavy steps making the big branch shake.

As soon as she was out of sight, Ketahn spun around and looked directly at the nest.

Ivy gasped and flinched back, releasing the cloth. She cringed.

You will be still, silent, and out of sight.

One out of three wasn't bad...right?

"I'm in so much trouble," she muttered.

It wasn't long before the nest was moving with that particular bounce that meant Ketahn was climbing along the web. Ivy backed away from the opening, sat down with her legs crossed, and placed her hands on her lap, resisting the impulse to wring the cloth of her shirt.

Claws scraped the exterior of the nest, moving closer and closer, until finally Ketahn's hand slipped in through the opening to sweep the cloth aside. He met her gaze with narrowed eyes and held it as he entered the nest.

Ivy smiled wide, giving him as innocent a look as she could manage. "How was your...visit?"

He tilted his head and let the cloth fall back into place, making the nest just dark enough that his markings and eyes glowed faintly. "She did not see you, but you did not obey."

She didn't think now was a good time to explain the saying *curiosity killed the cat*; she was sure Ketahn wouldn't take it very well. But his words confirmed her suspicion that the Ahnset was female.

"I was silent," she said.

His eyes remained narrow, and his mandibles twitched upward slightly—an *almost* smile. "But you were not still, and you were not out of sight."

"Ohhhh. I was supposed to do all three?" Ivy snapped her fingers. "Well, I guess I'll remember that for next time."

Ketahn chittered and lowered himself onto the floor in front of her, sliding a leg forward to brush along her shin. "It is good there may yet be a next time. If you had been seen..." He shook his head.

Did that mean other vrix might not be as kind as he'd been?

Okay, so maybe she should have listened. If Ketahn was worried, Ivy needed to be as well, and she had to take the necessary precautions.

She sighed. "I'm sorry. I was curious." She ran her fingers over the leg touching her shin. Though covered in the same hide as the rest of him, Ketahn's legs were harder—almost like antlers still covered in velvet—with soft, fine hairs covering them. "Who was that?"

"Ahnset." His gaze dipped to her hand. "She is my *okari'kija*."

"I don't know those words."

He braced his lower forearms on his leg joints and lifted his upper hands, running them back over his headcrest to comb his claws through his long, loose hair. "We have the same mother and father, and our eggs were laid and hatched at the same time. Our mother's third—and last—*okari*, her last group of eggs."

"Oh! Ahnset is your sister? *Kija* is sister?"

Ketahn nodded. "As you say."

"But she's so...*big*."

"She is a female."

Ivy's brows creased. "Are all your females big then?"

"Yes. Ahnset is one of the most big, but they are all close."

"And the queen?"

His mandibles twitched, and a faint but frustrated growl sounded in his chest. "She is more big than all."

Ivy slid her hand farther along his leg, relishing the feel of his soft hairs beneath her palm as she eased closer to him. "Why would Ahnset push you to mate with the queen?"

Again, his attention shifted to her hand. "Because she does not want to see the queen hurt me if I say no."

Frowning, Ivy settled down directly in front of Ketahn, leaned back into the curve of his lower arm, and looked up at him. "Hurt you more than the last time?"

Ketahn curled that arm around her, smoothing down her hair with his upper hand. "You do not need to worry, Ivy. I will find a way."

Ivy lowered her gaze, rested her hands on the forearm he'd wrapped around her, and stroked his skin. Faint scars marked his hide even there. She knew his life had been one of conflict and struggle, knew he'd hunted and worked hard every day, but she hadn't realized he was out here to escape all he'd been through, or that he'd lost so much—so many.

"Have you ever been happy, Ketahn?" she asked.

The hand in her hair stilled, and his embrace tightened. "Yes," he rumbled as his claws resumed combing through her hair. "I have known many happy days. But these last few eightdays have been my most happy."

Ivy smiled and rested her head against his chest. "The days I've spent with you are my happiest, too."

Chapter Twenty

Ivy's stomach fluttered as Ketahn tipped back and climbed higher. Though her hold on him already could've been considered a death grip, she somehow tightened it further, pressing herself flush against his hard, muscular back. The silk rope tied around their waists would hold them together. She trusted it because Ketahn trusted it. But that couldn't stop her reflexive reactions—especially while she was blindfolded, and it felt like the world was being turned and tilted to wild angles every few seconds.

If this went on much longer, her arms and legs would be so sore from clinging to him that she wouldn't be able to move come morning.

Not that her current position—sitting on Ketahn's hindquarters like he was her mighty arachno-steed—was a bad one. His body was hard all over, but it was warm, and there was a suppleness to his hide that she appreciated a little more every day. Pressing the side of her face against his back and listening to his hearts beating was always soothing. She could just do without all the times when he started climbing and she felt like she was on a roller coaster that was heading up an impossibly steep peak.

Her disorientation would've been assuaged by removing the

blindfold, but Ketahn had insisted she wear it. He'd said he wanted to show her something, but he only wanted her to look once he had her in the perfect place.

All she had to focus upon was Ketahn's feel and the sounds of the surrounding jungle. There was the usual rustling of leaves and the night calls of animals—many of which had taken on a certain beauty as they'd grown more familiar—but she'd also heard running water somewhere nearby for the last several minutes. That last sound seemed to be steadily growing in volume as Ketahn traveled.

"Are we almost there?" Ivy asked. It wasn't the first time.

"Yes," Ketahn answered. It also wasn't the first time.

She laughed, but it was cut off by a squeak when they suddenly dropped. It felt as though her heart had lodged in her throat. Ivy pressed her face more firmly against his back and dug her nails into his chest. Ketahn landed with a heavy thump, the impact jolting through him and straight into Ivy.

"Oh my God, did we just fall?" she asked breathlessly.

"I...intended to do that," Ketahn replied.

"I really hope that hesitation was because you had to think of the right word."

He responded with a thoughtful grunt and gently patted one of her hands before he continued moving.

Ivy frowned. "That isn't reassuring."

Ketahn chittered. "I will not let anything happen to you, Ivy."

Though she felt him climb a little higher, he thankfully didn't tip straight back again. Before long, the sound of running water had reached a dull roar, and there was just a hint of cool mist in the air.

Ketahn came to a stop and covered her hands with his, one of his thumbs stroking her skin. His other pair of hands settled on her legs, and he smoothed his palms up and down. "Now we are here. But do not look until I say."

His touch made her skin prickle in goosebumps and sparked heat low in her belly.

"Is it okay to get down?" she asked.

He released her hands and loosened the silk rope. As he drew the rope away, it sagged, running along her thigh to enhance the sensations created by his touch. She relaxed her legs and let them slowly fall until they hung straight down either side of him. Ketahn lowered himself enough for her bare feet to touch the ground. The earth underfoot was soft, spongy, and cool. Releasing her death grip on his chest, she scooted back on his hindquarters and swung one of her legs over, turning to slide off him and onto the ground.

Ketahn took hold of her arm as she did so, ensuring she didn't lose her balance. Once she was standing, he placed another hand on her hip and slightly adjusted the direction in which she was facing.

"Are you prepared?" he asked softly.

Ivy thrummed with anticipation. "Yes."

He stroked her skin ever so delicately as he gathered her hair and swept it over her shoulder. His clever fingers then rose, untying the blindfold. But he didn't let that blindfold fall; instead, he took both ends of it and slowly, *sooo* slowly, lifted it away. Ivy opened her eyes. Her breath caught and her eyes flared.

The waterfall ahead commanded her attention first. It was at least a hundred feet tall, the water sparkling blue and silver in the moonlight as it tumbled down over several tiers into a wide pool at its base. The mist rising from it glittered like it was full of diamond dust. Bare stone and clinging vegetation flanked it on either side.

Overhead, a large swath of the sky was visible, scattered with more stars than she'd ever seen and painted with the purples and blues of distant nebulas. Two moons hung nearby each other amidst those stars. The larger one was almost pure white, marked by only hints of gray and blue. The other, much smaller, shone a faint pink.

The jungle around the clearing was aglow not just because of the moonlight, but the bioluminescence of countless plants—leaves in iridescent blues, purples, and greens, and mushrooms and flowers adding more splashes of brighter color. All of it, along with the light from the night sky, was reflected on the rippling surface of the pool, which was a good forty feet below Ivy's current position.

Movement caught her eye. She turned her head to find several insects fluttering nearby. Their large, glowing wings were moth-like. The little creatures danced and flitted through the air, occasionally drawing together and twirling before breaking apart again. As Ivy swept her gaze around, she realized that those bugs —and similar creatures—were everywhere, as though reveling in the moonlight.

"Ketahn, this is beautiful," Ivy said.

"It is."

She looked up at Ketahn to find him staring down at her, his markings glowing more vibrantly than she'd ever seen.

"It took me a long time to realize it"—he brushed a finger along her jaw, stopping it on her chin—"but it is very beautiful."

Ivy's lips parted, and her heart quickened in response to his words and that thrilling, rough yet gentle touch. Was he...was he saying *she* was beautiful?

She stepped closer to him and reached up, cradling his jaw. He turned his face into her touch and closed his eyes. Though his face was not an expressive one, she could have sworn he appeared... content. As she slid her palm up along the side of his headcrest, he opened those eight glowing, violet eyes and raised his mandibles.

She could never call Ketahn handsome, not by any human standards, but he was striking and beautiful in his own right. Yes, he was alien to her—that couldn't be denied, couldn't be ignored, and it wouldn't stop being true no matter how comfortable she was around him. He'd always make her think of a spider. But that wasn't bad, wasn't frightening or upsetting. Not anymore.

Because he was Ketahn. His eyes were so deep, so mesmerizing, as capable of ferocity and intensity as they were of compassion and understanding. His hands, with their long, clawed fingers, could easily deal death—but they could also soothe away pain, work the finest threads, and rouse pleasure with their every touch. His plated chest was hard and unyielding, more like armor than flesh, but when his arms were wrapped around her, it was the warmest, safest place she could ever be.

Ivy smiled and smoothed her hand back until she could trail her fingers through the loose, silky strands of his ponytail, pulling them forward over his shoulder. "Thank you for bringing me here."

"You have taught me, Ivy. Not every moment in the Tangle must be a struggle." Ketahn turned his head toward the waterfall and lowered his mandibles. "After the queen's war was done, I would come here sometimes, and I would think. It was the only place that brought me peace...where the sound of the water could silence the spirits of the past."

She frowned, studying him quietly. In a way...Ivy and Ketahn were alike. They were both alone, both outsiders, both separated from the places they'd once called home. She could feel his pain and loneliness. He'd lost so much already, and Ivy wondered if he felt like he was losing his sister now, too.

Ivy glanced toward the waterfall, but her gaze soon rose to the sky, where beautiful, unfamiliar stars glittered against the bright nebulas. Of course she understood how Ketahn felt. Hadn't she left her home planet behind to move on from the past, to forget what she'd lost?

"I don't even know which direction to look if I wanted to gaze toward Earth," she said softly. "I don't know how far away it is, how long it's been since I left..." She looked up at Ketahn and flattened her palms on his chest, calling his eyes back to her. "But I know that I'm not alone. And neither are you, Ketahn."

He covered her hands with two of his and leaned down, gently touching his headcrest to her forehead. "I know, Ivy. Thank you."

After standing like that for a little while, Ketahn straightened and sank into a sitting position, dropping a hand to her hip to draw her down with him. She settled naturally between his spindly front legs, leaning back against his body with those claspers brushing her sides and hips.

With her head resting on his chest, she tilted her face toward the sky. "The stars are so different here than they are on Earth."

Ketahn wrapped his lower arms around Ivy, cocooning her in his warmth. "I cannot think what another world would be like. Or that there is even anything beyond the Tangle. What was your Earth like, Ivy?"

"Some places are like this. Of course, not *just* like this, but similar. There are oceans, too, where it's water as far as the eye can see, and deserts, which are hot, dry, and sandy. There are also mountains, giant rocks that go up to the sky, some covered in snow." She glanced at him with a smirk. "I bet you don't know what snow is."

He shook his head. "Tell me."

"It falls from the sky like rain, but it's lighter, softer. They're little white flakes that cover the ground."

"Is it like...ash, from a fire?"

"Yes! Except it's cold. So, so cold. And when it melts, it turns to water."

Ketahn looked up, tilting his head. "So...your world rains ash that turns into water?"

She chuckled. "Only in the winter, when the plants either die or sleep until spring, which is when everything wakes up and regrows. Not all places get cold, but it did where I was from." She nestled closer against him, curling her fingers around his forearms. "I was born in Wichita, Kansas, where everything was very flat. We didn't have giant trees, waterfalls, or mountains. But we had buildings. Think of them like your nest or...or a cave, but made with wood, stone, and metal, some even taller than any of these trees."

Ivy wasn't even going to get into cars, computers, holograms, and the countless other pieces of technology humans used every day. Explaining those things would be too difficult, and it wasn't like Ketahn would ever see any of that stuff. None of it really mattered anymore.

"Takarahl is shaped from the stone under the ground," Ketahn said, "and vrix in other places are said to have made stone *usilika* that stand tall in the jungle, but none so big as what you say. You must have lived among a great many humans to have dens so large."

"No, not really. Most of those places were used to work in or they were split up into apartments. Smaller...dens. I didn't live in those."

"Tell me of your Earth den, Ivy. Your broodmother and father, your broodbrothers and sisters. How many broods did your mother hatch?"

Ivy laughed. "Humans don't lay eggs, Ketahn. And it's usually only one baby at a time, but sometimes it can be two or three, or even more, but that's rare." She took one of his hands and placed it low on her belly. "We carry our babies here for nine months as they grow inside us."

His hand flexed, and a thoughtful rumble sounded in his chest, pulsing into Ivy. "There are creatures in the jungle that do the same."

"As for family..." She frowned, and that familiar tightness in her chest returned. "I don't have one anymore. I had a brother who was fourteen years older than me, so I never really knew him, and my mother and father... I wasn't planned for or wanted. I think they simply felt obligated to care for me, and when I look back, I don't know if they ever really loved me. And when I ended up angering and disappointing them when I was older, they saw it as a way to finally be rid of me. I was no longer their responsibility."

Ketahn was silent for a time—long enough that she wondered if she'd used too many words that he did not understand. When he finally spoke, his question caught her completely off guard.

"Did you pursue a mate?"

Ivy tightened her grip on Ketahn's arm. "There was a man who pursued me."

He stiffened around her, his hand clutching her stomach possessively. Even his claspers curled around her waist from behind. "Did you accept him?"

"I did. He...he was the reason I angered my parents. He said he wanted me, and I believed him. He always seemed to say the right things. Always had the right words. I thought he loved me as much as I had thought I loved him. But he just used me and threw me away."

Ketahn growled. "The right words do not matter if a male does not do the right things. He was not worthy of you." He caught her chin in his hand and angled her face up toward his.

"You are worthy of so much more than a male like him could ever offer, Ivy."

She smiled, and that tightness in her chest faded. "No, he wasn't worthy. It took me a long time to realize that. That I deserved better." Ivy looked toward the waterfall. Once more, a sense of peace drifted over her, and she let her head tip back against Ketahn, relishing the feel of his claws stroking her hair.

"When I was young," she continued, "I always dreamed of finding a man who'd love me completely, who'd sweep me off my feet and carry me right out of the lonely life I'd known. A man I would someday marry. I would wear the most beautiful white wedding dress, and we'd have the most beautiful ceremony in the spring, surrounded by a million flowers.

"But that never happened. After that guy, I struggled for several years, and then I joined the Homeworld Initiative so I could start over. I wanted to take part in this big, new adventure, to go to a new world where I could start a new life, a world where my past didn't matter."

Ivy looked down, grasped the hem of her worn, discolored shirt, and laughed. "Well, I can't say I'm wearing white anymore, but I'm definitely on a new, alien world where my past doesn't matter."

"What is *marry*, Ivy?" Ketahn asked.

Ivy glanced up to find him staring down at her. "For humans, it's when two people who love each other make a bond by exchanging vows and rings. They become mates."

"And a *wedding dress*?"

"A wedding dress is... It's... Here, let me show you." She gently pried his arms off her and disengaged his claspers so she could stand. She walked around him to a nearby bush with big leaves, each of which was at least as long as her arm. She broke several off at their stems and tucked them around the waistband of her shorts until she'd made a crude skirt, then picked one more leaf before returning to Ketahn.

"A dress is kind of like my shirt, except instead of stopping

269

here"—she touched the hem of her shirt with the side of her hand then dropped it down to her knees—"they are longer. And a *wedding* dress is made of finer material...like silk! And they'd have the sheer cloth like your sister wore. Except wedding dresses are white. And sometimes, they come with a long veil." She draped the spare leaf over the top of her head and grinned at him. "Do you like it?"

Ketahn rose slowly, unfurling his long legs and lifting his powerful body with entrancing grace. He closed the distance between them in a couple long strides. Ivy did not resist when he plucked the leaf off her head, turning it in his hand to examine it.

"I would see you clad in silk." He dropped the leaf and cupped the underside of her jaw, angling her face toward his as he took her hips between two of his hands. "I will see you clad in *my* silk."

Warmth flooded Ivy, and something fluttered low in her belly. Ketahn was not attractive by human standards, but that didn't stop her body from reacting to him. He towered over her, a dominating force, charging the air with raw lust and enveloping her in his presence, which was equal parts possessive and reverent.

And Ivy knew at that moment she'd wear anything he told her to—even if that meant wearing nothing at all—just to feel his heated touch again.

Chapter Twenty-One

HUNCHING OVER THE WORK SLAB, Ketahn carefully drew the thin bone needle through the fabric again. Since being pressed into battle during Zurvashi's war, he'd neither woven nor sewn anything so intricate as this. The weaving was easily the finest of his life. But it was this shaping, this stitching, that would determine his ultimate success.

Holding the stitching taut with the tip of a claw, he tied off the thread, ensuring it was as secure as possible.

Delicately, he plucked up the fabric, suspending it from its corners. The silk was pure white, but it had a particular sheen that gave it the illusion of being sheer. The folds and cut of the fabric were unlike anything he'd ever seen worn by any female vrix —and that was all the better, because Ivy was unlike any female vrix.

This was not meant to be worn as a wrap, draped over a head or a shoulder, or hung from a belt. This was a *dress*, and it was for Ivy alone.

He brushed the side of his thumb across the simple patterns with which he'd adorned the fabric; they mimicked the web that held up his den.

Ivy was no vrix, but why should she not go about clad in silk?

Why should her skin not be caressed by the finest cloth that could be woven by vrix hands? She was a slight, delicate creature. Better Ketahn's silk than the tattered clothing she'd been wearing since he'd taken her from the pit.

He slipped his lower hands under the bottom of what she'd called the *skirt*, sliding them slowly upward until they were at the dress's waist, where the fabric was cinched tighter. Curling his fingers, he touched the tips of his claws together, forming a rough oval with his hands. He hoped this would be the proper size; he'd made all the measurements by recalling the parts of Ivy's body compared to his own.

She would look beautiful in this dress, especially with her long, golden hair loose around her shoulders. He hoped it would match the flare of her hips properly, that it would not too greatly constrict her breasts, that she would find it comfortable.

His excitement to give her this gift had overcome even his distaste for Takarahl. Ketahn had not been so inspired in years, at least—but more likely he'd never been so inspired in all his life.

And this fabric was perfect for Ivy. Despite appearing thin and delicate, it was resilient and durable. Like his little human, it was far stronger than it looked.

Using all four hands, he attempted to fill out the dress as though she were wearing it, but he knew that would never come close to the real thing. If he were to leave soon, he could reach the den a little after sunfall, and he could see Ivy wearing this dress beneath the light of the moons. Though were he to be truthful to himself, even that was too long a wait.

Ketahn laid the dress on the work slab and set to it with needle and thread again to complete the final strip of web pattern, working with care and precision despite his impatience—and despite the torrent of thoughts and emotions that had been threatening to flood his mind since he'd left for Takarahl in the middle of the night.

His thoughts in the days following their journey to the waterfall had been...heavy. Though he'd not understood everything Ivy had told him, he'd drawn more than enough meaning from her words to feel as though he and she were connected in ways he could never have imagined. By the Eight, he understood her desire for change, for an escape from the past. He understood her longing for something new.

Was it foolish to believe that he and Ivy were, to each other, that something new for which they'd both yearned?

One thought had risen to the surface of his mind repeatedly these last few days—he'd never wanted a mate. *Wanted.*

That was no longer true, and it had nothing to do with Zurvashi.

What difference did human and vrix make? Ivy was his. She would be his mate—his nyleea.

He did not intend to give her any reasonable option but acceptance. If she had not realized it already, Ketahn would show Ivy that he was the only male worthy of her on this world or any other.

Something else had happened during those days, something he'd not been able to explain—something that had only intensified his desire for Ivy. Her scent had been growing stronger, fuller, sweeter. Though similar to the fragrance of her arousal, this was different...and, in its own ways, had been more maddening, piercing straight to his deepest instincts and constantly challenging his already tenuous self-control.

This was quickly surpassing a mere desire to mate and becoming a *need*.

He'd left the den today for two reasons—to deliver meat and make her dress. But he could not deny that escaping Ivy's increasingly potent scent was a welcome boon. Though he longed to fill his lungs with it even now, the time away had allowed him to recover his senses a little. That was good. He didn't want to frighten her by falling into a frenzy—but more, he didn't want to hurt her. As small as she was, as fragile as she was, it did not seem likely that she would make it through mating uninjured, even were he not in a frenzied state.

Yet another day in his den, breathing her in, would've shattered his resolve.

Ketahn made the final stitch, tied it off, and trimmed the thread. Tucking the needle against his palm, he smoothed his hands over the dress, flattening the fabric. It was impossible not to see Ivy's pale, smooth skin in his mind's eye as he did so, impossible not to imagine this silk sliding over the curves of her breasts, settling over her hips, brushing along her—

A sound in the tunnel outside the den caught his attention, just different enough from the dully echoing conversations and the noise of crafters doing their work—a whisper of movement, legs sliding over stone. He looked over his shoulder toward the den's entrance.

The silk hanging in the entryway swung aside. Ketahn quickly folded the dress to obscure its shape as Rekosh slipped into the den, the cloth falling back into place behind him.

Rekosh tilted his head, mandibles slowly squeezing closed. "I must have pricked my hide one time too many, or else I am bearing witness to a spirit. The real Ketahn would have departed long ago."

Ketahn chittered and turned to face Rekosh, bracing his hands on the work slab and shielding the dress with his body. "Perhaps he did, and I am but a reflection of your loneliness, Rekosh."

"Loneliness?" Rekosh huffed and moved toward his pile of furs and silk, lifting his tool-laden sash off as he went. "I speak to more vrix in a day than can be counted."

"I am aware. And they share a great many whispers, I am sure. But those are not the same, are they?"

"So, you are the true Ketahn," Rekosh said with a chitter, "for only he seeks to pierce so deep with every thrust."

"You bite, I claw. Is that not the way it has always been?"

Rekosh plucked his blackrock knife out of the pouch before placing the sash on a carved stone shelf. He reached to a nearby basket with one hand, lifted the lid, and removed a piece of moonblossom fruit from within. "Have ever I treated you with anything short of the greatest respect and admiration, my friend?"

Ketahn's mandibles twitched upward, but he stopped them before they could rise more than a finger's span; he'd been about to smile. Smiles were only for Ivy. Other vrix would not understand. "Yes. Most every time we have spoken."

"You know me nearly as well as your broodsister does." Rekosh sliced open the fruit's thick skin with his knife.

"Ahnset certainly does know you well. That is why she avoids you, Rekosh."

"I cannot argue that." Cutting a wedge out of the fruit, Rekosh lifted it to his mouth, caught it between his teeth, and tore the soft meat from the rind. "Perhaps I should embrace my loneliness, as you have, and go live in some mire out in the Tangle."

"Take care, Rekosh. You may find the idea of such a life too appealing to resist, should you consider it for long."

Rekosh sliced out another piece of fruit and slipped it into his mouth, regarding Ketahn as he did so. He folded his lower arms across his abdomen and leaned a shoulder against the wall. "What has truly brought you out of your exile today, Ketahn?"

Ketahn's fingers curled, and his claws scraped stone. If he'd not told Ahnset when she was twenty segments away from Ivy, he wasn't going to tell Rekosh now, but...he did not like withholding information from his friends and broodsister. It seemed to defile the trust they'd all built with each other over their lifetimes.

"I simply felt the urge to weave."

"Ah. Understandable enough." Rekosh lifted the remaining moonblossom fruit to his mouth and squeezed it, forcing the fruit within to separate from the rind and fall into his waiting gullet. Once done, he extended his red tongue, licked way the juice lingering around his mouth, and tossed the empty rind into a waste basket near the entrance. "That is, it would be understandable enough were I speaking to anyone else."

Ketahn narrowed his eyes, fighting back a wave of tension. "What do you mean, Rekosh?"

"You have not touched a loom in years, Ketahn, and you have not entered Takarahl of your own will in nearly as long." Rekosh snatched up a scrap of silk from the shelf and used it to wipe his hand and clean the blade of his knife. "So why would I believe that you showed up at my den before suncrest this morning and asked to use my tools because you had a sudden urge to weave?"

Raising an arm, Ketahn raked his claws through his hair until they met the tie keeping the strands pulled back. He longed for it to be Ivy's fingers doing this. Longed to be able to say so out loud. "There is more, yes, but you must trust that I cannot share it with you."

Rekosh's mandibles twitched, and his posture stiffened. "You know everything between us—all of us—remains so, Ketahn. I have not once shared your secrets with anyone."

Ketahn stepped forward and stretched a foreleg, touching it to Rekosh's. "I know that, Rekosh. I trust you with my life, my friend, but this matter..."

"You mean to bend to her will?" Rekosh asked softly. "To... win her, as she has demanded?"

Though Ketahn understood exactly who Rekosh meant, understood exactly what Rekosh was asking, the mere thought of it was so infuriating and alarming that he couldn't force a single word out of his throat in response. Especially being so close to... to something more with Ivy, the notion of mating Zurvashi made Ketahn's insides tight, knotted, and heavy, made furious fires spark in his chest, made him long to sink his claws into something and tear it apart.

"We all know this High Claiming will be different," Rekosh continued, speaking with uncharacteristic care. "All of this is building toward something, Ketahn, something...immense. And you cannot hi—"

Rekosh snapped his mouth shut at the sound of heavy steps and clinking metal in the tunnel outside, his gaze darting toward the entryway.

Ketahn's eyes moved in the same direction, his tension intensifying eightfold. Even without seeing, he knew what those steps meant. And with each one, Rekosh's unspoken words echoed through Ketahn's mind.

And you cannot hide from it.

Those steps moved directly to the opposite side of the entryway; at least four females, by the sound, if not more.

The hanging cloth jerked aside, and a huge figure filled the entryway, her gold jewelry shimmering in the light cast by Rekosh's crystal.

Prime Fang Korahla ducked low enough to peer through the opening. "Weaver, leave. Hunter, remain."

Ketahn met Rekosh's gaze briefly. He'd never seen his friend so tense, so concerned. He had never seen so uncertain a light gleaming in Rekosh's eyes.

"I would never dream of disobeying," Rekosh said, moving to the entryway. "I am not so foolish as to believe this den is my own."

"You are the one who likes to talk, are you not?" Korahla grumbled. "Resist the urge to do so until this matter is concluded."

The Prime Fang shifted aside to allow Rekosh through the entryway, who glanced at Ketahn over his shoulder before crossing into the tunnel and out of sight.

Ketahn backed up to the work slab again, which was just tall enough for his hindquarters to slip beneath, snatched up the dress, and held it behind his back. The queen's approach was heavy enough that he could feel the faint vibrations of it in the stone beneath his legs before she even appeared in the entryway. Zurvashi made that opening look as though it had been sized for a hatchling.

She leaned forward and twisted her torso, her golden adornments clinking and clanging as she drew herself through the too-small opening with a brutal sort of grace that was far more the result of strength than agility.

Once she was through, her body dominated the den, seeming to fill up every bit of space, to force out all the air. Her scent crashed into Ketahn even as her eyes settled upon him; it was stronger than ever, and it poured fire into his blood that had nothing to do with his anger or hatred.

"My Claws always pass along accurate information," she said, turning her head from side to side to glance around the small den, "but I did not believe them when they told me you had remained in Takarahl after bringing meat."

Ketahn's fist curled around the dress, but he stilled it before he could strengthen his hold any further. He would not damage it, no matter how overwhelming his emotions became—no matter how overwhelming the queen's scent became.

Zurvashi extended an arm and flattened her palm against the wall to the side of Ketahn's head. She didn't even have space enough to straighten her arm fully. "You seem tense, little Ketahn. Did you think I would not know? You can do nothing in Takarahl of which I will not be informed. This city is mine. *You* are mine."

He tipped his head back to glare up at her, keeping his shoulders squared and the dress securely in hand. "If I have learned anything during my time in the Tangle, Zurvashi, it is that nothing is certain."

"Do you truly believe that, Ketahn, even though you know me?" She leaned closer, caging him in by bracing another arm on the wall to his other side. "I am the queen. I will have what I desire. That is certain."

Her nearness forced Ketahn backward. His hindquarters scraped along the underside of the work slab, his back bumped into the slab's hard edge, and he was forced to bend his rear legs to harsh angles to fit them in the limited space. "So you have said more times than I care to count. Loudly enough that every vrix in the Tangle is sure to have heard by now."

"Then heed me, my little hunter." She leaned closer still, close enough that her mouth was less than a handspan from Ketahn's cheek and one of her mandibles brushed his neck. "The High Claiming will be upon us in four days. You know what I expect, and I will have little patience to spare should you fail to fulfill my desires."

He could smell nothing but her scent; it had become the very air around him, and it would either suffocate him or drive him into a frenzy right there. Her touch made his hide itch with unpleasant heat, and her breath was harsh against his skin.

Ketahn's arm trembled as he clamped the dress tighter. It was for Ivy, and Ivy was the one he wanted. Ivy was the one to whom he would be bound. He focused on the fabric, on its texture, its softness, on its connection to Ivy—on his connection to Ivy. And, slowly, the influence of Zurvashi's scent faded. It was not the fragrance he longed for. It was the not the fragrance he craved.

It would not be the fragrance that broke his resolve.

The queen grasped Ketahn's arm—the one tucked behind his back—and tugged it forward. His hearts stuttered with a fresh flare of heat, and it took every bit of his willpower to prevent himself from raising his arms and legs in challenge.

She leaned back as she forced his arm up, moving the folded dress into the scant space between them. "This had best be part of your efforts toward that end, Ketahn." With one of her free hands, she grabbed the dress and yanked it, tearing the fabric.

That sound filled the den with crushing finality, more stunning and penetrating than a crash of thunder from directly overhead.

Everything within Ketahn stilled. Hatred and rage roared at the core of his spirit, flooding his muscles with pure, raw, bloodthirsty strength. In his mind's eye, he surged forward to attack the queen.

But in reality, he just kept glaring at her, making no effort to disguise his emotions—and every effort to prevent himself from succumbing to them.

Zurvashi chittered; the sound was bitter, arrogant, and spiteful all at once. "It will take much more than a scrap of silk to fulfill your duty, Ketahn. I suggest you busy yourself. No more hiding in the jungle. No more pretending you have a choice." She lifted one of her lower hands, pressed the pad of a finger to the underside of his jaw, and forced his head back farther. "I will see you soon, sweet one."

She flicked her finger off him, clipping his chin with her claw and producing a flare of pain that was immediately drowned out by his fury. Releasing her hold on the torn dress, she shoved away from the wall, turned, and squeezed her way out into the tunnel, almost ripping down the cloth over the entryway in the process.

Ketahn watched her silk cloths ripple, her muscles bunch and stretch, and her golden ornaments gleam. He watched her, and he longed to snatch up his spear and plunge it into her back. So long as he could hit one of her hearts, she was unlikely to survive...and then his death would have been worthwhile.

But he cast that idea aside when his gaze fell upon the dress. He lifted it as the entryway covering fell into place and the heavy steps of Zurvashi and her guards started down the tunnel, staring at the torn silk, the ruined pattern.

All this anger, all this hate, all this pain, and what could he do with it? Of what use was it to him?

Mandibles twitching in agitation, Ketahn turned away from the entrance and laid the dress upon the work slab, spreading it to assess the damage. He ran his fingers delicately along the tear. It could be fixed—more importantly, it could be fixed without leaving much sign of the damage.

The hanging cloth rustled, and legs rasped over the floor.

"Are you all right, Ketahn?" asked Rekosh.

"Yes," replied Ketahn distractedly as he reached for fresh thread.

"You do not seem yourself..."

Something warm tickled Ketahn's chin. One of his hands snapped up, catching the drop of blood that fell from the small cut the queen had inflicted just before it could land on the pristine silk of the dress. Ketahn stared at the blood on his palm.

How much more would Zurvashi wring out of him before this was all done?

"Not another damned drop," he growled.

"What did you say?" Rekosh asked, shifting closer.

Once again, Zurvashi was keeping Ketahn from his Ivy for much longer than he'd hoped, but he would not return to his female empty handed. He would not allow the queen to deny his mate-to-be anything—not this dress, and certainly not Ketahn himself.

Ketahn closed his fingers over the blood and pressed the back of that hand against his chin to stem the blood flow. "I need to use your tools a while longer, my friend."

Chapter Twenty-Two

RUBBING her palms along her arms, Ivy stared out into the moonlit night. She knew she should've been sleeping. On any other night, she would've already been asleep, curled up safe, secure, and warm in Ketahn's arms. But it was now well past nightfall, and he'd yet to return from Takarahl.

Worry gnawed at her. What if something had happened to him? The queen had hurt him before; what would stop her from doing so again?

Ketahn will come home.

Home.

Was this nest she shared with Ketahn her home? Despite the conditions in which she lived, despite having to fight and work for everything in order to survive, Ivy's time with Ketahn had been the happiest of her life.

Ivy brushed her fingers over the woven branches around the entrance. "Home."

The word felt true. It felt right.

But it wasn't really the nest, was it? It was Ketahn. It was he who made this cozy nest a home, it was he who made her feel safe, who made her feel...cared for.

She shook her head and chuckled to herself. "I'm happier in a spider's nest than I was surrounded by modern conveniences. I'm crazy."

Rising to her feet, Ivy winced at a sudden cramp in her pelvis. She'd had a few of them since waking up this morning. At first, she'd wondered if she might finally be starting her period—which would really suck since she didn't have any of those *modern conveniences* on hand. Though she'd been lucky it hadn't happened thus far, she knew it was only a matter of time. But Ivy now wondered if she was simply ovulating. Her breasts were tender, as they usually were during that time, and there'd been no spotting to indicate her menstrual cycle had begun.

Cryosleep had many side-effects, most of which were short term. Her disorientation and weakness after waking had been amongst the most common and most fleeting, but the medical techs had told the colonists to expect their bodies to take time to recalibrate. Between the stasis, the drugs that they'd been injected with before going under, and being on a new planet, no one was supposed to feel like themselves right away. Everyone's hormones would be off for a little while. For the women, that meant potential delays in menstrual cycles—perhaps as long as six months.

Moving to the back of the nest, where they kept their food and water, she grabbed a waterskin and a spare silk cloth. Once the waterskin was open, she dampened the cloth, pressed it to her cheek, and closed her eyes. The coolness was welcome against her heated skin.

The night air was, as usual, muggy. At least during the day, she had the stream to swim in for relief. Nights like tonight made her long for a rainstorm despite her fears, just for the drop in temperature. It was surprisingly cold during those nighttime storms, but she didn't have to worry about the cold affecting her —at least not with Ketahn holding her.

With nothing to do but wait, Ivy removed her shirt and shorts and ran the cool, wet cloth over her body. It was wonderful to wipe away the sweat and feel clean. As she ran the cloth along her smooth legs, she couldn't help but smile to herself. She was incredibly thankful for the body hair removal that had been provided to all the colonists during training. She'd never have to worry about shaving her armpits, legs, or grooming between her legs again. All that remained was a small patch of hair above her pussy.

After taking a drink from the waterskin, she closed it and returned it to its place. Unwilling to put her threadbare, sweat dampened garments back on, Ivy nudged them aside with her foot. They could be washed tomorrow. She plucked up the large silk cloth she used as a blanket and wrapped it around her body. She'd just finished tucking the corner in when the nest rocked. Ivy started, a jolt of fear sweeping through her before it was swept away on a flood of elation.

Ketahn was back.

His claws rasped across the exterior of the nest, moving closer and closer to the entrance, until finally his body blocked out the night and he drew himself in though the opening. His markings lit up instantly in the blue glow of the uncovered crystal, and his eyes sparkled like amethysts.

"I was starting to worry you wouldn't come back tonight," Ivy said.

"I did not mean to be away for so long," he said as he swung off his bag, shifting it to his front to grab something from within. "I was..."

His words died, and he lifted his head, drawing in a deep breath through his nose slits. A long, low rumble sounded in his chest. Ketahn's gaze fell upon Ivy, and his whole body stiffened, his arm stilling in the bag.

Ivy took a step toward him, brow creasing. "Are you okay?"

He inhaled again and squeezed his eyes shut. "That scent..." One of his front legs shifted forward, brushing against her ankle before sliding slowly up and hooking under the blanket. The fine hairs on his leg teased at her calf, the side of her knee, and her outer thigh, sending a thrill through her.

Her sex clenched, and Ivy squeezed her thighs together as

289

though that could assuage the sudden ache permeating her core. She clutched the blanket to keep it from coming loose as she glanced down at his leg, which was partially hidden beneath it.

"What scent?" she asked, taking a step away and sniffing the air. All she could detect was the lush jungle flora, earth, and that spicy, woodsy, mahogany scent that she'd come recognize as Ketahn's. "I don't smell anything."

Ketahn huffed and shook his head sharply, withdrawing his leg. The claspers against his pelvis twitched as he returned his attention to his bag. He withdrew a piece of folded white silk from within. "I have this for you, Ivy."

"For me?" She closed the distance between them and accepted the silk. It unfurled. Tilting her head, she took hold of the other strap and gasped.

Ivy turned toward the glowing crystal and held the dress up. The material, while not transparent, was delicate and sheer enough to allow some light through, which accentuated the web-like patterns stitched into the fabric. She stroked her thumb over the soft material. It was sleeveless, with the straps running down to cross at the center, where they'd cover her breasts, and the skirt looked as though it would hang to midthigh.

"You made this? For me?" Ivy asked, though the answer was obvious. What vrix would wear something clearly made for a human body?

Ketahn's front legs extended, coming down to either side of her, and he eased toward her. "Yes, Ivy. Only for you."

Tears stung her eyes, but she refused to cry, even if they would've been happy tears. "It's beautiful." She looked at him over her shoulder. "Thank you."

He gathered her hair in one hand, drawing it aside to bare her neck, and leaned closer to take in another deep breath.

Ivy chuckled. "Do you think I stink?"

"No," he rumbled, meeting her gaze.

"Good. You had me worried for a second." Her smile

widened, and she turned her face toward the dress again, taking a step away from him. "I'm going to try it on."

Untucking the blanket, she let it fall to pool at her feet before bending down to step into the dress. She drew the silky material up over her legs and hips and slipped her arms through the straps, adjusting the coverings over her breasts. It fit perfectly. Like it had been made for her. Ivy smiled—it *was* made for her. The silk was cool to the touch but quickly warmed against her skin, and the delicate hem tickled her thighs.

"I love it, Ketahn," she said, running her hands down the skirt.

She felt him move up behind her again just before his hands settled over her shoulders. His rough palms were warm, their touch gentle and soothing, exactly what she needed after a long day spent alone in this place.

Slowly, he smoothed his hands down her arms. "I am glad, Ivy."

He lowered his head so it was beside hers and turned his face into her hair. When he inhaled, a sound rolled in his chest—one part purr, one part growl, one part chirrup.

Ivy arched a brow. "Ketahn?"

He placed his other set of hands on her hips, and they, too, trekked downward, brushing over the fabric of her skirt. They did not stop at the hem; his fingers dipped lower, to the bare skin of her thighs. They remained against her skin as he drew them up again, lifting the dress along with them. Ivy's heart quickened as he raised the skirt higher, his palms rasping over her skin.

His upper hands moved back up her arms, but they didn't return to her shoulders—they drifted to her chest, each covering one of her breasts and squeezing them. Her nipples hardened against his palms.

She sighed, her lips parting and eyes fluttering shut. His hands were hot against her breasts, swiftly heating up the silk between them, and her blood heated just as quickly, pooling fire low in her belly. She covered his hands with her own, pressing them more firmly against her breasts, delighting in the feel of silk stroking her nipples. A soft moan escaped Ivy as her head fell back against his shoulder. It had been so long since she'd been touched, so long...

But she'd never been touched like this, not by someone like Ketahn, not even in her wildest imaginings. Ketahn's caresses were infused with care, longing, desperation...with affection.

His lower hands bunched her skirt over her hips, baring her to the open air, which now felt cool compared to his heated touch. The hands upon her breasts kneaded harder, and his fingers caught her pearled nipples and pinched them. She gasped. Pleasure raced through her, spearing her clit, making it throb with desire.

Ivy's grip on his hands tightened. "Ketahn..."

He moved even closer to her, until his chest was against her back. Something thick, hard, and slick pressed along her ass and probed her thighs.

Ivy instinctively arched against it, needing more; she tilted her hips and moaned as it glided between her thighs and along her slick folds.

Ketahn growled. The sound pulsed into her and raced to her core, its thrill enhanced by the strengthening of his grip and the prick of his claws on her hips and breasts. His claspers crept around her waist, encircling it fully, and bent down to brush across the patch of hair on her pelvis. The tip of one grazed her clit. The delicious sensation it wrought was nearly strong enough to make her knees give out.

Ivy's breath caught, and her eyes snapped open. It was only then that she realized what they were doing. What *she* was doing. Everything felt so...so *good*, and she hadn't wanted it to stop, hadn't wanted those sensations to end. But this... Oh God, wasn't this wrong?

Was it?

She dragged his hands from her breasts and jerked forward, tearing herself out of his hold. Chest heaving, skin flushed, and sex pulsing in arousal with her essence dripping down her inner thighs, Ivy turned to face Ketahn.

"Ketahn, what are you—" Her eyes widened.

His cock glistened in the crystal's blue glow.

It protruded from his slit, long and thick, with two bulges on either side of its base. The shaft widened as it curved up toward the tapered tip, where there was a two-inch slit. Its skin was the same purple as his markings.

Nothing about it was human, and yet it aroused Ivy all the same.

Her core pulsed. She released a shuddering breath and rubbed her thighs together, which were coated in her slick.

That was what she had felt against her ass. That...that was what her body craved.

What *Ivy* craved.

Chapter Twenty-Three

THOUGH ALL KETAHN wanted in that moment was to be inside Ivy, to sate this consuming hunger, he remained in place and dragged his gaze over her body. The silk dress cradled her breasts and hugged her waist, following the curve of her hips. The bottom reached the middle of her thighs, leaving most of the pale flesh of her legs bare for him to appreciate. In the crystal's dull light, the fabric was a silvery blue that made her eyes seem all the brighter.

To see her wearing something he'd created, something he'd given her, made Ketahn's chest swell. It was his silk, his crafting, his gift, and it was on his female. She was not vrix, but she was beautiful.

Ketahn filled his lungs with Ivy; her scent dominated the air, that irresistible sweetness layered with the heady, demanding fragrance of her arousal, creating something stronger and more alluring than he could ever have imagined possible.

His stem throbbed, pierced by a deep ache that spread outward to the tips of his legs and fingers. In all his life he'd never needed anything as desperately as he needed her now.

And this time, he wouldn't fight it. He was done fighting it.

The Eight had led Ketahn to Ivy, and it was well past time to claim her.

He closed the distance between them. Her eyes flicked up to meet his, gleaming with uncertainty and yearning. With his upper hands, he grasped the straps of her dress at her shoulders; with his lower, he took hold of the bottom of the dress. The backs of his fingers glided across her warm, soft skin as he lifted the dress. Ivy shivered and raised her arms, not resisting as he removed her clothing. Her hair tumbled around her bare shoulders as it came free of the fabric.

The uncertainty in her eyes grew, and she crossed her arms over her breasts, catching her bottom lip between her teeth. She had not hidden herself from his gaze like this since their earliest days together.

Ketahn would not have that. He would not have her hiding from him.

He moved without thought, taking her wrists in two of his hands and prying them away from her chest. His spinnerets were already working as he raised her arms over her head and clamped her wrists together in one hand. He passed the thick strand of silk to his upper hand.

Ivy gasped and looked up, tugging on her arms. "Ketahn, what are you doing?"

"You are mine, Ivy," he growled, winding the silk around her wrists and arms, binding them together with a series of intricate, instinctual knots. Her skin grew impossibly warmer under his touch as he attached the strand to the ceiling of the nest, allowing her only enough slack to remain on her feet. He released her wrists.

She grunted and pulled down on her arms, attempting to back away from him. He easily dragged her back to him.

Ketahn wound the silk strand lower, using it to hold her close. He looped and crossed it around her torso and between her breasts, adding more knots so it ran beneath those full, fleshy mounds. His hands moved faster and faster as he lashed the strand around her waist, her hips, her thighs, and ankles, effortlessly overpowering her when she tried to kick at him or pull her legs away.

"Ketahn!"

He caught her jaw and lowered his face to hers. "I have conquered you, Ivy, and now I claim you."

Speaking required more effort than ever before, more focus and willpower than he'd thought possible. Between her feel, her heat, her beauty, and her scent—by the Eight, that scent!—Ketahn could barely form a full thought. His body had forced his mind aside. The desperation in his movements was as much from instinct now as from desire, and instinct demanded this—the Claiming. A female had to be overpowered, restrained, suspended. Conquered. And then he could make her his.

Somewhere in the deepest reaches of his mind, he knew what this was. He was succumbing to the frenzy.

There would be no stopping it now...not until he'd mated with her. Not until she'd taken his seed.

He spun her around so her back was toward him and wove the silk strand through the loops he'd made around her body, quickly crafting a web of interconnected anchors. His stem pulsed, the pressure within it so immense that he was certain it would burst before ever touching her again, and his heartbeats were like an unending peal of thunder.

Turning her to face him again, he raised his upper arms, stood high, and attached the strand to the ceiling at a dozen points, hoisting Ivy off the floor.

Ivy yelped, wriggling within her bindings, making herself shake and sway. "Please, Ketahn! Let me go. I don't know what this is but let me go."

The fear in her voice was the same as Ketahn had heard when she'd first looked upon him, and it pierced his lust-driven frenzy. Her cheeks were pink, her golden hair tousled, and her nipples hard and straining. The bindings he'd fashioned held her torso upright with her breasts jutting toward him, her thighs spread apart, and her calves bent back out of the way. Her weight was evenly distributed between the various loops around her body, ensuring the silk was not digging painfully into her skin anywhere.

Ketahn swept his gaze over Ivy. She was bared to him, exposed to him.

And she was afraid.

Drawing upon what little willpower he'd retained, he reached forward and buried a hand in her hair, cradling the back of her head. She met his gaze with rounded eyes.

"You are mine, Ivy," he said, his voice rough and raw. "My *nyleea*. I will not hurt you."

HER BROW CREASED as she searched his eyes. Slowly, some of her fear bled away, and a trusting light bolstered her gaze. "I know you won't. I...I just don't know what this is."

"This is the Claiming."

Gently, he swept her hair behind her shoulders, placed a hand on her chest, and trailed it down. He grazed her skin with his claws, his hunger intensifying each time she trembled, each time her skin twitched, each time tiny bumps rose on her flesh. When he reached her breasts, he stroked a budded nipple between his finger and thumb.

Ivy's lashes fluttered and she arched into his touch. "Ketahn..."

His chest rumbled in appreciation, but he didn't linger there; her scent was too much to ignore, drawing him toward its source, toward the center of her heat, her desire. Ketahn sank low, continuing the downward trek of his hand over her belly. He teased at the short triangle of hair that pointed down toward her slit.

Lifting his lower hands to her ass, Ketahn squeezed her yielding flesh and angled her slit toward him. Her heady fragrance struck him anew, and he breathed it in greedily, fixing his gaze upon the open pink petals of her sex. They glistened with nectar, and more of it was evident upon her inner thighs.

Her scent beckoned him, demanding he taste her. He opened his mouth, extended his tongue, and dragged it along her slit.

Ivy gasped, her body shuddering. "Oh God..."

She tasted sweeter than any fruit. She tasted unlike *anything*, tasted like she truly was from another world, like her essence was so pure and potent that it was never meant for the likes of Ketahn. His hunger flared, declaring itself in a fierce growl that made her shudder anew. The pulse in his stem was so strong now, so rapid, that it seemed impossible for him to hold back his seed, impossible to avoid giving in to the torrent of pleasure Ivy had granted him through this single taste.

He lapped at her thighs, grazing her skin with his mandible fangs and licking away all her nectar, unwilling to let any go to waste. Then he returned to her slit. He pressed his tongue between her folds and swept it upward, sampling every bit of that slick, pink flesh, seeking every drop of her sweet essence.

When his tongue flicked over the little nub at the apex of her slit, Ivy gasped again and bucked, her thighs quivering on either side of his head.

"Oh Ketahn, please..."

Ketahn had touched that bud when he'd first inspected her slit a lifetime ago. Her reaction had been similar but for one thing —this time, she did not say *no*.

He lowered his mandibles, pressing them to the undersides of her thighs, and ravished her slit with his tongue. He stroked that nub, he delved between her petals, he pressed the tip of his tongue inside her and growled at the tight heat of her channel.

All throughout, Ivy pleaded, begged, and moaned, straining against the webbing, but she did not tell him to stop. She wanted only more. He had never seen a female so responsive. Had never heard such beautiful, musical sounds as those his Ivy made while he pleasured her.

Clutching her ass, he returned his tongue to that nub and

299

circled it, flicked it, laved it with attention as he stared up at her face. Her brow creased, her lips parted, and her chest heaved with her panting breaths until, suddenly, her body tensed. She threw her head back and cried out, rocking her hips against his tongue as fresh nectar flowed from her channel.

Ketahn lifted her higher and positioned her over his face, drinking her essence as he continued to worship that nub with his tongue. He was eager for more of her, eager to watch her, eager to learn her every response to his attentions. Her cries escalated.

She writhed in his hold, struggling against the restraints, but she arched toward him, seeking his tongue. "Ketahn! Oh God, please, please, I can't... Ah!"

Her body stiffened again as she released another flood of nectar.

It was more than he could bear. His blood blazed hotter than a goldworker's fire, his hide was taut and tingling, and his stem was straining toward her with such desperation that it hurt. Though Ivy was the one restrained, Ketahn was the one bound— bound by his overwhelming, uncontrollable need for this female.

Ketahn rose, keeping his lower hands on her backside. He reached around her with his upper hands, banding one around her lower back and cradling the back of her head with the other, twining his fingers in her hair. His claspers extended on their own, wrapping around her hips. The tip of his stem pressed against her entrance.

Breath ragged, Ivy opened her eyes and met his gaze. The blue of her eyes was nearly engulfed by black.

Ketahn tipped her face up closer to his. "You are mine, Ivy."

Tightening his grip on her ass, he pulled her toward him hard as he thrust forward, forcing her entrance open to take his stem. He encountered none of the resistance he'd expected. Entry with a female vrix was a struggle, a fight, a battle of strength and will against muscles determined to keep everything out.

But with Ivy, he'd slid right in, aided by her slick nectar. As though her body welcomed him.

Ivy released a pained cry. Her eyes flared, and her body tensed, but she did not push him out. Her channel gripped him, hot and wet.

Ketahn shuddered against a wave of pressure and pleasure that threatened to shatter his mind. He tilted his head back and arched his spine, burying himself deeper in her and coaxing a ragged growl from his throat. Her silken heat clamped around his stem with surprising strength, but it still did not force him out—it only seemed to draw him in farther.

Nothing in all his life had felt so good. Nothing had been even a sliver as pleasurable. And he wanted—he *needed*—more. More of this, more of her.

"My *nyleea*," he rumbled. The heat inside him built to an unbearable degree, burning in his veins. His senses were clouded, overtaken by her scent, by ecstasy, by Ivy.

Ketahn's fingers flexed. He could hold it back no longer.

He let the frenzy take over.

IVY'S HEART POUNDED, its pulse echoing between her legs where Ketahn's cock stretched her. The initial hurt of his entry had faded, and now all she felt was incredible fullness—fullness and heat. Perspiration trickled down her spine, her neck, and between her breasts. Her skin was abuzz with sensation, and each time her nipples scraped against Ketahn's plated chest, another bolt of pleasure spiraled through her, making her clit thrum.

Ketahn eased back, withdrawing his cock and stretching her anew as its width expanded, only to thrust back into her. The angle of his thrusts struck her clit and G-spot perfectly. Ivy whimpered. He did it again and again, each time faster and harder than the last, sharpening her pleasure, making it coil tight within her core.

It was too much. She'd never felt so full, had never been so blasted by ecstasy, and she was certain she'd come undone, body and soul. But there was no escape; Ketahn was her world now.

His spicy scent filled her nose, his heat bathed her skin, his touch cocooned her, and his silk kept her bound and helpless but to feel *everything*.

She felt the rasp of his hide against her skin, his claspers anchoring her hips, his hands gripping her ass, and their claws pricking her flesh, all of it adding to the whirlwind of sensation swirling through her. Most of all, she felt his cock plunging in and out of her. It was pain and pleasure, a torment that scattered her thoughts into a million fragments and an ecstasy that fused them all together again as something new and powerful.

Ivy came apart, swept away by a roaring inferno that consumed her, its flames licking at every nerve, stoking her pleasure, building it higher and higher. Cries tore from her throat, and her body tensed as wave after wave of fire rushed through her. Her sex squeezed, clamping around Ketahn's cock and quivering as liquid heat flooded her.

Ketahn hissed and quickened his pace. His claspers clutched her hips, their tips digging into her skin. His hide slapped against her flesh, and Ivy's slick ran down her thighs. His front legs rose, darting past her on either side to slam against the wall, granting him only more leverage and making his thrusts all the deeper.

Unbelievably, another orgasm swiftly followed. Ivy's muscles strained against her bindings, and she clenched her teeth as powerful tremors rocked her.

"Ketahn," she rasped again and again.

His cock swelled, stretching her even more, and his already hard body tensed. Ketahn roared her name and pounded into her, his claspers clamping her in place. His shaft pulsed, somehow expanding further, and his hot seed exploded within her—but it was accompanied by a firm, fluttery sensation at the head of his cock. Something swept insistently against her cervix, stroking her inner walls.

That fluttering quickly grew in speed and urgency as the pulsing of his shaft intensified, turning into a vibration. Ivy's gaze met Ketahn's as her panting breaths escalated.

He touched his forehead to hers, shuddered, and growled. Another spurt of seed flooded her.

Ivy's skin prickled, and the sensations within her built higher and higher until Ivy could withstand it no more. She surrendered. Intense white filled her vision, blinding her. She squeezed her eyes shut as she was hurtled into another universe where only Ketahn and this intense, impossible pleasure existed. Her scream echoed into the jungle, raw with passion, with rapture, with pleasure so pure she'd been scorched to ash and reborn.

The white dominating her mind faded slowly toward black, and her awareness of both her own body and Ketahn's returned. His arms and claspers were around her securely, holding her with that gentle strength that seemed to come so naturally to him. His embrace was all that kept her from floating away. Without Ketahn, she'd be spiraling off into the stars, drifting through the vast emptiness of space in a state of stupefied bliss.

The beating of his hearts was a comfort, a soothing rhythm lulling her to sleep...

As the darkness behind her eyelids solidified, wrapping around her like a warm, soft blanket, Ketahn rumbled, "Now you are mine, my *nyleea*. My mate." He smoothed a hand over her hair. "My heartsthread."

Chapter Twenty-Four

IVY AWOKE to the sound of birds singing. Her lashes fluttered open. Though the cloth over the nest's entrance was closed, it flapped enough in the breeze to allow dancing beams of golden light in along its edges.

Inhaling deeply, she rolled onto her back with a sigh and stretched—only to freeze when nearly every muscle in her body protested the movement. More than that, her sex throbbed, and there was a heaviness in her core.

Ivy's heart quickened. Memories bombarded her in a flash, reminding her in vivid detail of everything that had occurred between her and Ketahn.

I had sex with a spider man.

She bolted upright, her blanket falling to her lap as she searched the nest, but Ketahn was nowhere in sight. Ivy wasn't sure how to feel about that. She would have liked for him to be here, to comfort her and ease her anxiety, but she was also grateful that he was gone so she could process the fact that she...that she'd had sex with Ketahn.

"I just had sex with an alien spider," she breathed.

Just as those words left her lips, she realized that she was sitting upon something incredibly soft—softer even than the lush furs Ketahn kept on the floor. She looked down to find herself atop what she could only describe as a nest of silk. Countless thin, fluffed threads were woven together to form a chaotic but intricate whole, resulting in something reminiscent of a huge cotton ball—and it was even softer than it looked.

Where had it come from? Had...had Ketahn made this while she slept? It was positioned in their usual sleeping spot, piled atop Ketahn's furs and spare silk cloths to form a pallet. She ran her fingers over the threads, marveling at how they didn't snag or separate much.

Ivy stilled when her eyes fell upon her wrist.

She held her trembling hands out in front of her. There was some redness around her wrists from the restraints Ketahn had created, and as she examined the rest of her body, she noticed a few other places where the silken strands had left their marks, but most of them had faded. There was some bruising and a few small scratches on her hips and thighs, undoubtedly left by his hands, claws, and claspers, but nothing serious. She looked like she'd recently survived a bout of rough, wild sex.

As she moved, something seeped from her pussy.

Keeping her breathing even and calm, Ivy slid a hand between her thighs and delicately touched her sex, feeling her tender flesh. There was something there, something thick and wet that also coated her inner thighs.

Ketahn's seed.

It was the final piece of evidence that made those memories a reality.

Oh God, she'd had sex with a spider alien and...and...she'd liked it.

No, she'd *loved* it.

Ivy hugged her legs to her chest and buried her face against her knees. She waited for the disgust, the self-loathing, the regret, waited for any sense that what she'd done was wrong, wrong, wrong...

But none came.

Every touch, every caress, every stroke of his cock inside her had felt right. Her body hadn't cared that he was an inhuman creature, hadn't cared that he had four arms, six legs, and eight eyes; it had simply craved the feel of his skin against hers, of his hands all over her body, of his cock buried deep in her pussy.

She had craved him.

Ivy ran a shaky hand through her hair. What...what did that mean? What did that make her?

Shoving those thoughts aside, she pushed herself to her feet. More of Ketahn's seed dripped down her inner thighs. She closed her eyes, took in a deep breath, and released it slowly. Her legs felt as though they'd give out at any moment. She didn't know if she was in a state of shock, or if this was a result of...her body having been well and truly loved.

She opened her eyes and extended a hand, using the wall as support as she made her way to the back of the nest. Grabbing a water skin and using the same cloth from the night before, she washed herself and scrubbed between her legs.

As she was walking back to the bed of fluffed silk, Ivy's eyes fell upon the dress Ketahn had made for her. It was folded neatly and laid beside the bedding. She picked it up, and it unfurled with a soft rasp. She never would have guessed that someone like Ketahn—so big, so dangerous, a predator at his prime—could create something so delicate, intricate, and fine. The threads shimmered in the erratic morning light that snuck in past the entryway cloth.

Ivy had just pulled the dress on when the nest bounced and rocked, signaling Ketahn's return.

The sunlight striking his hide as he entered made some of his scars stand out starkly; they were like a map of his past, of his battles and struggles, and she found herself suddenly longing to touch each one. To learn about each one.

When he met her gaze, he lifted his mandibles in his version of a smile, and Ivy couldn't help but smile back. He unslung his bag from his shoulders as he reached back to tuck the hanging cloth aside, allowing the full light to spill into the nest. The movements made his hair, which was pulled into a bundle of black, white, and violet, fall over his shoulder.

"Um, hi." Ivy turned her feet inward slightly, feeling more shy and awkward than ever.

Holding his bag by its straps, Ketahn approached her. He placed the bag on the floor in front of her. "Hello, Ivy."

Her feet were frozen in place as he extended an arm and cupped the back of her head. He leaned down, pressed his forehead against hers, and closed his eyes, releasing a contented trill. One of his front legs hooked around her calf, its hide warm and hairs soft. A moment later, he lifted his head and moved his face into her hair, where her neck met her shoulder, and breathed deep. A low rumble followed.

Ivy flattened her hands against his chest; his hearts thumped under her palms. Though he'd always been gentle with her, Ketahn had never been this affectionate. It was...nice.

Something wet trailed along the side of her neck, moving up to tease just below her ear. Ivy's breath caught. Her fingers curled against his chest, and her nipples hardened, turning into achy little points.

Just the memory of his clever tongue between her legs would've been enough to excite her, but the feel of it made her core clench and her clit throb.

"Your skin is sweet, my heartsthread," he said, "but your scent is sweeter."

She chuckled, her nerves making her laughter a little shaky. "Are you sure you're not going to eat me?"

He chittered and withdrew from her, albeit reluctantly, to sink down over his bag and open it. He removed two handfuls of fresh fruit from within. "We will have to settle for these. Ketahn no eat Ivy." Playfulness gleamed in his eyes, but it could not outshine their hungry light as he raked them over her. "But I will drink from you again, my *nyleea*."

Ivy's breath fled her in a rush. Her blood warmed, and heat

pooled low in her belly. She clamped her thighs together. "Ketahn..."

"First, you must eat." He plucked a moonblossom fruit from the food cradled in his lower hands and used the claw of his thumb to slice into its rind, producing a faint trickle of juice from within.

Her gaze settled on his hands as he deftly tore the rind away from the fruit and sliced a wedge out of it. The way he used those fingers and claws was so controlled, so precise; she longed to feel their touch on her body again. *Everywhere* on her body.

No. No, that was just a one-time thing. We're...we're not doing that again. I'm human, and he's...he's a vrix. An alien.

It isn't natural.

Is it?

"Ketahn, what...happened?" Ivy asked.

Ketahn tilted his head, mandibles twitching uncertainly. "What do you mean, Ivy?"

"Last night when you tied me up and we...when we..."

"We mated."

Cheeks burning, she glanced down. "I know that. But...what *happened*? Why did you suddenly...do that?"

"Because you are mine." He lifted the wedge of fruit toward her mouth. "Now eat."

Ivy looked at the fruit and blinked. *What?* Brow furrowing, she gently pushed his hand away. "What do you mean because I'm yours?"

"I conquered and claimed you. You are my mate." He moved the fruit toward her mouth again, more insistently this time. "Now eat, Ivy. I will not have my heartsthread go hungry."

"I'm not hungry," she said, taking a few steps backward. It was a lie—she was starving—but right now she was trying to wrap her head around his words. Had he... Was he saying them right? Did he understand them? Did he really mean... "So you're saying that you conquered me last night to mate. Because you wanted sex, right? That's all?"

"Because you are my mate," he said firmly, lowering his hand. "As I bound you, we are now bound. Our threads are entwined." He crossed two of the fingers on his free hand. "They are as one. We are as one."

"But you...you can't just decide that!"

His mandibles fell. He placed all the fruit on the floor and rose swiftly, drawing himself up to her in a single stride. Before she could react, he had his arms around her, and he pulled her against him. His claspers circled her waist and locked her there.

Ivy pressed her palms to his chest and stared up at him with wide eyes.

"The Eight willed that I find you," he growled. "And from the moment I saw you, touched you, scented you, I knew you were mine. None have gone to that dark place but me. None could have found you but me. Because you were always meant to be mine, Ivy. All my searching has been for you, though I did not know it. And all your waiting was for me."

"But you are a vrix, and I'm—"

"You are my female. My mate, my *nyleea*, my heartsthread." He captured her jaw with one of his hands, tilting her face up and forcing her to hold his gaze. His eyes blazed brighter and hotter than the sun, and all that heat—all that desire—was directed solely at Ivy. "And if I must conquer you again and again to make you understand, I will do so."

Ivy released a shaky breath. The ache that had suffused her core bloomed, spreading heat through her. The seeking touch of his claspers on her hips and ass through her dress sent an electric current over her skin. She grazed her nails down his chest. "Ketahn..."

"I smell your desire, Ivy." Ketahn released her jaw and eased his claspers, opening a sliver of space between their bodies—just enough for him to slip his hand between. One of his long, rough fingers slid along her sex, pressing between her folds to gather her slick. "You make this nectar for me."

Her brows creased, and she whimpered as whispers of plea-

310

sure coursed through her. She grinded against his finger, needing more, unable to deny the truth of her desires.

"Yes," she breathed.

Ketahn growled. His finger curled, putting torturous, rapturous pressure on her clit, sparking impossible heat inside her, and stealing her breath with anticipation. Before she could even gasp his name again, he moved—so quickly that she barely perceived what was happening.

He lifted her off the floor, spread her legs, and guided her thighs around his sides. His hands seemed to be everywhere for an instant, but she was most aware of them on her hips as he slammed her down onto his hard, slick cock.

Ivy cried out, raking her nails over his chest she arched her back. She threw her arms around his neck, needing something to hold onto. It was too much. *He* was too much. He stretched her, forcing her to take all of him, and it left her trembling.

She met his gaze and lifted her hips. His claspers and his hands pulled her back down. The initial burn of his entry was overpowered by a bolt of pure rapture. His claws bit at her ass, and he grasped a fistful of her hair in one hand, tugging her head aside and running his tongue along her neck again.

Ketahn pumped into her hard and fast, his movements fierce, possessive, unforgiving. The pleasure that struck her with each thrust of his cock was just as savage. She struggled to match his pace, but it was too much; her quivering thighs could not long support her, and all she could do was cling to him like she was adrift on an ocean of ecstasy and he was her life raft.

"You are mine, female," he rumbled. His fangs grazed the tender flesh of her neck, sharpening the pleasure that was spearing her core.

She squeezed her eyes shut and sagged against him, clawing at his back.

Ketahn's front legs darted out, slamming against the walls of the nest somewhere behind her. He reared back until she was nearly lying atop him; the altered gravity enhanced the force each time he hammered her down onto his cock.

He tugged her head back. "Look at me."

Her eyelids fluttered open, and Ivy found herself staring into his eyes, which shone like purple fire against his black skin.

"I have claimed you." He punctuated each word with a powerful thrust, plunging deeper and deeper, each stroke setting off a small explosion of pleasure within her. "You belong to me, my heartsthread. Only to me."

It was getting harder and harder for Ivy to keep her eyes open, to focus on his words. She slid her hands up his back, her fingers trailing over his scars and along his thick neck until, finally, she tangled them in his silky hair.

"Say it, Ivy," he snarled, the prick of his claws on her scalp forcing her eyes wide open again. "Tell me you are mine."

"Yes!" she cried as that fiery ball of heat in her core expanded. "Yes, I'm yours! Oh God, Ketahn! I'm yours!"

"Show me!" Somehow, he hammered into her even faster, even harder, matching the frantic rhythm of her heart. "Let me see how I have conquered you."

Ivy combusted. Rapture blasted out from her core, consuming her in delicious, maddening heat, engulfing her from head to toe. Moaning, she clung to him as her body thrummed with ecstasy and liquid fire overflowed from her core, burning ever hotter with each of his thrusts.

She felt Ketahn's shaft swell just before he let out a bestial roar that shook Ivy and the whole nest around her. His seed erupted with heat to match her own, the force of it complemented by the strange sensations of something unfurling at his tip and his cock vibrating.

Before she'd even begun to descend from the first, he blasted her to a second peak.

Ivy tugged his hair and scratched at his scalp as light flashed behind her eyelids. Her skin tingled with the rush of powerful sensations sweeping through her. She ground her sex against his pelvis and tightened her legs around him, seeking to take him deeper, to lock him inside.

His hands squeezed her ass, helping Ivy achieve her goal by pressing her firmly down on him. Ketahn buried his face against her neck. His breaths were hot and heavy against her skin, but it was his tongue that caught her attention and sent a thrill through her as he lapped the sweat from her flesh.

"My heartsthread," he rumbled, the fluttering at the tip of his cock intensifying briefly. He grunted, shivered, and another gush of seed filled her. "So sweet."

They held each other as they gradually descended from those towering peaks, sharing in one another's pulse, in one another's heat, in the lingering euphoria that had suffused them. For a time, it was difficult for Ivy to determine where her body ended and Ketahn's began...and she loved that. She'd never felt closer to anyone. She'd never dreamed it was possible to feel so close to anyone. So...connected.

Tears shimmered in her eyes, blurring her vision as she stared at the morning light streaming through the nest's entrance. How was it possible to feel more wanted, more *loved*, by something so alien than by those who should have loved her most?

Panting softly, she loosened her grip on his hair and combed her fingers through it. Her body was coated in sweat, and both her hair and her silk dress were damp with it. She was flushed all over. But she never felt so good as she did in that moment, with Ketahn's hands stroking her back and caressing her thighs and ass while his thick cock pulsed inside her.

A rumbling trill vibrated from him into her. "Now do you understand, Ivy? It was decided before ever we met. You were meant to be mine."

Ketahn raised his head, caught her chin in his fingers, and guided her face up toward his, forcing her to meet his violet eyes. They burned with possessiveness and passion, but they softened as he gazed at her. His mandibles spread, and he tipped his head forward to press his forehead against hers. "My *nyleea*."

Ivy closed her eyes, and the tears spilled over her cheeks. "My *luveen*."

Chapter Twenty-Five

THE WATERFALL WAS NO LESS impressive during the day, especially from the edge of the pool at its base. The mist in the air made the place seem like a mysterious land filled with hidden spirits—which it might have been, for all Ketahn knew—and the rainbow shimmering in the morning light overhead was like the bridge connecting this spirit realm to the real world. The leaves and flowers were vibrant, their colors more contrasted in the sunlight. In this moment more than ever the Tangle felt alive.

He stilled his hands, lowering the net he was mending.

Those times he'd been here alone, when he'd come to think, he'd sometimes wondered about the waterfall—about its size, its power, its...tirelessness. Vrix had wrought impressive things in Takarahl, but this waterfall was so much more. If the Eight truly walked in the forms of vrix, how immense were they to have crafted this waterfall? To have raised this jungle?

He turned his head to glance at Ivy, who was sitting on the rock beside him, weaving suncrest flowers into a delicate chain.

How huge and powerful were the Eight to have plucked Ivy's people from the stars?

Something sank inside him, and he shifted his gaze to look past her—to look in the direction of the pit. She'd asked him to

317

take her there so many times, and he'd always denied her. As the days had passed, she'd asked less and less, and each time, her hopefulness had been a little duller...and her reactions to his refusal, though less passionate, had troubled him more and more.

Had the Eight truly brought Ivy to the Tangle? Had they taken everything from her just so she could be Ketahn's? Or...had they merely guided him to her, to a female in need of a strong male to protect her, provide for her, and pleasure her?

She was his; he had no doubt of that and never would. And though *how* didn't matter, he couldn't help wondering at the forces that had brought them together. He could not help wondering whether he was right in refusing to bring her to see the place where he'd found her.

He looked down at the net draped over his forelegs and found himself suddenly without the will to continue his work.

Ketahn had chosen to live outside of Takarahl, to sever many of his ties to the vrix, and yet he could go see them whenever he wished. Ivy had not made that choice. She had not asked to be separated from the other humans. She had not asked to come to the Tangle, to be brought into this life. It was meant to be—she was meant to be with him—but how could Ketahn remain idle when his mate was troubled by this?

He returned his attention to her, watching her clever little fingers do their work. She'd come a long way since he'd first found her. She'd learned a great deal. Ivy was not the same as she had been, and neither was Ketahn. They had changed one another, and he believed those changes were good.

He'd not lied—the pit was dangerous. With the flood season approaching, it would be even more dangerous than on the day he'd found her. But if they delayed any longer, it could be several moon cycles before they could get into that...*ship* again, and that was only if this season's rains didn't finally prove too much and leave the ship completely flooded and impossible to enter.

Ketahn lifted his gaze to her face. She was wearing that look of concentration he'd come to admire so much—her eyebrows low with a little crease between them, her blue eyes glinting with focus, her lower lip caught between her flat, white teeth.

He did not fear the spirits in the pit. He did not fear the danger of the climb, or the beasts that prowled the surrounding jungle. He didn't fear the strange construction of the ship or the death that permeated it.

His true fear all along, his true reason for denying her request, was of losing her.

What if something went wrong and he failed to protect her? What if the spirits wanted her back?

What if she saw the male humans and decided she wanted them instead?

But now it was different. Now Ketahn and Ivy were mates, they were bound, they were ensnared by one another.

They'd spent the five days since he'd fully claimed her mating in every spot of the den and several places in the jungle, pushing their pleasure to new heights over and over again. She was his, and she had accepted it. She would not abandon him for a human.

Ketahn clenched his jaw and curled his hands into fists. He would not allow it—and he would not hesitate to challenge anyone, vrix or human, male or female, who sought to take her from him.

What remained to hold him back from taking her to the ship?

Certainly, it was dangerous, but every day in the Tangle was a risk. And, though she could not make the climb on her own, Ivy was far more capable than she'd been several eightdays ago. She would not be a burden. She never had been.

What was this one thing compared to what he'd already done? Compared to what he'd already risked, what he was willing to give up to keep her safe?

The High Claiming had been yesterday. He'd been expected in Takarahl, had known the potential consequences of his absence, and he'd spent the day with Ivy instead. Ketahn had made his choice. She was his mate, and he'd taken her several times without so much as a thought of Zurvashi.

If the time had finally come for him to leave Takarahl behind forever, he accepted it. He didn't think the queen would actually harm his friends and his broodsister; now that he'd made clear his choice, Zurvashi would assume they meant too little to him to be of any persuasion. And it would be a poor look even for the queen to turn upon one of her most respected and skilled Fangs for no apparent reason.

Regardless, there were ways to communicate with his friends and sister, and they all knew some of the queen's wrath might be directed toward them. They also knew how to care for themselves —and how to find him if they had to. They could leave Takarahl should it become necessary.

But Ivy had nowhere else to go. And there was nowhere else for Ketahn but with her.

Ivy glanced his way and raised her head, her lips curling into a smile. "Are you staring at me?"

He lifted his mandibles. "Always, my heartsthread."

"And what is it that is going through your mind, spider man?"

Ketahn growled and clacked his mandible fangs together. "The ways I might punish you for calling me that, human."

"Are you going to tie me up again?"

"Yes."

She grinned wider and withdrew her feet from the water. She twisted to face him, curling her legs behind her. The silk of her dress pulled taut around her breasts. "What if I don't consider that a punishment?"

"It is best you do not say that," he rumbled, sliding the net off his legs and placing it aside, "so we may both enjoy it."

Ivy laughed. The sound was a delight to his ears. Pushing herself up to her feet, she brushed away the moss, leaves, and petals that clung to her skirt and approached him, holding the woven suncrest chain in hand.

"You didn't tell me what you were really thinking," she said, standing in front of him.

"Only of you, my *nyleea*."

Her eyes softened as she looked at him. He did not miss the pink that tinted the pale skin of her cheeks. Ivy stepped closer, moving to stand directly in front of him, between his forelegs. Smiling, she raised her arms high and laid the ring of flowers atop his head. She giggled as she drew back.

"I don't think it makes you look any less fierce," she said.

Ketahn curled a foreleg around her. The ring of vines, leaves,

TIFFANY ROBERTS

and flowers was warm against his hide, and that warmth flowed down into his chest, spreading outward from there. "I must be fierce to protect you." He caught her hands with his lower ones, stroking his thumbs along her knuckles. "I will cherish this gift long after the blooms have withered. Thank you."

A look of surprise flashed over her face, but it quickly gave way to a more thoughtful and curious expression. She tilted her head and dipped her eyes to stare at his mouth. Catching her bottom lip with her teeth again, she shifted on her feet.

"And what is it you are thinking, Ivy?" he asked.

She met his gaze again. "I want to try something with you."

Now Ketahn tilted his head, raking his eyes down her body and then back up to her face. His stem stirred behind his slit, and his claspers twitched. Her words alone were often enough to excite him, but paired with that curious gleam in her eyes, he could not resist.

"What does my *nyleea* want to try?"

"I want to *kiss* you."

His mandibles twitched. "I do not know that word. What does it mean?"

"I...I think it would be better to show you." Ivy slipped her hands out of his grasp and lifted them to his face, cradling his jaw between them before she pressed her lips to his mouth.

Ketahn flinched back, uncertain of what she was doing. Touching headcrests was already a familiar, intimate gesture, but this seemed even more so. Her neck—her soft, elegant, delicate neck—was well within reach of his mandibles that way.

"What is this?" he asked.

Ivy drew back, dropping her hands to her middle and clasping her fingers together, but Ketahn prevented her escape by bracing his leg behind her.

"A kiss," she said uncertainly. "Did you not like it?"

He cupped her cheek in his palm and gently stroked her lower lip with the pad of his thumb. "I...did not expect it. For vrix, when we touch headcrests, it is a sign of great trust. The deepest

322

trust"—he brought his mandibles together, touching their tips— "because of the danger. This *kiss*...it is more than that."

"It can be. For humans, there are different kinds of kisses. We sometimes kiss another's cheek to greet them or show fondness or affection. But there are other kisses shared between...lovers. It's... it's like mating with our mouths."

A long, low trill rumbled in Ketahn's chest, and he found his eyes lingering on her pink lips. He had not known there were more ways to mate, but he was curious to discover them now— was curious to explore them with her.

Dropping his lower hands to her backside and his upper hands to her hips, he lifted her off her feet. Ivy's breath hitched, and she threw her hands up on his shoulders as though to steady herself. He slid his forelegs beneath her and bent them so their uppermost segments were jutting out straight before sitting her upon them, her thighs to either side of him.

"Show me again, my heartsthread," he said.

She smiled and brushed her calves along his sides. "Okay."

Leaning closer, she skimmed her hands toward his neck, her eyes drifting shut as she once more pressed those soft, warm lips against his mouth. But her lips didn't remain still. They lightly brushed back and forth, grazing his hide, teasing him with little whispers of touch. A thrilling shiver coursed through Ketahn, and his hearts quickened. Between the sensations she was creating and her scent cocooning him, he could not resist his excitement. His stem pulsed and began to ease out of his slit as his claspers circled Ivy's middle.

She applied more pressure and parted her lips, placing a lingering kiss first at one corner of his mouth and then the other. When she trailed those lips along his mouth in a slow, tender caress, they left fire in their path that only intensified his desire.

Ketahn's fingers flexed, eager to draw her closer, to spread her thighs wide and sink into her hot, wet depths and lose himself inside her. When her tongue flicked across the crease of his mouth, his breath hitched, and he lost that battle.

"Ivy," he growled, shuddering as his stem burst free.

He lifted her, and she immediately wrapped her legs around his waist, opening herself to him. With a hard thrust, he buried his stem in her slick, welcoming heat, pulling her down until she could take no more of him. Ivy gasped against his mouth, winding her arms around his neck and bracing her feet on his hindquarters.

Squeezing her ass with his lower hands, he worked her upon his length, chasing the strengthening waves of pleasure sparked by her hungry channel.

"Ketahn," she whispered, brushing her lips across his mouth again. "Kiss me."

Ketahn rubbed his mouth across her lips, scraping them gently, creating the soft rasp of hide against skin. When Ivy's tongue flicked once more across the seam of his mouth, he opened to her and extended his tongue, touching it to hers. Their tongues fell into an intricate dance—twisting, twirling, teasing, exploring one another's mouths with an intimacy he could never have imagined.

Just as he'd wanted, just as he craved, he lost himself inside his mate.

He felt the heartsthread that bound them together coil tighter and tighter inside him, felt their bond deepening with each passing moment, and knew without a doubt that it would never be severed—that he would make war against the Eight themselves if it meant keeping Ivy.

Chapter Twenty-Six

"SO, AGAIN...WHERE ARE WE GOING?" Ivy asked.

"As I said, you will know soon, my *nyleea*." Ketahn glanced at her over his shoulder, and his violet eyes glinted in what little sunlight managed to break through the jungle canopy.

She rose off his hindquarters just long enough to peck a kiss on his hard cheek, smiling all the while. When she'd first ridden on him like this, she'd felt a bit silly. Her feelings had changed drastically in the time since.

Ketahn's eyes narrowed in that particular way that meant he was smiling before he faced forward again.

Ivy sat down, making Ketahn's bag—which was currently slung over her shoulders—bounce on her back. She tightened her arms around his chest and turned her head to rest her cheek against his broad, plated back, where his largest purple-and-white markings were located. His hearts thumped in a steady rhythm; she could feel it through his back most clearly, but her sex was still sensitive enough to feel echoes of it in his hindquarters, too.

It hadn't taken her long to realize they weren't heading toward the nest after they'd left the waterfall. Ivy hadn't questioned Ketahn immediately. Her body was languid in the aftermath of their lovemaking, and she'd been content to simply enjoy the ride—and her continued closeness to him. Yes, she was a bit sore, but it was the best kind of soreness.

And the smooth movements of his thick hindquarters beneath her was equal parts soothing and arousing.

Of course, she wanted nothing more than to get back to the nest, nestle against him, and relish all the good feelings with which she was flooded. Contentment, happiness, euphoria, and, most of all, the feeling of being well and thoroughly loved.

Loved.

Was that what was happening?

She couldn't deny that she and Ketahn had developed a deep, meaningful relationship. He'd become her best friend—better than any human friend she'd ever had. He considered them mates, and she had accepted that, but it had only altered their relationship in a few ways.

There was the sex, of course, and God, it was mind-blowing. He'd also been more possessive since declaring his claim on her, and more affectionate. But none of that necessarily meant *love.* Could it be blossoming between them even now? Had it already? Did...did vrix believe in love?

She didn't even know exactly what being mates meant to Ketahn and his people. Was it a temporary state, or was it meant to be lifelong? Was it just about sex and reproducing or did it mean more?

And yet whenever she thought about somehow finishing the journey to Xolea or returning to Earth, something in her chest ached. That ache had only strengthened over time. Though she'd never wanted this, had never asked for it, she found that she didn't want to leave this planet—she didn't want to leave him. And she...she didn't want him to leave her.

Ivy had never been happier in all her life than she was in this alien jungle with her spider man. What did she have to return to on Earth but painful memories and meaningless struggle? What awaited her on Xolea? The work would never have bothered her, but there'd always been the implication that she'd eventually be expected to take a husband and have children, not because she'd fallen in love, but because it was necessary for the future of the colony.

Part of her had hoped things would've progressed naturally, that she would've met a decent man and built a relationship with him...but the scars of her past had still been too raw to really believe that, even years after Tanner.

She'd boarded the *Somnium* dreaming of a new life. There was no question that she'd found that here with Ketahn—and that it was impossibly, amazingly better than anything she could've imagined.

Her mate just happened to be a vrix instead of a human.

The surrounding shadows grew thicker, and Ketahn slowed his pace; the change was enough to jar Ivy from her thoughts. She lifted her head to glance around. They were close to the jungle floor, much closer than Ketahn normally traveled, where darkness pooled and the gnarled roots and branches seemed sinister. All the usual jungle sounds were muted here, like they were coming from a great distance—or even from another world.

Still, she was thankful that he'd not asked her to cover her eyes this time. As long as she was with him, she didn't care where they were headed. He'd protect her.

Ketahn halted abruptly, straightening his torso and twisting slightly to look back with his spear raised. He remained that way for some time, his muscles tense, his eyes visible only due to the tiny points of reflected light within them.

"What is it?" Ivy whispered.

A soft rumble sounded in his chest. "I heard something."

Eyes wide, she looked in the same direction he was, but all she could make out reliably were dark shapes amidst the shadows.

After a while, he relaxed and stroked a rough palm down her leg, easing her tension. "It is fine. The jungle makes many sounds."

He continued forward, his pace steady and unhurried as he navigated obstacles she could barely see. "Here we are."

She leaned to the side to look ahead. Pinpricks of sunlight were visible amidst the dense, black vegetation in front of her, each so miniscule and yet so brilliant in its contrast to the darkness.

Ketahn reached forward and parted the leaves with his spear.

Ivy squinted against the sudden light that struck her. This was more than a shaft breaking through the jungle canopy; it was pure, undiluted sunlight. As soon as her eyes began to adjust, she lifted her gaze.

The canopy overhead was torn wide open in a huge circle, baring the blue sky and fluffy white clouds in a space nearly as large as the one at the waterfall. The boughs around the edges of the clearing swayed in the wind, their leaves rustling.

Her gaze fell, and her heart sped. The reason for the huge break in the trees was impossible to miss—a huge pit gaped before her, its steep walls fraught with dangling roots and plants, spans of loose dirt, and jutting stone. Tangled vegetation had grown across the pit farther down, but it wasn't quite so thick as to hide the impenetrable darkness beneath it.

Ketahn stopped at the edge of the pit, bracing his forelegs on a large boulder. His mandibles twitched. "This is the place, Ivy."

"It's what place?" she asked, staring into that dark pit, but inside, Ivy already knew the answer.

"The place where I fell into my fate." He closed a hand around her knee and gave it a gentle squeeze. "Where the Eight led me to you."

She understood what she was looking at now—not a pit or a natural chasm, but an impact crater. "You're bringing me to the ship?"

"We will need to climb down." Ketahn leaned forward, angling his head to stare into the crater. He released a huff. "Take a rope from the bag so I can lash you to me, though you will still need to hold tight."

Ivy slipped the bag off her back and pulled out a length of silk rope. Excitement and trepidation made her hands tremble. After she slung the bag over her shoulders, she wound the rope around her waist and held the ends out to him. Together, they wrapped the rope around their torsos several times, with Ketahn adding knots and twists to keep it secure. When they were done, the rope was snug, but it left a little leeway between her and Ketahn.

He passed her his spear. She wrapped some of the rope attached to it around her hand and laid the weapon across her lap, tucking it horizontally between their bodies.

As Ketahn faced away from the crater and backed toward the edge, Ivy's heart stuttered, and she clung to him. It wasn't simply the idea of descending into this huge, dark pit that had her on edge—it was the question of what she would find when they reached the *Somnium*. She'd wanted this so badly, had asked him to bring her here so many times, but now that she was on the verge of getting what she wanted...

Would she be able to bear what awaited her? Perhaps she'd find closure, but it wouldn't likely provide her any comfort. There was a high chance that whatever hope she'd held on to all this time would be obliterated down there. That this would force her to accept the worst-case scenario as reality.

That...that she really was the only one left.

Her stomach lurched when Ketahn tipped back, and she squeezed him even tighter to fight gravity's insistent pull. Closing her eyes, she buried her face against his back, trying to focus on his scent, his heat, the feel of his rough hide. She tried to focus on him instead of the million what-ifs swirling through her mind with all the ferocity of a tornado tearing across the Great Plains.

She didn't let the little rasps of falling dirt and tumbling pebbles bother her. Ketahn would get them down there safely.

And whatever is down there, whatever we find...I'll still have him. That is enough. He will always be enough.

As Ketahn carried her lower, she became aware of a new sound, one that only occurred erratically but was nonetheless easily identifiable—the echoing *bloops* of tiny objects hitting water far below.

Ketahn slowed his descent to a stop. Ivy knew they hadn't reached the bottom yet, but she risked opening her eyes and pulling her head away from Ketahn.

She found herself looking straight up the steep side of the crater to the open blue sky. Vertigo threatened to make the world spin around her, but she clamped her jaw shut, took in a steadying breath, and kept her eyes open. Though she dared not look, she could feel the drop behind her. She could feel the distance to the bottom of the crater.

Ketahn won't let me fall.

That thought had barely finished when he began to rotate, turning his body like he was the spidery hands of an antique wall mounted clock. Ivy's eyes widened, and she squeaked, clenching her thighs around his waist and digging her nails into his chest in her desperate need for a solid hold. When he was done, they were both looking straight down.

The tangled vines growing across the crater were directly in front of Ketahn, but there were gaps aplenty for Ivy to see through. The darkness below wasn't complete—just enough light broke through to vaguely outline the debris at the bottom, to give her a ghostly hint of what would be there to catch them should they fall.

With his upper arms, Ketahn tore through the vines. Though he was taking care, each of his movements sent tremors through his body and into Ivy. Leaves, branches, and debris fell, clattering against the crater wall and plunking into the water somewhere below.

Once he'd opened a big enough gap, Ketahn righted himself and continued climbing down.

"You said you fell into this?" Ivy asked.

"From the trees above." If the climb was strenuous for him, there was no sign of it in his voice.

"How did you survive the fall?"

"I threw my spear, and it hit a trunk. It was enough to stop me, but only for a moment, and when it came free, I fell again.

The spear caught on these vines and stopped me again before I hit the bottom."

As they passed through the layer of vegetation, everything grew dark. Beneath the living growth was a tangled network of dead, dried branches; from the underside, it looked like the nest of some impossibly large bird. Watching those vines rise higher and higher above was surreal. The way the sunlight struggled to penetrate them was almost reminiscent of light shining down through the ocean's surface.

That was unsettling, but it was nothing compared to the smell—decay and stagnant water, a stink that hung thick as fog in the air beneath the vegetation. Ivy couldn't ignore it even by breathing through her mouth. Somehow, despite her stomach revolting, she managed not to throw up.

They reached the bottom without incident. Ketahn stretched his rear legs far behind him and pushed away from the wall. He trudged through the black water pooled at the edge of the crater, kicking up that foul odor anew, and followed a gradual incline that led onto land. Not dry land, but it was better than nothing.

An orange glow lit up the crater, bathing the debris in eerie light and casting solid black shadows.

A huge shape jutted up from the darkness and muck ahead, terrifying and familiar.

It was the *Somnium*.

Chapter Twenty-Seven

WELL, it was *part* of the *Somnium*, anyway.

The full ship was far larger than what stood before her. Or...it had been far larger. There was no telling if the entire ship was buried at the bottom of this crater or if this was just a piece that had somehow broken off. Regardless, the sight of it now, in this brief orange glow, made Ivy's insides twist into knots.

The wreckage was covered in dirt, moss, and vines; like everything else she'd seen in this world, it was being swallowed up by the jungle bit by bit. How many years had it lain here? How many years had *she* lain here?

For Ivy, the boarding of the *Somnium* had only been a couple months ago. The day before she'd woken in Ketahn's arms. She'd always known that time had passed—that years had passed—but it hadn't fully registered, hadn't felt real.

It felt real now. And that reality was so much harder to take when it was staring her in the face.

The orange light turned off. The afterimage of the ship danced in her vision for a second longer, haunting her.

"Can we go inside?" Ivy asked quietly.

Ketahn gave her knee another gentle squeeze and proceeded toward the looming wreckage. The ground was littered with rubble, mostly broken branches, rotting leaves, and stones of varying sizes, but Ivy was certain she saw bones scattered amidst it all.

The orange glow returned as they neared the ship. Ivy glanced up at the faded letters on the hull.

Somnium.

A dream that had been warped into a nightmare for thousands of hopeful colonists.

Ketahn stopped in front of a large tear in the hull that was edged with jagged metal. Vines and moss hung down over parts of it, tangled with dangling cables, wires, and pipes.

"Give me my barbed spear and tuck in close, Ivy," he said just before the orange light faded again. A red glow emanated from within the ship, only visible while the other light was off.

She passed him the spear, ducked down, and pressed herself firmly against his back, drawing her legs higher and more firmly around him.

He covered her legs with his lower arms and strode into the opening. He moved slowly, brushing aside the obstacles hanging in his path, turning and twisting to avoid jutting pieces of metal and the ship's internal support structure, and doing everything he could to shield her from all those little hazards with his own body. That selfless, caring act made her heart swell, and she pressed a kiss to his back.

Ketahn released a soft trill and brushed his thumbs along her calves. "You should have shown me kissing sooner, my heartsthread. I like it."

Ivy chuckled. "We can explore it more later."

They emerged from the break in a large room, where Ketahn said she could be at ease. Though reluctant to relax her hold on him, Ivy sat upright and swept her gaze around. Despite the damage, despite the mess and the water pooled on one side, despite the harsh slant of half the floor, Ivy knew they were inside one of the stasis rooms.

The emergency lights cast the room in a hellish red glow and made the broken cryochambers look like dark, ominous sarcophagi. None of those pods showed any signs of being operational.

Ivy swallowed thickly, took in a deep breath, and asked, "Can I...get down?"

Ketahn untied the rope binding them together, and Ivy helped him unravel it. Once it was clear, he sank down and lifted his arms off her legs, reaching a hand over his shoulder to offer her support. She took it and swung one of her legs over his hindquarters to slide off.

She had only taken one step when something jabbed the sole of her foot. She winced, clutching his hand as she leaned against him for support. Lifting her foot, she brushed away the dirt and debris to examine her sole—the skin hadn't broken, but a mean little pebble had come close.

Walking around barefoot all this time had definitely toughened up her feet, but apparently her calluses weren't quite tough enough to save her from unexpected pain.

Ketahn leaned down, took hold of her ankle, and examined her foot with a huff. "My delicate skinned mate."

He glanced around the room, and his mandibles clacked together. When he straightened again, he reached into the bag on her back and rummaged within, eventually producing a long piece of silk cloth that had likely been wadded up at the bottom.

He quickly tore it into two strips and, with speed and care, wrapped one around each of her feet. It was the closest thing to shoes she'd worn since before boarding this ship.

Ketahn didn't release her foot immediately. Stroking his thumb along the top of her foot, he said, "Walk with care, my *nyleea*. These will help, but they will not stop everything."

Ivy wiggled her toes and smiled. "I will. Thank you."

Bending down again, Ketahn brushed the seam of his mouth atop her foot—a soft kiss with no lips—and lowered her leg. The gesture made her heart ache all the more.

She stepped away from him with a mix of apprehension and

necessity. She didn't *want* to know...but she *had* to. The *Somnium* and its passengers would haunt her for the rest of her days otherwise.

Ivy reached the closest cryochamber and stared at the viewing window. Her blood turned cold. The glass was blackened and clouded from within, and a thin crust of mud had dried on the exterior, but she could see inside just enough to make out the shredded, stained padding of the pod's bed.

"Oh my God..."

Despite the damage to this room, the person who'd been in this pod had survived. And worse, they'd been trapped and awake long enough to try to claw their way out in desperation.

"I could have died while I was sleeping. I might never have woken up. I would have just been...gone." Ivy retreated a step from the cryochamber. "Or I could have died like this, trapped, terrified...suffocating."

Though she hadn't heard him move, she felt Ketahn behind her, his presence warm and comforting. He settled a hand on each of her shoulders and smoothed another over her hair. "But you did not. You are alive, and you are here with me, my heartsthread."

She turned to him and pressed her forehead and hands against his chest, sliding her palms up toward his shoulders. His hearts thrummed, their beat soothing, comforting, alive. She knew without looking that there was more death here, more tragedy, and no matter how prepared she'd thought she was to face it, she would crumble before long.

There was no one else to mourn all these lost souls, and Ivy didn't have the strength to do it all on her own.

"Show me where you found me," Ivy said, tipping her head back to meet his gaze.

Ketahn nodded, gently hooking a loose strand of her hair with a claw and tucking it behind her ear. He withdrew from Ivy and led her to an open doorway. The damage from the broken hull continued clear through into the adjoining hallway and the chamber on the other side, as though the entire ship had buckled and begun to break in half—likely due to the impact of the crash.

The corridor was flooded with water on one side and that red glow throughout the rest. Every doorway she could see had a solid red light over it. Dead. All dead. That's what it meant, she was sure of it, though she didn't know how she could be. And her heart broke further with every door they passed.

Ivy followed Ketahn down the corridor, away from the water. The dull, wooden thumps of the butt of his spear on the floor were the only real sound, slow and steady. Though the lighting was different, the cool air smelled off, and everything was wrong, she knew this corridor. She'd walked it on the way to her cryochamber. But then it had been pristine, almost gleaming. It had been as bright as the future they'd all been chasing.

When she first glimpsed a hint of green ahead, she thought it was her mind playing tricks on her. It didn't seem possible in this place of blood and shadows. But then Ketahn stopped at a closed door toward the end of the corridor and Ivy found herself staring up at a single green light over the doorframe.

"Here?" she asked.

"Yes. The door must have closed after I took you out of here." Ketahn shifted aside and gestured to a button on the doorframe. "Touching this opened it."

Taking a deep breath, she raised her fingers to the button, hesitated, then pressed it. After a soft chime and a drawn-out hiss —like an airlock depressurizing—the door whooshed open.

A gust of crisp, fresh air blew over Ivy, startling in how clean it was, but her breath caught because of what she saw. The difference between the corridor and the chamber ahead was stark. The light in the chamber was pure white, the floors and walls were clean and polished but for some faint muddy tracks, and holo displays glowed bright in several places.

It was almost as though this room had been touched neither by the crash nor by time. Only Ketahn had left his mark here.

She stepped into the room, immediately going to the nearest

cryochamber. Her heart raced when she saw a woman lying inside. Alive—in stasis. The woman had light skin, delicate features, long, black hair, and looked completely at peace.

Ahmya Hayashi.

Ivy remembered her. Remembered talking to the woman during training, remembered how shy and timid Ahmya could be, and how excited and animated she became when talking about her passion—plants and flowers. Ivy even remembered seeing Ahmya just before being plunged into cryosleep.

Moving away from the pod, Ivy continued down the center of the room, gazing back and forth at the cryochambers she passed. There were seven people still alive in stasis—three men and four women. The others... It seemed that not all the deactivated cryochambers had failed during the crash, given the varied states of some of the remains, but the result was the same. Twelve dead.

Ivy stopped before the eighth cryochamber. The lid was wide open, the bed inside was raised, and it was empty.

Vel. Eight.

"This was mine," she said.

Ketahn moved into place beside her. "Yes. I did not know if you were living or dead. You seemed as the others, caught in a sleep of death."

And she would have still been here sleeping had he not fallen into the pit.

Was fate real? Could he have fallen for a reason? To find her?

Ivy lifted her gaze to the holo display on the wall between her pod and the next. It was one of several displays that showed the vitals of the people inside the stasis chambers. Seven green human icons, twelve red, and one gray. That gray one was her.

She turned her head to glance to the far end of the room, where a large control console was positioned against the wall.

I need to know. I can't leave here without finding out.

Curling her hands into fists to steel herself, she strode to the console. Ketahn's legs thumped softly on the floor just behind her. The instant she touched the controls, the wide holo display flashed to life.

At the corner of her eye, she saw Ketahn flinch, and he growled. She couldn't imagine what this place was like for him, but...but they would have to deal with that later. There was no way she could explain everything to him while this tangled mass of emotion roiled in her chest.

The display was filled with alarms, warnings, and error messages, many of which were flashing dully—as though their urgency had long since passed but they were helpless to do anything other than persist. In front of all of them was a single larger window in which the numbers of errors and alarms were listed, both of which were in the hundreds. At the bottom was an icon marked *Status Report*.

Ivy lifted a trembling hand and touched the holographic icon.

"All systems critical," announced the computer through unseen speakers in a monotone, disinterested voice. "Auxiliary power ninety-four-point-one percent depleted. Total system failure in approximately two years, thirty-six days, and two hours. Navigation data corrupted. Current location unknown. Emergency signal inoperative. Immediate evacuation recommended.

"For further information, please enter crew clearance code."

Ivy stared at the display, unable to move, to breathe, to think, having never expected how hard the words she'd just heard would hit her.

Navigation data corrupted. Current location unknown. Emergency signal inoperative.

That meant no one knew where the *Somnium* had crashed. No one knew where its passengers and crew had ended up. That meant...that meant there had never been and never would be anyone coming to look for survivors. That there never would be any rescue from this planet for Ivy or any others.

And anyone left would be dead in two years.

She swiped her hand across the holo display, dismissing the alerts to reveal a generic log-in screen with the Homeworld Initiative logo as a backdrop. It was entirely unremarkable but for one thing — the date at the bottom.

June 23, 2284

Launch day had been the tenth of May, 2116. One hundred and sixty-eight years ago.

The journey to Xolea was supposed to take sixty years.

Ivy turned toward Ketahn, who was watching her from a few feet away. There was clear tension in him; his posture was stiff, his mandibles were raised and jittery, but she saw mainly concern in his eyes when they met hers.

"We need to wake them up, Ketahn," Ivy said.

He narrowed his eyes. "No, Ivy. We came only so you could see."

"You can't be serious! We can't just...just leave them here. They'll die!"

"And they will die in the Tangle if we wake them."

"I haven't. Why would their chances be any less?"

Ketahn closed the distance between them. He glared down at her and banged a fist against his chest. "You survived because of me, Ivy. Because you are mine, and I will care for you always. I cannot do the same for these others."

Her brow creased, and tears stung her eyes. "At least give them a *chance*. They deserve that much. Not to lay here, to never know, to never wake up, to just...rot when the ship loses power." Ivy crossed her arms over her chest, hugging herself. "Humans are stronger than you think we are."

"You are stronger than I thought, my *nyleea*. But for the rest?" He tore his gaze from her, ran it over the cryochambers, and hissed. "Here they will sleep. They will not know when they are dead. Out there, they will suffer. Whether they survive or not."

Ivy shook her head, and the tears spilled down her cheeks. "No. I...I can't accept that. You can't expect me to accept that."

His mandibles drooped, and an unhappy rumble sounded in his chest. "It is the truth, Ivy. Not just of the Tangle, but of life."

"Then why did you wake me?" she demanded.

"I did not know you would wake. Did not know you could." He took her face between his hands and wiped away her tears with his thumbs. "But I would do so again and again, if I had to repeat that night. Only for you."

Ivy's lower lip trembled as she stared into his eyes. She raised her hands and circled his wrists with her fingers, clutching him, needing something to hold onto. "They're my people, Ketahn. They are all that is left. How can I just leave them here to die?"

"Ah, my heartsthread," he said, tipping his forehead against hers, "you have a soft heart, but I—"

Ketahn pulled away from her and spun around in a flash, moving so quickly that he left her reeling—and she might well have fallen had he not braced one of his rear legs behind her. He stood in front of her, his spear at the ready, and stared at the open door, through which the red glow from the corridor beyond seeped.

In the sudden silence, Ivy heard only two sounds—that of her pounding heart and a light, barely audible scrape in the corridor.

They were not alone.

Chapter Twenty-Eight

WHATEVER WORDS KETAHN had meant to say fled him. The emotions remained in a raw, tangled, writhing mass lodged between his chest and throat, but they were distant—a discomfort for which he spared no attention.

The faint sounds in the hallway drew nearer to the entryway and ceased.

Ketahn should have trusted his instincts earlier, when he'd first suspected he was being followed. It would have been much easier to deal with a threat out in the Tangle. Now, he and Ivy were trapped in a chamber with only one way out. Yet he wasted no time admonishing himself. Regret could not undo what had occurred.

He raised his barbed spear in his upper right hand, readying it to throw. Turning his head aside just enough to see Ivy at the edge of his vision without losing sight of the doorway, he said in a low voice, "Take shelter."

Her skin was pale but for the hectic pink on her cheeks. Her big blue eyes glistened with tears, more of which trickled free when she blinked. She nodded, wiped the moisture from her face, and hurried to the nearest cryochamber. He watched until she had braced her hands against the pod's exterior and crouched down before turning his full attention to the doorway.

The pit would have deterred most of the Tangle's predators; few beasts would risk such a treacherous climb save in utter desperation. Ketahn knew of only one manner of creature likely to have followed him despite the danger.

Vrix.

And, more than anything else in the jungle, other vrix posed an immense threat to his mate.

Ketahn took a smooth, silent step forward as he called, "Show yourself."

The quiet that followed his command made the quick, steady rhythm of his thumping hearts seem eightfold louder. The ship's cool, oddly clean air was flowing out of the room, meaning he could not scent anything from the hallway, and the unnatural hum that pervaded this place—even this chamber, while the door was open—made it impossible for him to sense the subtle vibrations that might've signified movement in the corridor, but Ketahn knew.

Those sounds had been made by a vrix creeping closer.

He would not ignore his instinct this time, and he would not accept that it was too late to protect his mate.

"You are summoned, Ketahn," said Durax from the hall, his voice echoing off the ship's walls. "The queen demands your immediate return."

Ketahn's hand tightened around the spear shaft. He knew in that moment how this had to end, even if he didn't allow his thoughts to dwell upon it. Durax was too great a threat.

"Show yourself, Claw," Ketahn said.

Long, black fingers curled around the doorframe, grasping it. Durax's head came into view immediately after—half of it, anyway. Four of his pale blue eyes shifted as he surveyed the room in which Ketahn stood, widening slightly before they settled on Ketahn in a glare. His visible mandible rose and swept aside.

Durax raked his claws over the wall. "I would have expected

Takarahl's greatest hunter to have spotted me long ago. But it is as I have told our queen many times—you are not the mighty male she thinks she sees when she looks upon you, jungle worm. The Queen's Claw is already led by the most capable male amongst our people."

"You speak as though your hunt is over."

The Prime Claw chittered and drew himself into the doorway, exposing all but the ends of his legs. He held a barbed spear in one hand and the rope attached to it in another, the slack between the two drooping nearly to the floor. The head of the weapon was angled downward, and his axe hung casually at his belt.

With at least twenty segments between the two vrix and solid walls to either side of Durax, the fact was clear—the Prime Claw had ample time to evade should Ketahn thrown his spear.

"My hunt *is* over," Durax said. "You are trapped. Return peacefully to Takarahl, and I will inflict minimal pain upon you. Of course, the queen is not likely to be so merciful."

"I refuse."

"I will deliver you to my queen," snarled Durax. "I will lay you before her like you are nothing more than a chunk of meat, nothing more than ragged, rotting scraps."

Now Ketahn chittered, though the sound was harsh and humorless. "If Zurvashi truly wanted me in her presence, she would have sent someone capable of taking me."

Durax snapped his mandibles together. "You will return to Takarahl, grub belly, even if I have to drag you across the Tangle to get you there."

"Neither of us will be returning to Takarahl, Claw."

Extending his arm, Durax pointed the head of his spear at Ketahn. "When I bring you to her, the queen will finally know that I am the only male worthy of her. And when I toss her that ugly little creature"—he angled the spear in Ivy's direction—"and whisper all your secrets, she will forsake you once and for all."

Ketahn growled, mandibles spreading. The chaotic swirl

between his chest and throat thrashed with newfound ferocity, becoming impossible to ignore. "You will not touch my mate, you fangless coward!"

Durax reared back as though stricken, his blue eyes widening and his mandibles twitching. "You...you have *mated* that soft, pale, pathetic thing? I should not be surprised a jungle worm would thrust his stem into anything with a large enough hole. You are no better than the beasts you share the Tangle with."

"But still..." Durax brought his mandibles together slowly and extended his tongue to trail across their fangs. "Perhaps I will sample her meat and learn if it is as sweet and tender as—"

Something ruptured within Ketahn. The fury of ten thousand raging storms blasted through him, destroying every thought in his mind but for one, the only one that mattered, the only one that ever would—protect Ivy.

A ragged, thunderous roar tore out of his chest as he threw his spear.

Durax snarled and darted aside to take cover behind the wall. Ketahn was already charging forward, catching the rope to halt his spear's flight before it could pass through the doorway. The weapon clattered on the floor just short of the entryway. He yanked the rope back hard, making the spear leap off the floor, and plucked it out of the air an instant before he lunged across the threshold.

"I have always known your hearts are those of a traitor, but this..." Durax's spear was already in motion, speeding toward Ketahn in a twohanded thrust. But Ketahn was faster, deflecting the blow with a swing of his own weapon.

The corridor's light was redder than ever—but Ketahn would not rest until it was painted the deep red of Durax's blood.

He turned toward the Prime Claw and lashed out with his claws and spear in a relentless assault.

Durax defended himself frantically. He tore the axe off his belt as he backed away, legs skittering across the walls and floor, his ragged breaths broken by pained snarls and hisses each time Ketahn's blows landed.

The scent of vrix blood danced on the cool air.

Ketahn barely registered the damage he inflicted upon his foe —he was aware only that the threat to his mate was still moving.

"She offered you everything," Durax growled, swinging his axe in a quick arc that forced Ketahn to block with his own weapon. The blackrock head caught the barbed spear's shaft and sank into the wood.

With a twist of his spear, Ketahn wrenched the axe from Durax's grasp.

Durax switched his barbed spear to a single hand. "By the Eight, all I ever wanted was her. But spirits curse you, you blinded her to me!" He wildly thrust his weapon.

The blackrock spearhead glimmered in the red light as it darted straight for Ketahn's face. He swayed aside, and the sharp edge sliced across his cheek, leaving a trail of dulled fire behind.

But Durax had put too much force behind the weapon, and the glancing blow had not hindered his momentum. The spear shaft continued past Ketahn's head, and the Prime Claw stumbled forward until his forearm was beside Ketahn's face.

Ketahn snapped his head aside and clamped his mandibles down on Durax's extended arm. The large fangs pierced hide, shredded muscle, and crushed bone.

Durax's howl of agony echoed off the walls, its vibrations overcoming the ship's ceaseless hum. He grabbed his arm at the elbow and tugged back on it as his spear fell to the floor.

Ketahn bent his forelegs up, braced their tips on Durax's chest, and pushed with all his might, swinging his head away from his foe.

Even Durax's howling couldn't shroud the sound of tearing flesh and cracking bone as his arm was ripped off at the midpoint of his forearm. He staggered backward, spurting blood all over Ketahn, the floor, and the nearby wall, clutching his mangled arm.

Ketahn relaxed his grip on the severed limb and shook his head to dislodge it from his fangs. It hit the floor with a muted *thwap*.

Grunting and hissing like a maddened beast, Durax clumsily spun about and fled down the corridor, his legs clattering and scraping the walls and floor in his desperate struggle to remain upright and keep moving.

Ketahn could not allow that. No matter how bloodied Durax was, no matter how severe his wounds, he was a threat to Ivy so long as he drew breath.

Without conscious thought, Ketahn flipped his grip on his barbed spear and threw it.

The spear struck Durax in his lower back just as he neared the doorway that led into the chamber through which they'd entered the ship. His legs crumpled, and he tumbled to the floor, sliding past the doorway and down the angled floor on the opposite side of the break, stopping at the edge of the flooded portion of the corridor.

Ketahn strode after his foe, winding the rope around his hands to keep it taut as he approached.

Durax, face down, struggled to push himself up on trembling arms. He was able to raise his head barely a handspan above the water before Ketahn was there.

"Mercy," Durax hissed. "Broodmother instill you with mercy!"

Ketahn dropped down on Durax's hindquarters and grabbed the shaft of the barbed spear. When he pulled on it, the Prime Claw writhed and spat.

"The eightfold eyes of the gods are upon you," Durax choked out. "Spare me, and the queen shall never know! You...you will keep your creature, to do with as you please."

Bending his forelegs, Ketahn slammed them down over Durax's arms and leaned forward. He clamped a hand around either side of Durax's neck, the other two on the Claw's shoulders, and growled, "You will never so much as speak of her again."

"Never! By the Eight, never again!"

Ketahn shoved Durax's head down, plunging it into the thick, murky water.

The water bubbled and splashed as Durax struggled against Ketahn's hold. Ketahn simply clenched his jaw shut and leaned more of his weight onto Durax's upper body. His muscles bulged and strained with exertion as he squeezed his foe's neck with increasing strength.

Cold, stinking water splashed on his arms, chest, and face, contrasted by the warm droplets of blood that occasionally spattered his skin from Durax's savaged arm.

"No one will harm her," Ketahn roared. "No one will take her!"

His voice boomed along the corridor. He felt Durax's neck giving way to his crushing grasp but did not ease his hold. All Ketahn could perceive at that moment was red. The world, his body, his thoughts; all red.

"Ketahn?" That soft, uncertain voice seemed so out of place there, in that moment. It beckoned him, dragged his attention up and behind him.

Ivy stood several segments away, her back against the corridor wall, her eyes huge and rounded, and a barbed spear—Durax's spear—clutched in her shaking hands. Her brow furrowed as she met his gaze.

He realized only then that Durax had stilled—and had been still for some time.

"Are...are you hurt?" Ivy asked, taking a tentative step closer.

She was safe. She was alive, and she was unharmed. The fires in Ketahn sputtered and faded, leaving his body thrumming.

Ketahn released Durax and rose to stare down at the dirty, bloodied carcass. Durax's hair floated on the surface of the murky water like a tangled mass of webbing, and the blood oozing from his arm ran into the floodwater, indistinguishable from it under this light. Ketahn would not mourn this vrix, would not feel guilt for fulfilling the only duty that mattered—safeguarding his mate.

But when his eyes fell upon the filthy, matted black fur draped over Durax's shoulder, the fur that marked him as a Queen's Claw, heavy dread gathered in Ketahn's gut, threatening to drag him down entirely as it slowly sank.

"Ketahn?"

"The Queen's Prime Claw is dead," he rasped. "By the Eight, what have I brought upon us?"

Also by Tiffany Roberts

THE INFINITE CITY

Entwined Fates

Silent Lucidity

Shielded Heart

Vengeful Heart

Untamed Hunger

Savage Desire

Tethered Souls

THE KRAKEN

Treasure of the Abyss

Jewel of the Sea

Hunter of the Tide

Heart of the Deep

Rising from the Depths

Fallen from the Stars

Lover from the Waves

THE SPIDER'S MATE TRILOGY

Ensnared

Enthralled

Bound

THE VRIX

The Weaver

The Delver

The Hunter

THE CURSED ONES

His Darkest Craving

His Darkest Desire

ALIENS AMONG US

Taken by the Alien Next Door

Stalked by the Alien Assassin

Claimed by the Alien Bodyguard

STANDALONE TITLES

Claimed by an Alien Warrior

Dustwalker

Escaping Wonderland

Yearning For Her

The Warlock's Kiss

Ice Bound: Short Story

ISLE OF THE FORGOTTEN

Make Me Burn

Make Me Hunger

Make Me Whole

Make Me Yours

VALOS OF SONHADRA COLLABORATION

Tiffany Roberts - Undying

<u>Tiffany Roberts - Unleashed</u>

<u>VENYS NEEDS MEN COLLABORATION</u>
<u>Tiffany Roberts - To Tame a Dragon</u>
<u>Tiffany Roberts – To Love a Dragon</u>

About the Author

Tiffany Roberts is the pseudonym for Tiffany and Robert Freund, a husband and wife writing duo. The two have always shared a passion for reading and writing, and it was their dream to combine their mighty powers to create the sorts of books they want to read. They write character driven sci-fi and fantasy romance, creating happily-ever-afters for the alien and unknown.

Sign up for our Newsletter!
Check out our social media sites and more!
http://www.authortiffanyroberts.com

About the Author

Tiffany Roberts is the pseudonym for Tiffany and Robert Freund, a husband and wife writing duo. The two have always shared a passion for reading and writing, and it was their dream to combine their mighty powers to create the sorts of books they want to read. They write character driven sci-fi and fantasy romance, creating happily-ever-afters for the alien and unknown.

Sign up for our Newsletter!
Check out our social media sites and more!
http://www.authortiffanyroberts.com